RETRIBUTION

RETRIBUTION

DAVID HAGBERG

A TOM DOHERTY ASSOCIATES BOOK

NEW YORK

RETRIBUTION

A Forge Book
Published by Tom Doherty Associates, LLC
175 Fifth Avenue
New York, NY 10010

www.tor-forge.com

Forge® is a registered trademark of Tom Doherty Associates, LLC.

The Library of Congress Cataloging-in-Publication Data
is available upon request.

ISBN 978-0-7653-3155-7 (hardcover)
ISBN 978-1-4299-2259-3 (e-book)

Forge books may be purchased for educational, business, or promotional use. For information on bulk purchases, please contact the Macmillan Corporate and Premium Sales Department at 1-800-221-7945, extension 5442, or write to specialmarkets@macmillan.com.

First Edition: January 2015

Printed in the United States of America

0 9 8 7 6 5 4 3 2 1

FOR LORREL, AS ALWAYS

ACKNOWLEDGMENTS

Special thanks to my eldest son, Kevin Hagberg, for this nifty idea and others over the years.

AUTHOR'S NOTE

Some of the characters and situations in this novel, especially in the prologue, are based on actual people and events. I've changed the names and changed the sequence of some events for the sake of the story and, of course, to protect individuals and the actual tactics of DEVGRU—Naval Special Warfare Development Group—also known as SEAL Team Six.

That team does exist, but the events portrayed in this story in no way depict their actual names, personalities, or situations.

The name Pam Schlueter is a real one, but she in no way is connected with the business of this novel, nor does she resemble in any way the truly evil character I've portrayed.

Retribution is a complete figment of the author's imagination, except for the incredibly unsettling fact that indeed 25 percent of homeless men in this country are combat veterans. It is a terrible way to treat our homecoming heroes. Unconscionable. This book is dedicated to all of them. Their motto is: The only easy day was yesterday. Maybe we should think about changing it for when they are discharged from the service!

RETRIBUTION

PROLOGUE

□

Abbottabad, Pakistan

An hour and a half from their staging area at the airbase outside of Jalalabad, just across the Afghan border, Chalk One with eleven SEAL team assaulters crashed on the outer wall of Usama bin Laden's compound.

It was late, after midnight, and pitch dark under a moonless sky.

Barnes and Tabeek were first off the UH-60 Black Hawk helicopter, dropping eight feet to the ground, just avoiding the still spinning main rotors. No one had been hurt but it had been close.

This was the big deal that all twenty-two SEAL assaulters, their CIA translator, one explosive ordinance tech, and a combat dog had been waiting for ever since 9/11. The president had finally given the green light to take out UBL and the mission barely underway was going south.

The team aboard Chalk Two, the second Black Hawk, was tasked for fire support inside the compound as well as security along the outer wall. The Pakistani military academy and police barracks were less than a mile away. And those guys could be showing up at any moment.

Tony Tabeek, called "Tank" because of his solid build, raced across the inner courtyard and set the first breaching charge on the iron gate to the inner courtyard. "I'm going explosive," he shouted.

The downed chopper no longer mattered, all that counted in Peter Barnes's head was staying on mission, something he'd trained for his entire career. All of them were senior operators, in their thirties, well experienced in Iraq, Afghanistan, and other hot spots over the past ten years or so, and they'd all worked the mission plan over and over again, until no one had to give orders, everyone knew his job.

The other assaulters stacked up behind Barnes, all of them turning away and lowering their heads as Tony hit the detonator. The charge went off with a very loud bang, blowing a large hole in the gate.

Tony was first through and within ninety seconds of the crash the team was back on mission. Anderson peeled off to race up the outside stairs to clear the roof of possible snipers.

It was believed that bin Laden and perhaps two or more of his wives had an apartment on the third deck of the main house. The problem was no one knew how heavily armed they might be, how many soldiers or relatives might also be in the building, and who of them—especially the women—would be decked out with suicide vests ready to pull the pin as soon as the house was breached.

Don, Bob, and Greg the Ratman raced across the courtyard to the north door while four other operators went to the south door.

Barnes, who at five eight with a slender build, a scruffy beard and long hair, was the smallest member of the two teams on the crashed bird, glanced over his right shoulder in time to see Chalk Two disappear behind the north wall. They were supposed to hover over the main building to let at least one team fast-rope to the roof. But they knew that Chalk One had crashed and made the right decision to put the operators on the ground outside the perimeter.

In their final briefing the admiral had stressed the absolute importance of placing boots on the ground ASAP. The team was at its most vulnerable point in the air, and especially fast-roping into the compound.

The troop net lit up with radio calls as the team aboard Chalk Two piled out of the chopper and headed toward a gate on the north side of the compound.

Tony raced across the inner courtyard to the guesthouse, where it was believed that Ahmed al-Kuwaiti, who was one of bin Laden's important couriers, lived with a wife and two or three kids.

A pair of sturdy metal doors with barred windows above and on either side were locked solid.

Barnes stepped aside as Tony pulled a sledgehammer from the back of his vest, extended the handle and hit the lock with three sharp blows, doing nothing but denting the metal.

He broke out one of the windows, but the bars wouldn't budge when he tried to pry them apart.

By now anyone anywhere inside the compound or in the fairly upscale neighborhood who wasn't dead or totally deaf knew that something was going on.

"I'm going explosive," Barnes said softly, thinking that whispering at this point was the dumbest thing he'd ever done. He pulled the breaching charge from his kit.

There was an explosion from the north side of the compound, and a second later Chalk Two's team leader radioed that the breach had failed.

"We're moving to the Delta compound gate at this time."

Barnes dropped to one knee, peeled the adhesive strip off the back of the breaching charge, and stuck it in place on the door.

Don, their translator, the last man out of the chopper, raced across the compound toward them when someone inside the guesthouse opened fire with the unmistakable rattle of an unsuppressed AK-47.

Tony returned fire from the left side of the door as Barnes moved to the window on the right, smashed out the glass with the barrel of his Heckler & Koch 416, and fired several short bursts inside, walking the rounds left to right.

Don was right behind Barnes. "Ahmed al-Kuwaiti, come out now!" he shouted in Arabic.

No one responded.

Barnes was on autopilot now—in the zone—no stray thoughts, not even curiosity about how all of this was going to turn out. He was on mission, following the plan.

He went back to the door, made sure the explosive charge was in place, and pulled a detonator out of his kit. He was about to attach it to the charge when someone inside opened the lock and cracked the door.

Barnes stepped back. There was nowhere for the three of them to take cover. If al-Kuwaiti tossed out a grenade it would be game over.

A woman appeared at the open door, a bundle of something in her arms. She was crying.

Barnes raised his rifle. The laser pointer on her forehead lit up like day in his four-tube night vision goggles. For just a moment his finger tightened on the trigger, until he realized that the bundle in the woman's arms was a baby. Three other children stood behind her.

"Come here," Don told her.

"He is dead," she said in Arabic as she stepped out of the house. "You shot him. You killed him."

Don translated.

Barnes patted the woman down, and he and Tony entered the house, which smelled of heating oil. Al-Kuwaiti lay on the floor in a pool of blood, and Barnes fired several shots into his body to make sure he was dead.

It took less than one minute to clear both rooms, and when they were finished Barnes activated an IR chemical light stick at the front door. It could only be seen by someone wearing NVGs and it indicated that the place was clear.

"C One is secure," Barnes radioed on the troop net.

The team from Chalk Two had breached the gate to Delta compound and had already reached the main house in A One where it was believed that UBL and his brother Abrar al-Kuwaiti lived. Another breaching charge blew and moments later one shot was fired, followed by several more.

By the time Barnes, Tabeek, and Don reached the west side of the building and stacked up behind the other assaulters waiting to enter through the north door, Stew reported that a metal gate blocked access to the second floor and he was going explosive.

Barnes and the others could only wait and pull security, laser points dancing just about everywhere in the A One courtyard, especially along the second- and third-floor windows and rooflines.

The mission commander from Chalk Two, realizing that the Chalk One chopper was never going to fly, got on the satellite radio and called for one of the Quick Reaction Force CH-47 Chinooks standing by for refueling and help if needed.

Stew had set the breaching charge on the gate, and since the blast was going to be inside a structure and would create a very intense pressure wave, most of the assaulters took cover. The charge blew with an impressive bang, and the chickens in the wire coop next to where

Barnes and the others were waiting started raising hell. It was like a three-ring circus inside the compound. All they needed now were klieg lights and a ringmaster with a bullhorn.

Everyone in the stack hustled inside and started up the spiral staircase, all of them trying to be as quiet as possible.

When Barnes reached the second deck, just about everyone ahead of him was already clearing four doorways down a long corridor.

An assaulter was halfway up the stairs to the third floor when a man stuck his head around the corner. He was clean-shaven. The intel briefings they'd been given made it likely that he was one of UBL's sons.

"Khalid," the assaulter called softly.

The man appeared around the corner again. The assaulter shot him in the head and he fell down the stairs all the way to the second deck.

Barnes and the others stepped over the body and headed up the stairs where they found Khalid's AK-47 propped against the wall. If the guy had held his position and fired down the stairs they would have been bottled up and it would have been an entirely different game.

But Barnes had seen random shit like that happen all the time—and not always for the team's benefit.

It was very dark inside the house, but with NVGs everything was lit up green. Skip Faircloth, the lead assaulter, was the point man, and Barnes was next; several others were stacked up on the stairs. They moved slow.

If UBL was on the third floor he'd had plenty of time to strap on a suicide vest or at the least arm himself.

This had become nothing more than a CQB—close quarters battle—drill, that Barnes and every other operator on the mission had done hundreds of times.

Just a few steps from the top deck landing, Skip fired two suppressed shots at a head poking out of an open doorway.

Barnes was right behind him, their rifles at the ready as they approached the doorway and looked inside.

Two women dressed in long gowns were wailing and crying over a man lying on his back at the foot of a bed.

One of them looked up and suddenly charged Skip. It was impossible to tell if they were wearing suicide vests, but Skip deflected her charge, and hustled her and the older woman to the other side of the room without thinking what could happen if either of them were wired.

The downed man lay on his back, blood and brains leaking out of the side of his head where one of the shots had entered his skull. He was dressed in a white T-shirt, loose slacks, and a desert-colored vest.

It was bin Laden. Same build and height, same face, same nose, same hair and beard, though it appeared as if he'd dyed away the gray. He was twitching, still not quite dead.

Barnes was sure of the solid ID, and he and another assaulter fired several rounds into the man's chest, killing him.

It was over, finally.

They cleared an adjoining bathroom and a room that looked as if had been used as an office. The women and three children were hustled out. The team leader securing the rest of the third deck reported all clear when Barnes came out.

"Secure," Barnes said, and the team leader reported the situation on the troop net.

UBL was dead. It was time to gather up intel, including papers and hard drives, plus samples of the dead man's body fluids for positive DNA proof, then bag the body and boogey out before the Pakistani military finally woke up and came charging.

PART
ONE

Four Years Later

O N E

Atlantic coast Florida in mid-July lived up to its reputation as hot and muggy, the wind off the ocean doing nothing except increase the humidity, which Dieter Zimmer, driving north from Miami International, found almost unbearably oppressive. It was a few minutes after noon, and although he had the rental Impala's AC cranked up to the maximum, he was sweating profusely and hating every second of it.

At around six feet, with a thick barrel chest and a broad circular face under a spectacularly bald and shiny head, he stood out. It was something every trainer he'd had in the German army and for five years starting in '96 with the Kommando Spezialkräfte—the elite special forces—promised would make him stand out.

"You're the first stupid son of a bitch that the enemy will shoot," Sergeant Steigler told him the first day of training. "You're going to die for your country."

"No, sir, that dumb son of a bitch will be the first one I shoot. He'll die for his country."

"Ah, we have a General Patton amongst us," the sergeant said, and the name had stuck, finally shortened to Patton.

He turned off I-95 at the Fort Pierce exit and on the other side of the town drove across the bascule bridge onto Hutchinson Island and headed north on A1A, the Atlantic almost ominously calm, big thunderheads off in the distance to the east. Past a spate of condominium towers right on the beach, and a mobile home park on the land side of the highway, he slowed for a driveway to the right. The sign on the fence read UDT/SEAL MUSEUM.

Parking just outside the chain-link fence, the gate onto the grounds open, he sat for a moment watching as a Mercedes sedan passed on the highway. His target, he was told, would be driving a Ford pickup, dirty green with Florida tags, and wasn't expected to show up down here from Tampa until between one thirty and two. He was bringing something for the museum, and he definitely wanted no announcements. Since he'd gotten out of SEAL Team Six he'd supposedly wanted nothing to do with any publicity.

"I just want to get on with you, you know," he'd said. He'd been talking to an old friend and neither of them had any idea their phone call was being recorded.

Dieter had listened to the entire conversation two months ago in a hotel room in downtown Munich with the others. They'd been in the final planning stages for the first part of the operation they were calling *die Vergeltung*—the Retribution.

And he was here now, the countdown clock to the start at less than minus sixty minutes.

It was a Tuesday, and the only cars were those of the two attendants inside. No maintenance was scheduled for Tuesdays or Thursdays, and the likelihood of a casual visitor dropping by was slim. But Dieter was ready for that possibility.

He'd always hated the U.S. and everything about it. The prejudice came from his father who'd been an ordinary soldier and complained constantly about the American occupation forces with boots all over Germany. Taking up valuable real estate with their bases, especially the massive one at Ramstein.

"Fucking our women. Driving fancy cars. Paying twenty-five cents—one mark—for an entire four liters of gasoline while we have to pay fifteen times as much. Eating enough meat in one meal, which they buy at their commissaries, to feed a German family for a week."

He'd felt the esprit de corps in the KSK, which solidified his resolve, Germany for Germans, and had hoped in those end days of the cold war for the Russians just to try to come across the border. They would kick some serious ass all the way back to Moscow.

Getting out of the car, the heat slammed at him, especially at the top of his bald head. He realized that he should have worn a hat after all. Something else to be bitter about. And there was a long list in his mind.

He wore a Cuban-style guayabera shirt, yellow and a little thicker than the normal cotton ones, to hide the silenced subcompact conceal-and-carry Glock 26 with a suppressor. The pistol fired the small 9×19 mm round, but the magazine held ten shots, plenty for a close-order gun battle, which he intended this one to be.

Inside the gate a crushed-gravel path led through the grounds, toward the low-slung building. River patrol assault boats made of plywood and painted olive drab that had been used in Vietnam were set up on concrete stands, as were an original towed submersible that had been used in World War II to ferry the underwater demolition teams to find and blow up the mines just below the water line, a Huey chopper—also Vietnam era—and even a Mercury capsule, which had splashed down in the Pacific and was secured by a SEAL team.

A curved ramp led up the side of the museum's main building. There used to be a huge brass globe on the roof, on which all the countries were engraved. It had symbolized the battlefields since World War II on which the UDT teams, and later the SEALs, had fought and died. A lot of them heroes, some of them Medal of Honor winners. But it was gone now and Dieter couldn't understand why it had been removed.

Less than ten meters to the east, beach installations of the sort that had been used in World War II to repel the Allies from landing in places like Normandy—the ones the UDT guys were sent in to blow up—were on display to show what an impossible job they had. In fact this stretch of the barrier island had been used to train U.S. forces for the landing.

Dieter was a solider—or had been one—and a very large part of his thoughts were with these guys. They had balls, no doubt about it, and he had a real admiration for them. The only problem was they were Americans.

He had been taught to hate them, and yet sometimes when he tried to really examine his true feelings, he couldn't say why his hatred had become so intense, especially in the past couple of years working with Pam Schlueter. But she was a convincing woman, with connections to big money and a track record to prove her worth among men. He thought that she was probably nuts; they all did. But all of them thought they understood why her hatred ran so deep,

and none of them could find any fault with her. Anyway it was because of her that they were in the business of killing—a business
that all of them loved.

At the bottom of the ramp he walked past models of a pair of
World War II UDT operators in bathing trunks, fins, and round masks.
Their equipment had been crude at best, but they'd gotten the job
done.

Inside he went straight back to the reception area behind a glass
case displaying books and patches and other souvenirs that were for
sale. A stack of the book *No Easy Day*, written by one of the SEAL Team
Six assaulters who'd taken out Usama bin Laden, was laid out on the
counter next to the cash register. An old man seated behind the counter looked up from a newspaper he was reading and smiled pleasantly. He was dressed in khakis and a blue polo shirt with U.S. NAVY
embroidered over the pocket.

"Did you sign in? The book is by the door."

"I'll catch it on the way out," Dieter said.

"You're German."

"Yeah. No longer the bad guys."

The old man's name tag read PAVCOVICH. "Ain't it the truth."

Dieter figured the man was in his mideighties, maybe older, and
had probably fought in the war. "You alone here today?"

"Charlie's out back. Doing some painting this morning. We've got
a VIP coming in today. One of the SEAL Team Six guys who blew bin
Laden away."

"I heard."

It took a moment for the old man to understand something wasn't
right—the visit was supposed to be a secret. He started to open his
mouth.

Dieter pulled out his pistol. "Let's go back to the office."

"You fucking kraut."

"Now," Dieter said, the pistol pointed directly at the old man's
face.

"Screw you."

"If I have to kill you I will. But all I want is to duct-tape you to
your chair and tape your mouth shut."

"And then what?"

"Then I'm going to have a talk with your VIP."

The old man got up from his stool and shuffled from behind the counter and down a corridor that led to the displays, to a small office. The door was open.

"Have a seat," Dieter told the man.

"You don't have any duct tape."

"*Nein*," Dieter said, and he fired one shot into the back of the man's head.

TWO

☐

Dieter checked to make sure that the old man was dead, careful not to get any blood on himself, then went back out into the museum, closing the office door. He quickly went through the several rooms of displays to make absolutely certain that no one else was there, sorry in a way that it was totally impossible for him see the place the way it should be seen.

Two large rooms—almost warehouse size—were in the back. One of them displayed big pieces of war machinery—like an armored Hummer—while in the second room a young woman with earbuds sat listening to music behind a counter. The room was filled with racks of souvenir hats, T-shirts, and other UDT/SEAL kitsch.

She looked up and smiled when Dieter came in. He shot her in the forehead and she fell back, the smile still on her lips.

Maybe in another time, next year or something, he would come back. But he was lying to himself, something he'd been doing ever since he was a kid growing up in a small lake village south of Munich. He'd lied to everyone at first, and so often, that he'd begun to believe his own stories, so when he discovered how to cheat on exams in school, he didn't think of it as cheating. He was passing tests. He was telling people what they wanted to hear. He was telling himself what *he* needed to hear.

He holstered his pistol and checked the front door again to make sure no one had shown up. Then he let himself out the back way and followed a path to the corrugated metal shed at the rear of the property. The big service door was open. A Chevy pickup truck painted dark blue, the U.S. Navy markings blanked out but still legible, was parked just inside.

Holding up at the door he looked inside. "Charlie?" he called softly. "You around here someplace, buddy?"

No one answered, so he went in and took a quick look around. The place was a mess, but it was a fairly well-equipped machine shop, with a metal lathe, a table saw, a drill press, and other tools, including an electric welder and a portable air compressor.

Back outside he glanced at his watch. It was a little past one, which still gave him a margin of at least thirty minutes before the retired SEAL Team Six assaulter was due to show up, but he wanted to be in place well before then.

No one was in the yard within the fence with its tank traps and machine-gun installations. He started down the white shell path. Almost immediately he caught the smell of someone smoking a cigarette, and it instantly brought back memories of when he was a kid stealing his father's Ernte 21 unfiltereds and sharing them with a couple of his friends on the way to school. He'd given up the habit once he'd joined the KSK because they'd robbed his wind. But they still smelled good to him.

He pulled up short. A bucket of red paint, a brush balanced on the rim, was set next to a log revetment about twenty feet long that protected a machine-gun nest behind a narrow slit. Barbed wire was coiled around the front and sides of the installation, and it looked to Dieter as if someone had been touching up the heads of the spikes or the bolts driven into the logs with Rust-Oleum to protect them from the corrosive salt-laden air.

The guy was nowhere to be seen, but the smell of his cigarette was strong on the very light breeze.

He'd been painting, but he'd put down his brush and had left for some reason.

"If it doesn't feel right, it probably isn't," the instructors had drilled into their heads. "Recognize when you are walking into an ambush. It only takes one determined son of a bitch to fuck up your day."

The SEALs had a saying that incoming rounds had the right of way. It amounted to the same thing he'd been taught.

Dieter pulled out his pistol and, concealing it behind his right leg, headed to the machine-gun emplacement. The smell of smoke was fading, and for a moment he was pissed off. Both guys were supposed to be inside the museum, waiting for their VIP to show up, and he was running out of time to deal with this kind of shit.

"Mind the wet paint," someone off to the left said.

Dieter turned in time to see a fairly short man with a large beer belly, maybe in his sixties or early seventies, with only a fringe of white hair around his ears, dressed in paint-splattered white coveralls, walking over from behind an assault boat set up on a concrete stand. He was grinning.

"You a former SEAL?"

"No, you?"

The man stopped short. "You're German."

Dieter shrugged deprecatingly. "Can't help who my parents were." The American was too far away for a decent pistol shot. "I was in the German special forces, and I've always wanted to get over here to see the museum."

"KSK?"

"Right. You must be Charlie. Pavcovich said I'd find you down here somewhere." Dieter stepped forward and raised his left hand as if he wanted to shake.

Charlie stepped back a pace. "Something wrong with your other hand?"

"Not at all," Dieter said and he brought his pistol out. "In fact I'm a rather good shot."

"I'll be goddamned," Charlie said. "We got a call a couple of days ago that someone like you might be showing up. Didn't say who he was or who the hell you were, but he was a German too."

"Someone like me?"

"He said to call the cops if you did."

"Maybe you should," Dieter said. The only Germans he thought who might have given such a warning were from the BND—the German secret service. Pam had raised the possibility—no matter now slight—that the Bundesnachrichtendienst might come snooping around at some point. But not this early. Not before they'd even started.

Charlie suddenly turned and sprinted to the open gate in the tall fence. He crossed the narrow parking lot and disappeared through the sea oats toward the beach, jigging left and right as he ran.

Dieter stepped around the machine-gun emplacement and began firing, steadying his gun hand against the top log, one measured shot after the other. On the third shot the American yelped and staggered to the left, blood on his left thigh.

The fourth shot struck the former UDT operator high in his back, just below and to the left of the base of his neck. But the man would not fall. He hobbled over the rising sand dune.

Dieter went after him.

Charlie reached the waterline on the beach and then turned and looked at Dieter, an odd expression that was mixed with pain, but no fear, on his broad face. "You're here about our bin Laden SEAL. But why? You're not al-Qaeda?"

"Purely business," Dieter said, and he shot the man in the middle of the forehead at nearly point-blank range.

Charlie Saunders fell back into the water, the light rippling waves washing over his face, carrying the blood away, his arms splayed out to either side.

No boats were anywhere to be seen. Nor were there any people on the beach. Dieter reloaded his pistol as he started back up to the main building to wait for the first bin Laden SEAL he would kill. The first of twenty-two, plus the CIA translator and the one EOD tech. The dog would get a free ride.

THREE

☐

Peter Barnes glanced over at his wife Sally, her face scrunched up in the neutral expression that meant she was bored out of her skull, wanted to be anywhere except in a ratty old pickup truck heading to Fort Pierce, and was merely going for the ride because she owed him. Which in his mind wasn't really so.

She'd gotten sick almost to the day two years ago when he'd mustered out of the navy, and as it turned out his bone marrow was a match for hers and he'd saved her life. The problem was that their marriage had been on rocky grounds because of his three-hundred-day-per-year deployments, and nothing either of them could say or do seemed to make much difference.

Sometimes civilian life was a bitch. No one was shooting at you and you didn't have to watch for IEDs. No one was giving you orders—sometimes shitty ones that made no sense—nor did you have the responsibilities of looking out for your guys. And that was the problem: there was nothing to prepare for, nothing to get the heart beating, no actual reason for getting up in the morning.

One of the guys from Chalk One had written a book about taking out UBL, but Barnes's discharge after eighteen years landed him a job as a maintenance man for a condo association on St. Pete Beach. He'd thought about going to work for Xe or one of the other contractor services, but he knew that he would feel guilty as hell leaving Sally again. Yet he was drowning.

They'd come across the state through Orlando and were finally on I-95 heading south, just a few miles from the exit to Vero Beach; from there they'd take A1A south. Already they were late.

"We'll spend a half hour there, tops. Then I'll take you to lunch someplace," he said.

"You coulda just mailed it," Sally said without looking at him.

She was still pretty, still had her body because they'd never had kids—and in a way she was even more beautiful because her cancer had left her skin almost translucent.

"I want to hand it over in person," Barnes said. The UBL book had been a big bestseller, but the journal that he'd kept was, in his mind, a hell of a lot more personal. And there was no one else right now that he could share it with except the guys who ran the museum and the people who visited every week.

"Whatever."

He held his silence until they got off at the SR 60 exit into Vero Beach. "You okay, babe? Need to stop to take a pee?"

She shook her head.

Sometimes he felt so goddamned guilty because he wanted to get back into it, while at the same time he wanted to be there for her. He'd held friends in his arms on the battlefield and talked them through dying. He understood, he really did. And he'd been there for Sally as she nearly died.

He glanced over at her again. But looking into her eyes was different than looking into the eyes of a badly wounded SEAL. He loved her but he'd never felt the same camaraderie he felt with his teammates. And that drove him even crazier.

"We can stay at a hotel tonight. I can call and make an excuse. Nothing much is happening tomorrow. We'd be back by noon anyway."

She finally looked over at him. "I just want to forget the years you were gone. Maybe if we'd had kids it might have been better, or maybe worse, I don't know. It's just that I always waited for someone to show up in a navy car, ring the bell, and tell me that you'd been killed somewhere in the mountains, or at sea, or in the middle of some fucking desert."

Barnes tried to say he was sorry, but she went on.

"They couldn't even tell me what you were doing. I wouldn't know why you had died. Whether you'd thrown your life away for some bullshit political reason, you know. Someone signs an executive order and my macho husband runs off, jumps out of a plane, and gets his ass shot off."

He had nothing to say. It was over; he was out of the navy and never going back. She was suffering from post-op depression and maybe even post-traumatic stress syndrome from waiting at home for the shoe to drop. Guys had committed suicide, but so had a lot of their wives.

"And then what?" she cried, tears welling in her eyes. "What about me? What was I supposed to do with the rest of my fucking life?"

"I'm back, sweetheart. I'm not going anywhere."

"What about right now?" she demanded.

It was the same argument they'd been having for the past two weeks. "It's something I have to do. When we drive back home, it'll be over and done with. For good."

"But not forgotten," she said, and she turned away.

"No," Barnes said, and he concentrated on his driving.

It was a long way into town from the interstate, and then past the power plant on the Indian River waterway and onto the barrier island—Orchid Island here, but called Hutchinson Island south across the St. Lucie County line.

Past the condos and beach developments, they finally reached the point where A1A was less than fifty yards from the water. The Atlantic was almost flat calm this afternoon, but way out in the east thunderheads were building, some of them into anvils, the tops blown off by the jet stream seven miles or so above the surface. They would be having some nasty weather by evening, and he made the decision to drive back to Vero when they were finished at the museum and check into the Holiday Inn Express just off the interstate. Tonight they could splurge on a nice dinner at the Ocean Grill right on the beach. He would make sure that they got a window table so they could watch the storm.

Once he'd been accepted into the elite DEVGRU, which was the Naval Special Warfare Development Group—SEAL Team Six—he begun making entries into his journal every day. Sometimes he bitched about the workload, especially on the Green Team, which was the nine-month training evolution. But at other times he was excited, especially during CQB—close quarters battle—drills that were a whole lot better than any 3-D video game, and his writing showed it.

During his first deployment to Iraq his writing became closer to the bone, especially about friends dying, their bodies shot to hell, brains leaking out of their eyes or where their noses used to be; scraping bits and pieces off the dirt road after an IED went off; dragging a bullet-ridden body back to a defensible position so that the ragheads wouldn't take it and mutilate it and hang the pieces from some roadside pole.

The journal had helped him get rid of a lot of his feelings, but sometimes at night in bed, or like now when he was driving practically on autopilot, a lot of that crap still came back in living color.

"You're doing it again," Sally said.

He looked up out of his thoughts. To the south were the condo towers on the beach just beyond the museum.

"I knew this was going to happen. I would have bet good money on it."

"Sorry," Barnes said. There was no use arguing because she was right, and she knew that he knew it.

"Yeah."

"We're almost there. One half hour, tops, and we'll haul ass. Promise."

But she did not answer.

F O U R

□

Wolfhardt Weisse could have been Dieter Zimmer's older brother. Tall, broad chest, round face, intelligent eyes, and a bald head that looked as if it had been waxed and buffed. The difference was this: Zimmer was a German terrorist, while Weisse was a captain in the German intelligence service.

Driving up from Miami he had taken his time following Zimmer, whom he had traced all the way from Munich. The BND had evaluated his threat as interesting but not likely imminent. The real problem was the lack of follow-up intelligence: Zimmer was part of a suspected terror cell called the Black October Revolution, which for the past three years had been nearly impossible to penetrate.

The organization had nothing to do with any sort of a revolution. Apparently, it was a murder-for-hire group, mostly dirty ex-cops and former Bundeswehr soldiers, led, it was believed, by a woman, nationality so far unknown—maybe German, maybe American—who either had a lot of money or a well-connected banker.

The best they'd been able to do so far was to work out from wiretaps, the names of five suspected members, Dieter Zimmer among them, and their involvement in several contract killings in Afghanistan and Iraq and possibly one in the U.S. But without any proof of wrongdoing on German soil they could only follow the five. Wolf had been assigned Zimmer, and no one at BND's new headquarters in Berlin near the Reichstag had been more surprised than he when Zimmer had suddenly flown to the States. Wolf had managed to get one of their tech people down from the German embassy in Washington to meet Zimmer's flight and place a GPS tracking beacon on the car the man had rented.

For the last twenty minutes it had been stopped at a location on a barrier island just north of the city of Fort Pierce.

The briefing he and the others had received six months ago by Oberst Hans Mueller, their project chief and liaison with the BfV, which was the domestic intelligence service, had been very specific.

"Do not crowd them until we have proof of wrongdoing. All we have now are suspicions."

"Sorry, sir, but I'd say that's exactly what we do to the bastards. Make them look over their shoulders twenty-four/seven," Wolf said. "Force the fuckers to make mistakes."

The colonel, who had come up through the ranks, smiled. "Personally I agree with you, but everybody takes orders." His nickname was the Iron Man, because he wasn't afraid of getting his hands dirty in the field.

"Even you, sir?" someone asked from the back of the briefing room.

"Especially me," Mueller said. "Probable cause, ladies and gentlemen. It's in the constitution."

Which in Wolf's estimation was a load of horseshit. He couldn't think of any intelligence agency field officer in the world who gave much thought to probable cause. Nobody but the Americans actually talked about waterboarding and the like—enhanced interrogation methods—but everyone used them because they worked.

Ten minutes with Dieter Zimmer and they would start getting answers.

Like why the hell he had dropped everything and suddenly flown to the States, and what the hell was he doing stopped out in the middle of nowhere—lying on the beach and getting a tan?

Wolf got off the interstate at the Fort Pierce exit and headed east with the fairly heavy workday traffic, something bothersome niggling at the back of his mind.

In school, starting when he was about seven, he'd been outstanding at chess. He'd taught himself from a book of matches played by chess masters through the ages, and after one year he was his class champion, then the school's champion and finally the all-city Baden-Württemberg champion.

He'd lost interest by then because the game and his opponents seemed too predictable. Playing became a bore.

But he'd never lost his edge—his ability to see around corners, to work out the next dozen or so moves that his opponents were likely to make and come up with the countermoves to defeat them. When he tested for the Bundeswehr they'd wanted to make him a cryptographer, but in his head working out codes was just like playing chess. He wanted to be physical—blow up things, get into hand-to-hand combat—which in the end landed him in the secret service. He could figure things out and he could kill a man if need be.

These days the only people he played chess with were his ex-wife Renate and their two boys, Jared and Eric, and just for fun—though Eric at six was already showing an inventiveness.

Zimmer had most likely come here to meet someone. But it was apparently a rendezvous in the middle of nowhere, perhaps with the woman who was possibly an American.

The middle of nowhere. The one piece of the puzzle that made no sense.

He phoned his contact at the German embassy in Washington, and when he had identified himself he was put through instead to Gottfried Lenz, chief of the BND's Washington station.

"I'm glad you called, Captain, because I don't like being in the dark, and I especially don't like you co-opting my assets."

"Yes, sir. If you wish to call Oberst Mueller to verify my orders, I'll wait. But I need a piece of information."

"I don't give a shit what you need. But I'll call Mueller and find out what this is all about."

Just now relations with the United States were on the tight side, because of the continuing debt crises over the euro. Germany wanted to let Greece, Spain, and several other members who were in serious trouble because of mismanagement opt out. Sink or swim. Wall Street was in a minor tailspin because the American bankers feared the move would spark a recession in Europe, which would naturally spill over to the States. The White House was putting pressure on Merkel to back down. No one wanted to add to the tense relations.

And Lenz had the reputation of being a hidebound bureaucrat who always followed orders to the letter. He wanted no ripples in his operation.

Wolf called the embassy again, this time asking for the travel and tourism section. A young woman answered. Speaking in German, Wolf identified himself as a tourist on the way up from Miami to Orlando.

"I'm just passing Fort Pierce now and I thought I'd drive out onto the barrier island and take the highway north. I have all day and I was wondering if there might be something to see other than the ocean and some sand."

"I'm not personally familiar with the area, but one moment please and I'll bring it up."

"Fine."

She was back after just a few moments. "Did you serve in the military, sir?"

"Years ago," Wolf said. It was an odd question.

"Then you have probably heard of the U.S. Navy SEALS. They're a corps of special operations soldiers. Commandos. Their museum is just north of the city on the barrier island highway A1A."

"Thank you very much, it sounds interesting. Do you have an exact address?"

"Yes, of course," she said, and she gave it to him. "Will there be anything else I can help you with?"

"No," Wolf said, and he broke the connection. He plugged the museum's address into his GPS and the location came up with a match for Zimmer's car, which made even less sense.

The man hadn't suddenly flown to the States simply to visit a museum. A military museum. A SEAL museum.

A few years ago the SEALs had become world-famous when they'd swooped across the Afghan border into Pakistan and killed Usama bin Laden and flew off with his body. At the time he remembered thinking that the operation sounded like something the Israelis might have pulled off. It was a lot more daring, with a lot more political risk than most American presidents were willing to sanction. Jimmy Carter had taught his successors that lesson with the botched raid to free the American embassy hostages being held in Iran.

He passed through the downtown area and turned east again over a bascule bridge onto the barrier island when his cell phone chirped. It was Lenz from Washington. He ignored the call.

Zimmer had served in the KSK, getting out on an other-than-honorable discharge. Wolf had seen the man's jacket. He'd not been guilty of anything terribly wrong. He had no court-martial on his record, only a series of bad fitness reports because he couldn't follow orders. He was a big mouth—a braggart, according to one of his supervisors. Very unpopular with his fellow operators. Not a team player. But his marks for CQB drills were all superior. He knew how to fight. His attitude was his only problem.

The man had disappeared for several years, until he'd shown up as a name on a series of random cell phone intercepts. A file had been started on him and eventually the four others, plus the woman, and now he'd come here to a SEAL museum in an obscure corner of Florida.

Why?

To assassinate someone?

Wolf sped up.

FIVE

A battered old Ford F-150 pickup turned onto the gravel driveway and parked next to the red Impala. From his vantage point on the roof Dieter watched a man dressed in khaki shorts and a black T-shirt get out on the driver's side.

He reached back inside and took out what looked like a thick manila envelope and said something to a woman on the passenger side.

Because of the angle of the sun it was almost impossible to make out any of the woman's features except that it was a woman. Almost certainly Barnes's wife.

Barnes turned away, closed the door, and started toward the open gate, but then he turned and went back to the truck and opened the door again.

At first Dieter wasn't sure if this was the right guy. Most of the photographs he'd seen of the SEAL Team Six operator showed a man with long scraggly hair and a week's worth of beard, dressed in the usual tan patterned Crye Precision uniform. This one's hair was a buzz cut, and he was clean-shaven. Which was to be expected considering the condo association he worked for now. The man was no longer a killer. Now he made sure that the lawns were mowed, the palm trees trimmed, the pool cleaned, and everything that needed to be painted was painted. Hinges did not squeak, cracks in sidewalks and walkways were filled, window screens were repaired, and no light in a public place ever stayed burned out for long.

Barnes did not seem happy. It was clear even at this distance that he and his wife were having an argument.

He turned away, then back again, said something else, then slammed the door and marched through the gate and up the gravel path.

Dieter moved a little farther back until Barnes was out of sight below; then he went down the ramp.

From where it was parked the pickup truck was not visible from the front door of the museum. Nevertheless Dieter glanced once over his shoulder as he headed in an even stride down the path, as if he were in no hurry. Just a man leaving the museum on a fine summer afternoon.

Sally Barnes had rolled down her window and was staring off toward the sea oats and other grasses along the dunes in front of the beach. She didn't notice Dieter until he came around to her side of the truck. She looked angry.

"If you want to shake my husband's hand he's inside," she said. Her voice was high and thin. Dieter got the impression that she was sick, or had been recently.

He smiled. "Actually it's you I came to see," he said.

She scowled. "What?"

No one was passing on the highway. Dieter looked over his shoulder again to make sure that Barnes wasn't coming back, then he pulled out his pistol and shot her in the forehead, driving her head back against the window.

The 9 × 19 mm load was light enough that, combined with the effects of the suppressor, the bullet did not exit from the rear of her head, making a mess. She slumped over in the seat, her eyes still open.

Holstering the pistol, he opened the door, and shoved her body down onto the floor so that it would be out of sight to anyone walking by. Then he closed the door and headed back to the museum.

The woman had been unexpected. Had she stayed home she would have lived to mourn her husband. But it was of little consequence to Dieter. She was his fourth kill for the organization; her husband would be the fifth. For the moment he was actually enjoying the heat of the day, with no thoughts about returning to Germany to plan for the next phase.

Today was just a warning. It was foolish, he and the others had agreed, but Pam had insisted.

"I want the bastards to squirm," she told them in her sharply clipped German.

"They'll go to ground once they realize what is happening," Rolf Woedding, the first man she'd hired, suggested languidly. He was from Hamburg. He'd been a major in the Bundeswehr and had won a couple of medals in Iraq.

He'd been accused, though never convicted, of the slaughter of a dozen civilians, after which he had quietly taken his discharge. For two years he'd worked as a contractor back in Iraq and Afghanistan, but his methods had become even harsher, and his contract guarding Afghan government officials had been terminated.

And he came to the attention of Pam Schlueter.

"No," she'd disagreed. "They're arrogant, all of them. I know these Americans, who they are, how they react."

"Their capabilities?"

"Will be their undoing. They work as teams. They don't know how to operate on their own."

"Once we've taken out the first few, won't the rest coalesce?" Woedding had pressed. "Some of them are still in the service; they'll just as likely return to their bases where we can't get to them."

"They'll come out when we start killing their families," Pam said. "Or don't you have the stomach for such things now?"

Woedding had merely smiled, and Dieter remembered thinking at the time that the man's expression was that of a cobra waiting patiently to strike.

No one else said a thing. Woedding outranked them all, and he was almost certainly the most out-of-control son of a bitch in the group. Everyone respected him, but more than that, all of them except Pam were afraid of him.

Just inside the front door, Dieter took out his pistol again and stopped to listen. He happened to glance at the sign-in book where Barnes had written his name and the date, when he heard someone toward the rear of the museum say something.

The words were indistinct, but the tone of voice was clear. Barnes had discovered Pavcovich's body in the office.

Moving to the end of the short corridor, Dieter stopped at the point where he could see the glass case in the reception area. At that moment Barnes came around the corner, his head down as he punched numbers into a cell phone.

He looked up, his eyes widening, and moved to the left the instant before Dieter fired, the shot smashing into a framed photograph of a SEAL Medal of Honor winner.

Dieter fired again, but Barnes disappeared around a corner into one of the display areas.

In any sort of action scenario Dieter's heart rate actually dropped. He became as calm as a man strolling along a beach without a care in the world, though he was capable of moving incredibly fast if need be. Afterward he'd always been able to tell his debriefers details that he never remembered noticing. He had an almost preternatural awareness of his surroundings.

It was not likely that the ex-SEAL Team Six assaulter was armed; nevertheless Dieter moved with caution down the corridor to the entrance into the first display room when he heard the sound of breaking glass. For just a moment he was confused. There were no windows in the front of the building through which Barnes could escape. But then it struck him: he was inside a museum of specialized warfare, with weapons on display. Certainly not loaded, but some of the stuff in here would be deadly in the right hands.

Dieter cautiously peered around the corner as the lights at the far end of the room went out behind one of the display counters. He fired one shot in that general direction, merely to see if he could get a reaction, but Barnes did not respond.

It was possible that the man was trying to reach the back door, which was farther down the corridor beyond the office. Dieter turned to head him off, but Barnes was right there with a World War II M1 Garand rifle, the bayonet fixed.

For just an instant Dieter stood looking into the ex-SEAL's eyes, and for just that instant his resolve weakened. The son of a bitch was a killer, and he was in the zone.

Barnes lunged from just a couple of feet away, but instead of stepping out of the way, Dieter moved forward, batting the tip of the blade away with his left hand. He fired the Glock into the man's neck, just below his chin, the round plowing upward into his brain.

SIX

□

Wolf had come through U.S. customs on a diplomatic passport, his one check-on bag sealed. He pulled into a condo parking lot less than fifty meters from the SEAL museum's fence, unlocked the bag in the trunk and took out his big SIG Sauer P226. He loaded it with a fresh magazine of 9mm hollow points, screwed the suppressor barrel on the end, and jacked a round into the firing chamber.

Back behind the wheel of his rental Camry, the pistol on the seat next to him, he watched the main gate and building in the rearview mirror. Zimmer's Chevrolet was parked next to a green Ford pickup truck with a Florida plate. The gate in the tall chain-link fence was open, but no one was about. The yard was deserted.

If they were right about Zimmer and the others working as contract killers, then it was very possible whatever was going on here today could be something more than a meeting. Wolf got a hollow feeling in his stomach.

He'd spent time in the hills of Afghanistan and in Iran's mountains helping set up suites of electronic surveillance equipment that could intercept military transmissions and relay them to an orbiting ComSatBw-2 satellite, which, combined with synthetic aperture radar images from the SAR-Lupe satellite monitoring the region, would give German military intelligence a lot of real-time information.

The problem came the night an Iranian patrol stumbled on their position. In the intense firefight that followed, all six Iranian commandos plus two of Wolf's people were killed.

Finishing their mission that night they had loaded all the bodies in the back of a pickup truck and driven eighty kilometers out into the desert, where they dumped the Iranians. They made their rendezvous point another one hundred plus kilometers to the north near the town of Babol near the Caspian Sea. When they were picked up by the patrol boat, the crew thought they were all mortally wounded because of their bloody uniforms.

He'd had a strong gut feeling just before the attack, and it was that feeling that saved most of his squad. Ever since then he listened.

Waiting until an AC service van heading north passed, Wolf drove to the SEAL parking lot and slowly passed the pickup truck and the Chevy to the end of the chain-link fence.

He turned around and drove back, parking behind the Impala, so that if Zimmer managed to get past him he would not be able to make his escape, at least not by car.

Grabbing the pistol he got out of the car and walked around to the driver's side of the Chevy and took a quick look through the window. The car was empty, no bag or anything else, no key in the ignition.

He looked across toward the museum to make sure no one was coming up the path; then he glanced inside the pickup. A woman lay on her side on the floor; a little blood from a bullet wound in her forehead had dribbled down the side of her nose.

But her death made absolutely no sense. As far as they'd been able to determine the organization Zimmer belonged to probably specialized in assassinations of high-profile targets, not some woman in an old pickup truck. Not unless she was someone important, or the mistress or wife of someone important, and the truck was merely a disguise.

The plate on the back was Hillsborough County, Florida. Moving cautiously toward the open gate, completely focused on what he might be walking into, scanning the roofline, the edges of the building and the corners of the boats and other things on display in the yard, Wolf almost missed the plate on the front of the truck.

He looked over his shoulder to make sure that somehow Zimmer hadn't come around on his six, when he spotted the circular emblem of the U.S. Navy Special Warfare Development Group. SEAL Team Six. The ones who had taken out bin Laden a few years ago.

One of them had apparently driven here with his wife or girlfriend and had gone inside. Zimmer's target? Which made even less sense unless the group was working for al-Qaeda. But there was no money there. The only effective cells still able to function were in backwaters like Somalia and, lately, Ethiopia and Sudan. But they were poorly equipped and had no real connections outside of their little groups. The leaders of the other larger, more important units, mostly in Afghanistan and Pakistan, had been killed by U.S. drone strikes.

Wolf made his way off the path between the boats and the Huey chopper, until he had a sight line on the front door. Everything from here looked normal.

The problem was Zimmer. They wanted him alive, if possible. If he could be taken, Wolf was to call his operations handler in Berlin, who would in turn make contact with the FBI. From there the situation—except for a debriefing—would be out of his hands. Mission accomplished. Or at least his part of it done. It would be up to the intelligence directorate to put all the pieces together.

He sprinted the last fifteen meters to the front door and flattened himself against the wall next to it. It was summer, and Florida's low season. It was possible that someone from the nearby condos might spot a man running around the museum yard with a pistol in his hand, but unlikely. Most of the people on islands like these were snowbirds—they came down from the snow in the northern states during the winter months and went back home in the summer.

In any event he had Interpol credentials and a permit to carry his weapon across the borders of member states. By agreement, deadly force was to be used only to protect his own life or the lives of innocent bystanders.

He'd been too late to protect the woman in the truck, and almost certainly the docents inside the museum, but he suspected that Zimmer would find dealing with a SEAL Team Six operator was an entirely different matter.

Wolf took a quick glance through the glass door. Nothing moved inside, nor were there any obvious signs of violence. But the short corridor that led maybe eight or ten meters back to a glass display case was a killing field. No place for someone coming through the door to take cover.

He turned and went to the east corner of the building, the scents of the sea at low tide strong on a chance breeze, the day easily as hot and humid as the lowlands along the Tigris River in Iraq. Moving fast and low, he made his way to the rear corner, where once again he held up for just a moment before chancing a quick look.

A man was running flat out, heading down a narrow path through a back gate in the tall fence directly toward the ocean. He was large and bald, and he was wearing a yellow shirt. The same man from the plane.

He disappeared over a rise, and Wolf headed after him at the same moment he heard the first siren from a long ways off. Someone had called the police. But if they were local cops, they wouldn't have a chance against Zimmer.

Near the top of the low dune, Wolf hunched down and cautiously took a look at what appeared to be a beach bunker of some sort. Big logs, barbed wire, of the sort the Japanese had used in the South Pacific during the war.

But there was no sign of Zimmer.

Rising up, he sprinted the rest of the way down to the bunker, at the same moment Zimmer appeared around the corner, his pistol pointed directly at Wolf's chest.

The siren was closer now, and in the distance there were more.

"Who the hell are you?" Zimmer asked in English.

"BND," Wolf said. His pistol was away from his side, pointed down.

Zimmer reacted, but his aim didn't waver.

"Put down your weapon and you might live out the afternoon. I followed you from Munich, and we have surveillance operations on the rest of your group. I'm only sorry that I wasn't in time to save the poor woman in the pickup truck. Was killing her really necessary?"

"You'll never know," Zimmer said in German.

He raised his pistol.

"Killing a SEAL. That why you came all this way?"

"You can't guess the half of it," Zimmer said, and he fired two shots.

Wolf staggered back, both rounds hitting him in the chest. As his legs went out from under him he managed to bring his pistol up and pull off one snap shot that hit Zimmer in the face just below his nose.

SEVEN

□

Wolf was sitting up trying to catch his breath from the impact of the two rounds on his Kevlar vest. He'd holstered his weapon and held up his Interpol credentials when the first cop came over the rise.

"Drop your weapon, put your hands together at the back of your head," the cop shouted. He was young and nervous.

"I'm a police officer," Wolf said. "Interpol."

"Put your hands together at the back of your head."

Wolf dropped his ID wallet and did as he was told. "There is a woman dead in the pickup truck, and at least two more dead inside the museum. This is the man who committed the murders."

The cop came down the slope and placed handcuffs on Wolf's wrist. But he was clumsy—it would have been child's play to take his weapon and shoot him.

He radioed something that Wolf didn't quite catch, and a minute later two more cops came over the rise. A lot more sirens were close now.

The young cop stood aside as one of the others picked up Wolf's ID, while the second kicked the pistol away from Zimmer's body.

"Are you armed?" the cop with his ID asked.

"Yes. Holster under my shirt on the left."

One of the new cops took his pistol. "You've been shot."

"I'm wearing," Wolf said. "Can you get these things off me?"

"In a minute," the cop said. His name tag read Fischer; he was a sergeant. He stepped a few yards away and spoke into a lapel mic.

"The man is Dieter Zimmer," Wolf said. "He's a German citizen I was following. We think that he works for a terror cell of killers for hire."

Two more cops showed up, but Fischer held them back and came over to Wolf.

"Passport?"

"Back pocket, right."

Fischer took it and read the number into his lapel mic.

Another set of sirens came from the south, their tones more high-pitched than the police cruisers. Wolf figured them to be ambulances.

"Take off the man's cuffs," Fischer said at length.

The younger cop did it and helped Wolf to his feet.

"Do you need a doctor, Captain Weisse?" Fischer asked. He was a short black man, his face glistened with sweat.

"No. But I need to contact my office in Berlin. They'll want to know what's happened here."

"My lieutenant is speaking with someone; they want to know if you're okay. Your embassy is being contacted."

"Good. May I have my things?"

Fischer handed over his passport and credentials wallet. "I'll hold the weapon for just a bit."

Wolf pocketed his ID and passport and went to search Zimmer's body, but one of the cops stepped in the way. "Sorry, sir, but for now he's our dead guy."

"I'd suggest that you get one of your ordinance disposal people down here. These guys are known to sometimes wear explosives, booby-trapped to go off if a first responder isn't careful."

The cop stepped back.

"Go ahead and deal with it," Fischer said from a respectful distance.

Wolf bent over Zimmer's body and carefully probed the areas of the armpits and groin. But he found nothing. He checked the pockets, coming up with about one hundred U.S. dollars, car keys for the Chevy, and a wallet with a driver's license and credit cards and a German passport, all of them in the name of Rheinhardt Schey.

"The passport is a fake. We'll provide you with the proper identification, and I'm sure that the BND or someone will want to claim the body. This is an ongoing investigation."

"Into what?"

"He was an assassin."

"There are two people dead up in the museum. One of them is a docent, the other is a younger man, we're working on his ID."

"He was a navy SEAL."

"I saw the front plate," Fischer said, and he cocked his head and stepped away, apparently listening to something in his earbud.

One of the cops had walked around to the other side of the machine-gun bunker. "We've got another one down here," he called up.

There were now six cops on the dune, and Fischer motioned for one of them to check it out. He was still talking into his lapel mic.

Wolf couldn't make out what he was saying, but the guy seemed a little surprised. None of this made sense to any of them. The killings were not random; Zimmer had gone through a lot of trouble to come all this way to kill a SEAL Team Six operator. Somehow he'd known that the man would be here at this particular moment in time, which meant the Black October Revolution had pretty sophisticated intelligence contacts here.

He stood staring at Zimmer's body, when Fischer came over and handed him the SIG.

"Any ideas?"

"His group is called the Black October Revolution, contract killers of high-profile targets—the four hits we know about were businessmen who weren't in the EU. The hits happened off German soil, one of them, in fact, in Atlanta. Tony Aldrich, who was a big player in the real estate market in Spain and in Monaco."

"Last year," Fischer said. "It was in the news. There've been no arrests, but his girlfriend was a suspect. They have a penthouse in Palm Beach, so there was a Florida connection." He glanced at Zimmer's body. "You think it was this guy?"

"I don't know, but we think it was the same organization."

"Motive?"

"Money."

"Killing a navy SEAL doesn't fit the profile."

"No," Wolf said.

Fischer looked at him. "Your English is good."

"I spent a couple of years at UC Berkeley a while back."

"Party time?"

Wolf had to smile, remembering how different it was there than at Kaiserslautern or even Heidelberg. "Yes."

"I've never been anywhere except a couple of cruises to the Caribbean with my wife."

"Come to Berlin and my wife and I will show you around. Professional courtesy."

"Sounds good," Fischer said. "Your embassy wants you in D.C. They've booked a flight for you on American Airlines, leaves a little after five. Someone will meet you at the gate."

"This wasn't what I expected," Wolf said, glancing up the dune toward the museum.

"You didn't pull the trigger."

"No, but if I had got here a little quicker, I might have prevented the woman's death. No reason for her."

"We might need you for the coroner's inquest," Fischer said. "Anyway, good hunting."

EIGHT

☐

The flight was early, around quarter to seven when they arrived at the terminal. Walking down the Jetway, Wolf was struck by the fact that Washington was even hotter and more humid than Florida. He could never live here.

A trim attractive woman in her early twenties with short dark hair met him just beyond the counter in the arrivals gate. She introduced herself as Lise Meitner, his BND embassy contact.

"Do you have a checked bag, sir?" she asked.

"Just one. My weapon."

"Yes, sir."

He followed her through the busy terminal down to the baggage arrival hall, where they didn't talk while they waited. Five minutes later his leather overnight bag showed up, once again sealed with diplomatic tape, and they went across to the parking garage and up to the third floor.

"Lenz is not very happy with you," she said, as they get into a plain gray Ford Taurus four-door. She was grinning. "He even raised hell with the *Fremdenverkehr* girl who gave you directions."

"I'll see if I can make it up to her."

"Herr Ritter was informed, and he had a little chat with Lenz." Hans Ritter was the ambassador.

"He won't like what I'm going to tell him either," Wolf said.

"I'm not taking you to the embassy. Colonel Mueller set up a meeting for you at the CIA. Apparently he's been working with someone over there ever since the thing in Atlanta, and they're interested in what happened this time in Florida."

Wolf looked at her. Traffic was heavy leaving the airport, and on the parkway heading north to Langley, but she was a good driver, easily pacing her movements. "What's your position here?"

"Scientific liaison. My namesake was my great-grandmother, the Austrian nuclear physicist, and the knack runs in the family. I'm the only one in three generations who hasn't become a scientist or a science teacher, and no one is happy I ended up with the BND."

Scientific liaison was intel-speak for industrial spying. "How's it going?"

She shrugged. "I don't have to shoot anybody, if that's what you mean."

"Right," Wolf said, and he suddenly realized how tired he was. He'd been on the go for thirty-six hours. He'd never been able to sleep on airplanes, especially not heading into a situation.

Lise glanced over at him. "I didn't mean it like that. It's just that I don't like spying on a friendly country, and I know I sure as hell would never want to face someone with a pistol."

"No one in their right mind wants to, trust me."

"I suppose not," she said after a beat.

They drove again for a while in silence, and Wolf tried to piece together something that would make sense to whomever he was supposed to meet with at the CIA. He hadn't been involved in the Atlanta operation, so he hadn't been required to work with the agency—that had fallen to Mueller who had friends over here. But he had worked with a number of their field officers in Iraq and Afghanistan, and on the one mission inside Iran. The ones he'd met had seemed steady, if a little arrogant around the edges, though not as cocky as some of the Mossad officers he'd known.

Zimmer's last words had been bothersome, and Wolf had thought about them on the plane all the way up. The man hadn't been the least concerned that he'd killed an innocent woman, and that he'd come all the way from Germany simply to murder an American who'd served in the U.S. Navy. *You can't guess the half of it*, he'd said.

Half of what?

The only connection Wolf was making was the bin Laden raid, which continued to make no sense.

They turned off the parkway and followed a road through the woods to a visitors center with two lanes, one on the left for credentialed employees and the other for nonemployees. They had to show their passports and were given a visitor's pass for the dashboard.

"You may drive Mr. Weisse to the drop-off point in front of the OHB, after which you will return here. Do not go beyond that point, ma'am. You will be timed."

"May I wait for him?"

"Back here once you have turned in your visitor's pass."

On the way up the winding road the seven-story original head-quarters building appeared through the woods. The parking lot in front was full this afternoon.

"I've never been out here before," Lise said. "But it looks just like in the movies."

"I don't know how long I'll be, so there's no need for you to wait."

"Lenz told me to stick with you."

"Well, you can't come inside, so tell him that," Wolf said. She was a sharp girl, but naïve. "Tell him I gave you a direct order."

She pulled up in front. "Are you going to come to the embassy afterward?"

He had to laugh. "No, but don't tell him that. He'll probably have a heart attack."

"I wish," she said.

"Drop my bag off at the gatehouse, if you would," Wolf said, and he went up the broad stairs and into the big marble lobby, the CIA's logo in the floor.

A very attractive woman in her mid- to late thirties, short dark hair, blue eyes, and a voluptuous movie-star figure came across to him. She was dressed in khaki slacks, a white blouse, and a dark blue blazer. "I'm Pete Boylan. You must be Wolfhardt Weisse."

"I am," Wolf said and they shook hands. Hers was tiny compared to his, but it was cool and her grip was firm. High marks in his esti-mation.

She handed him a visitor's pass on a lanyard. "You look like you could use some sleep."

"I don't get much on airplanes."

"I'll make this as brief as possible, but there might be someone else who wants to have a word with you."

They went through the security arches, past the Starbucks and down the broad corridor that served as the agency's museum, with displays of equipment starting with the OSS during World War II. Radios, weapons, explosives, hidden cameras, and miniature tape recorders, as well as insects about the size of a man's thumb that were actually remote-controlled drones equipped with tiny cameras.

"Makes us think that we're actually James Bonds around here," she said.

They took an elevator up to the sixth floor and walked down to a small conference room pleasantly furnished with a table for a half dozen people, some pretty pictures on the walls of places like the Eiffel Tower, the Colosseum, the Sydney Opera House, Niagara Falls.

Pete flipped a wall switch. "We're recording audio and video—is that okay with you?"

"Fine."

"You were involved in a shooting in Florida. Walk me through it."

"We've been monitoring an organization that we think may be an assassination-for-hire operation specifically targeting high-profile people."

"We have the summary from Colonel Mueller. But the thing in Fort Pierce doesn't seem to fit the profile."

"No. And the only way it makes even remote sense to me would be if the SEAL Team Six guy he took out had been on the bin Laden operation."

"He was," Pete said.

"Anything special about him?"

"Nothing except that he was one of the men up the stairs who actually fired shots to make sure of the kill. But the group the BND is investigating hardly seems the type to be working with al-Qaeda."

"No," Wolf said.

"But?"

"Something Zimmer said to me just before I shot him. I asked why the guy and his wife? He said I'd never guess the half of it."

Pete picked up the phone and made a call. "Otto, I want to bring Captain Weisse down to have a chat. Are you decent?" She nodded. "We're on our way."

ΠΙΠΞ

□

Pete's key card wasn't programmed for Otto Rencke's security lock, so she had to buzz. Very few key cards other than the director's and deputy director's gained entrance to what most people on campus considered the holiest of computer inner sanctums. Fact was that most people who even knew about Otto and his "darlings," as he called his search and analysis programs, were frightened out of their wits thinking what harm he could do to the entire U.S. cyberstructure if he had a mind to.

Wolf had heard stories about the CIA's resident computer genius and the man's long-term friendship with Kirk McGarvey, a former DCI and a legend in the intel business himself, but he was not prepared for the tall, somewhat ascetic-looking man who opened the door for them.

"Oh, wow, I've been working the problem all afternoon, and you guys aren't going to believe what shit I'm coming up with."

"Otto Rencke, Captain Wolfhardt Weisse, BND," Pete said, and the two men shook hands.

Rencke's long red hair was tied in a short pony tail. He was dressed in ragged jeans and an old KGB sweatshirt "Bad business down there, involving a man's wife—believe me, I could write the book on shit like that—but what'd you think Zimmer was up to?"

They went into Rencke's suite of offices, a space he shared with no one that was filled with wide-screen computer monitors, some of them as big as one hundred inches, hanging on the walls, other smaller ones at a dozen workstations, and in the middle of the innermost office a horizontal touch screen as long and as wide as a conference table for sixteen people.

"We had no idea," Wolf admitted. "But I was assigned to keep track of him. Maybe he was meeting someone. We just didn't know."

"Not even a glimmer when you got to the SEAL museum?"

"It wasn't making any sense to me, and whenever that happens I get nervous."

"Good instincts," Otto said.

Most of the monitors were blank, showing only colors: white, blue, red—even a couple of violets. Otto led Pete and Wolf to the table-top, on which were displayed several dozen photographs of three men and one women.

"The name Pam Schlueter mean anything to you?"

"We think she may be either the director or the power broker for a group based in Munich that calls itself the Black October Revolution. Assassination for hire."

Otto moved the two photographs of her to the center of the screen. One showed her sitting on a blanket on a beach, with what appeared to be an aircraft carrier in the distance.

"That's her in Virginia about fifteen years ago. Photo was taken by her husband, Dick Cole, who is now a captain, acting chief of staff with JSOC—Joint Special Operations Command in Virginia."

"We weren't aware that she was married to an American naval officer."

"Not now. They met twenty years ago in Munich when he was a youngish lieutenant commander and she was a poli-sci student at the Ludwig Maximilian University. She was doing a paper on military liaisons between Germany and other NATO countries, and at some point she ran into Cole, who even then was in JSOC. They apparently hit it off, because they got married within six months. A year after that he was rotated back to the Pentagon and she followed."

"We knew none of this. Much of her background has been wiped clean."

"In Germany," Otto said. "But over here it's easy. Anyway, their marriage went bad, and about the time they moved to Virginia Beach they got a divorce. She took her maiden name and moved back to Germany. I came across a couple of civilian police reports of domestic violence. From what I could piece together he wasn't a very nice guy. Lots of physical violence, on both their parts. She broke his arm in one fight."

"Tough lady," Pete said.

"Apparently she's developed a thing for Americans," Otto said.

"SEALs in particular?" Wolf asked.

Otto smiled and shrugged. "If she was calling the orders on this one, it would seem so."

"Revenge against an ex-husband? How likely is that?"

"More likely than you might think, Captain," Pete said.

"Friends call me Wolf."

The other photograph of her, dressed in plain desert camos, showed her coming out of a building. The shot had been taken from across a busy street. "Pakistan's intelligence service headquarters in Islamabad," Otto said.

Wolf was taken aback. As far as he knew the BND had none of this. "When?"

"September fifteenth, three years ago. It's the only shot of her, taken by chance because we were looking for someone else. We don't know why she was there, who she spoke to, or the subject of their meeting."

"But you came up with her ID."

Otto gazed at the photograph. "It's the stray bits that sometimes make the most sense." He looked up. "I went searching for connections with SEAL Team Six after I was told about your shooter, and one of my darlings came up with her. And you know her name. Nails it, don't you think?"

"Nails what?" Wolf asked.

"Her group's target this time is the SEAL Team Six that took out bin Laden."

"Al-Qaeda doesn't have the money."

"Pakistan does. The three guys are Pakistani intel—ISI."

"Definitely makes it our problem," Pete said.

"If I'm right," Otto said.

"Have you ever not been right?" she asked. She picked up a phone and called Marty Bambridge, who was the deputy director of operations and told him that she and Otto were coming up to his office with the BND officer.

Wolf stepped closer to the table and stared at the two photographs of the woman. The one on the beach showed Pam Schlueter, somewhat reminiscent of a young Judi Dench, the British actor. She was smiling, apparently still happy with her husband, who had most likely taken the picture.

But in the second photograph, the determined, angry expression on her face, clear even though the photograph had been taken from a distance, was the same as in the photos the BND had managed to come up with.

In the first she was a happy young woman, but she had changed. Somehow in the past fifteen years she had become radicalized, and Wolf felt that it had taken more than an abusive husband to do it.

TEN

The DDO's secretary announced them and Bambridge told her to send them in. He was an officious little man, with narrow shoulders and a nearly permanent look of surprise on his dark face. Backroom gossip was that despite his name, he behaved more like a Sicilian and therefore was probably connected with the Mob. His temper was legendary, but he was a good organizer, though almost always by the book.

He rose from his desk as they came in. "I'm sorry that your colonel's courtesy call came too late; otherwise we might have been able to help out."

"The captain was on a surveillance mission," Pete said. "The assassination of a former SEAL came as a surprise."

"I should have known better," Wolf said.

"Yes," Bambridge said, and they all sat down. "What brings you up here at this hour? I was getting set to finally go home."

For as long as she could remember Pete had wanted to slap the officious bastard in the mouth. And a couple of years ago she'd said as much to McGarvey, who'd laughed.

"No one would blame you, but the man does a nice job pushing papers. Stay on his good side and you'll get promoted. One of these days he'll be gone."

"Walt loves him, and he's got a couple of intelligence oversight committee members on his side. Maybe he'll end up as DDCI, or even DCI, God forbid." Walter Page was the director of central intelligence.

"Won't happen," Mac had assured her.

That was last year, but now she wasn't so sure. Rumor was that

Page was considering him for the deputy directorship, which was only a heartbeat from the DCI's chair, at least on a temporary basis.

"Otto has come up with a couple of interesting connections," she said.

"No doubt interesting," Bambridge said. He'd had a troubled relationship with McGarvey over the last few years. Otto and Mac were longtime friends, and therefore in Bambridge's mind, Otto was also a wild card.

"The guy Captain Weisse was following shot and killed a former SEAL Team Six operator who was on the operation to take out bin Laden," Otto said. "He'd written a memoir of his time in the navy and was bringing it to the UDT/SEAL museum."

"How do we know that?"

"The police found it inside the museum," Wolf said.

"Any of it in the media? Was he hyping for a book contract or something?"

"Not that we know of," Otto said. "But the fact that the shooter knew that Barnes would be there at that exact time means the group that hired him has some damned good intel contacts here in the States."

"Who, for instance?"

"I don't know that part yet, but my guess would be somewhere within the Pentagon, or perhaps inside JSOC at Fort Bragg or down in Virginia. I'm digging into Barnes's phone and travel records to see if he still has some buddies up there. Maybe someone with a grudge or someone in financial trouble."

Bambridge turned back to Wolf. "Who did he work for?"

"A group calling itself the Black October Revolution, specializing, we think, in the assassinations of high-profile targets for some fairly serious money. It's run by a woman who was actually married to an American naval officer."

"Ended in divorce," Otto said.

"The SEAL in Fort Pierce was hardly a high-profile target," Bambridge said. "So why is it I have a funny feeling that you're going to tell me this woman's ex is or was a SEAL himself and this assassination was just for revenge."

"He's a captain now in JSOC—DEVGRU, Virginia Beach."

"And the connection is what?"

"Not really a connection, not yet," Otto said. "Let's call it a coincidence, like having a photograph coming out of ISI headquarters in Islamabad a few years go—just after the bin Laden raid."

Bambridge's eyes narrowed, and he held up a hand. "This stops right now. Unless Captain Weisse has been buried underground in one of the old bunkers in Berlin, he, like you, should be perfectly aware that Pakistan is our chief ally fighting the Taliban and al-Qaeda. Without them we'd be dead in the water, wide open for another nine-eleven."

"Come on, Marty, Pakistan is no ally," Pete said, her anger coming to the surface as she'd known it would even before she'd stepped into his office. But he was the DDO and he needed to know what was going on, even though he was an asshole. "Anyway most of those people were Saudis. Pakistan is helping us because they need our military aid, without which India would steamroller them."

"That's a good bit of analysis for an interrogator from housekeeping."

"I have photographs of three ISI officers who were seen entering the ISI building at the same time she was inside," Otto said.

"A lot of people work there. What's your point? Another coincidence?"

"All three of those officers were very vocal at that time in their anger over the bin Laden raid right under their noses."

"So were a lot of them," Bambridge said. "So what?"

"The day after the woman was seen leaving, their complaints stopped," Otto said. "Another coincidence, wouldn't you say?"

"Coincidences do happen," Bambridge said, and Pete started to object, but he held her off. "Any supposed link to the ISI or to any person in specific—any Pakistani—is a nonissue as of this moment. And that is a standing order from the top. In the meantime, several murders were committed on U.S. soil, two of which Captain Weisse has himself admitted to. The local police have already requested help from the FBI, and a team has been in place since late this afternoon."

"I imagine they will want to interview me," Weisse said.

"You have been ordered home. Your embassy has made the arrangements."

"There'll at least be a coroner's inquest," Pete said. "And Captain Weisse has told me that he is willing to share his file on the Schlueter woman."

"The Black October Revolution and its aims are of no concern to this agency at this time."

"For Christ's sake, Marty, one of their people killed several U.S. citizens, including a decorated war hero—and we're not interested?"

"Naval intelligence has been notified, and they are on the case as well, though it's my understanding that Barnes was no longer on active duty. Captain Weisse will be deposed at home, and that comes directly from his Colonel Mueller."

Pete suddenly realized that Bambridge was frightened. She almost called him out but thought better of it. Someone above him, either the DCI himself or Robert Bensen, the deputy director, had given the order to back off, and Marty was a team player to the end. He followed orders even if they stank.

"Okay, Marty, you want us to drop it, we will."

Otto was clearly surprised.

"The situation is being handled," Bambridge. "Is there anything else that I need to know at this time?"

"No," Pete said, and they all got up.

Bambridge shook hands with Weisse. "Give my regards to your colonel. I'm sorry for your agency's sake that things didn't work out as you might have hoped they would."

"Thank you, sir," Wolf said.

"What the hell was that all about?" Otto asked in the elevator on the way down to his office. "The silly bastard was lying out his ass."

"You're damned right he was," Pete said. "Someone got to him, someone high enough up the food chain to scare him witless."

"Someone from across the river? The White House?"

"Or the Pentagon. Someone on the SecDef's staff."

"Should I be hearing any of this?" Wolf said. "I'll have to report it to my boss."

"You might as well, because we're not done with you and your investigation of the Schlueter woman and her group."

"Isn't the man we just talked with your boss?"

"Yup, but Otto's going to let his computer programs loose while I go talk to an old friend, who'll probably contact you at some point."

"Off the grid?"

Pete and Otto laughed. "Definitely off the grid."

"Who's the old friend?"

"Kirk McGarvey. Can you delay going back? I think he's going to want to talk to you?"

"Twenty-four hours?"

"Plenty of time."

"I'll give you my encrypted cell phone number."

"I already have it," Otto said.

ELEVEN

Kirk Cullough McGarvey, Mac to his friends, ran along the river in Georgetown's Rock Creek Park just at sunrise. He was a man of about fifty, in superb physical condition from years of heavy workouts, long swims, weight training, and fencing at épée with the Annapolis navy team when he was in town. A little under six feet, a little under two hundred pounds, he could still move as gracefully as a ballet dancer if the need arose. Which it often had during a long career with the CIA.

A few other joggers, some walkers, and other folks on bicycles used the park just about every decent morning, and several of them recognizing McGarvey waved or simply nodded, but he was otherwise occupied, thinking about his wife, Katy, and their daughter, Liz, who had been brutally murdered just a couple of years ago.

He thought about them every day. But lately he was sometimes having trouble seeing Katy's face, though her scent was still strong in his mind. And every day, just like this morning, he wanted to lash out, hit back at all the darkness in the world that thought taking lives was the right thing to do.

He'd actually met bin Laden a number of years ago in a cave in Afghanistan, and the man had looked him in the eye and with a straight face lectured that no one was innocent. Infidels—men, women, or children, it made no difference—were all to come to Islam, the one true faith, accept Mohammed into their souls or die.

Mac had begun years ago as a field officer for the CIA and had risen to special black operations, which was the forerunner of the company's elite Special Activities Division. He'd worked for a short time as deputy director of operations and had even briefly served as the agency's director.

But neither desk job had suited his temperament. He hated bullies; it was as simple as that. In the field he could even the odds, take down the bad guys who preyed on the innocents. Unlike bin Laden he firmly believed that just about everyone who went about their business in a peaceful way, respecting the rights of others, was an innocent.

His father had instilled only one hard and fast rule in Mac as a child, and that was no hitting. Yet despite that golden rule his father had worked on nuclear weapons development at Los Alamos and Mac had killed bad people.

The creek and the path crossed under the P Street NW bridge and McGarvey pushed himself. Katy once asked if by running or swimming to just this side of total exhaustion he wasn't trying to atone for what he thought were his sins, namely, assassinating people?

He'd had no answer for her then, nor did he think he would have one if she were alive to ask him now.

A hundred yards later, just at the edge of the Oak Hill Cemetery, Pete Boylan, who'd been doing stretches against a park bench, turned and intercepted him. She wore spandex tights and a white T-shirt that was soaked with sweat, and she looked really good.

"Want some company?" she asked.

"If you can keep up."

She laughed, the sound husky, all the way from deep inside, and warm. "If it gets too tough, I'll just knock you down and sit on you."

They ran for a half a mile or so in silence all the way up to Massachusetts Avenue, traffic already building, where they stopped and did more stretches. Mac felt good, better than he had for the past several months, and the heat and female sweat smells coming off Pete's body reminded him of a lot of things out of his past.

"You didn't come down here just to get your exercise," he said.

"I work out at the gym on campus and sometimes down at the Farm. I'm here because I need your help."

It's about what he'd figured, not only by her unexpected presence but by the expression on her face; she seemed puzzled and a little pissed off. "Where'd you park?"

"Just off M Street." It was a little over a mile back the way they had come. "I brought someone with me who I think you might want to talk to."

"Anyone I know?"

"Otto's met him. He was involved yesterday with a shooting at the UDT/SEAL museum in Florida."

"I suppose that you and Otto took whatever it was up to Marty and he ordered you to back off."

"Yeah."

"You'd better explain," Mac said, and they started back at a slow jog as she went over everything she'd learned from Weisse and what Otto had come up with. He found that he almost had to agree with Bambridge.

No one in the administration or inside the U.S. intelligence community trusted Pakistan, and especially not the ISI, its secret intelligence service, any further than they could throw the Washington Monument, but the Pakistanis did provide a launching point for U.S. drone strikes on al-Qaeda leaders. Government spokesmen in Islamabad complained loudly about the U.S. military's violation of their borders, and especially their airspace, but that was all about keeping their public satisfied. In the meantime the United States continued to subsidize their military—in a delicate balancing act with India—for the right to continue operations.

He told Pete as much.

"You're right, of course," she said. "But this is different. I think that someone in the ISI—someone high on the food chain—is funneling money to the Schlueter woman to field assassins to kill the key SEAL Team Six guys who took out bin Laden."

"Why?" Mac asked, though he knew the answer.

"Because we embarrassed the hell out of them."

"What would killing the shooters—or maybe all twenty-four of them who went on the raid—accomplish? Washington would sure as hell sit up and take notice. So would the Pentagon, so would Walt Page, so would the FBI, so would the State Department. Think of it: killing all those guys—even if it could be done, because they're damned good at close order battle—would cause a firestorm to fall on Islamabad. Or at least on the ISI."

"Not if it were an arms-length operation. It would give the government plausible deniability. Could be someone they intend to throw under the bus if something goes wrong."

"They'd have more ways to lose than gain," Mac said. He was playing devil's advocate and they both knew it. But the first rule of operational planning was to poke holes in every detail and keep filling them until they all disappeared. And even then it was the unknown that always seemed to jump up and bite you in the ass—like the crash of the SEAL's Chalk One helicopter.

"They want to save face," Pete said. "They want retribution."

Wolf was sitting at a picnic table smoking a cigarette. When Mac and Pete showed up he got to his feet and tossed the cigarette into the creek. Pete introduced them, and after they shook hands they sat down.

"I understand that you've been ordered home," Mac said.

"I'm supposed to be on the way to Reagan."

"I'm driving him over," Pete said. "But we don't have a lot of time."

"We can dig out what we need to know about the Black October Revolution, and Pete tells me that Otto's already started a file on the Schlueter woman, but it's not completely clear to me why you followed the shooter out of Germany."

"We think that Schlueter has hired a team of five men and one woman—most of them ex–special services—to work as assassins for hire."

"KSK," Mac said. They had a good reputation.

Wolf nodded. "We think we can connect the team to at least four killings, all of them off German soil. One of them in Atlanta. Plus the SEAL in Florida, who I was assigned to follow, his wife and the docents."

"Do you have minders on the others as well?"

"We didn't think that it was necessary. But this hit came as a total surprise to us. To this point the team has targeted only high-profile people. Barnes hardly fit that description. And his wife definitely did not."

"She was collateral damage, as were the docents in the museum," Mac said. "Pete thinks the group might have a contract from the ISI to take out the SEAL Team Six guys who brought bin Laden down."

"That's what she and Otto came up with, but I don't know if I can sell it to my colonel. We have our own operations in Pakistan. Certainly much more limited than yours, of course, but Berlin would be put in the same position as your government if we actively went after them."

"It's either that or they take out those guys one by one," Pete said. "The least we can do is warn them."

"I can just hear what the navy would say, and what the White House would do," Mac said.

"We can't turn our backs on this thing," Pete said.

"Of course not. One of Schlueter's people is dead. Can we get the files on anyone else associated with her? Without making noise?"

Wolf nodded. "I'll see what I can do," he said. "But maybe you should come to Berlin to speak with the director."

Mac glanced at Pete, who shrugged. "Marty has closed us down, so we're not going to get any help from the agency. Not unless we come up with something concrete."

"Will your colonel agree to talk to me?"

"As long as it's not official," Wolf said. "I can arrange the meeting."

TWELVE

□

Warsaw's Zoological Garden was situated on the Vistula River almost directly across from the Royal Castle, the old Market Square, and other attractions including churches and museums in the ancient part of the sprawling city. The early summer evening was lovely; a lot of people were out and about. The zoo was anonymous.

Pam Schlueter was a somewhat husky woman in her late thirties, with a pleasant round face, a short no-nonsense pixie haircut, and expressive eyes that, like the set of her mouth, showed her anger and impatience. She was dressed plainly in a short-sleeved yellow shirt, jeans, and Nikes, a brown leather bag over her left shoulder, leaving her right hand free to withdraw her subcompact Glock 26 pistol, the same weapon as everyone on her team carried.

She'd left Berlin this morning before lunch for the four-hundred-mile drive, taking a great deal of care to make certain that she wasn't being followed. Twice she'd gotten off the E30, once to fill up the tank of her Volvo and the second to have a beer at a small *Gasthaus* and look over her shoulder. But if she had a tail they were very good. Coming into the city she made several abrupt turns, but each time she came back on her original track she'd detected no one following her. Which in itself was disturbing after the mess Zimmer had made in Florida.

She made her way directly back to the Hippopotamus House where ISI Major Ali Naisir was standing in front of the glass wall, watching two of the big animals swimming underwater. He was a short, slightly built man of about forty, dark with a thick mustache, dressed in khaki slacks, a white shirt buttoned at the collar, and a dark jacket. As she walked up to him she could see that he was watching her reflection in the glass.

That he had come here to Warsaw and had asked for the meeting in public was extraordinary in itself, but when he turned, gave her a big smile, and pecked her on the cheek before offering his arm, she was blown away. In the months Naisir had been her handler, he'd never smiled at her, nor had he ever made any physical contact, not even a handshake.

"Congratulations in Florida," he said as he led her out of the house and down the broad walkway in the general direction of the elephant exhibit.

"I don't know what you're talking about. It was a disaster. My operator was shot to death."

"Yes, but he managed to achieve his objective."

"At a very high cost."

"The cost doesn't matter," Naisir said, looking at her. "It's the same with collateral damage. If he had used a bomb to wipe out the entire museum and every living soul within a half-mile radius, still the price would not have been too high."

There was nothing to say in reply. It was one of the many things she did not understand about the Pakistani males, especially those who could trace their lineage back to the Pashtuns, primarily from Afghanistan. They were an ancient people who loved poetry and dance above everything else. But they were short of temper, never forgave a sin against them, and would go to the ends of the earth for retribution. Their potential for cruelty was all out of any normal proportion. A perceived slight at a wedding ceremony could result in the deaths of the entire party.

"Negotiating terms was not the reason I called you here," he said. "You must hurry with the rest of the assignment. The timetable must be moved up."

"Mistakes are bound to be made."

"We're aware of that possibility."

"Likelihood."

They stopped. "Are you saying that you cannot do this for us?" he asked.

"No. What I'm trying to tell you, Major, is that when the U.S. Navy realizes that a coordinated attack is being made against the Neptune Spear people, our chances for success will drop like a rock."

Neptune Spear was the SEAL Team Six code name for the bin Laden raid.

"That may already be the case, Ms. Schlueter. We believe that Captain Weisse, who is a field officer for the BND officer, was the man who shot Mr. Zimmer to death. He was released by the police and flown to Washington, where we think he was debriefed by the CIA. But that's not all."

The news was nothing short of stunning to her. She'd known, of course, that the BND had been snooping around her organization, but to have sent a field officer on a specific assignment—this specific assignment—was stellar. It put the entire operation in extreme jeopardy.

She managed to focus on Naisir. "What else?" she asked.

"He met this morning with Kirk McGarvey, who at one time was the director of the agency."

"Former DCI. It would make him an old man now. Old and soft."

"Anything but," Naisir said. "We've dealt with the man and we know something about him. What we don't know is why he met with Captain Weisse and why the meeting was held at a public park. But shortly afterward, a woman who we're certain works for the CIA, drove the captain to the airport, where he flew back to Berlin."

Pam tried to work it out, to make some sense out of what Naisir was telling her. The BND was snooping around, but if she was being warned now that the German spy agency knew about her and the shooters she had hired, then it was probably time to make a one-eighty and close down the operation.

But even as she had that thought she knew damned well it was simply impossible for her to do so. Like the Pashtuns, she had been done wrong, and nothing on earth would stop her from getting revenge.

The abuse her husband had thrown at her had begun within months after they'd gotten married, and years later she had to wonder what had possessed her to stay with him when he was rotated back to the States for duty at the Pentagon. It was in a pleasant ranch-style house in Temple Hills just across the river from Washington where his abuse had turned from emotional to physical.

At first it was watching porn with him, much of it S & M, and he would make her reenact it while he videotaped the "action," as he called it. When his promotions slowed to a crawl he began seriously beating her with sopping wet bath towels and lengths of rubber hose. But it was always on her body and upper thighs so that no marks were visible when she was dressed.

The abuse had progressed so slowly, and with what she thought was even some innocence on his part—he said he loved her and that he wanted only pleasure for both of them—that she'd gone along with it.

But then there were water hoses up her vagina and rectum, and broom handles, and electric shocks to her nipples, and she'd finally had enough. After an entire weekend of abuse that seemed as if it would never end. She got a knife from a kitchen drawer and tried to stab him to death. But he was a lot bigger than her, and quicker and stronger, and she was weak from her injuries. He took the knife away and calmly beat her into unconsciousness even though she'd managed to break his arm.

The final straw came on Monday afternoon when he telephoned from his office and asked if she wanted to go out for a bite somewhere and then a movie. It was as if nothing had happened. Within a couple of hours she was packed and checked into a motel near Dulles Airport. Two days later she was on a plane back to Munich, and he never looked for her, never tried to contact her, never even bothered with a divorce. And her deep-seated anger began to grow, first against him and then against the navy and finally everyone and everything American.

The last she'd heard he was with DEVGRU. She'd hatched the plan to kill the SEAL Team Six members who'd taken part in Neptune Spear and approached Pakistan's intelligence for the funds to get retribution for both herself and them.

But at arm's length. After her first meeting in Islamabad, Major Naisir had been her only contact.

They had reached the elephant exhibit, where two of the females were standing near one of the pools. Two children had purchased elephant food from a dispenser and were throwing the pellets over the fence, but the animals were ignoring them.

"I'm going to need some spot-on intelligence if there's any hope of pulling this off," Pam told her handler. "The exact locations of every one of those guys."

"For now we want you to limit your efforts to the other ten operators who actually entered the main house where Usama was living with his family. Most of them are retired, and we think that at least two of them are currently on some form of federal assistance."

"They're still well-trained killers."

"You will send overwhelming force where it is needed," Naisir said. "In the meantime I will personally see to silencing Captain Weisse."

"If you assassinate him it'll prove to the BND that something is actually going on and they'll come after us with everything they've got."

"He'll be beaten to death by hoodlums on the street. Another act of random violence that Berlin has always been so famous for."

Pam nodded. The killing would be senseless, and she said as much.

"This goes back to the captain's meeting with McGarvey. Depending upon what was said McGarvey could very well become a major problem."

"We'll kill him as well," Pam said.

"That might not be as easy as you think."

"Everyone is vulnerable; businessmen, SEALs, presidents, even former CIA directors," Pam said. "We'll start immediately. But I'll want a bonus."

Naisir nodded. "For McGarvey alone we will pay you an extra one million euros. Will that do?"

"Nicely," she said.

THIRTEEN

□

McGarvey came down to the lobby from his room in the old but fashionable Bristol Hotel Kempinski on the Ku'damm in the middle of Berlin. It was just before nine in the evening and Wolf was waiting for him.

"Did you have a good flight over?"

"Not bad," McGarvey said.

"I figured that you would come in under a false passport, so I didn't bother trying to find you at Tegel. I thought I'd wait until you called."

"Colonel Mueller has agreed to talk to me?"

"He has a place on Oranienstrasse, right on top of where the wall used to be. I think it's a point of pride with him. He had family stuck on the east side."

"Wife and kids?"

"They went to Munich for a holiday. We'll be quite secure."

Driving over to Mueller's apartment the city was alive with traffic, people out on the streets, in the shops and restaurants and sidewalk cafés. The last couple of times Mac had been here the city had seemed dark, even ominous. There'd been a lot of financial problems and readjustment issues when the wall came down. Just trying to come up with a reasonable match for the two standards of living had at times seemed insurmountable. East Germans, especially East Berliners, were needy. It seemed like the West was pouring marks down a bottomless rat hole. Everyone had been tense.

Oberst Mueller met them at the front door of a heavily rebuilt three-story brownstone and took them back to a small book-lined study that overlooked a rear courtyard that had once been bisected by the wall. Now rose bushes blossomed where the concrete sections had stood.

The colonel was a tall man, something over six feet, with an unremarkable build and face that marked him as anything but a military officer and high-ranking member of Germany's secret intelligence service. He was dressed in corduroy trousers and a khaki shirt, the sleeves buttoned up above the elbows. The room smelled of pipe tobacco.

"Thanks for agreeing to see me," McGarvey said.

"Captain Weisse tells me that you may have come up with something disturbing that might make some sense after the incident in Florida and you could use some help. I'm all ears."

"This would be a nonofficial request."

"I understand."

"The situation between us and Pakistan is delicate, and my government doesn't want to increase the strain if at all possible."

"But you personally have a situation. And considering what I know about your background, it could mean that you're going to become involved in something violent. Something that neither my government nor yours wants to happen."

McGarvey wasn't sure that he liked Mueller, though the man had agreed to hear him out. "Captain Weisse came to the United States and gunned down a man you suspected of being a terrorist. First blood was shed on our soil by your agency, not the other way around."

"Point taken. Did the captain brief you on our ongoing investigation?"

"Yes. And until Florida it seemed that the group you've been investigating was nothing more than assassins for hire, targeting non-Germans off German soil. Not pretty, but considering everything else the BND is faced with, not a high priority."

"Killing the ex-SEAL was an anomaly," Mueller suggested.

"I don't think so," Mac said. "In fact I think that someone hired the organization to assassinate all the SEAL Team Six people who took part in the raid on bin Laden."

"Al-Qaeda no longer has the money or the influence it once had."

"No."

"There are, however, wealthy Islamists in the United States, and of course in Saudi Arabia, who might want to retaliate."

"They would have nothing to gain."

"Which leaves Pakistan," the colonel said heavily, as if it had been a foregone conclusion of his from the very beginning. He got up and turned to the window. "As you pointed out, the situation between your government and that of Pakistan's is delicate. The balance of power—of nuclear power—between Pakistan and India is disturbing to us as well. That said, Islamabad would have absolutely nothing to gain by carrying out such a monstrous plot, which could only end in failure."

"Retribution," McGarvey said.

The colonel turned back. "For an extrajudicial assassination. I can see their justification, can't you?"

"We did not attack civilian targets in their country. Nine-eleven is significant for us."

"Just as the firebombing of Dresden was for us."

"Yes, and just as the London blitz was for the British," McGarvey shot back, tired of the game.

"The Nazis are gone," Mueller said sharply.

"Will you help?"

"Operationally, no."

"With information, nothing more."

"We would expect a quid pro quo."

"Of course," McGarvey said. "I'd like a copy of your files on the Schlueter woman, along with the Black October Revolution and its members."

Mueller considered it for a moment. "In return for what?"

"Our file on her, and on the twenty-four SEAL Team Six operators who took part in the raid."

"The file on the SEALs is of no interest to us."

"It will be once you come to accept what the Schlueter woman's mission is and why she went to the ISI for backing."

This caught Mueller's attention.

"We have a photograph of her coming out of ISI headquarters. Until the incident in Florida we had no idea who she was or what she was doing in Islamabad, but now we think we know the connection."

"Go to your navy. Tell them to take those people into protective custody."

"That's not going to happen," McGarvey said. "At least not for now."

"Just what are you suggesting?" Mueller asked.

"Schlueter and her organization are creating trouble for Germany as well as for the United States. Share the files and I will eliminate it."

Mueller shook his head. "My government will not allow you to run around Germany shooting people. Point them out, get the proof, and we will arrest them."

"I would be operating on my own, without the sanction of Berlin or Washington."

"You will have your files, Herr McGarvey. But once you leave this apartment you will be totally on your own. Do you understand?"

"Yes."

"If you commit a crime on German soil you will be arrested and prosecuted. Is this in any way unclear?"

"No."

"I'll take you back to your hotel and bring the files over as soon as I can arrange copies," Wolf said. "Probably not till morning."

FOURTEEN

☐

Major Naisir sat in a C-class Mercedes across the street from the Bristol Hotel watching the front entrance. It was a little after ten in the evening, and traffic was heavy. Berliners were gearing up for another night on the town, for which the Ku'damm had always been famous. Personally, he found the city to be garish, some parts of it even revolting.

"It grows on you," Hamid Jatyal, the ISI chief of Berlin Station, had confessed in his office at the embassy on Schaperstrasse not far from the hotel. But then the man was a Punjabi, a tribe in Naisir's estimation never to be trusted.

"Have you taken care of the little job I asked you to do for me?"

"Yes, the BND captain," Jatyal said, handing over a slim folder. "As a matter of ordinary routine we keep a loose watch on the BND's headquarters, and we picked up Captain Weisse coming into the building from a rear entrance this morning a few minutes after eight, as you can see in the report. He left for lunch with a friend at the Hansa-haus Bierstube a few blocks away, after which he returned to his office."

"Has he left for home yet?" Naisir asked. That was forty minutes ago.

"He left the office at approximately eight o'clock, but he went to the Bristol Hotel, where he was inside for a brief period before he emerged with a gentleman whose identity we don't know."

"Were photographs taken, I hope?"

"Of course. I'll bring them up," Jatyal said. He opened a program on his desktop. In the first frame Wolf was coming out of the hotel with a somewhat husky man in a dark blue blazer and jeans. In the second shot the man had turned so that he was directly facing the camera. Naisir was shaken, though he did not let his reaction show. It was McGarvey, here in Berlin with the man who had followed one of Schlueter's operators to the States and killed him.

"Where did they go?" he asked.

"To an apartment building on Oranienstrasse that we believe is occupied by a BND colonel. They went inside, and as of five minutes ago were still there."

"Have your team report to me as soon as they leave the apartment building," Naisir said.

He'd tried to reach Schlueter, but the number he had was no longer answering. She had changed it again as a precaution, which was sensible. She would contact him when she thought it would be safe.

Sitting in the car Naisir thought about the mission, and the extra task he had given to her to assassinate McGarvey for an additional one million euros. It might be possible to accomplish the task tonight and save the money, he decided.

The same older model Audi A6 as in the photographs pulled up in front of the hotel, and McGarvey got out. He said something to Wolf behind the wheel and then closed the car door. But instead of going directly inside he waited until the BND officer drove off and looked across the street directly at Naisir.

The windows of the Mercedes were tinted enough that it was impossible for McGarvey to see inside, yet Naisir shrank back. The American's reputation was legendary. He was a killer, and by all accounts very good at what he did. Or had been once upon a time.

McGarvey walked down the driveway to the curb and waited for a break in traffic as if he were about to cross the street.

The little prick was challenging him. Naisir, powered down his window and looked directly across the street for a long second before he slammed the car in gear and took off, just making the light at the corner and turning right. His last glimpse in the rearview mirror showed McGarvey still at the curb, watching.

Two blocks from his embassy he pulled into a parking garage and drove to the top level. He called Jatyal's cell phone. The COS answered on the first ring. "Yes."

"I need two men tonight within the hour," Naisir said.

"Our field officers? I think I can accommodate you."

"Not countrymen. This has to be a totally deniable operation. Germans."

"What exactly do you have in mind?" Jatyal asked.

Naisir told him. "I want this to look like an ordinary street crime. Robbery leading to the unfortunate murder of an American citizen."

"The American from the photograph with Captain Weisse?"

"Exactly."

"He has been identified as Kirk McGarvey, a former director of the CIA. Killing him will send shock waves to the highest levels."

"That's why this can never be traced back to Islamabad."

The phone was silent for several long beats. Naisir could almost hear the man's brain furiously working out all of the ramifications— not for the operation itself but for his own career.

"I'm not going to do it without authorization from the ambassador," Jatyal said at length.

"He is not to be involved under any circumstances, and that is a direct order," Naisir said. "You work for the ISI, not the ambassador. And if you refuse to carry out my orders, I shall have General Bhutani telephone you in the next fifteen minutes." Lt. General Tariq Bhutani was the director general of the agency.

"My God, it's after two in the morning there."

"Yes, it is."

This time Jatyal did not hesitate. "It won't be Germans. I'll send Turks. Four of them."

"So many?"

"For this job, yes. How do you want to arrange it?"

Naisir told him the location of the garage. "Have them park on the fifth level, in the northeast corner." It was one level down. "How will I know what they're driving?"

"As soon as I arrange it I'll call and let you know. But you mustn't let yourself be seen by them. This cannot come back to the embassy under any circumstances."

"It won't. Just see that you send me four capable men who are not afraid to get their hands dirty."

"The ones I have in mind are already so filthy it's probable they have never been clean in their lives. After all, they're nothing more than Turks who're involved in the drug trade and bringing young girls from Romania and Bulgaria. Enforcers."

"Have you used them before?"

"These four yes, once."

"Will five hundred euros each be enough?"

"Yes, but don't identify yourself."

FIFTEEN

In his room at the Bristol, McGarvey was sipping a snifter of very good Napoleon brandy—his first for the evening—as he talked to Otto and Pete back in Langley. Despite the hour they were still at the OHB.

"Sounds like Mueller gave you enough rope to hang yourself," Pete said.

"At least they didn't kick me out, and Weisse is going to get me copies of their files on the Schlueter woman and her organization. Might be something for us."

"Tonight?" Otto asked. "Send the stuff to me and I'll get started."

"Probably not till morning. In the meantime something else has come up."

"The Schuleter woman's people?" Pete asked.

"I'm not sure," Mac said. He told them about the Mercedes across the street from the hotel. "The guy rolled down his window and looked right at me before he took off. Dark complexion, black hair, mustache. Definitely not German."

"Pakistani?"

"Be my guess. Which means the ISI knows I've taken an interest."

"If it's the Pakistanis," Pete cautioned. She was a charming woman, and among the best interrogators the CIA had ever known, because she was not only patient and kind with her Johns, as she called her subjects, but she was skeptical without letting it show during the typical interview. She gave the outward appearance of being positive about everything, while in reality she trusted nothing—especially anything that seemed like a sure bet.

"Point taken," Mac said. "But whoever it was had a definite interest in me, and I'd like to know why."

"Are you coming back in the morning, kemo sabe?" Otto asked. "I think I might be able to come up with something that makes sense."

"I'll get out of here as soon as Wolf brings me the files."

"Do you think this guy will show up again tonight" Pete asked, and it sounded as if she already knew the answer.

Mac's suite was on the fifth floor, the windows looking down on the Ku'damm. He was watching the heavy traffic as the Mercedes pulled into a parking spot across the street and a slender man in a dark jacket and jeans got out.

"He just got out of his car."

"It's a trap."

"Almost certainly."

"Are you armed?" Pete asked.

"No," McGarvey said, and before she or Otto could object he hung up.

He got his black blazer and went downstairs. The lobby bar was busy. The hour was coming up on midnight by the time he got outside.

The man from the Mercedes had already started away on foot when McGarvey crossed the street and looked inside the car. But the doors were locked, and nothing was on the passenger seat in front or in the back.

The Pakistani, or whoever he was, had just made it to the end of the block when McGarvey hurried after him. He wanted to crowd the man. That he was being led into a trap was a foregone conclusion—he wanted to see what might happen if the guy knew that he was being pressed.

In the next block McGarvey had closed the gap to less than thirty meters. The zoo was not far, and though it was closed at this hour of the night, it would make a perfect place for an ambush. But the Pakistani turned left and entered a parking garage.

Mac was just a few seconds behind; inside he stopped for a moment to listen. From somewhere on the ramp above he heard faint footfalls. The guy had left his Mercedes parked in front of the hotel, so he hadn't come here to retrieve a parked car. Someone was waiting for the hare to lead the hound to slaughter.

Turning, he sprinted across to the down ramp and headed to the second level, making as little noise as possible. The garage was mostly dark; the concrete pillars cast long shadows. And it was quiet, the only noise coming from traffic on the Ku'damm.

Just at the top Mac quickly crossed to one of the pillars, where he stopped.

The Pakistani was about twenty meters away, just around the corner from the up ramp, obviously waiting for McGarvey to appear. After several seconds, he took a quick look over the barrier before he ducked back.

McGarvey stepped around the pillar. "Looking for me?" he asked.

Startled, the man turned and stood flat-footed for just a moment, like a deer caught in the headlights. But then he reached inside his pocket.

Mac moved back, ready to duck behind the pillar again.

But the man pulled a cell phone out and spoke briefly to someone, before he put it back in his pocket. "Clever of you, but not clever enough," the man said. He spoke with a British accent.

"You're a long ways from Islamabad, but then I would have thought that you would have arranged a meeting with Pam Schlueter on neutral ground somewhere outside of Germany."

A car started up from the next level above, and tires squealed on the concrete floor.

McGarvey walked over to the next concrete support column, and Naisir warily stepped back into the deeper shadows.

A dirty yellow Mercedes panel van shot off the down ramp, its headlights flashing as the the driver hauled the wheel left and accelerated the van directly toward McGarvey.

At the last moment he stepped to the side, expecting the driver to run him down, smash his body against the pillar, but the van skidded to a halt, the side door opened, and three very large men leapt out.

They were dressed in dark clothing, their faces bare, not worried that their descriptions might given to the police. But they were not armed, or at least they had not drawn weapons, which meant this was going to look like a simple assault and robbery.

The guy McGarvey had followed from the hotel was gone, his part of the operation finished.

"You gentlemen might want to get back in your van and drive away," Mac said, stepping out in the open. "That is, if you're smart enough."

The three of them spread out, one left, one right, and one directly facing McGarvey. They were dark like the man from the Mercedes but their features where rough. Working class, possibly Albanians, maybe Turks, a lot of whom had immigrated to Germany for good-paying jobs. But these three were bullyboys, someone's enforcers. And though they were big men, they were light on their feet, like professional boxers.

"You should have stayed home and minded your own business, you fucker," the one in the middle said, his accent thick.

The three of them advanced. But instead of retreating, Mac strode directly toward the one in the middle, but at the last moment he shifted right and slammed the second man backward into the concrete column.

The middle man leapt forward, saying something under his breath, and McGarvey turned toward him, ducking a roundhouse punch and smashing his fist three times into the guy's chest, just over his heart.

He skipped to one side as the third man rushed forward. Grabbing the guy's coat sleeve he propelled him into the one who'd pushed away from the pillar, blood streaming down the side of his face.

The middle man was trying to catch his breath, when McGarvey turned back, got behind him and twisted his head sharply to the left, breaking his neck.

Turning on his heel he was in time to see both men fumble under their jackets, bringing out pistols—what looked like older Glocks.

He was on the first man. Grabbing the guy's gun hand he pulled the Turk around and, using him as a shield, he snatched the pistol and fired two rounds at the other man, hitting him center mass and dropping him to the deck.

Mac shoved the Turk away and pointed the pistol directly at his face. "Who hired you?"

The man said something unintelligible.

With a squeal of tires the van shot backward, turned left, and raced to the down ramp, careening off the concrete wall with a hail of sparks before it disappeared.

"Just you and me now, and I have a gun," Mac said. "You can tell me who sent you, in which case I let you walk away. Or you can refuse and I'll kill you, in which case it'll be me who walks away."

"You'll shoot me anyway."

"No need," McGarvey said. He ejected the pistol's magazine, tossed it aside, ejected the round in the firing chamber and let it fall to the deck, and threw the gun away. "Who hired you?"

The Turk glanced at the two bodies. "I don't know. It was a blind number, as usual. Money always shows up the next day at a drop box in a whorehouse not far from here."

"Who was the man who set up the ambush?"

"I never got a clear look at his face."

"Get the fuck out of here," McGarvey said.

The Turk turned and headed for the ramp.

"How much to take me out?" McGarvey called after him.

"Five hundred euros," the Turk said. "Each." He disappeared down the ramp.

Mac gave the man a full five minutes to get clear, then he walked down the up ramp to the still busy street and headed back to his hotel. He would have bet just about anything that the guy from the Mercedes was a Pakistani; the English they learned was British, and the best field officers spoke it with a proper upper-class accent. And he would have bet just about the same amount that the three guys he'd come up against were Turks hired by someone—most likely ISI—from the embassy.

The two-tone dee-dah of police sirens sounded not too far away. Mac crossed the street with the light so that he was on the same side as the Bristol and picked up the pace. The Pakistani from the Mercedes had probably called the police for insurance in case the muscle he'd hired wasn't successful. At the very least Mac would be taken into police custody and held for a time.

SIXTEEN

Brian Ridder missed SEAL Team Six, the camaraderie, the bullshit practical jokes, the nearly constant ragging on each other, the adrenaline high coming off a successful op with all your pieces in the right places, no holes leaking. At five eleven and a hundred and seventy pounds, he was still in good shape, but a lot of the time his head wasn't straight.

But he was glad that he was finally out, because his knees hurt most mornings, his back gave him such hell that even a half dozen extrastrength aspirins every day didn't do much but dull the pain back to a near-constant Niagara Falls roar, and because he was finally a full-time husband and dad of three boys.

It was two in the morning in Virginia Beach. Brian was sitting up in bed, his body drenched with sweat, his sheets so wet again that his wife Cindy was going to accuse him of pissing himself, and they would have another of their ferocious arguments. He thought that he was losing his mind, but he was more frightened these days than he'd ever been in Afghanistan or Iraq or any of a dozen hot spots where he'd been dropped. Usually into the middle of some serious shit.

The hell of it all was that he thought he missed the action, and yet he knew that he shouldn't. He knew that he loved his wife, and yet a lot of a time lately he couldn't stand her. And the boys; he loved them with every fiber of his being, and yet a lot of the time they got on his nerves so badly that he wanted to smash the little bastards in the face.

"Man up, for Christ's sake," he'd shouted in his sleep a couple of nights ago, and Cindy had grilled him about what he meant.

"Are you losing your fucking mind or what? she'd screeched. "Because if you aren't, I sure the fuck am."

Besides his being wigged out half the time, money was their biggest problem. He'd gotten out of the navy after seventeen years—three years short of his pension. No monthly payments, no base exchange privileges, and even worse, no medical or dental. Larry, their youngest, needed braces they couldn't afford. Cindy's teeth were giving her fits, and the dentist she'd gone to wanted fifteen thousand to put her mouth right. But there was absolutely no money for any of that.

He had no real trouble getting jobs—he'd driven a bus for the city, had worked on a road-repaving crew, had even done some rough construction, mostly framing for garages and other small buildings. But he'd trained all of his career to be stealthy. Hide in broad daylight. He'd practiced swimming five miles in the open ocean, jumping out of aircraft flying at thirty-five thousand feet, and free-falling down to a couple of thousand feet before opening his chute. And he'd been trained to blow up shit, and to kill people with a variety of weapons, including his bare hands.

He had skills that didn't translate into civilian jobs, because he didn't know how to keep his mouth shut when he figured something was wrong.

For a few months he thought about applying with one of the major contracting companies to go back out in the field. Afghanistan, Iraq—there were high-paying jobs out there. But he could not think about picking up a gun again. Ever again.

He got out of bed and took a pee without turning on the bathroom light. Cindy had rolled over, but if she was awake she didn't say anything. He went down the hall to check on the boys, all of them sleeping soundly, and then padded into the kitchen, where he got a gallon bottle of milk from the fridge and took a deep drink. It was another of Cindy's pet peeves, his drinking out of the bottle like that. Now the boys were doing it. And leaving the toilet lid up, not picking up after themselves, never bothering to put their dirty clothes in the hamper or their dirty dishes in the sink.

The kitchen looked out on the small backyard, where he'd planted a couple of apple trees a few years ago when he was on leave. They were big now, and in the summer they were great for shade.

He started to go back to bed when he thought he saw something moving near the eight-foot-tall wooden fence that separated his yard from the Digbys', who were on vacation. Their five kids—three girls and two boys—liked to come over, especially on weekends, so he and Roland had put in a gate. It was ajar now, or at least it looked like it, and his anger spiked.

A couple of months ago Cindy had told him that she was sure she'd seen some guy in their backyard. A Peeping Tom. It hadn't been Roland, but whoever it was had come through the gate.

She'd wanted him to call the police, but he'd told her that she'd been dreaming, and that had started another terrific fight.

He went to the window and, keeping to one side so that he wouldn't be so easy to spot, looked out across the yard. If anyone had been there, he was gone now. But the gate was still half open and that was bothersome. Either the guy had left and not bothered to close the gate, or he'd come around to the north side of the house, where he could look into the bedroom windows.

"Son of a bitch," he said under his breath. He debated for just a split second whether he should warn Cindy and call the cops or take care of it himself.

He went through the hall and into the laundry room, where he unlocked the back door, eased it open, and poked his head outside for just an instant. Nothing moved, so he slipped outside and headed past the kitchen windows to the corner of the house.

Someone was tapping on something. For just an instant it almost sounded like Morse code, but it dawned on him that what he was hearing was someone tapping on a window. With a piece of metal. The muzzle of a pistol.

Time slowed down, and his heart, which had been pounding, settled into an even rhythm as it did when he was about to walk into a close-quarters battle somewhere in Badland.

He peeked around the corner. A tall man dressed in dark clothes stood at the bedroom window. He was tapping the muzzle of what even in the darkness at a distance of twenty-five feet Brian recognized was a silencer tube.

The bastard was trying to wake up Cindy and he meant to shoot her.

Keeping low, Brian stepped around the corner and raced silently toward the guy, who at the same moment fired two shots through the window.

"No," Brian shouted at the last instant.

The shooter turned and fired once directly into Brian's chest, and then stepped aside.

Brian's knees gave out and as he fell his momentum carried him forward and onto his side, at the shooter's feet. The man's eyes were lifeless, no expression in them whatsoever. The pistol was a 9mm subcompact Glock 26. A toy, but deadly in the right hands. And the son of a bitch had shot Cindy with it.

Breathing was getting tough, but all he could think about was the SEAL's dark humor: incoming rounds have the right of way and sucking chest wounds were nature's way of telling you to slow down.

"Why?" he managed to croak.

"For Usama."

Everyone on the assault team that night in Abbottabad knew something like this was possible. A couple of days ago Pete Barnes and his wife had been shot to death in Florida. But his old boss over on the base coming up on his thirtieth year, told him that the word from the top was that the hit in Florida was an anomaly: "Some son of a bitch redneck with a grudge against the world opened fire at the museum. If he'd been targeting you guys he wouldn't have taken out Pete's wife." Taking revenge on the assaulters was one thing, but killing the wives was stupid.

The shooter pointed his pistol at Brian's head.

"Why our wives?"

"Not just the wives," the shooter said. His English had an odd accent that Brian couldn't quite place. Maybe German. This guy wasn't a redneck with a grudge. He was a pro.

But then what he had just said suddenly registered. *Not just the wives.*

Brian started to roll over so that he could reach the bastard's legs and bring him down, stop him from hurting the boys, when a thunderclap burst inside his head.

SEVENTEEN

☐

McGarvey met Weisse for breakfast at eight in the Bristol's smaller dining room. It was a weekday and the place was filled with businessmen, making it an anonymous venue. But the German BND officer seemed ill at ease.

"There was a bit of excitement last night at a parking ramp a few blocks from here," Weisse said. "Two Turkish gentlemen who the Berlin police believe were involved in the drug and prostitution trade were found murdered. One had his neck broken. The other was shot to death, and his pistol was unloaded and field-stripped."

Their waiter came and took their orders.

"I think that someone has taken notice that I'm here," McGarvey said.

"It was your work?"

"Yeah. But what puzzles me is, why me? Why now? I don't see the connection."

"I'm investigating the murder in Florida, and you've come to meet with me. Someone's watching."

It's exactly what McGarvey figured Weisse would say. "Homegrown terrorist organizations usually don't have the wherewithal to keep tabs on intelligence officers."

"But governments do. Pakistan?"

"I haven't been able to convince the DDO at Langley. Maybe you'll do a better job of it with your colonel."

"Not without concrete proof, which the director says he needs before he can make his recommendations," Weisse said. "You and I are in the same boat. But what the hell were you doing in that parking ramp?"

McGarvey told him about the dark-complected man across the street from the hotel. "I'm just about certain he was a Pakistani."

"But you can't prove it."

"No, but I think he was an ISI officer."

"We have photos of just about everyone who works at their embassy. Would you mind looking at them?"

"He won't be there. Unless I miss my guess he came to Germany specifically to take me out."

Weisse looked away for a moment. "He would have to have some good intelligence from your side of the pond. Who knew that you were coming here?"

"You," McGarvey said.

"But I didn't know your work name, or where you were staying, until you phoned."

"You did know that I was coming. If the leak came from your shop they could have posted a team with my photograph at the airport."

"Did you spot anyone?"

"I wasn't really looking," Mac said. "Anyway, if they'd doubled or tripled me they would have been hard to pick out."

"How about at the CIA?"

"Only two people, both of whom I would trust with my life. And have in the past."

Weisse nodded. "The only other possibility that I can see is that you became a target from the start, in which case you could have come under surveillance in Washington."

McGarvey conceded the point.

"What's your next move?" the German asked him.

"Have the police been given my name?"

"No. As far as anyone is concerned it was good riddance to scum."

"Then if you'll give me the files, I'll go back to Washington and see what I can piece together. My flight leaves around noon."

Weisse took a CD jewel case out of his jacket pocket and handed it over. "We're stepping up our investigation of Schlueter and the people we've already identified in her organization. But once again our hands are tied without hard evidence. None of which we've been able to come up with yet, except for the incident in Florida. And we haven't been able to find any clear chain of evidence tying Schlueter to the kill."

"But he worked for her organization."

"We think so, but again there's no evidence that his act wasn't rogue."

McGarvey's cell phone rang. It was Otto.

"Can you talk?"

"I'm with Captain Weisse."

"It's happened again, this morning in Virginia Beach. A shooter or shooters unknown killed Brian Ridder—he was one of assaulters at Abbottabad. Also shot his wife to death and killed their three boys."

"No witnesses?"

"No one's come forward so far."

"What's Marty saying?"

"Not a word."

"How about the navy?"

"Nothing. Both Barnes and Ridder were out of the service. No longer the navy's problem."

"The other twenty-two guys need to be warned."

"I was given strict orders twenty minutes ago to stay out of it. Came from State."

McGarvey gave him his Air France flight number, which got to Dulles around 6:30 P.M. "Have someone pick me up. I think this time we'll meet at your place. But tell whoever you send to watch their back. They came after me last night."

"You okay?"

"Yes. I'll give you the details when I get back, but someone is definitely taking notice. And I have a feeling they're going to speed up their timetable now that I'm in the mix."

"I'll try a guy I know at JSOC," Otto said, and he rang off.

"Another one?" Weisse asked.

"Yeah, along with his wife and three kids."

"Doesn't make any sense."

"It does if you look at it from the ISI's viewpoint. They were embarrassed by the raid on bin Laden but they couldn't do a thing about it for fear we'd cut off their military aid. This operation is the next best thing."

"Retribution."

"It's looking more like it every day. I need you guys to put some pressure on Schlueter and her gang."

"I'll have to pull some strings."

"Pull them, Wolf, before it's too late."

Pete was waiting for him just outside the customs and passport control area, a serious look on her pretty face. "As best as I could tell I came in clear," she said. "Otto's already at his house waiting for us."

"Audie?"

"They sent her back to the Farm."

Audie was McGarvey's granddaughter; Otto and his wife Louise had adopted her after Mac's daughter and son-in-law were assassinated. It had been a staggeringly horrible time in his life, and in the lives of Otto and Louise; as a result, everyone doted on the girl, who still wasn't old enough to start kindergarten. Her go-to place when the bad guys were out and about was the Farm, which was the CIA's training facility on the York River, south of Washington.

They went outside to where Pete had parked her Nissan Altima in the arrivals area, a metro police card on the dash. On the way out to Otto's safe house in McLean, McGarvey adjusted his door mirror so that he could watch for a tail. But if anyone was back there he couldn't make them out.

"Otto said that you ran into a little trouble in Berlin."

"The Pakistanis are definitely involved. But whether it's an independent group working with Schlueter or an ISI-sanctioned operation I don't know yet."

"But your guess is ISI."

"At arm's length. Plausible deniability and all that."

"So if we catch the bastards with their hands in the cookie jar, it won't go any further."

"Something like that."

Pete glanced at him. "Doesn't matter to you either way."

"Twenty-two guys are still on the line. They've done their part; now it's time for us to do ours."

EIGHTEEN

□

Louise, tall, all arms and skinny legs, had a good cognac waiting for Mac at the McLean house, and they all sat around the kitchen table looking out over the backyard filled with a swing set and slide and other kid's toys. They'd tried to spoil Audie, but she never changed. She was a combination of her mother and grandmother—sweet and gentle most of the time, unless she was putting her foot down because she thought she was being treated like a baby.

"The guy you followed to the parking garage was Pakistani—you're sure of it?" Otto asked.

"His accent was right, and as far as I can see, the Pakistanis are the only ones with a vested interest in taking out the SEAL Team Six assaulters."

"What about the Schlueter woman?" Otto asked.

"Probably financial, but she has her own ax to grind," Mac said. He handed Otto the disk from Wolf. "The Germans know that she was married to an American naval officer stationed as a military liaison to the BND in Munich. Apparently they don't know the details, except that it turned out badly for her, and she could be looking to settle old scores."

"Hell hath no fury like a woman scorned," Louise said. "Is this guy still around. Do we know who he is?"

"Dick Cole. He's acting chief of staff for DEVGRU down in Oceana, Virginia."

Louise made a sour face. "DEVGRU is SEAL Team Six, and I don't think I'm liking this very much. Are you suggesting this guy is helping his ex in some way?"

"The BND doesn't think so. I went through the stuff on the disk

at an Air France biz center at Tegel, and it looked to me like the connection with Schlueter and her ex was nothing more than a motiva-
tor. Evidently, she not only hates her ex, but she hates Americans in
general. The SEAL Team Six thing is just her way of earning a big
payday from the Pakistanis."

"You don't think it's coincidental, her going after the SEAL Team
Six guys with or without the ISI's help and her ex's connection?"

"I don't know, but it's something I'm going to ask her the first
time I get the chance. As far as I'm concerned, the connection stinks,
but to believe that her ex is somehow working with her is a stretch."

"Maybe you should ask him," Pete suggested. "At the very least he
might be able to tell us something about her that we can use."

"If he'll talk to me," McGarvey said. "But someone higher up the
food chain may have put a muzzle on him and everyone else having
anything to do with the team."

"Well, it is about money," Otto said. "I've found that much out.
Schlueter has collected two million euros over the past several months,
paid into half a dozen accounts in places as far away from Germany
as the Caymans and as close as Warsaw. The problem so far is the
source. I'm coming up with blanks, which tells me that the encryption and remote remailers her paymasters are using are damned
good."

"Government grade good?" Mac asked.

"Yeah, but new. Could be one of those hackers from Amsterdam.
Some of those kids were pretty good. State-of-the-art shit."

"The ones who hacked into our power grid?"

"Could be. But I'll find them, and if there's a connection back to
Islamabad I'll nail it too."

"If we can cut off the lady's funds, maybe she'll back off," Pete
said.

"Don't count on it," Louise said.

"In the meantime I'm going over to see Walt, and get his take,"
McGarvey said. "If someone is putting on the brakes, he'll at least tell
me who it is."

"Do you want me to tag along?" Otto asked.

"For now I want you to stick with the money trail. But see what
else you can dig up on Captain Cole. Check his financials."

"Tread lightly, Mac," Pete said. "He might have been a son of a bitch and a wife beater, but it doesn't mean he's a traitor."

Walter Page, the DCI, had a young guy in a white polo shirt and jeans waiting for McGarvey in the lobby of the OHB to escort him up to the seventh floor. He introduced himself as Dr. Steve Ellerin who'd been brought over from Harvard to help work out a political and intelligence scenario that made any sense for our future with Saudi Arabia.

"I've been given an office and a staff—better than mine at Harvard—and the run of the place, but for some reason they won't trust me with a gun," he said grinning.

"Welcome to the club. They don't trust anyone else around here with guns, except for the security people."

They were alone on the elevator up and Ellerin kept looking at McGarvey. "I've heard about you," he said, just before they reached the seventh.

"Any of it good?"

Ellerin chuckled. "All of it interesting. You ever think about writing a book?"

"Not about this," McGarvey said as the doors opened.

They went down to the DCI's suite where the Harvard doc left him. "Nice to meet you, sir."

Page's secretary announced him and he went in. Page sat behind his big desk. Carleton Patterson, the CIA's general counsel who'd been with the company for as long as anyone could remember, sat across from him.

"I take it that you've already heard about the second killing," Page said. "Police have it down as a robbery gone bad."

"Bullshit," McGarvey said, and he sat down next to Patterson.

"It would seem so, after the Florida incident," the lawyer said dryly.

Page was angry. "I understand that you went to Germany to meet with an officer in the BND, and that there was an incident in which two men were killed. Were you involved?"

"Yes. It was a setup—four of them sent to take me down. Turks with connections to the drug trade."

"And you let two live?" Patterson asked.

"I wanted them to take a message back to the people who hired them."

"The bureau wants your passport," Page said.

"Which one, Walt?"

Page sat back. He was clearly frustrated. "Why did you come to see me? What do you want?"

"Two of the twenty-four SEALs who took part in the raid on bin Laden are dead, along with their families. The one in Florida was murdered by a German who most likely works with a group of professional assassins for hire. The second one had nothing to do with a robbery."

"Is this what the BND believes to be true?"

"Officially no. But they did send one of their officers to follow the Florida shooter. And we've learned that in the past several months two million euros have been paid into bank accounts belonging to the leader of this group."

"It's up to the Germans to arrest her."

"Not without proof. And possibly for the same reason that Marty ordered Pete Boylan to back away from the investigation."

"What reason is that?" Page asked.

"The two million came from the ISI."

Page held up a hand. "This stops now, Mac, and I mean it. No more of your running around on your own shooting anyone who gets in your way."

"Who ordered you to leave Pakistan out of it?"

"This conversation ends now," Page said. "Someone from the bureau will want to interview you, and I suggest that you cooperate this time." He got to his feet, but McGarvey remained seated.

"Can you tell me what the navy is doing? Has the ONI at least given the other guys the heads up?"

"The Office of Naval Intelligence is not this agency's business."

"Christ, what if I'm right? How many other assassinations are going to have to happen before you get your head out of your ass?"

"Get out of here."

McGarvey got to his feet. "Have I ever steered you or this agency wrong?"

"A piece of advice?" Patterson asked.

"Sure," Mac said. He hadn't thought that he would get very far this morning, but he was glad he'd come; the company was on notice.

"Whatever you do, stay as far away as possible from the Senate's Select Committee on Intelligence."

"Anyone in particular?" McGarvey asked. There were fifteen members on the committee.

"I think you know the two or three I'm talking about."

McGarvey nodded. "Thanks for your time, Mr. Director," he said to Page, and walked out.

ПINETEEП

At the Alt-Collner Schankstuben restaurant Pam Schlueter took one of the small tables on the sidewalk and ordered a Martini & Rossi red vermouth with an orange peel. It was the signal that she'd come in clear, which just now was a great puzzle to her. One of several she was faced with.

About a month ago she'd noticed that someone was following her, and it didn't take long to figure out that her minders—there were three on single shifts—were almost certainly BND officers. It was a BND officer who'd followed Dieter to Florida and gunned him down on the beach outside the UDT/SEAL museum. And Friedrich Heiser had had to lose another BND officer before he made the hit on the Ridder SEAL and his family.

And as of yesterday she was still being followed. But all of a sudden this afternoon, when she'd taken a test run to the Marx-Engels Plaza in preparation for tonight's meeting, she realized that her minders were gone.

For a couple of hours she wandered all over the city, sometimes on foot, sometimes by bus or taxi but no one was behind her. She'd even become so obvious as to suddenly stop and reverse direction or walk into a shop and go out the back way. But still nothing. Nor had there been anyone in front of the apartment she was using for the past several weeks or anyone to follow her here tonight.

Only a few diners were in the pub, and the small table next to hers had a reserved sign on it. Naisir came around the corner and sat down at the reserved table. "You had no trouble this evening?" he asked conversationally.

"No. But what the hell are you doing here?" Pam demanded, keeping her voice low. His calling her for this meeting was another of the puzzles.

A waiter came out and Naisir ordered a grilled ham sandwich and a beer.

"I can't eat like this in Islamabad," the ISI officer said. "I've come to warn you that I arranged to have Mr. McGarvey taken out but the idiots who were to have done the job failed. In fact, McGarvey actually killed two of them."

Pam had seen the back-page newspaper article about a disturbance in a parking garage just off the Ku'damm. The police had called it a robbery attempt, which was common these days. "I had the contract, I was waiting for you to tell me where he could be found, and now you're saying that he was here in Berlin?"

"Yes. It was thought to save you the trouble so that you could concentrate on your primary assignment. How are you progressing?"

"I still have Heiser and four other operators in the States, all of them in the Norfolk area."

Naisir frowned. "If they're working together, they're bound to be noticed."

"For now none of them knows of the existence of the others. They're each working independently. In fact, one of the DEVGRU operators and his family have already been eliminated."

"Yes, I'd assumed that was your work. What about the others? There's been nothing in the news over the past twenty-four hours. You've not run into any trouble you're not telling me about?"

When Pam had realized that she was no longer being tailed by the BND she had debated keeping Naisir in the dark. But she depended upon him for up-to-the-minute intelligence, and of course for the money—one million euros up front, plus five hundred thousand for each SEAL assaulter taken down, plus an additional bonus if all twenty-four of them were eliminated.

"The BND is no longer following me," she said.

"They're very good. You can't be certain."

"But I am," she said, and she told him about her activities this afternoon and evening.

Naisir's sandwich and beer came, and Pam ordered another vermouth. When her drink came and the waiter left, Naisir was actually smiling.

"Perhaps it's better that we let Mr. McGarvey return home unharmed after all," he said.

"I don't understand."

"Don't you see, my dear, the man has actually helped us—you in particular."

"No, I don't see."

"Why he became involved no longer matters. But he is, and his first step was to come here to talk to the BND officer who took your Herr Zimmer out. But the meeting took place at the private residence of Weisse's control officer, not at headquarters. Afterwards, the team tailing you was ordered to stand down. The same thing is happening at this moment in the United States. Only the local police are involved in the murders, but not the FBI or the CIA."

"I'm still not following you," Pam said.

"Mr. McGarvey has convinced the German intelligence service as well as his own CIA that the attacks on the SEAL Team Six assaulters is being orchestrated by us. By the government of Pakistan. To exact retribution."

"Which is the truth."

"Of course it is. But neither Berlin nor Washington could ever admit to something so monstrous. We provide the United States, and to a lesser extent the coalition forces, including Germany, with the right to do battle with the Taliban and al-Qaeda leadership. Of course we condemn the attacks publically, but we allow them."

"Including the raid on bin Laden's compound?"

"Especially that one," Naisir said. "And in return we are given money to help fund and equip our military."

Pam understood perfectly. "India is a friend of the United States. So we're talking about a delicate balance."

"An extremely delicate balance, one that neither Washington nor Berlin wishes to upset."

"Stupid that they would allow their war heroes to be assassinated."

"The actual reason for the balance is to prevent a nuclear war between us and India—a war that would almost certainly spread, perhaps to something totally out of control."

"It's still stupid," Pam said. Even through her deep hatred she could see it—a country not protecting the soldiers who served it.

"I agree. But they have McGarvey. He won't get any official help, but he's bound to come after your assassins and eventually you."

"I thought you said that he's helped us."

"Yes, he has. But just remember he will come after you, and when he does, you'd best be prepared to deal with him."

"Unlike your clumsy effort."

"I agree," Naisir said. "Even I underestimated the man. Don't you make the same mistake."

"When the time comes he will be eliminated for an additional fee."

"Yes, one million."

"Two million."

"Agreed," Naisir said without hesitation.

"Then the next step is to kill the remaining twenty-two SEALS."

TWENTY

□

A young ensign in desert tan Crye Precision battle dress was waiting for McGarvey at the front gate of the U.S. Naval Special Warfare Development Group—DEVGRU—at Virginia Beach. He wore no name tag, only his insignia of rank and the SEAL Team Six patch. Slight of build, with long hair tied in a ponytail, he had the thousand-yard stare of the warrior who has seen close-quarters battle.

"Mr. Director, welcome to DEVGRU, I'm Ensign Mader. Captain Cole asked that I bring you up to his office."

McGarvey parked his car in the visitor's lot outside the main gate and then got into a navy Hummer, with Mader at the wheel.

On the way up, the windows were down. Mac heard two sharp explosions and then a lot of small-arms fire in the distance through the woods, "Busy day."

"Yes, sir."

They stopped at an intersection to allow a pair of armored personnel carriers to pass. Seconds later a Black Hawk helicopter roared low overhead and disappeared toward the sound of the shooting to the east.

A few blocks later they passed the post exchange and the cluster of buildings normally associated with a military installation, finally pulling up and parking in front of a three-story building with a small signboard and an American flag in a grassy area.

"I'm surprised that your flag isn't at half mast because of the two operators you lost," McGarvey said.

"That takes a presidential directive and we've received none," Mader said sharply.

Inside they bypassed the elevator and took the stairs up to an office on the third floor, where a young clerk, also dressed in Cryes, picked up the phone. "The gentleman from Washington is here, sir." He hung up. "Captain Cole will see you now, sir," he said.

Cole's corner office looked down a long grassy slope to what appeared to be an urban setting of several two- and three-story concrete block buildings. Several battered cars and a couple of pickup trucks were parked on the street. Two men were spraying foam on one of the cars, which was on fire.

The captain, dressed in Cryes like everyone else McGarvey had seen this afternoon, got up from behind his desk. "Glad to finally meet you, Mr. Director," he said, though his attitude and inflection said differently.

"I won't take up much of your time. I expect you're a busy man."

"That I am," Cole said, motioning to a seat. He was half a head shorter than McGarvey and lean, with a scar that ran down the left side of his weather-beaten face from just below his ear to the bottom of his chin. His eyes were narrow, as if he was getting ready either for bad news or for an attack.

"Would you like a cup of coffee?"

"No. I'll get directly to my reason for wanting to see you. It's about your ex-wife, Pamela Schlueter. Have you had any contact with her in the past few months?"

Cole got to his feet, furious. "Get the hell out of my office."

"If need be I'll have you ordered to Washington, and we can conduct this in an ONI facility."

Cole reached for the phone.

"I don't much care for men who beat up on their wives. Especially a man with your training."

"Unproven allegations."

"But not your presence on any number of porn sites," McGarvey said. Otto had dug that up last night. "At least you have the good sense never to use government computers."

"You can't prove a thing," Cole said, no longer so sure of himself.

"I think you know I can."

Cole sat down.

"Thing is, you're doing a damned good job down here. Five to go for your thirty years, though you've been passed up twice for your star. It's possible that a recommendation from the CIA might help the next time around. Especially if we prove that your ex is involved with the people who murdered the two SEAL Team Six operators."

"Can't be her," Cole said.

"Why not?"

"She was from Bad Aibling, a small town outside of Munich. She was a village girl when I met her and still a village girl when I brought her back to the States. I had a job at the Pentagon and she never fit in. Bitched all the time about the weather, the food, the traffic, the people. Nothing was right for her."

"Including you?"

"Especially me."

"Which is why you got rough with her?"

"Actually it was the other way around. She was a farm girl, no sisters, only four older brothers who she roughhoused with from the time she could walk. At least that's how she explained it to me."

"The SPs were called to your quarters more than once."

"Believe me, McGarvey, I could have killed her, so I was very careful not to let her take things too far. In the end in Washington she'd gotten so aggressive that one night I had to let her break my arm. The next day I moved over to the BOQ on Andrews and sent her home. She filed for a divorce from Germany."

"Was watching porn her idea too?"

"It was mine, something we did together. And that's as far as I'll take that issue. But if you think that Pam was somehow behind the murders of those two DEVGRU operators and their families, you're barking up the wrong tree."

"You say she was aggressive. Was she crazy?"

"Clinically nuts?" Cole asked. He shook his head. "I'm no shrink, but at the end she was having some pretty big mood swings. I put it down to her being pissed off living in the States. She never made friends, not one, never even tried."

"Would you know if she might have played around, maybe had an affair?"

"Maybe, but I don't think so. Wasn't her style."

"While you were married, did she ever go home, visit old friends or family?"

"Twice."

"Has she still got people in Bad Aibling?"

"Her parents and one of her brothers are dead. The other three are married, living in Munich I think, but I'm not sure," Cole said. He sat forward. "I'm more motivated than you to figure out who killed two of our people, but my hands are tied. If they'd been on active duty it would have been different."

"Were you given direct orders not to try to find out what happened?"

"No," Cole said, and McGarvey thought he was lying.

"Of the other twenty-two operators, only three are still on active duty, and all of them are stationed here."

"What twenty-two?"

"The others on the Neptune Spear raid. I think that all of them have been targeted by a group led by your ex-wife and financed by the government of Pakistan."

"What brought you to that conclusion?"

"The guy and his wife in Florida were murdered by a German, who was being followed by a BND officer. They got into a shootout, and the BND officer killed the assassin. When I went to Germany to talk to the BND, someone tried to take me down. I think that it was a Pakistani who arranged it."

"What's the connection with Pam?"

"The BND believes she's the head of an organization that hires out as assassins."

"Bullshit," Cole said, getting to his feet. "Get the hell out of here."

"Would you know how to reach her if need be? A phone number, an e-mail address, something like that?"

"With all due respect, Mr. Director, you don't work for the CIA any longer, so whatever the hell you're doing here has no official sanction."

McGarvey got up. At the door he turned back. "It'd be too bad if I found out that you were still in contact with your ex-wife."

"If that's a threat, I would suggest that you tread with care. I've recorded this conversation."

Otto had warned about that as well. He had given McGarvey a device that looked like an ordinary cell phone, but one that broadcast the equivalent of a white noise signal, which made recordings impossible. "Keep him guessing after you leave and he tries to play it back," Otto had said.

"We'll keep in touch," McGarvey said.

"I don't think so."

"Count on it."

TWENTY-ONE

Pete had come over to the Renckes' safe house in McLean, and after they'd finished lamb chops, a very good potato galette, and a nice salad that Otto had learned to make from online recipes, she asked McGarvey what was bothering him. "You've been quiet ever since you got here. Something troubling you?"

"Cole's reaction wasn't what I thought it would be," Mac said. "He's absolutely sure that his ex-wife couldn't be behind the killings."

"Maybe he's a liar."

"Not that good."

"How'd he react when you told him that you knew he was doing porn on the web?" Otto asked.

"He didn't deny it."

"The question is, did he agree to either call the other nineteen ex-SEALS back to base for their own protection or at least convince the ONI to get involved?" Louise asked.

"They're no longer on active duty. Not his problem."

"None of them did their full twenty," Otto said. "As far as the navy is concerned they're on their own. Every one of them on the raid was over thirty at the time—all of them with beaucoup experience. The trouble is that just about every one of them have screwed-up backs, blown-out knees, and serious rotator cuff problems because of crap they had to do not only in the field but during training. A lot of them are suffering from some form of post-traumatic stress syndrome, their hearing is shot from the constant firing of weapons and use of explosives, and their eyesight is crap because of hours looking though night vision oculars. But they can't use the navy's medical service because they weren't wounded or disabled, and they can't get any decent health-care insurance that they can afford because of their disabilities."

"What about VA hospitals"

"From what I've learned, those guys are way too proud to stand in line."

"Hell of a way to treat our war heroes," Louise said. "Can't we get the bureau or at least the local cops involved?"

"They're investigating the two attacks, but no crimes have been committed against the others, nor have the guys gotten any threatening letters or e-mails or phone calls," Otto said. "Their hands are tied."

McGarvey had thought about exactly that problem on the drive up from Virginia Beach—that and the likelihood that the United States and Germany had backed away from making any waves that might implicate the government of Pakistan in the killings.

"Has Marty or Walt Page made any noise to make me back off?" he asked.

"Not a word," Otto said. "I think they *want* you to get involved. Have from the start. Means they're willing to stand aside, but they won't offer you any help. Neither will the bureau."

"That's about what I figured."

Pete was staring at him. "There's something else," she said.

"I picked up a tail just north of Williamsburg. A white Lexus SUV, so far as I could tell, only the driver. He was good, matching my speeds, keeping at least three cars behind me. I got off the interstate at Richmond and drove around town. Three times I pulled into parking lots in tough neighborhoods and got out of my car. Come get me. But each time the guy in the Lexus didn't take the bait. And each time when I got back on the highway he was there. So I just lost the bastard."

"How?" Pete asked.

When he was at his apartment in Georgetown, McGarvey drove a modified Porsche Cayenne SUV; the computer code that limited a car's top speed in the United States to 130 miles per hour had been removed. The machine could do in excess of 180 on its Y-rated racing tires.

"He couldn't keep up."

Pete grinned. "You'll have to take me for a ride one of these days."

"Any idea who it was?" Otto asked.

"Picking up a tail coming out of the meeting with Cole was no coincidence, or at least I don't think it was. It's something I'm going to find out tonight."

"How?"

"I'm going to drive back to Georgetown and wait for him to show up."

"I'll come with you," Pete said.

"I want you to hold down the fort here for at least tonight. As soon as I get this issue settled I'm going down to Norfolk to be near where most of the nineteen guys are living. In the meantime Otto is going to give all of them the heads-up. If something starts to go down I want them be on their toes, and if all else fails push the panic button."

"You're not keeping me out of that show," Pete said. "Not a chance in hell."

"I'd hoped you say that," McGarvey said.

"Watch yourselves tonight," Louise told them.

McGarvey headed straight across to the CIA campus before he picked up the GWM Parkway. Within a couple of miles the white Lexus was in his rearview mirror; he took his time, finally crossing the river into Georgetown on the Key Bridge.

His apartment was on the third floor of a brownstone that overlooked Rock Creek Park. He parked his Porsche in the first available spot on N Street Northwest, about a block out, and walked the rest of the way.

Traffic was light, mostly concentrated several blocks south on M Street, where all the bars and restaurants and shops that drew the tourists and locals were located. At Twenty-seventh Street, instead of turning left to his apartment, he waited for a delivery van to pass, then crossed the street to the park.

A dark, vaguely familiar figure came around the corner, hesitated for a few moments, and then came across.

McGarvey lingered in plain sight long enough for the man to spot him; then he turned and hurried down to the parkway, where he lost himself in the deeper trees near the river's edge. No joggers or strollers were out here at this hour, which was the main reason Mac had led his quarry to the park. If there was to be a shootout he wanted the action to be isolated so that no innocent bystander would be involved.

But he did not want to kill whoever it was who'd followed him from Virginia Beach unless it was absolutely necessary. He needed some answers, not another body.

For a full two minutes the night was nearly silent. The man had disappeared.

Edging around the trunk of a tree, Mac took out his pistol and cocked his ear to listen for something, anything, some sound that did not belong here. Something other than the gentle burbling of the slow-moving creek and the distant traffic. A twig breaking, the rustle of a branch as someone passed, footfalls on gravel.

He caught a slight noise off to the left, upstream, and moved five yards to the trunk of another tree where he held up. Someone was ahead, perhaps twenty yards away, but closer to the creek.

Mac angled back toward the road to a spot he figured was just above where he'd heard the last noise. He stood absolutely still. After several moments he picked out the outline of a man in dark clothing, one hand on the trunk of a tree. The man was facing downstream, less than fifteen feet away. He had something in his free hand that was likely a pistol.

Raising his own gun, Mac stepped out from behind the tree. "If you are very careful you just might survive this night," he said.

"McGarvey?" the man said, his voice soft, his accent German.

Mac knew the voice. "Let your gun fall to the ground."

"I'm not armed," the man said. He raised his right hand and switched on a flashlight, the red beam pointed downstream.

"Captain Weisse?" McGarvey asked.

Wolf turned. "I came to warn you that Pam Schlueter has disappeared and her next target is almost certainly you."

McGarvey holstered his pistol at the small of his back and walked down to Wolf. "Why like this? Why not a phone call or an e-mail? Why come here and follow me?"

"I've been suspended and all my wireless accounts are being monitored. I had a hell of a time getting out of Germany and then here."

"Same question: why?"

"Because we both know that Pakistan's government, or at least the ISI, wants to take out all the SEAL Team Six guys who hit bin Laden. But I've been ordered to cease and desist. So here I am."

McGarvey smiled. "You'll probably end up in jail."

"We'll see," Wolf shrugged. "In the meantime I've come to help. What's our next move?"

TWENTY-TWO

□

Flying in over Washington and banking sharply to come in for a landing at Washington's Reagan National Airport just after noon, was déjà vu for Pam Schlueter; her skin prickled and the hair at the nape of her neck stood on end.

Getting off the plane and passing through customs under a Canadian passport in the name of Monica DeLand she had to control her blinding anger, everything she'd gone through here coming back to her in vivid Technicolor.

As an officer's wife ten years ago she should have been flown military to Andrews, but instead she'd been stuffed into the economy section of a Lufthansa flight from Frankfurt to National and had to catch a cab to their temporary apartment on base. There'd been a hassle at the main gate before she was allowed through, and when she arrived at the married officer's quarters she'd been appalled at how filthy the place was.

Dick had not come home until nearly midnight, drunk; he'd flopped on the couch and gone to sleep even before she could come out of the bedroom to say hi. In the morning he was up and gone before she woke up and it wasn't until the weekend when he was free that they went apartment hunting together.

But he'd had time Friday night for his little S & M games that they'd begun in Munich, and that whole week and weekend had been the beginning of the end for them, though she didn't know it at the time.

The easier solution would have been to assassinate him and be done with it. But even that small an operation took planning, and especially money, of which she had very little. Until she'd contacted the ISI she'd worked as an editor for a number neo-fascist under-ground newspapers. Most of them spread the anti-Turk and anti-Muslim message, but one called for the wall to be put back up. West Germany could once again be the Germany, while the sponges and leeches in the East could form their own government and go back to doing what they did best: live off the dole.

Working around people like that did little to help her bank ac-count but a lot to fuel her anger. She'd become a sharply honed woman of devious intent. She got to know the disaffected Germans. The ones with permanent grudges. The ones filled with hatred like hers.

At one of the shops in the terminal she picked up a prepaid cell phone before she went down to the Hertz counter and rented a Chevy SUV. Within thirty minutes of landing she was on Highway 50 heading southeast to I-95 and Norfolk.

Naisir had warned her never to have all of her operators in one place at the same time. It was common intel tradecraft that deep-cover field officers usually never knew of the others' presence, and especially never met face-to-face.

But these were not normal circumstances in part because of the enormity of the operation—killing a lot of SEALs within forty-eight hours or less—and because of Kirk McGarvey, the loose cannon that none of them had expected. Killing him for the two million euro bonus did not seem as attractive as it had at first, yet there was no doubt in her mind that he would have to be dealt with.

In fact he had become priority one in her mind: hence the meet-ing with her five operators who had flown over from Paris, London, Rome, and Madrid separately and were already in place at the Shera-ton Waterside in Norfolk.

She had initially contacted the four men, plus Zimmer, to work for her under the Black October Revolution banner. Their job was to take on fairly high-profile assassinations for large, though fair, sums of money for those kinds of things. Finding the six men had been easy because of her underground contacts, and finding the assign-ments even easier. The business world, especially in Europe and es-pecially in these times of global financial meltdown, needed pruning from time to time. And her people—all German KSK-trained—were eager not only to earn some money but to kill people. It had been their specialty in the Kommandos, and as civilians they had felt useless until Pam came along.

Once her reputation was solid, the ISI had jumped at the chance for retribution. And her Kommandos had also signed on, but with some reservations. American SEALs were in a sense their comrades-in-arms. Yet the challenge of going up against men as well trained as they were was too interesting to pass up. And in the end they were willing to do anything that their paymistress wanted them to do.

She pulled into a rest stop outside of Fredericksburg to use a pay phone to activate her new cell phone. She was back on the highway in less than ten minutes.

By the time she had driven another twenty miles south on the interstate she had telephoned each of her five operators, giving them the same message. She was to meet with them in her suite at seven sharp.

Pam pulled up to the valet parker at the Sheraton Waterside in Norfolk just before six. A bellman took her bag and inside she checked in under the DeLand name paying for four nights in the presidential suite with a platinum American Express card that had been arranged for her by the ISI.

"A package was to be delivered to me this afternoon. Has it arrived?"

"Yes, madam. It has been placed in your suite."

It was a large leather case that had been sent down from the Pakistani embassy by courier. It contained six Glock 26s with suppressors, six magazines of ammunition for each pistol, and $100,000 in one-hundred-dollar bills, plus six new U.S. passports and supporting documents including driving licenses, family photographs, AAA memberships, and credit cards.

When she was finished at the desk, and her suitcase was sent up, she walked across to the concierge.

"I will be having a meeting with five business partners in my suite at seven this evening," she told the young man. "I want water and soft drinks, plus sandwiches and other snacks sent up no later than six forty-five. Will there be a problem?"

"Of course not, ma'am. Would you also like beer and wine? The hotel maintains an excellent cellar."

"No alcohol."

"Yes, ma'am."

She handed him a hundred-dollar bill, the same amount she had tipped the desk clerk and the bellman, and headed to the elevators. Tipping was so incredibly stupid, but it was expected, especially in the United States. Another on a very long list of things she hated.

TWENTY-THREE

Otto arranged for a CIA Gulfstream VIP jet to get them down to Norfolk's international airport. Once they were airborne, McGarvey brought Pete and Wolf up to speed.

"Of the nineteen remaining SEALs, fifteen live in the Norfolk–Virginia Beach area, close to the base where they were trained. Three are still on active duty, presumably on base, but Otto hasn't been able to find out if they've been deployed somewhere. Two others are in the San Diego area, one is down in Tallahassee, and the last one is running a small hotel in the Virgin Islands. St. Thomas."

"The police still won't help?" Wolf asked.

"Otto keeps trying, but unless there's a legitimate threat, which there hasn't been so far, their hands are tied."

"But two of them, plus their families were gunned down in cold blood."

"Your people in Berlin aren't cooperating with Interpol, so our cops still don't have a positive ID on the guy you shot and killed in Florida."

"Insanity," Wolf said.

"Welcome to the club," Pete told him.

"It'll be impossible to keep watch on all of them—even the fifteen in Norfolk—without help," Wolf said.

"Otto caught us a little break," McGarvey told them, though Pete already knew. "He convinced all of them that trouble was coming their way right now, and eight agreed to call nine-one-one if something came up."

"Leaves us seven," Wolf said.

"Three cars will be waiting for us at the airport. Two of the guys—Dan Lundien and Barry McDougal—live within a couple of miles of each other on Sandbridge Road. You and Pete will keep a watch on them."

"For how long?" Wolf said. "Twelve hours, twenty-four, thirty-six? We can't keep it up forever. And these guys probably won't stay barricaded in their houses. Kids have to go to school. Wives have to go to the grocery store."

"It's going down tonight," Mac said.

"How the hell did you come to that conclusion?"

"I'd do it tonight, just in case someone like us convinces the ONI or the bureau or at least the local cops to keep a heads-up."

"What about the other two?"

"Sam Wiski and Jayson Wonder—Double Shot and Wonder Bread—are next-door neighbors. Wiski lives with his wife and two teenage daughters, but Otto thinks it's likely that Wonder is in the middle of a divorce. His wife and son are out in Seattle."

"If this goes down tonight, like you think it will, how many shooters do you think the woman has sent?" Pete asked.

"We think that there were five of them," Wolf said. "Four now, unless there are others we know nothing about, which is certainly possible."

"They must have good papers."

"Zimmer did. First-class."

"So for now let's assume there are at least four guys, plenty to take out the fifteen if no one gets in their way," McGarvey said.

"It gives us one-in-three odds that someone will come gunning for the four we're going to shepherd," Pete said. "But if any of them start elsewhere and one of the guys pushes the panic button, or maybe starts shooting back, it could slow them down a bit."

"Could be there'll be more than four of them," Wolf said. "And these guys are pros."

Pete suddenly got it. "He's right. If someone calls nine-one-one, whatever cop shows up could be running into a buzz saw without a clue what he's dealing with."

McGarvey got on the aircraft phone and called Otto, who was

working from his house. "Pete came up with something we need to think about. If one of these guys actually dials nine-one-one, the first responder won't have a clue what he could be up against."

"Got it covered, Mac," Otto said. "One of my darlings is watching the nine-one-one systems for the entire area. If a call comes in from any of the fifteen numbers, I'll let you guys know and I'll give the cops the heads-up."

"Let the bureau and the SPs on base know if something starts to go down."

"You're sure it's going to happen tonight?" Otto asked.

"Yeah."

"That's something else that doesn't make a lot of sense," Wolf said when McGarvey hung up. "I was a Kommando, and I bought into the esprit de corps ethic. I work with guys from my old unit—or at least I did until yesterday. And I'm telling you that if someone started coming after me, my old unit would activate in a heartbeat."

"The KSK fields some tough guys, there's no disputing it," McGarvey said. "But it's different on this side of the pond. I know, because I worked with a couple of their teams a few years ago."

"Your SEALs are tough; they have the reputation. I'm not arguing that point."

"But the guys who hit bin Laden weren't ordinary SEALs. They were DEVGRU—SEAL Team Six—the cream of the crop. They're recruited from the pool of regular SEALs to train for eight or nine months with what they call the Green Team. A lot of them wash out and are sent back to their old units because they can't make it. And there's no shame attached because everyone in the regular SEALs knows just how impossible it is to graduate."

"What's your point?"

"By the time those guys make it through their initial training and do the first couple of ops in the field they're the most competent and confident guys in any special ops unit anywhere in the world. They're deployed on average three hundred days a year, and between missions they constantly train. After a while most of them start to believe that they're invincible. On top of all that the guys we're dealing with were all in their thirties when the bin Laden raid went down.

Every one of them were seasoned pros. Every one of them came back from the op. One two three, just like clockwork, even though one of their helicopters crashed. That team just jumped to the ground, between the still spinning main rotor, and stayed on mission."

"They worked as a team."

"That's right. And right now not one of them can conceive of anyone coming after all of them."

They taxied over to the private terminal operated by Landmark Aviation. Clifford Blum, the night manager who'd arranged for the three rental cars to be brought over, was waiting for them on the tarmac.

McGarvey told the crew to get some rest but stand by to take off again within an hour's notice, possibly less. "We could be in a hurry."

"We'll refuel immediately," the pilot said. "Are we going back to Washington?"

"If I'm lucky, we'll fly down to Miami with an extra passenger."

The pilot glanced at the black leather bag that contained a sedation kit used to calm reluctant passengers. Otto had it sent over. And it was obvious that the crew knew what it was.

"We'll be here, Mr. Director."

"Stay frosty," McGarvey said, and he went down the stairs.

Blum shook his hand. "May I log your flight, sir?" he asked. The aircraft's markings were navy, and the Landmark manager had to be curious about what a navy aircraft was doing landing at a civilian field, but he didn't press it.

"No," McGarvey said. "Our crew will need to refuel tonight."

"Will they need help with weather or flight planning?"

"Won't be necessary," McGarvey said.

"Yes, sir," Blum said, but he didn't sound disappointed, and he practically ran back inside.

"At least he was convinced to stay out of it," Pete said.

"All the better," McGarvey agreed. "Don't take any stupid chances tonight. If it looks as if you're getting in over your head, do a one-eighty and let Otto know. He'll have an open line with all of us, and he'll call whoever he needs to call. If you need to talk to each other or to me, tell Otto and he'll make it happen."

"These bastards aren't going to get away with it," Pete said with feeling.

McGarvey gave her a smile. "Watch yourself."

TWENTY-FOUR

□

The last of the five to arrive at Pam's suite was Steffen Engel, the only one to have been court-martialed out of the KSK—because he'd killed three recruits during CQB drills. Though it was never proved to be deliberate murder, he was cashiered because it had been his obligation as a drill instructor to make sure no serious harm came to his trainees.

"Didn't expect to see you here," he said.

"I brought your weapons, papers, and walking-around cash," Pam said. "And I brought something else."

Like the others on the team, Engel stood under six feet, and except for an almost permanent scowl on his square face and deep-set eyes under thick dark hair, he was unremarkable-looking. He easily passed for everyman wherever he went, and he was just enough of a chameleon to smile pleasantly whenever the need arose. But like a lion he lived for the kill, and even Pam understood that he was a force to be handled with care. It was the main reason she'd picked him from the applicants whose résumés she'd read on *Soldier of Fortune*. If anyone could finish an op no matter the trouble, it was Engel. She didn't like him, but he was perfect for her kind of wet work.

"The operation is on?"

"Yes, come meet the others you'll be working with. They're in the dining area."

The other four were seated around the table large enough for six: Rolf Woedding, the first she'd hired and the most ruthless; Friedrich Heiser, at twenty-four the youngest of the team; Klaus Bruns, whose mother was Russian and father was East German; and Felix Volker, five eight, the most heavily built of the men, and, in Pam's estimation, completely insane. He actually believed that he was Hitler and Eva Braun's grandson. She never disputed the belief with him.

Volker looked up. "Steffen, I thought I caught a whiff of something rotten coming through the door."

Engel scowled; it was obvious that he was surprised. "Fuck you too, and the rest of you as well."

"This is the team," Pam said, from the head of the table. "I don't much care if you get along on your own time, but for now pay attention because the most important mission of our op is on for tonight."

"It's a definite go, then?" Engel asked.

"Yes," Pam said. She passed each of them an iPhone. "Programmed are the names, addresses, and brief bios of your targets. You'll each do three tonight. They're all in the immediate Norfolk–Virginia Beach area and I've grouped them in the general vicinity of each other to minimize your travel time. Once you've eliminated one target you will immediately go to the next, erasing the first from the phone on the way."

"Fifteen in one night will create a hell of a stir," Volker said, the happiest anyone had seen him in a while.

Pam passed out their new passports and other papers, as well as tickets on separate airlines for destinations ranging from Mexico City to Caracas. They were to make their own arrangements for getting to San Diego for the next phase. "You'll be leaving first thing in the morning, and I'll send word when I expect you to be in California. But the delay will not be very long."

No one objected.

She passed out bundles of cash, $15,000 to each of them, along with the Glock pistols, silencers, and ammunition.

All of them checked the pistols' actions and loads before they looked at the passports, papers, travel documents, and cash. The KSK had trained them to be thorough. First priority: make sure of your tools.

"Fifteen tonight—if nothing goes wrong—which makes seventeen," Heiser said. "Leaves seven more? From the original team."

"Plus one."

They all looked up.

"Kirk McGarvey," Pam said. "Anyone heard of him?"

"Former CIA director," Volker said. "Supposed to be some kind of badass. But I'd heard that he bought the farm down in Cuba a while back."

"You heard wrong. And he's gotten himself involved in trying to save some lives. He might even be here in Norfolk tonight, the white knight in shining armor."

"Could be a problem."

"Whoever takes him down gets a bonus—four hundred thousand euros."

"I'm looking forward to meeting the gentleman," Bruns said.

"Good to know, Klaus. But you'll have to earn the bonus before you spend it."

"The bastard is ancient."

"Fifty."

"*Leicht*," Bruns said. Easy.

"I hope you're right. It'd be the best bonus I've ever paid."

"Do you think this man will be a problem?" Volker asked.

"It's a real possibility," Pam said. "One that we have to consider. But think on this: the man did serve as the CIA's director, but before that and since then, he's been involved in what they call 'special projects.' Black ops."

Volker nodded. "The man is an assassin."

"A very good one."

"I understand. He's just like us."

Pam nodded. From what Naisir had told her, McGarvey was nothing like her operators. The man was a killer, for sure. Like a James Bond. But he worked for his country, not for money.

"Of course one can never be certain about that aspect, because the man is wealthy in his own right," Naisir had said. "Worth at least several millions."

"Yet according to you he teaches philosophy at some small college in Florida. How much sense does that make?"

"From our way of thinking, not much. But be very careful, Ms Schlueter, that his study of Voltaire does not blind you to his formidable abilities."

TWENTY-FIVE

Wiski and Wonder lived next door to each other in matching one-story bungalows, with carports, ratty little lawns, and roofs that needed repairs in a Norfolk neighborhood called Hollywood Homes, which was a subdivision of Lake Edwards. Their houses were at the end of a dead-end street within sight of the lake.

The neighborhood was quiet, lights on in almost all of the houses, but no traffic, no one outside, quiet except for someone's stereo playing in one of the houses.

It was two when McGarvey showed up, backing his dark blue rental Taurus in the driveway of a house with a FOR SALE sign on the lawn.

No cars were parked on the street; though many of the carports were filled with junk, the cars, and in two cases pickup trucks, were parked in the driveways or on the lawns. Even in the dark the neighborhood looked unkempt, and he thought that it was a hell of a place for people who had served their country, especially at the level these guys had, to end up.

He lowered the window and sat back low so that only the top of his head would show and settled down to wait.

A dog barked somewhere. He sat up ten minutes later when he heard two pistol shots from the apartment complex across the lake. He waited a full five minutes listening for sirens, but if the police were ever summoned they weren't responding.

His cell phone vibrated. It was Otto.

"I picked up a nine-one-one call from one of our guys south of Naval Air Station Oceana four minutes ago and gave the cops the heads-up. Turned out to be a false alarm; one of the neighbors came over with a six-pack."

"Did they ask who you were and how you hacked into their system?"

"I didn't give them the chance, and there's no way they'll trace my call. But so far the rest of the numbers have been quiet. How about you?"

"Someone across the lake fired a couple of shots, sounded like a pistol—nine or ten millimeter—a few minutes ago."

"Nothing showing on any of the police channels in your area."

"Maybe the neighbors over there are used to it," McGarvey said. "Anything from Pete or Wolf?"

"They showed up about fifteen minutes ago, but I haven't heard anything."

"Give them a call and make sure everything is okay. Something starts to go down, I want to hear about it immediately."

"You've got the willies?" Otto asked.

McGarvey was about to reply when the hackles on the back of his neck rose. He turned in time to see a dark figure darting between two houses across the street on the side facing a strip of woods away from the lake, three doors down from Wiski's place.

"Might have something," he said softly.

He waited for a few moments to see if whoever it was showed up on the other side of the house. It was possible that one of the neighbors was out and had gone back inside.

"Mac?"

The figure darted across the open backyard to the rear of the next house.

"Looks like it's going down now," McGarvey said getting out of the car.

"I'll give Pete and Wolf the heads-up. Do you want backup?"

McGarvey ran across the street and headed toward the cul-de-sac. "I'm going to try to take this guy alive. But if it starts to get noisy and someone calls the cops, let me know."

"Will do," Otto said.

McGarvey took out his pistol and made it to the end of the block; the neighborhood was almost deathly silent. A couple of lights were on in one of the houses behind him, but all the others were dark. Even the one streetlight was burned out.

He pulled up behind a pickup truck in the driveway of the house next door to Wiski's and listened for a long ten seconds, until he thought he heard a quiet shuffle of footsteps on gravel.

Easing to the left, he crossed to the front of the SEAL's little house, and at the east corner he peered around the side in time to see a man dressed in dark slacks and a dark shirt of some kind doing something to a window.

"Not this time," McGarvey said, raising his pistol.

The man leaped to the left almost as agilely as a ballet dancer, pulled a pistol and fired two silenced shots, both of them plowing into the side of the house.

Mac fired once, aiming low for the man's legs, but missing as the figure disappeared around the back of the house, firing a third and fourth shot over his shoulder.

Sprinting back to the opposite side of the house Mac was in time to see the figure dart between the two houses. He gave chase, stopping briefly at the rear corner to take a quick look. But the yard was empty. Nothing moved in the darkness.

"I don't mean to kill you unless it's necessary," Mac said, scanning the shoreline.

Something moved behind him.

"How kind of you, Herr McGarvey," a man said, in a heavy German accent.

Mac rolled around the side of the house an instant before a pistol was fired inches from the back of his head; the shot, even though suppressed, was very loud at such close range.

The man grunted something.

Mac rolled back around the corner, the muzzle of his silenced pistol connecting sharply with the man's broad forehead. Engel reared back and Mac stepped forward, keeping the pistol in direct contact with the guy's head. He got the instant impression that he was in a cage with a wild but calculating animal.

"Drop your weapon," McGarvey said.

Engel moved his head left at the same moment that he batted McGarvey's gun away. He raised his own pistol, firing off one snap shot at hip level, just missing McGarvey.

Mac managed to grab the German's gun hand and, with his other in the guy's face, forced him back against the side of the house. Except for the silenced shots this was all almost completely noiseless.

Slowly Engel slumped back, releasing his grip on his pistol, letting McGarvey take it from his hand and toss it aside.

Mac stepped back. "How did you know that I would be here tonight?" he asked, though he didn't expect an answer that would be of any use. It wasn't going to be that easy.

Engel was outwardly calm. He shrugged. "What now?"

"You and I are going someplace where we can have a little talk about SEAL Team Six and Frau Schlueter's interests in them."

"I don't think so," Engel said, and he produced a Glock 81 field knife, which looked something like a slimmed-down version of the U.S. Special Forces KA-BAR. Deadly in the right hands.

Mac stepped back out of range, his hands to either side. "The KSK fields some sharp operators, but of course the stupid ones like you and your pal down in Florida and the others out tonight usually riff out. That your story?"

Engel said something in German under his breath and charged, feinting first to the right. McGarvey waited for the actual thrust from the left and managed to deflect it, hooking the German's arm under his left, and bending the man's wrist back nearly to the point of breaking.

Wordlessly Engel tried to smash his fist into the side of Mac's head, but each time Mac slipped the blow and increased the pressure on the man's knife hand, forcing him back against the side of the house again.

"A jail cell is better than a pauper's grave, don't you think?" Mac said.

Engel hooked a leg around McGarvey's and they went down, Mac on the bottom. Engel slowly brought the tip of the knife around so that it was inches away from Mac's throat.

For a long beat or two, McGarvey resisted, but then all at once he caved in, rolling left as the knife came down. This time he snatched the blade out of the German's hand, flipped it end over end, and rapped the heavy pommel sharply against the man's forehead, momentarily dazing him.

Getting out from underneath, McGarvey pulled the syringe kit out of his pocket and injected a few cc's of methohexital directly into the side of Engel's neck. He needed the man docile for what came next. The German was struggling out of his momentary daze, but the powerful sedative took hold almost immediately and he lay back, his body going slack except for the rise and fall of his chest.

McGarvey found both pistols and pocketed them, then quickly searched the German, coming up with a cell phone.

The neighborhood remained quiet.

He hit the speed dial and a woman answered immediately. "Steffen?"

"I have your man. Call the other two off and go home, Ms. Schlueter. It's over for tonight."

The woman was silent for a long time. When she spoke it sounded as if she was talking in her sleep, her voice dreamy and distant. "For tonight," she said and she was gone.

Mac phoned Otto and told him what had happened. "Nothing from Pete or Wolf yet?"

"No. You okay?"

"Fine. Have them meet me at Landmark and have the crew standing by for immediate takeoff."

"Do you want me to call Martinez?"

"I'll do it," McGarvey said. "We dodged a bullet this time, but it's not over."

"It never is, kemo sabe," Otto said.

Engel was heavy, but not impossibly so. McGarvey managed to heave him off the ground into a fireman's carry and headed back to where he had parked his car.

TWENTY-SIX

☐

Raul Martinez was waiting for them at a government hangar on the side of Miami International Airport opposite the civilian terminal. The morning sun was not up yet; the airport just starting to come alive with the first commercial flights out.

On the way down from Norfolk, Wolf had identified their prisoner as Steffen Engel, a former KSK hand-to-hand instructor, one of the serious badasses in the Kommados who'd been kicked out for excessive force.

"Definitely one of Schlueter's handpicked shooters," Wolf said. "But there's little or no chance he'll cooperate with us, no matter how persuasive you think you are. At least not here in the States. Maybe the Saudis would have better luck."

McGarvey glanced at Pete, who had a little sad smile on her lips. She'd told him once that sometimes she might not like the method, but if the reasons were strong enough she'd have no problem.

"It's the real world," he'd told her.

"Shitty."

Martinez, who was the CIA's chief of operations in Miami's Little Havana neighborhood around the Calle Ocho, was a slender dark man who knew just about everyone in south Florida and the Keys, along with most of their secrets. But Cuba was fast becoming a cause of the past. Fidel was dead, his brother retired, and the exiles were getting old; memories were fading, becoming less urgent each year.

He'd arrived with two husky Cubanos in coveralls in a light gray panel van with FROSTPROOF AC SERVICE and a Hialeah logo on the sides. When McGarvey came down the stairs Martinez gave him a hug.

"Otto said that you were bringing someone special."

"Nothing to do with Cuba this time," Mac said.

"Nothing much does anymore, comp," Martinez said. "We lost the revolution, could be we're losing the peace. Who'd you bring?"

McGarvey explained about Engel and Schlueter and SEAL Team Six. "Last night was just a temporary fix."

"The bastards just keep coming, and yet they expect us to treat them like they've got civil rights," Martinez said with disgust.

Pete, who Martinez knew, came down the stairs with Wolf. Mac introduced the German BND officer.

"Have you ever been involved with this type of interrogation?" Martinez asked.

"No," Wolf admitted.

The Cubanos went aboard and brought Engel out between them, the man's feet dragging on the ground, and loaded him into the van.

"We can find you a secure hotel. Might be best for your career all around if you don't get involved, you know what I mean?"

"It's too late for that, I think," Wolf said.

Martinez shook his head. "Where the hell do you find these people, Mac?" he asked, but there was no answer, because none of them knew if he was talking about Engel or Wolf.

Little Torch Key, about one hundred miles from Miami, was a series of low mangrove islets that extended northward up into the Gulf. Isolated, lightly inhabited, and nearly impossible to reach by road or water without detection, Government 312 was a listening post for Cuban radio and television broadcasts. It had figured big during the Bay of Pigs invasion, but ever since then it had languished.

Outwardly. But before and since the Bay of Pigs the tiny facility— only three concrete block buildings, a generator shed, and a diesel tank on stilts behind a tall razor wire fence—had in fact been used as an enhanced interrogation outpost. Far from the prying eyes of the media or other governmental agencies, the CIA, which denied its existence, had from time to time made use of the place. Completely extrajudicially.

It was broad daylight when they showed up, the morning steamy, already in the nineties. The Cubanos brought Engel inside one of the windowless block buildings furnished only with a leather-covered interrogation bench complete with straps. A single lightbulb hung from the ceiling, and a hose was connected to a faucet in one corner. In the middle of the floor directly beneath the bench was a drain hole covered by a grate.

The Cubanos laid Engel on the bench and secured the straps around his legs, hips, and torso so that that he couldn't move to defend himself.

Martinez went out and started the generator and the light came on. He brought back a thin towel and a bucket, as Engel was starting to come around.

"You guys might want to wait outside," he told his Cubanos, and they left without a word. "You too," he told Pete.

"This guy would have killed two of our people and their families if Mac hadn't stopped him," she said. "And there would have been even more deaths tonight." She looked at Engel and the others. "I'll stay."

Mac closed the door; almost instantly the room became stifling.

Martinez filled the bucket with water, and Pete went to Engel's side. "I'll do this," she told Mac and the others.

McGarvey stepped aside with Wolf. Pete's reputation inside the CIA was beauty and brains. Only a handful of fellow officers who'd watched her in action during interrogations realized that she was much more than that. She was fierce enough that no one felt right about giving her a nickname. She made most people who knew her nervous. But not McGarvey because he of all people understood that what she was giving up for her country was every bit as dear as what the SEAL Team Six guys had given up.

She patted Engel on the cheek a couple of times. "Hey, Steffen, can you hear me?" she asked gently.

Engel's eyes were open, fixed on hers.

"You were given a sedative. It's wearing off now. Do you understand?"

After several moments he nodded. He turned his head as far as the restraints would allow and looked at McGarvey and Wolf, and then at Martinez.

"I'm going to ask you a few questions," Pete said, her tone still reasonable. "If you cooperate this will be easy. You'll be transferred to a federal cell somewhere in the D.C. area where you'll be held until your trial for attempted murder and acts of terrorism."

Engel looked at her again, the expression in his eyes and face one of utter contempt.

Pete patted him on the shoulder. "But it's not going to be easy, is it?" she said. "Let's start with your name, please."

Engel said nothing.

"Give me just that much, okay?"

He looked away.

"So here's the deal. We're going to waterboard you, which you understand will not be pleasant. In some cases subjects have actually died. At the very least you will be faced with pain, of course, but also possible damage to your lungs, some brain damage because of oxygen deprivation, and perhaps even a few broken bones as you struggle against your restraints."

Her tone was sad, her voice apologetic, low, even sexy. She understood what he was about to experience, and she conveyed the feeling that she was genuinely sorry for him, even afraid.

"What is it we want to know?" she asked, not turning away from Engel.

"We know that you and the others were hired by Pam Schlueter to kill the SEAL Team Six guys who took out bin Laden," McGarvey said. "We want to know who hired her. Who is her paymaster? Who is her contact?"

"You heard, so I don't need to repeat the question," she told Engel. "A name is all Mr. McGarvey needs, and then it'll be off to a jail cell—pleasant compared to your present circumstances."

Engel stared at her but said nothing.

"No?" Pete said. "Too bad for you."

She took a towel from Martinez and draped it over Engel's face. He flinched.

"One name, Steffen. It's all that we ask of you."

Martinez placed a strap across Engel's forehead; despite the man's struggles he managed to tighten it down, holding the assassin's head firmly in the face-up position. He began pouring water directly onto the towel covering Engel's face. Slowly, but in a steady stream.

The German lay perfectly motionless for nearly fifteen seconds, his training and control perfect, until suddenly his chest spasmed and he bucked violently against the leather straps.

Pete, her mouth set, motioned for Martinez to continue pouring water on the towel, and Engel convulsed more violently. His brain was telling him that he was drowning, and he could no longer control his body, which had dropped into a primal defense mode.

Mac, who had been waterboarded himself, knew what it was like, what was at stake, and he felt the man's pain. But he didn't give a good goddamn. Engel was an assassin for hire. A freelance. Not for a country or a religion or even for an ideal, but simply for money.

Martinez stepped back and Pete pulled the towel off Engel's face. "Here we are at the start of a long road. Are you ready?"

Engel was working to catch his breath.

"Steffen?"

"Fuck you," Engel said.

Pete replaced the towel, and Martinez, who had refilled the bucket, poured the water again, with the same results.

"A name," Pete said when she'd removed the towel for the second time.

Engel tried to say something, but Pete draped the towel over his face again. This time she got the hose, turned it on to an even flow, and held it a couple of inches above his mouth and nose. She held it there, seemingly forever, until Engel's movements began to subside as he lost consciousness.

Tossing the hose aside, Pete ripped the towel off the German's face and got close. "Last time, Steffen. A name, or I set the hose on you again and walk away."

Wolf stepped forward, but McGarvey held him back.

"*Sprechen zu mir, Kommando!*" Pete said. Speak to me! "A name. Just that."

The sound of the running water falling on the concrete floor, and just then an osprey or some other hunting bird flying overhead, dropping for a kill, seemed suddenly loud in the close confines. Even louder than the noise of the diesel generator, and of Engel's desperate gasps for breath.

"Steffen," Pete whispered close to his ear.

"Naisir," Engel croaked, his voice barely audible, scarcely under-standable.

"Naisir who?"

"Major Naisir. ISI. In Berlin, Warsaw. Guernsey."

Pakistan

Ali Naisir had led a charmed life up until August 2008 when Pervez Musharraf was forced to resign from the presidency of Pakistan and leave the country because of death threats from the Taliban, and other political considerations.

Naisir was a lieutenant in an ISI special detail tasked with protecting Musharraf not only from the Taliban and the angry mobs outside parliament, but from himself and his own ambitions as well.

"The general has done Pakistan a great and honorable service, but it is time for him to step aside," Colonel Akhtar Ahmed told him. Ahmed was director of the Joint Intelligence Bureau, which was responsible for collecting political intelligence inside and outside the country.

Naisir had been called to the colonel's office at headquarters in Islamabad, though he had no earthly idea why. "Yes, sir."

"In fact he means to leave this very night, and already various parties want to stop him from going. By any means."

"I can arrange for a military detail to escort him every step of the way, sir. He still has many friends at the PMA and NDU." The PMA at Kakul was Pakistan's military academy and the NDU—the National Defense University—in Islamabad was where officers learned strategy, leadership, and statecraft. Nearly all the powerful officers in the military and the ISI were graduates of both institutions. Naisir was in his fourth year at the NDU and was considered one of its rising stars—which was why he'd been given the important job of seeing to the overall welfare of a president.

Ahmed waved his response aside. "That would call too much attention to him. He wants to make the pilgrimage to Mecca, and you will see that he makes it safely to the border, at which point your obligation will be completed. Is this clear, Lieutenant?"

"A private flight—"

"Would be shot down within sight of the airport. He'll be expected by friends in Jalalabad."

"A convoy?" Naisir suggested, though he knew what the colonel would say and why.

Ahmed shook his head. "You'll leave under darkness tonight. Just you and a couple of men, no fanfare, no special precautions."

Through Peshawar, which was a hundred and fifty kilometers from Islamabad, it was another one hundred plus klicks over the mountains to the relative safety of the Afghan town—the highway in many spots nearly impassable and almost always choked with truck traffic.

It had dawned on Naisir that he was never expected to cross the Khyber Pass into Afghanistan, let alone reach Jalalabad. And when his body was found with Musharraf's, he would be branded as a traitor.

"Do you understand, Lieutenant?"

"Perfectly," Naisir had said. He got to his feet, crashed his boot heels together, and saluted in the British fashion—palm out.

"Understand something else. In this case the mission is as important as the man. What happens in the next twenty-four hours will have a great effect on the future of our country, and on yours."

Naisir drove a Range Rover, an indifferent even aloof Musharraf alone in the backseat, while three enlisted men rode behind in a Toyota pickup truck, one of them in the back manning a machine gun on a swivel mount.

Their departure from Islamabad shortly before midnight had gone without incident and although Naisir had been extremely nervous on the run west to Peshawar, the last big town before the mountains along the Afghan border, the drive was a nonevent.

To that point traffic had been reasonable, but then the highway began its climb up to the pass which at a bit more than three thousand feet was one of the most heavily traveled highways in the world—and had been since the days of the ancient Silk Road—and everything slowed to a crawl.

Trucks were backed up as far as the eye could see in either direction. Those heading into Afganistan were transporting fuel and other supplies for the American war effort, while the trucks heading into Pakistan were empty, returning for supplies.

The Taliban had controlled much of the highway over the past several years, sometimes closing it for days at a time, despite the Pakistani military presence.

Naisir figured that if they were going to run into any sort of trouble it would be on the last stretch before the actual summit, which was about three miles inside Pakistan. Once across the border, the highway was controlled by American forces and would be relatively safe.

The mountains rose steeply on the other side of the road. Around one switchback Naisir caught a glimpse of the big stone gate that straddled the highway; a short distance to the right was one of the squat towers that the Khyber rifle detail used as a lookout.

Most of the trucks were pulled over and parked just on this side of the gateway, but Naisir could not make out any people; no truck drivers nor the soldiers who manned the border were anywhere in sight. His inner radar came alive.

He got on the walkie-talkie to warn Sergeant Brahami that something might be coming their way. "Unit Two, copy?"

"This is Two."

"Something odd is going on at the border. Keep alert."

The pickup was ten yards back, and behind it the line of supply trucks had begun to slow down and spread out. Naisir had the strong feeling that they were heading into a trap.

"I see it, Lieutenant," Brahami radioed back. "What do you want to do?"

Naisir had never worked with the sergeant or the other three men in the pickup. They had been assigned to him for this detail at the last minute with written orders.

He glanced at Musharraf in the rearview mirror. "There may be some trouble at the border crossing, Mr. President. Are you armed?"

"No. Should I be?"

Musharraf had had a distinguished career in the military, even winning the Imtiazi Sanad medal for gallantry because of his battlefield conduct in the second Kashmir war of 1965. He was an officer who, when given an order to hold his position, did so no matter the odds. After that he'd joined the Special Service Group, which was Pakistan's elite special forces unit, where he again showed his bravery under fire.

"Yes, sir," Naisir said, and he handed back his 9mm Steyr GB pistol as they came around the last switchback, less than fifty yards from the gate. "It's possible that someone is waiting to assassinate you."

"What do you propose?"

"I'm not going to stop until we reach the border. If need be we'll shoot our way across the summit."

"It won't do your career much good," Musharraf said. He rolled down the windows on both sides.

Naisir got back on the walkie-talkie. "I'm not stopping for the summit."

Brahami didn't answer.

"Sergeant, copy?"

They were coming up on the gate. No one was anywhere in sight. The trucks and a few cars, sitting idly off the side of the road, were surreal in the harsh overhead lights.

Naisir picked up the 9mm Ingram MAC 10 from beside him on the seat and turned the cocking handle ninety degrees to unlock the bolt; then he slammed the pedal to the floor and the Range Rover surged ahead.

He glanced in the rearview mirror at the same moment the pickup truck went up in a fireball, almost certainly hit by an RPG fired from above and to the right, the explosion completely destroying it.

Four men armed with AK-47s, dressed in the leggings and long shirts of Taliban fighters, came around from behind the gate and stood shoulder to shoulder in the middle of the road.

Musharraf started firing, one measured shot at a time, hitting two of the Taliban shooters as Naisir closed the distance to less than ten yards, holding on to the steering wheel with his right hand, while firing out the window with his left.

The men opened fire, blowing out the Range Rover's windshield but directing their aim at Musharraf, who weaved and ducked as he continue to fire his pistol one shot at a time.

At the last possible moment, with only one of the Taliban left standing, Naisir plowed into him, his body slamming up onto the hood of the SUV, still alive but bleeding heavily from wounds in his forehead and neck.

Naisir tapped the brakes hard. The Taliban rocketed off the hood, and Naisir ran over his body, the Range Rover nearly rocking out of control, until they were on the other side and descending into the valley toward the border crossing.

Three days later, Naisir reported as ordered to Colonel Ahmed's office. He had been relieved from duty without explanation the morning he'd returned from Jalalabad, and he had remained confined to his quarters in the bachelor officer's wing at the school.

"You exceeded your orders, Lieutenant," Ahmed shouted. "And in doing so you got the three men under your command shot to death."

"It was an RPG, Colonel, fired I'm certain by Taliban forces—the same ones who attacked my vehicle in an attempt to assassinate President Musharraf."

"It does not matter who attacked. What matters is that you violated two sovereign borders—ours and Afghanistan's. And now we have the Americans breathing down our backs once again."

"What would you have had me do, Colonel? Die on the highway?"

"It would have been for the best," Ahmed blurted angrily before he realized what he was saying.

"I was ordered to get the president safely out of Pakistan, which I did. I'll accept a court-martial on the issue, sir."

"Get out of my sight, Lieutenant."

"No, sir. Not until my position has been clarified. Am I to be returned to my unit and be allowed to finish my degree, or am I to be discharged from the service? I have a right to know which, sir."

Ahmed sat back and toyed with a thin file folder on the desk on front of him. "If you wish to resign you will be allowed to do so. Without prejudice."

"I do not wish to resign."

"You are relieved of your present position and will devote your-self to completing your education, at which time—if you graduate—you will be assigned to Joint Intelligence Miscellaneous, at the rank of captain."

Naisir held himself in check. That directorate of the ISI was responsible for espionage operations, including offensive intel missions in other countries. The crème de la crème.

Brilliant careers could be made in the field, but men's careers could also come to fiery ends.

Problem officers were sent to that directorate, where they either shone like bright stars or crashed like meteors.

Naisir understood the risks, but he could not foresee what was to happen in the coming years. Then again, no one could.

"Thank you, Colonel," he said, forcing his expression to remain neutral.

Ahmed hand him the file folder. "Your orders, Lieutenant. And don't be so quick to thank me; you may change your mind before long."

PART
TWO

Ten Days Later

TWENTY-SEVEN

☐

Pam Schlueter's Alitalia flight from Rome landed at Tehran's IKA—
Imam Khomeini International Airport—at four thirty in the afternoon local and she was among the first out of the first-class exit,
thoroughly discouraged and angry, mostly with herself.

She carried only one overnight bag, which passed through customs as did her Danish passport in the name of Inga Paulson without
bother. Fifteen minutes after landing she was waiting with a few
others at the taxi queue, though she'd half expected Naisir to pick her
up or at least send someone.

He hadn't sounded happy when she'd telephoned him with the
news, but he agreed that it would be best if they met.

"I'm coming to Islamabad," she told him.

"That would not be a very good idea. The situation here is becoming unstable. Your presence would not help."

"Unstable?"

"There are some in the government who believe that it might have
been a mistake hiring you. There've been some back-burner feelers
from Washington about certain recent events."

"I'd imagined there would be," Pam told him. "It's why we need
to talk face-to-face. No bullshit now, because the mission has
changed."

"Perhaps the mission has become untenable for the time being."

"It's worse than that."

"Come to Tehran, if you must. I have friends there. Book a room
at the Esteghlal Hotel."

"Tomorrow," Pam had told him. "Under the name Inga Paulson,
Danish passport."

"We'll have an early dinner, and you can leave first thing in the morning. Come alone."

"You too."

"And, Ms. Schlueter, I'll want the truth about everything."

"So will I, Major."

The hotel was located in the northern section of the city, facing the foothills of the Alborz Mountains, which formed a natural barrier between the capital and the Caspian Sea. She wore a head covering to hide her short-cropped graying hair, but unlike in some Muslim countries she did not have to cover her face.

She paid the indifferent cabbie well, and inside at the desk she paid for her suite with an Amex platinum card, which she loved doing. Most of her life, including when she was married, she'd lived on a budget. Especially in Germany, in the first few years of her organization, she lived frugally. Now that she finally had serious money, she was enjoying herself. And she meant to continue to do so.

She refused the services of a bellman and went up to her suite on her own. The sitting room on the tenth floor looked out over the hills, which were dotted with the homes of the more affluent Tehranians, all of them sporting more than one satellite dish, not only for television signals but for connections with Wi-Fi networks. The hotel was first class even by international standards. Surprisingly, the minibar, which needed the room key to access, was stocked with beer, wine, and several liquors in addition to mixers, bottled water, and soft drinks.

She opened a Heineken and turned on the flat-screen television; the channels included the BBC and CNN in English and Deutsche Welle in German. She turned to CNN and watched for a half hour to see if there was any mention of the assassinations, but there was nothing. She got the feeling that the CNN broadcast was censored.

The phone rang. It was Naisir and he sounded rushed.

"I'm here," he said. "Let's talk before dinner."

"As you wish."

. . .

Pam actually knew very little about Naisir, except that he was a major in a directorate of the ISI that dealt with special projects outside
of Pakistan, mostly in the West, especially Europe and the United
States. When she had first approached the ISI about her project, she'd
been immediately sent to meet with him, and his had been a sympa-
thetic ear. He'd understood exactly what she wanted to do, why she
wanted to do it, and the benefit it would have for his country. But he
had his doubts.

"You're new at this," he had said. "You've not done much."

"But what we've done, we've done well. You would not have been
directed to meet with me otherwise. And now we've come to the next
step."

"Yes, assassination on a much larger scale. Twenty-four of them,
to be exact. But why, Ms. Schlueter? Not simply for money. What is
your motivation?"

"Why not money?"

"You have greater zeal than that," Naisir had said. "A passion for
revenge, I think. Your ex-husband? Is he that much of a thorn in
your side?"

Pam remembered the spike in her anger. She'd wanted to lash out
at the bastard, but she'd controlled her temper. She'd shrugged. "The
money is sufficient for our purposes, wouldn't you agree? I will provide you a service, for which I will get paid well and for which your
government will be able to claim no knowledge. In fact I suspect it
will be to your benefit to denounce the acts."

Naisir had actually smiled. "But not too loudly, because no one
would believe it wasn't something we wanted. Retribution."

Pam had let it hang there for several beats. Naisir wore a gold
wedding band, and she had the urge to ask him if his was a more
successful marriage than hers had been, but she refrained. "Yes," she
said. "Retribution. Do we have an agreement?"

"Of course. But let me caution you that if unseen circumstances
should arise, you will deal with them on your own."

"I might ask for intelligence."

"That would be possible, but we could not provide any overt
assistance. You must understand that would be a condition."

"Of course," she assured him.

.   .   .

The doorbell rang and Pam got up to answer it. Naisir, dressed in a Western business suit, the collar of his white shirt open, no tie, a four- or five-day shadow on his face, walked in.

"You came in clean?" he asked.

"As far as I know."

"Do you have another one of those?" he asked, indicating the beer.

"Of course," he said. She got him the beer and they sat across from each other at the coffee table.

He took a drink. "What do you want?"

"McGarvey has become priority one," she said.

"I warned you."

"Yes, you did. In the meantime your retribution has to go on hold until we can deal with him."

"What happened?" he asked.

She explained about the Norfolk operation and McGarvey's call from Steffen Engel's cell phone. "I immediately recalled my other operators and told them to get the hell out of there."

"Where are they now?"

"Back in Berlin, where they will stand by until I give them their next assignment."

Naisir thought about it for a long moment. "He knows who you are."

"It's possible, but there was nothing on Steffen's cell phone that could have led directly to me. It was a prepaid phone—they all were."

"What about your Herr Engel? If he's not dead, can he be made to talk?"

"Not likely."

"Actually, what I'm asking is, how much of our arrangement is he aware of?"

"If you mean does he know your name? No, he does not."

"Would you be willing to stake your life on it?"

"Yes," Pam said without hesitation, even though she knew that she wasn't sure. Steffen, like the others, was a professional who had his own contacts. Anything was possible.

"What is it that you want of me?" Naisir asked.

"That you understand the delay for the primary objective, that your offer of two million for McGarvey still stands, and that if you learn anything that might be useful to me you will let me know."

"Yes, to all of it."

"Then we will kill Mr. McGarvey before we proceed any further."

TWENTY-EIGHT

☐

Coming home, Rawalpindi Airport was always a crush, though this time Naisir had not checked a bag, and his ISI-issued diplomatic passport parted the waters as usual. He hadn't logged his trip, so he hadn't signed out with his office nor would he have to sign back in. In fact he'd taken yesterday and today off, his first in several months, to try to figure out what might be coming up behind him and what his options were.

The cab ride back up to Islamabad was choked with traffic as usual, but although the two cities just ten kilometers apart were called twins, they were nothing like each other. Rawalpindi was filthy; by comparison, Islamabad was showroom-clean. Rawalpindi was where the ordinary people lived and worked, while Islamabad was were the government functionaries did their thing. The embassies were here, along with the diplomats and their families. All the government buildings were also grouped in the restricted sections of the city; the Parliament, the Secretariat, the Interior Ministry, the Supreme Court, the state bank, and the ISI.

Naisir maintained two homes—a small one behind tall walls near the airport in Rawalpindi, which he used as a safe house where he met in secret with field officers who were never allowed to come anywhere near ISI headquarters. And the other, the home he shared with Ayesha, his wife of nine years, behind spotless white walls in F-10, just west of the expansive Fatima Jinnah Park in F-9.

Islamabad was considered a green city because of its tree-lined avenues and many parks, and it was always a great pleasure for Naisir to come back to it, to his modern open-plan home, and to Ayesha, who was not only his wife but his best friend, major confidante, and chief adviser.

It was she who agreed that he should take the assignment to kill the SEALs who had violated Pakistan's sovereignty when they'd taken out bin Laden. All of Pakistan would rejoice, especially those in the president's inner circles. "But with care, Ali," she said.

They were in each other's arms in bed, the house staff retired for the evening, no children to disturb them. "It's a great deal of money," he'd said.

"That little sum of is of no consequence; it is the response of the American government that's vital. The money they give us in military aid is about all that stands between us and the Indians."

"Plus our nuclear arsenal."

"Which we would never have achieved without the inadvertent help of Washington."

"What are you saying?"

"If the CIA can prove that Pakistan is behind the deaths of the SEALs, it will go very badly for us. Our diplomatic response—whatever it might be, no matter how mild it might be—would anger our people."

"Which is why we hired an outside team for the operation. They will be blamed."

"You're not listening to me. If it goes bad you will throw the Schlueter woman and her operatives under the bus, but do you honestly believe that if they are arrested and interrogated, they wouldn't point their fingers at you."

Naisir had considered the possibility from the beginning, which was why he'd taken such care to hide the money trail, and his physical meetings with Schlueter. "She and her people might point fingers, but without proof it would be meaningless," he told his wife.

"Just a hint, a suspicion on the CIA's part would be enough," she'd pressed.

"Enough for what?"

"For General Bhutani to feed you to the wolves." Lieutenant General Tariq Bhutani was the director of the ISI and maintained a warm relationship with Walter Page, the CIA's director.

"It's possible," he'd conceded.

"In that case, my husband, we need to think about our survival. Inside of Pakistan if possible; outside if need be."

"It's a little early for such dark thoughts," he'd said, stroking her thigh.

"It's never too early, because when the sword falls there won't be time," she'd replied. "Think on it. I will."

It was early afternoon when he got home. Ayesha met him at the door, and after they embraced she looked critically at him and nodded. "Let's talk."

"Yes," Naisir said.

Ayesha's family was well-to-do; her father, two brothers, and an uncle owned three rug factories and eleven outlets in Pakistan and in six major European cities, in addition to New York, Washington, and Miami. Because of the family fortune Ali and his wife were able to afford to buy the house when he'd still been a first lieutenant, and to afford a cook, a housekeeper, and a gardener, even on a major's pay.

The inner sanctum was the only wing of the house that didn't face in the large central courtyard and garden, but instead faced toward the park. Here was his study and hers, plus a pleasantly furnished sitting room separating the two, a modern Western bathroom, and a wet bar. It was the only area of the house that none of the staff were ever allowed to enter. And it was the only place that was protected from electronic eavesdropping, where they could speak freely.

"Would you like a glass of wine?" she asked when the door was closed and they were safe.

"A brandy, I think."

"Tell me everything," she said as she poured him a nice Rémy in a crystal snifter. She opened a Coke for herself, which she always drank straight from the bottle.

"Something's come up involving the CIA, as you expected might happen."

"Are they working with the Germans?"

"Not from what I can gather. But I once mentioned to you a man who used to be the director of the CIA, Kirk McGarvey."

"There was something about his family being involved in an attempt on his life that went wrong. Has he become involved?"

"It looks like it," Naisir said. He briefly outlined the Norfolk operation that had gone bad even before it had fully developed. "McGarvey's gotten himself involved for some reason. He personally either killed or took down one of the operatives and used the stupid man's cell phone to call Schlueter and warn her to back off. Which she did."

"So now what? Has the mission been canceled?"

"Postponed."

"Until when?"

"I've promised a two million euro bonus to Schlueter to eliminate the man."

Ayesha's face dropped and she put her Coke on the table. "You cannot be serious. McGarvey was the CIA's director, and that's a presidential appointment. Men who have reached that status are untouchable. The kind Prophet's wrath would come down upon you like a storm from the desert beyond anyone's imaginings."

"If it were ever to be traced back to me."

"If the Schlueter woman is successful, and somehow manages to kill McGarvey, the CIA will move heaven and earth to find her and then you. There would be nowhere for us to go. We would be as good as dead. Surely you must see this."

"But he has to be eliminated," Naisir said. "Somehow he knew about what was going to happen in Norfolk, and he was there—at exactly the right place at exactly the right time."

"Which is exactly my point, my dear husband. The man has an intelligence resource—almost certainly he still has friends inside the CIA. If he's somehow tapped into Schlueter's communications with her team, he may already know your name."

"Not likely," Naisir said, but the doubts he'd already had were being reinforced by his wife's.

"If he's followed her movements—say, to Tehran—then he knows that you're involved."

"He'd need proof."

Ayesha looked away for a longish moment. "The SEAL Team Six were not one hundred percent sure of Usama's location at the compound. They have publicly admitted it themselves. It did not stop them from flying across our border and against impossibly long odds accomplish the mission and get out with his body."

Naisir said nothing, because he knew what was coming.

She looked back. "You are only one man, Ali. Nowhere as well protected as Usama was, and certainly much easier to find. Think on it. If McGarvey is assassinated someone could very well come here for you—in retribution."

TWENTY-NINE

□

It was very early in the morning and Otto Rencke was in his element back at his suite of offices at CIA headquarters; he had been given a task to find out things, and the task had been given to him by the only friend other than his wife he'd ever had in his life—Kirk McGarvey.

Mac and Pete, with Wolf in tow, got back up to Washington last night and had gone directly to Otto's safe house, where they'd hashed out the Schlueter operation. It would probably have gone off spectacularly if it hadn't have been for them, and the two names they'd learned—Steffen and Naisir—along with the cell phone.

Martinez had personally taken the German down to the lockup at Quantanamo Bay, where he would be held in an isolation cell until this mess was straightened out, after which it would be up to the AG what to do with the man.

Which was of no concern to Otto at the moment. When Kirk got involved with something, the eventual outcome, though not always neat and tidy, was an outcome. Things got resolved. Shit happened, as the kids used to say.

Otto had set several of his search programs to work on the issue when Kirk had first brought the problem to him. He added the name "Steffen" as most likely a German citizen, possibly ex-military, and the name "Naisir" as a Pakastani ISI officer.

While he waited for something to pop up on one of the screens, he took a look at the phone. It was a basic Samsung with a SIM card that would work either in Europe or the United States but not in Japan or Korea. It, along with five others, had been purchased at an airport kiosk in Paris four months ago with a Barclays credit card under the name Monica Lawson. The phones were on one-year prepaid plans that included four hundred units of voice and text time.

As he suspected, someone had tested them during the last month; five of the phones had called the sixth. There was no record of any conversation or text sent, just the numbers. The last call made from the one Kirk had taken from Steffen had been to the same sixth number. Presumably the one Pam Schlueter carried.

He tried calling that number, but it did not ring, nor did the other four. When he tried to call the phone in his hand nothing happened, not even a busy signal.

As he'd also suspected once the operation in Norfolk had fallen apart, the service to all of the phones had been canceled.

He used an evidence kit to swab the microphone and then bagged the swab and the phone. Later he would send the bag to a lab to see if any DNA other than Mac's could be found.

Within less than a minute one of his programs came up with a dozen Steffens that more or less matched his broad search parameters, two of them starred. One was for Steffen Engel, who'd been a tactical instructor in the German KSK, and the other for Steffen Voss, who was an analyst for the BND special signal intelligence directorate, which was still outside Munich.

He phoned Martinez, who answered on the first ring.

"*Si.*" There was a roaring noise in the background.

"Where are you?"

"About ten minutes from Gitmo."

"I want you to take a picture of your guy and send it to me ASAP.

"Are you at work?"

"Yes."

"Hold on. It'll just take a minute," Martinez said.

While he waited, Otto pulled up the files, including the government ID card photos of both Steffens. Both men had the same general Teutonic square-jawed look, an intensity in their eyes, almost of hatred. Otto's bet was on the ex-KSK sergeant.

"Here it comes," Martinez said. "Keep me posted, would you?"

"You got it, Raul. Thanks."

Even before he transferred the image from his cell phone to a computer screen he knew the man Mac had picked up in Norfolk was Steffen Engel, and he immediately queried his program to find out everything about the man in just about every computer in the world. Beyond the man's basic military records he set his machines to look specifically for incidents that would give them a more rounded idea of who he was, how he operated, and where he'd been in the past year or so.

Naisir was a very common Pakistani name: eighteen of them in the ISI alone, and one hundred more in the military and other governmental agencies. Otto concentrated on the ISI because he did not think that the Schlueter woman was acting alone. Someone was directing and financing her, and the only logical choice was the ISI.

He'd brought a carton of half-and-half from his private stash at the house and had stopped at a 7-Eleven to pick up a couple of sleeves of Twinkies, something that he'd had a lot of trouble finding until last year. Louise didn't know that he had fallen back on old habits; if she had, he figured that she would skin him alive. But when times got tough, a guy needed something to fall back on. And in his case it wasn't alcohol.

He sat back, his sneakered feet on the edge of the desk as he ate his Twinkies and drank his cream, the screen racing through hundreds of databases with backgrounds of the eighteen ISI officers his program had picked out.

Ten minutes later he sat forward all of a sudden. Several photographs of a major in the service's Directorate of Joint Intelligence Miscellaneous by the name of Ali Naisir popped up and something resonated in the back of Otto's head, though he didn't really know why.

Naisir's background was pretty normal. He'd joined the military out of high school. After a short stint of active duty, he was accepted into the Pakistan Military Academy's two-year program, after which he'd studied for four years at the National Defense University.

He'd been set for a general court-martial for insubordination, but in the fall of 2008 the charges were dropped and he was allowed to return to the university, after which he was promoted to captain and assigned to the Joint Intel directorate.

The timing struck Otto. In the late fall of 2008 Musharraf had resigned his presidency, and it was almost certain that some faction of the Taliban would assassinate him. But he'd managed to escape, it was rumored, with the help of the ISI, where he turned up in Jalalabad, and from there to Mecca for his pilgrimage.

The timing of Naisir's dropped court-martial was most intriguing to Otto, because the date of Musharraf's escape matched perfectly.

He was a major now, which meant he had more autonomy than as a captain, and he was still with the Joint Intel directorate, which was notorious for causing new officers to crash and burn—many of them within the first year or two.

But Naisir had legs; he had a history.

Otto studied the man's official photograph and looked into his eyes. Something was there. Not innocence, exactly, but more like honesty. No guile. He was a man who was saying: I am what I am, give me a job to do and get out of my way so that I can do it.

Sorta like Mac.

And despite himself Otto found that he admired the man.

THIRTY

CIA director Walt Page and deputy director of operations Marty Bambridge, who was an officious, self-important bastard in just about everyone's opinion, sat across the coffee table from McGarvey and the agency's general counsel, Carleton Patterson, in the DCI's office. The late afternoon sun streaming through the windows did nothing to dispel the somber mood.

"I imagine something new has come up, otherwise you wouldn't have asked for this meeting," Page said. He'd been the CEO of IBM before the president had tapped him to run the company, and by all accounts he was the best in a lot of years. But he was a strictly by-the-book DCI. He and McGarvey had formed a truce of sorts over the past year.

"Yes, and before I head to Islamabad I wanted to bring you up to speed," Mac said.

"I'm not going to listen to this," Page said sharply. He was suddenly angry. "If you make an attempt to reach Pakistan you will be subject to immediate arrest. I think I made that perfectly clear just a few days ago."

"The situation has changed, Mr. Director."

"This meeting is over," Page said. He started to rise, but Patterson motioned him back.

"Perhaps we should hear him out. He's almost always over the top, but he's never been wrong."

"Outside the law, in a word," Bambridge said. He and McGarvey had never gotten along.

"There was another attempt on the SEAL Team Six guys in Norfolk. We think that there were four assassins, at least one of whom we know for a fact was an ex-KSK German commando by the name of Steffen Engel. Had they been successful, they might have wiped out at least ten of the guys plus their families."

"You were there," Patterson said.

"Yes."

"Extraordinary."

"How many people did you kill this time?" Bambridge demanded.

"None," McGarvey said. He hoped that Bambridge would be included in the meeting; he wanted to get a few things out in the open with the deputy director. "We wanted to stop the attack and I wanted at least one of them alive."

The DDO smirked. "We?"

"Doesn't matter for the moment—"

"It goddamned well does, mister."

"The German commando?" Patterson said mildly. He was an old man, and he'd been around the company through a half-dozen directors. His was one of the most respected voices in the OHB.

"I managed to take him down before he could make the hit. He had a cell phone, which I thought he and his teammates would have been given in order to communicate with their boss, the Schlueter woman."

"The one you say was married to a SEAL officer. A still-serving SEAL officer," Patterson said.

"That's right," McGarvey said. "I used the phone to call her, and told her that it was over and to go home."

"What about your prisoner?" Patterson asked.

"He's in an isolation cell at Gitmo."

"Martinez is involved again?" Bambridge asked, fuming. "The son of a bitch needs to be fired." But then something else dawned on him. "You were in Norfolk, so you flew with your prisoner not directly to Guantanamo Bay, but to Miami to see your old pal. And to do what?"

McGarvey wanted the DDO to figure it out on his own.

"You got his name, but you apparently got a connection to Pakistan. Christ." Bambridge looked at the DCI. "They took him to Little Torch Key," he said. He turned back to McGarvey. "Didn't you?"

"Not only that, Marty, we waterboarded the bastard. And we got a name."

"Torture has never been a reliable source of information. Everyone knows it except you."

"Save it for CNBC. We didn't give him a name and ask for confirmation; he came up with it on his own."

"Who else was there besides you and Martinez?"

"That doesn't matter. What does is the name."

"It matters to me," Bambridge practically shouted.

It was exactly the reaction McGarvey had expected.

"The name?" Patterson prompted.

"Ali Naisir. He's a major in the ISI's directorate of Joint Intelligence Miscellaneous."

"Rencke," Bambridge said. He was beside himself.

"I would tread with care, Marty," McGarvey said.

"No one is above the law. Not you, not Martinez, and certainly not Otto Rencke."

Everyone was silent for what seemed like a long time. McGarvey bided his own, letting all of them, especially Page, work out the ramifications.

It was finally the DCI who spoke. "You believe this information is reliable?" he asked.

"It all fits. Pam Schlueter, who had an unsuccessful marriage to one of our naval officers, apparently hatched a plan to strike back at him. But she wanted to do it in a very big way, and for that she needed some serious muscle, which these days costs serious money. I think she approached the ISI with her scheme to kill the SEAL Team Six guys who violated Pakistan's airspace to take out bin Laden. Nothing the government in Islamabad could do about it, except swallow its pride. Which had to hurt like hell. Schlueter gave them salvation. She would organize a team to take out the SEALs—all of them—but as an operation totally independent of Pakistan. And they bought it because she had the motive and they had the money."

"Has Otto found any traces of the money trail—any link no matter how small back to the ISI?" Page asked.

"Not yet. But he's working on it."

"The man needs to be reined in, Mr. Director," Bambridge said.

Page ignored him. "You want to go to Islamabad to talk to him, nothing more?"

"If the connection exists—and I'll ask him in such a way that he'll tell the truth—it means that Pakistan is killing our people. Not just the SEAL operators who took out bin Laden but their families as well."

"The proof?"

"I'll find it."

"Pakistan is the Wild West," Patterson said. "Have you ever considered that you'll get yourself killed one of these days?"

"All the time," McGarvey said.

"Marty, Carleton, leave us, would you please?" Page said.

Bambridge was startled, but he and Patterson got up and left.

Page went to his desk and dialed a number. "It's me," he said when someone answered. "It's the McGarvey situation. It's come to a head as we thought it might. I'm bringing him over to brief you."

THIRTY-ONE

McGarvey had never met John Fay, the president's new adviser for national security affairs. When he and Page were shown into the NSA's West Wing office, the man got to his feet and shook hands.

"I've heard a great deal about you, Mr. McGarvey, and I've wanted to meet you for some time."

He was a very lanky man, over six eight, but unlike many tall men he did not slouch. On the way over in the DCI's limousine Page had explained that Fay had been a center for the Rutgers basketball team—long before the coaching scandal, of course, but he still took the mess personally. He was a proud man.

"The man is a fixer," Page said. "It's why the president picked him. He knows the international situation like the back of his hand, and for three years he acted as a special adviser to Congress on all the major intelligence-gathering agencies in the world, including ours. He told me not so long ago that he loved to read spy novels."

"I hope he doesn't believe what he reads," McGarvey had said. "Anyone who gets their intel from novels gets the intel they deserve."

"He's anything but that sort of a fool," Page said. "In fact he's one of the smartest men to ever hold that position, and he's liable to ask you some penetrating questions. I suggest that you give him your honest assessments."

"I always do," McGarvey had said.

"Would either of you like some coffee, or perhaps a soft drink?" Fay asked, motioning them to take a seat.

"Not for me," McGarvey said.

Page waved it off. "The situation with the SEAL Team Six continues to develop, and in fact Mac came to me with a couple of disturbing events and a recommendation that, frankly, I find problematic."

Fay was instantly troubled. "My God, don't tell me there was another shooting?"

"A near miss," McGarvey said. And he explained in detail the events in Norfolk, only leaving out Pete's and Wolf's names.

"You actually spoke with this woman on the phone?"

"I told her it was over."

"How'd she sound?" Fay asked. "Mad, surprised, confused?"

"Determined. She said that it was only over for now."

"You're suggesting that despite what happened in Norfolk, and the fact that you and the agency know what she's trying to accomplish, she won't give up?"

"Yes," McGarvey said. "Because there's most likely a great deal of money at stake and she's carrying out her own personal vendetta."

"She was briefly married to a still-serving SEAL officer," Page explained. "It was about as bad as it can get, and apparently she's been nursing her hatred ever since the divorce."

"Is this officer aware of what she's trying to do?"

"I told him, but he didn't believe she was capable of something like that," McGarvey said.

"Did he tell you why he was skeptical?"

"No."

"There is still some passion there, you think?"

McGarvey had thought about it. "He might think that he's somehow responsible."

"What does he suggest?"

"He's buried his head in the sand. It's easier for him."

Fay nodded thoughtfully. "What do you suggest? How do we stop her?"

"Cut off her source of money," McGarvey said.

"Who is her paymaster?"

"The ISI."

"Oh," Fay said. "I see. In retaliation for Neptune Spear." But then he had another thought. "Do you have proof that the Pakistanis are financing her? Do you have a direct link, a name, anything?"

"Major Ali Naisir."

"And you got this name how, exactly?"

Page had warned that the NSA would ask penetrating questions. "We took the man I captured down to a facility in the Florida Keys, where we waterboarded him until he gave up the name. We've done some research since and came up with Naisir's position within the ISI, which is consistent with this sort of an operation."

"Where is he at the moment?"

"Gitmo."

"I meant Major Naisir."

"Islamabad."

McGarvey's reply hung on the air.

President Langdon, in shirtsleeves, his tie loose, appeared at the door. "Gentlemen," he said mildly. "Is this something I need to be in on?"

Fay looked up. "No, sir. Not at this moment. We're still in the preliminary stages of a what-if exercise."

"We're not committing any assets or considering committing any?"

"Nothing important, Mr. President."

The between-the-lines was huge. The president glanced at McGarvey, whom he'd never really gotten along with, then back to his NSA. "Keep me in the loop if and when the time comes."

"Of course," Fay said, and the president left.

"How deeply has he been briefed?" McGarvey asked after a long beat.

Fay almost laughed. "Are you kidding me? This isn't another Neptune Spear. If you go over there looking for this major, you're strictly on your own. Deniability, Mr. McGarvey. Especially if something goes wrong. Do you understand?"

"No," McGarvey said. He'd faced this kind of crap nearly his entire career. We lamented the Pearl Harbors and the 9/11s, but beforehand, when we could have done something to stop the attacks, we sat on our hands. We looked the other way. It was the fair thing to do. It just wasn't right. Not the American way.

"Bullshit," Fay said. "You occupied Walt's office, you know how delicate and necessary our relationship with Pakistan is. Without its cooperation we have absolutely no chance of defeating the Taliban over there."

"So we allow them to finance the assassination of all the guys and their families?"

"Of course not, nor will the navy sequester them on some base somewhere, even if they'd go for it. There'd be no telling how long they'd have to stay cooped up."

And McGarvey did understand. He stood up. "Thank you for your time, Mr. Fay. I'll keep you posted."

"Do."

THIRTY-TWO

They sat drinking beer at the kitchen counter in the Renckes' McClean safe house. Mac and Pete seated, Otto and Louise standing across from them, and Wolf, bag in hand, at the door. He had been ordered back to Germany.

"I don't know how much help we can give you," Mac said.

"I'll get a letter of reprimand in my personnel file, but it won't be the first or last. Anyway I think it's for the best that I keep an eye on Schlueter. It's a sure bet she's not done."

"It's too bad you can't take her into custody," Louise said.

"She's done nothing wrong on German soil. But if the CIA or FBI were to make an official request, we could do something."

"Won't happen," McGarvey said. "Fay made it perfectly clear that I was on my own, and if something went wrong I would be cut loose. And Walt told me the same thing."

"Wouldn't be the only time politics got in the way," Otto said.

"No. So that issue isn't on the table. But I'm going to need some help from you guys. Wolf will keep an eye on Schlueter, and if she makes a move back here, or if she simply disappears, I'll want to know immediately."

"I don't know how much manpower I'll have at my disposal, but I'll do my best."

"In the meantime I want to make Naisir sit up and look over his shoulder."

"Is that such a good idea?" Pete asked. "If he knows that you're coming he'll just order your arrest and they'll stick you in a jail cell somewhere and you'll disappear. That is, if you're not shot trying to escape."

"I don't think so," McGarvey said. "He'll probably have someplace to go to ground. But he'll be just as constrained as we are. His government will deny that there ever was a deal between one of its ISI officers and a German terrorist group."

"That won't matter. They'll treat you as nothing more than a rogue spy—maybe an independent contractor on your own vendetta but with absolutely no connection to Schlueter."

"I hope that'll be the case," McGarvey said. "I've been thinking about it. Besides giving notice to Naisir that I'm coming after him, Otto's going to build a legend for an American wheeler-dealer living in Karachi. Some guy selling arms to the Taliban, maybe bomb-making equipment that they use to attack not only American targets but Pakistani ones as well."

Otto saw it immediately. "We'll call him Poorvaj Chopra, born in Calcutta but emigrated to the States with his parents when he was five. Served in the Army Rangers but got kicked out for some shit I'll figure out. Maybe smuggling, gambling, whores—whatever. Anyway, his father went back to Calcutta a few years ago and got mixed up in a Hindu-Muslim riot in the slums and got himself killed. Ever since then Poorvaj has had a hard-on for Pakistanis. Figures he can stick it to them by selling arms to the Taliban while at the same time making some money. Now we want to put a stop to him."

"Not for any love of Pakistan but because the Taliban have been attacking our people as well," Louise said. "But Naisir's not likely to believe it."

"Doesn't matter," Mac said. "If the legend is strong enough and my assignment is to come to Pakistan to take the guy out, he won't be able to pass me off as an enemy of the state. Someone who needs to be picked up or shot. If he wants me dead he'll have to do it himself."

"He might have friends," Wolf said.

"We'll deal with those issues as they come up. In the meantime, I have all the credentials I'll need. But it's become next to impossible to carry a weapon aboard an international flight, especially one going into a country under siege like Pakistan."

"Weapons," Pete said, but McGarvey didn't catch it.

"Best if I fly commercial, probably from someplace neutral like

Poland or the Czech Republic. Soon as I get back to my apartment I'll call you with my passport number."

"Give me a name, I have all your documents in a database," Otto said, and McGarvey nodded.

"Leonard Sampson."

"Got it."

Louise was staring at Pete. "Did you mean what I thought you meant when you said 'weapons'?"

"I'm going to Islamabad too," Pete said. "I'll need a weapon, and papers under the name Doris Sampson."

"Not a chance in hell," McGarvey said.

"She has a point," Louise said.

"No."

"You're just the sort of figure Naisir and whoever he'll have helping him will expect to show up," Pete said, her tone of voice reasonable. "But if you show up with wifey in arm—wifey with a scarf to cover her hair like a dutiful Muslim woman—you might fit in. At any rate, if Naisir is likely to have friends, you might as well have a second gun hand."

"He's already seen my face in Berlin."

Pete turned to Otto. "I need the passport and a flight over. Doesn't have to be the same flight as Mac's. Might even be better if you can get me there first so I can be waiting for him. It'll be harder for him to ditch me."

"Goddamnit," McGarvey said. All of his professional life he had lived in mortal fear that what he did would boil over into his personal life, affect the people he loved. And it had. Two women he'd been involved with after his divorce from Kathy had been killed because of him. And then once he got back together with his ex she had been assassinated along with his daughter and son-in-law.

The same bullshit fear came roaring in at him again. He didn't want to be responsible. And he said as much.

"Bullshit, as you're fond of saying," Pete said. "I'm a grown woman, capable of taking care of herself. I think I proved that a couple of years ago right here in D.C., you macho bastard."

"It's not that."

"What, then?" Pete demanded. "Tell me."

McGarvey turned to Otto and Louise for support.

"Your creds will be waiting for you at Dulles first thing in the morning," Otto said. "I'll have the flight number before you leave here tonight. I think Atlanta first, then Warsaw and finally Rawalpindi. I'll have the name of a guy who'll meet you with weapons and anything else you might need."

"We'll need to know where Naisir lives, and his family situation. I really don't want to barge into this guy's house while he's having dinner with his wife and kids."

"I'll have that for you as well."

It was a nightmare to McGarvey. "Don't I have anything to say about this?"

"No," Louise and Pete said simultaneously.

He took a pull of his beer, looking at both of them. Otto's expression was neutral.

"I won't cut you any breaks," Mac said.

"When did you ever?" Pete shot back.

"Shit," he said. "Naisir works for Joint Intel Miscellaneous."

"Yes," Otto said.

"Means he meets with field officers from time to time. Like our NOCs who never show up at headquarters."

"Right, right, right," Otto said. "He's got a safe house somewhere. Could be when you show up he'll run to ground."

"If for nothing more than to insulate his family." McGarvey said.

Pete gave him an odd look, but she nodded. "If we know where it is, we might get there first and wait for him. It would keep the whole op clean. Keep the collateral damage to a minimum."

"Eliminate it completely if possible," Louise said. She'd always been the conscience of the group. She kept Otto centered, and sometimes reminded McGarvey that what he was doing—what he'd always done—was the right thing.

"You guys are right, of course," McGarvey said. "But I can't help thinking about the families of the two SEALs they killed.

THIRTY-THREE

☐

Naisir was made to wait for nearly an hour in the ISI director's outer office before the secretary motioned him to the door.

"You may see General Bhutani now, Major," he said.

Naisir had taken the call in his office fifteen minutes ago, thankful that he had worn a decent uniform this morning. Ayesha had insisted, telling him she had a hunch, and once again she was right. Over the years he had learned to trust her feminine intuition, and at this moment he was especially glad of it.

General Butani was seated behind his mammoth desk in front of the broad windows that looked down on a pretty courtyard and fountain. A short, slender man dressed in civilian clothes, one leg crossed over the other, was seated in an easy chair in a corner across the room.

Naisir stopped directly in front of the general, clicked his heels, and saluted. "Major Ali Naisir reporting, as ordered, sir."

The general, who was reminiscent of Musharraf, with a round smiling face, neatly trimmed mustache, and graying sideburns, returned the salute but did not offer a chair.

"I am a busy man, so allow me to come straight to the point. Trouble is heading your way, which is exactly what Pakistan cannot afford to have happen."

Naisir's gut tied in a knot. "Sir?"

"You are currently involved with a delicate project in the United States, if I've been informed correctly."

"It was thought to keep the project at arm's length from the service."

Bhutani let it hang for a moment. "Are we speaking of the same project?"

"SEAL Team Six, sir? A proposal was made to us some months ago that it could be possible to eliminate the Americans who took part in the operation they called Neptune Spear."

"Why?"

"Retribution."

"Who gave you this assignment?"

"My section chief, Colonel Sarbans."

The general glanced at the civilian, who merely shrugged but said nothing.

"The assignment was completely on my shoulders," Naisir said. "In case something went wrong I was to take full responsibility. Personally."

"There have been two attacks recently, both of which included the murders of the men's families. Was that your doing?"

"I did not order the killing of innocent civilians, but sir, it was my doing."

"Who is—or are—the assassins? Certainly not ours?"

"No, sir. I hired an outside contractor, who put together a team."

The general was relieved. "Was it expensive?"

"We've made partial payments of around one million in U.S. dollars. More has been committed."

"Where has this money come from?" The civilian asked.

"I have a draw on the Special Projects fund."

"You live in a fine house near the Jinnah Park," the civilian said. His voice was very soft, his accent southern—perhaps Karachi.

Naisir knew instantly what was going on, what he was being accused of. "My wife's family is wealthy and generous. The transactions for the house and the two cars and our staff, are quite transparent."

"Perhaps too transparent."

Naisir turned back to the general. "Sir, am I being accused of stealing state money?"

"Not exactly," Bhutani said. He took a photograph from a folder and handed it across. "Do you know this man?"

The eight-by-ten black-and-white photo date-stamped yesterday showed a slightly built man, dressed in a Western-cut business suit, coming out of the airport at Rawalpindi. He was carrying an attaché case and what appeared to be a matching leather suitcase on rollers.

"It's not a clear shot, but I don't think I know him. Who is he, sir?"

"He flew up from Karachi and booked a suite for six days at the Serena Hotel. Do you know this place?"

"Yes, sir," Naisir said. He was confused. Something not good was coming his way, but he couldn't guess what.

"Your wife's family is wealthy. Have either of you ever stayed there, or perhaps had a meal at one of the restaurants?" the civilian asked. "The Dawat is one of the best in town. There is even music."

"No, sir, we've never been."

"The man in the picture is an Indian-born American. Emigrated with his parents when he was very young. He served in the American Army Rangers, but he was dishonorably discharged when it was found that he was having affairs with several of the top-ranking officers' wives on base. Apparently he has an apartment in Karachi, and we think that he may be involved in a number of illegal activities, among them supplying the Taliban with the materials to make IEDs."

"That would come under the SS directorate."

"Normally yes," the general said.

"If the proof is there, why hasn't he been arrested?" Naisir asked.

"His name is Poorvaj Chopra," the civilian said. "The thing is, no one has ever seen him coming or going from his apartment in Karachi, nor has his bed here at the Serena been slept in. It would appear that he is a mysterious man who is able to come and go without being spotted."

"We have his photograph."

"Supplied to us by the CIA, who've had him under surveillance in the United States."

"I'm sorry, sir, but I have no idea who this man is or what you think his connection to me might be."

"He's made three calls to your home and one to your office," the civilian said.

Naisir was rocked. "I took no calls from this man."

"Yes, we know. Each time he let the telephone ring once and then hung up. We think that all four calls were made from a cell phone. Four different cell phones."

"Can you explain why this man called you?" Bhutani asked. "Why he has come to Islamabad?"

"No," Naisir said. "Sir, am I being charged with a crime?"

"Not at this time, Major," the civilian said. "But if Mr. Chopra does make contact with you, for whatever reason, we want to know about it."

"Then why are you monitoring my phone?"

"We're not," General Bhutani said. "The CIA is, perhaps in connection with your operation against the SEAL team we were informed."

"If that were the case they would not have shared that intelligence with you, sir," Naisir said.

"No. But obviously something is going on. I suggest that you deal with it, Major. Perhaps if Mr. Chopra were to suddenly disappear permanently, it might be best for you. For all of us."

THIRTY-FOUR

At this point time was not really of the essence as far as McGarvey was concerned. For the moment they figured that Schlueter's primary target was no longer the SEALs but Mac himself. And they wanted to let Naisir stew in his own juices. Keep looking over his shoulder until he got lazy.

Otto had booked them one of the longest routes from Dulles to Atlanta and from there overnight to Warsaw via Amsterdam. They took a Polish Airways LOT flight to Frankfurt, where they picked up an Etihad flight to Abu Dhabi and from there at last to Islamabad, where they were scheduled to touch down at two thirty in the morning local, three days after leaving Washington.

They'd flown first-class on Mac's nickel, and on most of the legs they'd had seats that folded flat, allowing them to get plenty of rest. The food had been reasonably good, and Mac had cut back his drinking so that by eight in the morning according to his watch they were less than a half hour out of Islamabad and he felt good.

A flight attendant had brought them warm moist washcloths and hand towels, along with their customs declaration forms, which Pete had filled out for both of them.

"This is a first for me," she said.

"Filling out a customs form?"

"No, going into badland."

"I warned you."

She gave him a look. "I'm not frightened. I'm excited."

"You might want to rethink that, Pete. A little fear goes a long way. Makes you aware of what's going on around you. Makes you a little sharper."

"Naisir will be waiting for us?"

"He knows my face, but it's been three days since Otto planted the Chopra legend, and he may not have made any connection yet. No reason for him to be watching for me to show up. In any event he won't be expecting you."

"I'm part of the disguise, but what about you? You could have done something with your hair, maybe worn glasses, aged your complexion. You've done it before."

"I want him to know that I've come, and why," McGarvey said.

Pete turned away and looked out the window. In the distance the lights of a large city were visible. "Silly me," she said. "I thought you'd say something like that."

"I'm not going to dance around with this guy. We already know that he's involved with Schlueter, and that he's an ISI officer, which makes him the center of my target. I want him to come to me, and the sooner the better."

"You're going to kill him," Pete said.

"If need be."

She nodded. "Once he knows you're here he'll try to do the same."

"I hope so; it'd prove his involvement."

"And afterward? What about Schlueter?"

Once through the complicated customs, which included a thorough credentials and baggage check and a pat-down, they went out to the cab stand, where a late-model Mercedes C-class sedan with a light on the roof pulled to the head of the queue. A tall, lanky driver jumped out, opened the rear door, and took their bags.

"Welcome, lady and gentleman, to the Islamic Republic of Pakistan," he said in English marked by a thick Punjabi accent. "Please to get in my most excellent taxi, and I will take you wherever you wish to go."

Pete hesitated, but Mac handed her into the backseat and got in behind her.

The driver, who was dressed in faded jeans and a stained sweatshirt with the Manchester United soccer team logo, closed the door, put their bags in the trunk, and got behind the wheel.

A few of the other cab drivers had begun to honk their horns because he had cut the line, and a cop started in their direction, but their cabbie pulled out and headed at breakneck speed to the highway to Islamabad, which was busy despite the hour.

Their driver kept looking in the rearview mirror until they were clear of the airport. "Did you have any trouble getting in?" he asked, in very clear English with a slight Texas drawl.

Pete was startled.

"San Antonio?" McGarvey asked.

"Corpus, actually, Mr. Director," the driver said. He glanced in the rearview mirror again. "Looks like we haven't picked up a tail. Name's Milt Thomas. I work for Don Simmons, he's the Islamabad station chief."

"Aren't you exposing yourself picking us up?" Pete asked.

"I'm too low in the pecking order for anyone to take much notice. In fact I'm actually part-timing with the cops looking for bad guys coming in. They send over a list every week or so, we mine it for anything we might use, and once in a while I'll send them a bone and everyone's happy."

"Our names on the list?" McGarvey asked.

"Yours; not Ms. Boylan's."

"Do you have a package for us?"

"Nine millimeter Walther PPKs with silencers and several extra magazines. Antiquated, if you ask me. But Don said it'd be what you wanted. Had a hell of a time digging them up. Five small bricks of Semtex and acid fuses, plus a package from Mr. Rencke. It's all in an attaché case in the trunk. Combo lock, 7534. Get it right or the entire package will melt down in a big hurry. Lid's wired with couple of hundred grams of thermite. Won't cause the Semtex to blow, but it'd cook a lot of meat standing anywhere within eight or ten feet."

"Where are you taking us now?"

"Mind if I ask you a question, Mr. Director?"

"Friends call me Mac. What's your question?"

"Do you know anything about a guy named Poorvaj Chopra? Supposedly he's an Indian-born American working out of Karachi brokering arms deals for the Taliban."

"Never heard the name," McGarvey said.

"The ISI is real interested in this guy, and so are we, because the ragheads are killing our people too with IEDs that Chopra is selling them the materials for."

"What's the connection with us?"

"We thought that maybe it was your operation. I'm taking you to the Serena Hotel, where you guys have a connecting suite with his, and I have to warn you that the ISI should be crawling all over the place. But . . ."

"But what?"

"We've taken a couple of passes, but there's been no sign of the guy, nor were we able to pick up any ISI activity. Strange."

Their passports under the name Sampson raised no eyebrows at the front desk, and they were taken up to their suite immediately. The rooms were very well furnished, the walls and especially the ceilings were replica works of ancient Islamic art. The huge bathroom was world-class, as was the sitting room. But there was only one bedroom, equipped with a walk-in closet, a flat-screen television, ornate chests, a seating area next to the tall windows, and a single king-size bed.

"Cozy," Pete said at the door.

"Right," McGarvey said.

He opened the attaché case on the bed, took out the pistols, the magazines—three each—and the suppressors. He and Pete field-stripped the weapons, checked the actions, and loaded them.

He set aside the blocks of Semtex and fuses and took the manila envelope into the sitting room, where he got a beer from the minibar and sat down on the couch to see what Otto had sent.

Several photographs, including an official portrait used for internal records, showed the man that McGarvey had briefly met in the parking garage in Berlin. He was handsome, with large dark eyes, and a fine-featured face. In one he was coming out of a restaurant with a very good-looking woman of slender build on his arm. They were laughing about something and they seemed very happy.

She was Ayesha, his wife. Her family was wealthy, while his relatives were comparatively poor. But he had been well-educated at several state schools, including the military academy, and from what Otto had managed to gather, he had a fine service record.

He and his wife—there were no children—lived in a house in an upscale neighborhood near the Fatima Jinnah Park. The place, their two cars—a Fiat and a BMW—plus a small staff were way over the top for a major's pay, but they had been subsidized from the start by his wife's family.

Just as McGarvey had suspected, Naisir maintained a safe house in Rawalpindi where he met from time to time with his deep-cover field officers. The only reason Otto had been able to find out anything about it was because the place was financed by the ISI as a line item in the directorate's black budget.

Otto had included Google Maps images of and driving directions to both places.

"What do we do now?" Pete asked.

McGarvey handed her the package. "We stay here till eight to see if ISI has taken any notice of us, then we rent a car and drive down to Rawalpindi."

"To do what?"

"Apply a little pressure."

THIRTY-FIVE

□

Pam Schlueter sat by the window in her one-room apartment in the immigrant neighborhood of Kreuzberg drinking schnapps and worrying about her next move. She wanted the money for taking McGarvey down, but more importantly she didn't want him or some ISI goon to come up behind her one night and put a bullet in her brain.

Once you started these kinds of operations, you could never back out, not until they were finished. Only this time she'd managed to grab a tiger by the tail, and she still wasn't quite sure exactly how she was going to eliminate him.

Certainly not by any frontal assault, with her four remaining operatives coming at him in force, all at once, guns blazing. From what she'd managed to learn about the man, he'd survived plenty of fights where the odds were overwhelmingly stacked against him.

Nor did she think she could trust any of them to do the job one-on-one. Steffen was one of the best, and he'd had a lot of respect from the others, but he was gone, evidently taken out by McGarvey—the fifty-year-old they all thought would be easy.

Yet as she turned that notion over she decided that one-on-one would be the only way of getting to him. With a woman's touch.

Someone knocked softly at her door. She snatched her Glock 26 from the table and went barefoot across the room. She was dressed only in jeans and a plain white T-shirt, no bra.

"*Wer ist es?*" Who is it, she said, just above a whisper.

Someone downstairs was playing American country-and-western music, and the couple on the right were having their usual nightly row, but other than that the building was quiet.

"Felix," a man said.

Felix Volker, one of her shooters—the crazy one. She recognized his voice.

She opened the door and let him in, locking it behind him. He had been drinking, his face a little flushed.

"Did you know that someone has been sitting in a VW across the street since twenty-one hundred hours?"

She turned and started for the front window.

"He just left," Volker said. "But I think it was that BND officer who's been sniffing around for the past few months."

"The bastard who killed Dieter in Florida?"

"Maybe."

Steffen's name came into her head. It was possible that he wasn't dead. It was possible that the CIA had made him talk. But if that had been the case, and the CIA had passed the information to the BND, the agency wouldn't have simply sent one man down here merely to watch her. More likely he'd come to check out one of the Turkish or Greek immigrant families who lived in the neighborhood. They'd been causing a lot of problems over the past year and a half; that, along with the Muslim issue, was driving the government crazy.

"Did he spot you?" Pam asked.

"I don't think so. But I think you better get the hell out of here tonight before he comes back. You can stay with me."

Pam laughed. "You talk as fucking nuts as you look," she said. "Get the hell out of here." She turned away, but Volker grabbed her by the arm.

"When are we going to finish the job," he demanded.

She tried to smash the butt of the small pistol into the side of his head, but he deflected the blow and grabbed her by the neck, squeezing hard.

Bringing the pistol around again, she jammed the muzzle into his temple and started to squeeze the trigger.

He released his grip and laughed. "Here we are, then, an impasse, when all I wanted was the green light to finish the operation, and maybe to fuck you."

"I don't like men."

"I don't like you," he said. This time his laugh was low, but wild, crazy, and completely out of control. "But a piece of ass is a piece of ass. Even you."

She lowered the pistol and laid it on the small table beside the door.

Volker tried to kiss her; his breath smelled of garlic and beer. She turned away and went to the small bed across from the window, took off her T-shirt, her back to him, then pulled off her jeans and panties and lay down.

"You want it, let's get it over with, pig."

"Fucking whore," Volker said. He took off his trousers and shorts, but didn't bother with his shoes or shirt.

She spread her legs for him, and they had sex, just about as rough as it had been with her ex, and just about as pleasurable. When he was done he got up and looked down at her.

"I'm sorry that I called you a whore," he said. "At least they fake liking it." He got dressed and at the door he looked back at her. "When do we go operational?"

"Soon," Pam said, and he left.

She lay there for five minutes, a little sore, but not at all unhappy because she didn't think Volker would give her any further trouble. Men were almost always so easy that way. It had been a hard lesson for her to learn when she was young.

Her encrypted cell phone rang. It was Gloria, her U.S. eyes and ears, and the only woman in the world with whom she had a real and lasting connection. They were sisters in a very large way, and depended on each other: Pam for information, and Gloria for what Pam promised she would do when the time was right.

"McGarvey has shown up in Islamabad."

"How do you know?"

"We have someone on the ground—you know that. But there's something else going on that no one can get a handle on. Someone else is already there, and the CIA and ONI and just about everyone else wants to know what the hell he's doing there."

"You're not making any sense."

"He's an arms dealer by the name of Poorvaj Chopra, works out of Karachi. But he flew to Islamabad a few days ago and booked a suite at the Serena Hotel. Thing is, no one has actually seen the guy. Driving everybody nuts."

"What's your point?"

"McGarvey showed up a little while ago with a woman who we think is a CIA operative. They checked into the Serena under the name Sampson and took a suite adjoining Chopra's."

As amazing as the extent of Gloria's connections and her knowledge was, Pam found the gaps frustrating. It was like looking through a window partially covered by venetian blinds. She'd once explained that she was just one small part of a girls club mostly of frustrated wives: "We know lots of stuff, but not everything."

"What else?"

"Another thing that doesn't make any sense to me. McGarvey and the woman—I still haven't found out her real name—took about the longest way possible to get to Islamabad. Three days from Washington. Not only that: they flew first-class all the way and the CIA didn't pay for it; McGarvey did. It's almost as if he wanted just about anyone who was interested to know he was on his way, and give them plenty of time to think about it."

That's exactly what he was up to. Pam saw it in a flash. "I have to go, luv, but keep me posted. Especially about this Chopra character. My guess is, he's another CIA NOC in place over there to help McGarvey."

"Have you done any more thinking about what I'm going through over here?"

"All the time, believe me. And as soon as I get this project straightened out you're next on the list—and you know the reason."

"I'm really counting on you," Gloria said, and Pam could hear the desperation in her voice.

"I know," she said.

She called Naisir and left a message on his voice mail, but it wasn't until twenty minutes later after she'd booked her flight to Islamabad and had begun packing that he called back.

"Do you have news?" he asked.

"Yes. McGarvey showed up there with a woman—most likely a CIA operative. I think he's there to meet a guy by the name of Chopra who's probably a CIA NOC."

"Where the hell did you get this?"

"Never mind that part. But I think that they must have taken Steffen alive and made him talk. It's possible he knew your name and gave it up."

"Bitch," Naisir said softly. "Which would mean McGarvey, the woman, and the other bastard are here to take me down."

"Are you aware that McGarvey and his broad are staying at the Serena in a suite adjoining Chopra's?"

"We think Chopra is an arms dealer working out of Karachi."

"Do you have him under surveillance?"

"No one has actually seen him. All we have to go on is one photograph."

"Let me guess—it came from the CIA," Pam said.

"Yes."

"It's a setup. Killing you on Pakistani soil could have a lot of unintended consequences for your people as well as for me and the operation. But if you were somehow to be discredited, maybe link your name with Chopra's and maybe the CIA, you could be taken down by your own directorate."

Naisir was silent for a long beat. When he came back he sounded unsure. "It may already be happening. Chopra made four calls—three to my home and one to my office."

"Did you talk to him?"

"No."

"Are your people monitoring your telephones?"

"We got it from the CIA, who say they're after Chopra as well, because the stuff he's selling to the Taliban is being used to kill American ground troops as well as Pakistanis."

"I'm on my way," Pam said. "I can be there sometime tomorrow afternoon."

"What the hell are you talking about?" Naisir practically shouted.

"We're going to set a trap for the three of them. Who knows, maybe the CIA will give you a medal. Crazier things have happened."

THIRTY-SIX

Wolf was on suspended duty with pay pending an investigation into his actions in the United States and here in Germany. He'd been required to turn in his credentials and his weapon, but he'd not been restricted to his apartment in the quiet neighborhood of Dahlem, which was known as the university district—nor, so far as he'd been able to determine, had a tail been placed on him.

He sat in his VW Jetta parked a block from the Schlueter woman's apartment where he'd been forced to move when one of the woman's goons had shown up and went inside. The man, who Wolf was pretty sure was a guy named Volker, had stayed less than twenty minutes.

He'd probably come for orders, not trusting the phone, which could mean that the operation against the SEAL team was still in play.

Wolf lit a cigarette, a habit he'd taken up when his wife Renate had left him six months ago—for the second time—because she couldn't live with his constant nights out and mysterious trips abroad for which he could give her no explanation. She'd discovered his pistol and several diplomatic passports in different names when he'd stupidly forgotten to close and lock his floor safe for just a few minutes when he went to take a shower after a trip.

"Are you some kind of a spy, then?" she shrieked, holding up the weapon and documents.

He'd taken them from her without a word and locked them in the safe.

"You bastard, answer me or I'll take the boys, walk out the door and never come back."

"I can't," he told her. "And you're never to mention anything about this ever again."

"Or what?" she shot back.

"My life could depend on it."

She'd packed a bag that night, and moved in with her sister down in Potsdam. Three days later she'd called to apologize for her outburst and promised that she would never breathe a word about what she'd found.

"Then come back," he said. "I miss you and the kids."

"I can't. I'd be forever listening for the phone to ring, someone calling to tell me that my husband had been shot to death by some unknown gunman in some unknown city in some unknown fucking country. Can't you see, Wolfhardt, that I'm frightened?"

"Yes," he'd said. "Can't stop me from loving you."

"Or I you," she said. "We can still be friends. Maybe."

"Of course. Dinner once in a while?" he'd asked, and she'd agreed.

This evening was to have been one of the dinners, but he'd canceled. He'd heard the disappointment and resignation in her voice, which had actually given him some hope that they might still get together again.

"Give me a call when you get back from wherever," she said. "And take care of yourself."

A taxi passed Wolf's car and pulled up in front of Schlueter's apartment. A moment later she came out carrying a small green overnight bag and got in the backseat. The cab immediately took off and Wolf followed it, not at all surprised twenty minutes later when it took the Stadtautobahn highway exit to the Tegel Airport, where it pulled up at the Terminal A departures entrance.

Wolf had kept his police placard, which he placed on the dash and parked across from where Schlueter got out.

When the cab left he hurried across the street and into the terminal, in time to see Schlueter queue up at the Air Berlin counter. He held back, but the line was short at this hour of the night. It took less than five minutes for her to reach one of the ticket machines and only two minutes to get her boarding pass. She headed down the broad hall to the gates.

He followed her at a discreet distance, pulling up when she

showed her boarding pass and passport to the security agent and went through the screening process. As soon as she had disappeared down the corridor, Wolf pulled an envelope from his pocket and, cutting ahead of everyone else, rushed to the security agent.

"The woman with the green bag who just came through here forgot this," he said.

The agent, an older man, shook his head. "May I see your boarding pass and identification, sir?"

"You don't understand. I'm not flying tonight. But she needs this information."

"I'm sorry, sir, but I cannot let you pass."

"Damnit, you don't understand."

"I'll have to call security."

"How do I get this to her?"

"Go to the airline ticket counter; perhaps they can help."

"But I don't know which gate she's boarding from," Wolf said. He half turned away. "I'll be skinned alive," he muttered.

"Green suitcase?" the security officer asked.

Wolf turned back. "Yes."

"Twenty-six. Have them send it there."

"You just saved my life," Wolf said, and he turned and headed back the way he had come, stopping at the first overhead monitor he came to that was out of sight of the security entry. Twenty-six was an Air Berlin nonstop flight to Abu Dhabi; it left in thirty-five minutes.

Outside he called McGarvey's cell. It was answered on the third ring.

"Yes?"

"It's Wolfhardt. I have some information for you."

"Are you in Berlin?" McGarvey said.

"Yes, at Tegel. Schlueter is taking a flight to Abu Dhabi that leaves in a half hour. I think she's on her way to Islamabad. Maybe you should contact someone there to watch out for her."

"Pete and I are already here."

"Could be that she and Naisir talked. And it could mean they've bought into the Chopra legend."

"We've not seen any sign of it yet. But we're going down to his safe house in Rawalpindi in a few hours, to see if anyone sits up and takes notice."

"Don't underestimate her and her people. One of them showed up tonight, and within a half hour she was out the door and on her way to the airport. Whatever he told her had to be significant. And I think she's probably on her way to help Naisir."

"With what?"

"I think she might know that you're there, and why you're there, and I think it's possible that she's been hired to deal with you, if for no other reason than retaliation for what you messed up in Norfolk."

"If she knows that we're here, she has to have an intel source in the CIA. No one else knows we left."

"It could be anyone. Your rep is your worst enemy at this point."

"We'll look out for her," McGarvey said. "In the meantime, you're still a part of this operation as well. You took out one of her operatives in Florida, and if they have your name, they're likely to come after you before they go ahead."

"I hope someone tries. I want my creds back."

"Watch your back," McGarvey said.

"You too," he said, and then pocketed his phone. As he stood waiting for the traffic to clear so he could cross the road to his car, he thought about laying everything out for Colonel Mueller. But he knew damned well that there'd be no chance of getting orders to go to Islamabad to help Mac. All that was left at this point was to do what Mac had advised, and watch his own back.

He took the Stadtautobahn back into the city and drove directly to Schueleter's apartment building. As he pulled up at the curb a figure loomed up from the back floor and the muzzle of a pistol was placed almost gently on the back of his head.

"I thought you might come back here," Volker said.

Wolf looked at the man's face in the rearview mirror. "It's a pretty big deal killing a federal cop. There'd be no hole deep enough for you to hide in. Except maybe a grave."

"You used your cell phone at the airport. Who did you call?"

"My mother. It's her birthday."

"As you wish," Volker said. "Let's go then."

"Where?"

"The parking garage at the airport where I left my car."

Wolf slammed the gas pedal to the floor and took off with squealing tires. He figured his speed and erratic driving would make Volker hesitate to shoot and sooner or later attract the attention of some cop.

Squealing around a corner he narrowly missed a parked car when a thunderclap burst inside of his head.

□

THIRTY-SEVEN

Naisir stood on the balcony of his inner sanctum looking toward the park; there was very little traffic at this hour of the morning. He was nursing a Rémy and deep in thought, so when Ayesha came up behind him and brushed a finger across the nape of his neck, he practically jumped out of his skin.

"You scared me half to death," he said, turning to her.

"I heard the phone. Who was it?"

"Schlueter. She knows that McGarvey's here."

"What's her source?"

"She wouldn't tell me, but she knows about Chopra. Thinks he's a CIA NOC."

Ayesha thought about it for a moment, then nodded. "If that's to make any sense it would have to mean that the CIA is running some sort of an operation. Possibly against you because of the SEAL operation."

"I thought the same thing. Problem is, I don't have the proper resources to monitor McGarvey's movements."

Ayesha looked at him. From the beginning she'd had the ability to read his thoughts: from the expression in his eyes, she'd explained. "What else?"

"Schlueter is on her way here. She wants to help me set a trap for them."

Again his wife hesitated a moment, lost in thought. "That also could make some sense, if it's handled correctly. Afterward you could get rid of her."

"The SEAL operation is still on. I'm not going to drop it now."

"Kill her and hire someone else. Her people have only managed to take out two of the twenty-four, and you said yourself that they bungled the operation in Norfolk. There're others out there willing to do the job."

"But none with her motivation."

"Allah save us from motivated people. They're the ones who strap on suicide vests, which doesn't make them exactly sane. Given the right push they could turn around and bite the hand that feeds them."

"My orders are to eliminate Chopra even if he does work for the CIA."

"Then do it."

"He and McGarvey know each other. They're in adjoining suites at the Serena."

Ayesha turned and looked at the hideous German grandfather clock one of her sisters-in-law had given them. It was four. "Most of the hotel's guests are asleep at this time of the morning. Go over there now, get a universal key from the night manager, and take care of the Indian. No one on the hotel's staff will complain about letting on ISI officer in, nor will the death of a guest receive any publicity. And you won't be in any trouble at work because it was exactly what you were ordered to do."

"McGarvey's right next door. And he brought another officer with him—a woman."

"He's an entirely different issue. But I have an idea that we can use the Schlueter woman to do the dirty work for you."

"Killing two CIA officers in the hotel would be something entirely different."

"I agree. Which is why you'll lure him to the safe house. Use your contacts on the street. Someone who could help. And if by some chance he does manage to escape it will be because he and his woman have murdered two agents of the government of Pakistan in their pursuit of a woman who was responsible for the deaths of two American SEALs."

"You're devious," he said, with admiration.

"It's the years of business training from my father and uncles. Know your goal and do whatever it takes to achieve it. All other considerations are without merit."

They went back to their bedroom where she laid out his jeans, a white shirt and black blazer. He loaded his 9mm Steyr GB, holstered it beneath his jacket, and pocketed the silencer tube, all in under fifteen minutes.

Putting on a robe she went down to the door to the rear courtyard where both their cars were parked—his a BMW 5-Series, hers a new Fiat 500 convertible in bright green.

"As soon as I dress I'll drive down to the safe house and get it ready," she told him.

"Come back here immediately, in case this develops sooner than I think it will."

"Don't worry about me," Ayesha said. "Go with Allah."

"And you," he said and they embraced.

It was nearly five by the time he got to the hotel. He showed his credentials to the clerk at the desk and was immediately brought into the night manager's office. The officious little man in a cutaway morning suit glanced at the ISI identification book.

"How may I be of service to the state?" the man, whose name tag read Suri, asked.

"I need a universal key card."

"I can show you any unoccupied room that you wish to see."

"I want a universal card that opens any door in the hotel."

The night manager stood his ground. "That would be quite impossible."

"A citizen of India is a guest here. If you are harboring a spy against the state and don't want to cooperate, I will place you under arrest this minute. I have people who will find out from your own lips your involvement before breakfast."

The manager paled visibly. "His passport was American."

"Forged."

Suri got an ordinary-looking plastic key card with the hotel's name printed in English and Punjabi and handed it over. "I want no violence in my hotel."

"Then I suggest that in the future you mind who you admit as a guest."

"I must warn you, sir—"

Naisir stopped and gave the man a hard look.

"I mean to say that although Mr. Chopra—the gentleman I believe you are referring to—is a guest in this hotel he has not actually been seen by either me or any of the staff since he arrived on Monday."

"How is that possible? He had to have checked in. Got his key, had his bags taken up."

"His key was sent to the VIP lounge at the airport, and his bags were delivered that afternoon."

"Has he slept in his bed, eaten in any of the restaurants?"

"He may have lain down on the couch, but the housekeeping staff isn't sure."

"He must be a spy," Naisir said.

"If you say so, sir."

The soaring ornately decorated lobby lounge beneath massive crystal chandeliers was open, but only one person was seated reading a newspaper and drinking a coffee at a small table. The man didn't look up as Naisir crossed to the elevators. Nor did the desk clerk pay any attention.

On the fifth floor Naisir turned left. At Chopra's suite he listened at the door for a moment or two. Hearing nothing, he withdrew his pistol and screwed the silencer on the threaded barrel; then unlocked the door and stepped inside.

The sitting room was in darkness, except for some light coming through the tall windows covered only in gauze drapes, and utterly silent.

The king-sized bed had not been slept in, nor did it seem to Naisir's eye that the bathroom had been used. Naisir began to realize that Chopra was nothing more than a legend created by the CIA to distract him. Divide his attention, lead him to believe that his only enemy wasn't McGarvey. Even General Bhutani had bought in to the story.

Unscrewing the silencer, pocketing it and holstering the pistol, he put his ear to the adjoining door but no sounds came from McGarvey's room. It was even possible that he too was a phantom guest.

He called the hotel operator and had him call the Sampsons' suite.

After a moment the phone in the adjoining room began to ring. McGarvey answered on the third.

"Yes."

"I'll meet you in the lobby lounge at seven," Naisir said, and he hung up.

THIRTY-EIGHT

□

McGarvey went to the door and looked through the peephole just as a blurry figure passed by in the corridor. He waited a second and opened the door a crack in time to see Naisir round the corner into the elevator alcove.

Pete came to the bedroom door, a pistol in her hand. She was wearing nothing but a nightshirt down to just above her knees, her hair tousled. "Trouble?" she asked.

"Major Naisir tossed Chopra's suite, just like we thought he would."

"Was that him on the phone?"

"Yes. He wants to meet me in the lobby lounge at seven. Seems like he's taken the bait."

"Why didn't you just kill him? We could have stashed his body in Chopra's suite and bugged out on the first flight to anywhere. It's why we came here, isn't it?"

"I want to talk to him first. And then I want to talk to Schlueter."

"You're not going to get anything out of them."

"We won't know that until we talk to them," McGarvey said.

"Okay, how do you want to play it?"

"Get dressed; then set up your laptop."

Pete went back into the bedroom, and McGarvey called Otto on his cell phone. "Naisir's taken the bait. He just left Chopra's suite. He phoned and said he wants to meet me in the lobby lounge at seven. Gives us a couple of hours."

"Was he alone?"

"He was when he passed my door."

"He'll have some muscle standing by, maybe even cops. They

could arrest you guys for entering the country on fake passports, even though they're diplomatic. But he doesn't want that. He wants you dead."

"That's exactly what I want him to try, but it won't happen this morning in the hotel. First, he wants to know what I know about the ISI's involvement with Schuleter and the operation. He made a mistake coming after me in Berlin, and he knows it."

"The guy's motivated," Otto said. "His boss is probably putting pressure on him to get the mess he created straightened out."

Pete came out and set the laptop on the desk. She had put on a pair of jeans. Last night McGarvey had slept on the couch, on his insistence, and she promised not to flounce around half-naked. A sexual tension between them had begun to build the moment their plane had pushed away from the gate at Dulles.

McGarvey switched to speaker phone. "We have the laptop set up. Can you task a bird to take a look at Naisir's safe house?"

"Already on it. In fact Louise set it up two days ago, one of our Jupiters. But she only uses it for three-second bursts out of every three minutes. She wants to minimize the chance that someone will notice that the bird isn't doing what it's supposed to be doing. For those three seconds the digital file will only show what happened beforehand. So far there's been no activity down there. I'll bring it up and check the last six hours or so, and then pull up the real-time images."

"We'll log on to your site," Pete said.

"I'll take care of it," Otto told her.

A few seconds later the laptop came alive, and a house and courtyard behind tall walls appeared on the screen in a series of images that included the road that passed in front. It was like watching an extremely slow stop-action film, in which cars and a few people seemed to stream by at very rapid speeds. Six hours went by in about six minutes.

"Nothing," Otto said. "I'm bringing it up in real time."

The image on screen was the same, only enhanced by infrared. Two cars and a truck flicked past, and the sampling mode went to sleep for the next three minutes, only a static view of the safe house being transmitted.

Suddenly headlights flashed on the front gate and a car appeared.

Three minutes later the car was parked in the courtyard and a figure in dark clothes was at the door.

In the next three-second burst, one of the windows in the house was lit up.

They watched for another fifteen minutes, but nothing changed.

"Go back to the image of the person at the door and freeze it," Pete said.

Otto brought it back and began enhancing it, first by centering on the person, then by enlarging it, and finally by adjusting the light scales, though it was difficult in the satellite's infrared mode.

"It's a person," Pete said. "But I can't tell much more than that."

"Let's see what one of my darlings can tell us," Otto said. His darlings were his special analytical programs that he had developed over the past ten years or so. No one in the company really understood their algorithms; nevertheless many of its programs were at the heart of the agency's computer system.

A series of markers on the figure showed up, followed by a series of alphanumeric strings along the right side of the screen.

"We're pretty sure that it's a slightly built woman. Height about one hundred seventy centimeters—makes her about five feet six."

"Or a very small man," Pete suggested.

"We can model the heat distribution," Otto said. The figure of a person showed up on the screen. Its hips were somewhat prominent as well as its chest area.

"A butt and boobs," Pete said. "Not much smaller than me and definitely a female. But who, and what the hell is she doing there?"

"Naisir's wife. I got a grab of the rear license plate. Car's registered in her name. She drove down to open up the place for her husband and possibly set some sort of a trap for you."

"It had to have taken her a half hour to get there, which means he sent her down even before he came to the hotel," McGarvey said. "He must have known that the Chopra legend was a ruse."

"It also means that he's expecting you to show up down there at some point," Otto said.

"Not until sometime after our meeting at seven," McGarvey said.

"I'll get dressed," Pete said and she went back into the bedroom.

"Keep an eye on the place. The moment anything changes let Pete know first, then me."

"Take it easy, kemo sabe."

"If this fully develops by the time Schlueter gets here, we may have to make a run for it."

"I'll work on it. But goddamnit, watch your ass."

They took one of the service elevators down to the basement laundry room, and McGarvey went with Pete out the back way. She was going to walk past the loading dock, and once she was a block or so away from the hotel she would get a cab back to the airport, where she would rent another car.

"No fooling around," McGarvey warned her. "If something doesn't look right, get the hell out of there.

Pete nodded. "I'm a big girl."

"Yes, you are. But this is badland, so watch your ass."

THIRTY-NINE

□

Naisir went to the hotel's business center on the mezzanine floor, empty at this hour of the morning, and telephoned a man he only knew by the Punjabi name of Gakhar, who was a dacoit, one of the more lucrative part-time jobs in Pakistan. By day most of them held ordinary positions as shopkeepers or taxi drivers or construction workers. During their off-hours, however, they moonlighted as professional bandits or enforcers.

He'd never actually met the man, or any of the dacoits, but Gakhar ran a string of part-timers, and Naisir called on him from time to time for jobs that the ISI or local cops didn't want to handle.

The call was answered on the first ring. "Yes."

"Do you know who this is?"

"Of course."

"I need four bullyboys who have some brains."

"When and for how long?"

"They would have to be in place within the next hour and remain possibly overnight. Will this be a problem?"

"None whatsoever, except for the price. I have four specialists in mind. Very strong, very good. They have no limits. What is the nature of the assignment?"

"It concerns one man and one woman, both of them professionals."

"Professional what?"

"Let's just say they are contractors who work for the CIA. Armed and very dangerous."

"Is this to be a public execution, or can a place of privacy be arranged? The price will vary with the conditions, you understand this."

"Of course," Naisir said. As much as he would have liked to gun down McGarvey and the woman right here inside the hotel, or just outside on the street, in full view of dozens of witnesses to make a statement to the arrogant American government, he did not want to endanger his own position, nor did he want to jeopardize Retribution. "It will be at a place of complete privacy."

"Tell me," Gakhar said.

Naisir explained about the safe house in Rawalpindi. "I think that I can guarantee at least one of them will be there sometime within the next few hours. Probably the man, who in any case is our prime target."

"And if it's the woman instead? Shall we kill her?"

"I'd leave that to your discretion. She could be useful as a lure for the man."

The phone was silent for several beats. "One hundred thousand U.S."

"The bodies will have to be disposed of."

"One hundred twenty-five thousand."

"There will be no payment if it is just the woman alone."

"One last thing, I must know who these people are, exactly."

"I don't know who the woman is, except that she works for the CIA."

"But you know the man."

"His name is Kirk McGarvey."

"The former director of the CIA?" Gakhar demanded. He sounded impressed.

"Can you handle the job?"

"Yes, of course. The bodies will have to be taken to friends in the northwest, where their beheading will be taped for television. But there will be repercussions; you must also understand as much. The Americans will stop at nothing to find their murderers. There will be drone strikes up there, many of my friends will lose their lives. And if your involvement were to come out, even your life would be forfeit. So you will have to pay not only for the deed but for the collateral damage, as well as my discretion."

"I don't care how it's done, but do understand me, Mr. Gakhar. My reach is longer than yours."

"One million dollars."

The amount took Naisir's breath away. He had access to such amounts from the same black ops fund—ironically money from the Pentagon—that he was using to pay Schlueter. But questions would be asked, especially when the United States began its retaliatory raids, which were inevitable unless McGarvey and the woman were simply to disappear and Chopra was the one to have his head chopped off. The man was nothing more than a CIA legend, after all. His death would be the supreme irony.

"Agreed," Naisir said. "But I have another idea."

"I'm listening."

And Naisir told him.

It was only a few minutes after six when Naisir, watching from the mezzanine balcony, spotted McGarvey getting off the elevator, crossing the now-busy lobby, and heading out the front doors. The woman wasn't with him, but Naisir waited to see if she was covering his back. After a full minute when she didn't show up, McGarvey appeared in the door and looked up to the mezzanine balcony.

Even at this distance, Naisir got the same shock of recognition he'd had in Germany. The man standing just inside the doors was a dangerous animal, far more deadly than anyone Naisir had ever met, or even knew of. And he instantly had the thought that no matter how many bullyboys Gakhar sent, they would be not enough.

McGarvey headed across to the lobby lounge, and Naisir took the stairs down, reaching the table just as McGarvey was ordering a coffee.

"You're early," Naisir said, sitting across from the American. He ordered a coffee, sweet.

"So are you, but then it pays to be cautious in our line of work."

Naisir almost asked, what line of work, but he didn't. "What are you doing in Pakistan?"

"I came to try to talk some sense into you. We know that you work for the ISI, of course, and that the twenty-four SEAL Team Six operators and their families have been targeted for assassination because of the raid in Abbottabad. And I want you to call it off before your involvement goes public and the White House is forced to react."

"None of that is true, of course," Naisir said evenly. He had the almost overpowering urge to pull out his pistol and shoot the smug bastard in the head here and now.

"You didn't pull the trigger, of course, though you tried to have me taken out in Berlin. But your subcontractor, Pam Schlueter, has hired a team of specialists to do the job for you. We know this for a fact because we have one of them in custody, and he provided us with her name. And yours. So here I am."

"Speculation."

"I don't work on speculation, Major," McGarvey said. "So what's next for us?"

"I reiterate that I am in no way involved in any attack against your military personnel in any theater, and demand that you and the woman you came here with leave Pakistan at once or I will have you both arrested."

"I don't think so. You were in Mr. Chopra's suite a little while ago, so you know by now that he is a phantom. But your superiors still want you to bring him in, or more likely have him killed. Arresting or killing a former director of the CIA would be another thing. Something your government could not allow to happen."

Naisir continued to hold himself in check. He hated this man more than he had hated any other man or thing, and he promised himself that he would make every effort to piss on the corpse after Gakhar's men were finished and before they took it up north. "Leave within the next twenty-four hours or you'll never get out of here alive."

"That'll give us plenty of time to meet Ms. Schlueter when she arrives. I'd like to have a little chat with her as well."

Naisir jumped up, his heart pumping hard. "I can promise you one thing, you son of a bitch."

McGarvey looked up at him. "Yes?"

"You will rot in hell," was all Naisir could think to say, and he turned on his heel and stalked away, certain that the bastard American was laughing at his back.

FORTY

□

Naisir's safe house was a plain two-story cinder block building that had once been painted white. It was protected by a tall wall, also of cinder block access through which was an iron gate off the street. This was a middle-class neighborhood of cab drivers, people who worked in shops or factories, people who made rugs, hammered silver, or worked construction. At this hour of the morning the narrow street was devoid of all but the occasional delivery van or bus.

Pete took one pass in the blue Chevy Aveo she'd rented at the airport and parked just around the corner in a spot where she could watch the front gate with the passenger side–door mirror.

She phoned Otto. "I'm in place."

"Is that you in the Aveo at the corner?"

"Yes. Is the wife still inside?"

"She hasn't moved, but she's made three phone calls in the past hour. A pretty fair encryption system, Chinese I think, but I'll have it shortly."

"Any idea who she called?"

"No, but I'll have that too."

Pete checked the load on her pistol. She would have preferred something a little heavier, perhaps a Glock or a SIG, but the Walther in the 9mm version had some decent stopping power, even if fired with the suppressor attached. "Anything I should know about before I go calling?"

"It looks clear from my vantage point, but we don't know much about the wife, except that she comes from a wealthy family."

"Besides her husband's connections she'll have some of her own. But I want to know what she's doing here."

"Naisir just left the hotel, so he might be on his way down. But I think he sent her ahead to get the place ready."

"For what?" Pete asked, even though she thought she knew the answer.

"For you and Mac to get there. For Schlueter to arrive. They figure that you guys will probably show up in the middle of the night, so they think they've got all the time in the world."

"Do you think the cops will be here too, or maybe some muscle from the ISI?"

"No one official for now. They'll want to keep this thing as quiet as possible while they decide what to do about the SEAL contract."

"Now that we're here, they can't seriously be thinking about going ahead."

"People have done crazier shit," Otto said. "So watch yourself, and she's just the guy's wife, nothing more sinister, as far as we know."

"As soon as you decrypt her phone calls let me know if trouble might be coming my way. Otherwise I'm just going to hold down the fort till Mac gets here."

"Lots of stuff could go wrong, so maybe it'd be better if you waited for Mac no matter what happens."

"I'm not going in to shoot it out with her, if that's what you mean," Pete said.

"That's exactly what I meant, plus all the shit that we haven't thought of yet," Otto said. "One good thing on our side is that as far as I can tell there is no surveillance operation on the place. So you're going in clean, although there might be someone else in the house with her. But I don't think so."

"I'll find out," Pete said.

She sat behind the wheel for a full minute watching the house and the neighborhood. Somewhere a dog was barking. A jet took off from the airport, which was only a couple of miles away. Nothing moved on the street, nor were there any people out and about, though she had the distinct feeling that she was being watched.

The iron gate swung open on its electric motor, which came as a surprise to Pete. She started the car, expecting to see Naisir's wife drive out in her green Fiat convertible. When the woman didn't come, Pete switched off the engine and walked across the street, where she stopped just at the gate.

Ayesha's car was parked to one side in the narrow courtyard. Nothing moved, and after a couple of seconds Pete slipped inside and started across to the door.

The top of the wall was embedded with sharp spikes about eighteen inches tall set at three- or four-inch intervals, so climbing out of here would be just about impossible. For just a moment Pete thought about phoning Mac, but only the wife was inside, and as far as Otto had been able to determine the woman was not on the ISI's payroll. Nor was she any sort of a agent for any other intelligence or law enforcement agency. She was nothing more than a housewife whose family happened to be wealthy.

Pulling her gun, Pete went the rest of the way to the door, which was unlocked. She pushed it open with the toe of her sneaker and paused for a moment to listen for any sounds from inside. But the house was quiet.

Stairs went up from a narrow vestibule. A corridor ran back to the rear of the house. She went to the second floor. Three doors led from the hallway, all of them closed.

Downstairs she paused again to listen for anything, the slightest noise that Ayesha was somewhere close. But the place remained silent, and Pete began to get a little spooked. Pointing the pistol down and away from her leg, she started along the corridor, careful to make absolutely no sound, trying to keep her breathing even, though her heart was racing.

The smart move would have been to turn around and find another way out of here till Mac arrived, but she kept telling herself that she was armed, and she'd faced worse situations working with him.

The end of the corridor opened to the right into a broad living area furnished in the Western fashion, with couches, wingback chairs, and a flat-screen LED television. Tall sliding glass doors faced a small garden backed by the rear wall that, like the one in the front, was topped with sharp metal spikes. Several small lime trees were in full bloom, but the rest of the garden looked as if it had been neglected for a long time.

Ayesha Naisir rose up from one of the wingback chairs that faced away from where Pete was standing. She was a short, slender woman with long black hair and wide dark eyes. Beautiful in an exotic way, even in jeans and a snow-white peasant blouse that revealed her bare shoulders, she smiled and stepped away from the chair, her tiny feet bare, her nails painted bright pink.

"I wondered who would show up first, you or Mr. McGarvey, though I really didn't expect either of you until sometime tonight, or perhaps in the early morning," she said. Her English was flawless with a hint of British accent.

"Who else is here with you?" Pete asked.

"No one, though my husband should be here soon. He called and said that he and Mr. McGarvey had a pleasant chat at the hotel, though the outcome was anything but."

"Then I guess we'll just sit down and have a little chat of our own while we wait for them to show up," Pete said. She motioned toward the couch.

"It might be a little more complicated than that, I'm afraid," Ayesha said. She came around to the coffee table in front of one of the couches and picked up what looked to Pete to be a television remote control, pushed a button, and then set it down.

Too late Pete realized it wasn't a TV remote, but the control to close the gate.

Ayesha came forward and Pete raised the pistol.

"Are you going to shoot me?"

"If need be."

"Then you would be in very grave trouble," the woman said, stopping an arm's length away.

Pete pointed the pistol at the woman's head. "Your husband has hired a team of assassins to kill twenty-four American servicemen in the United States, along with their wives and children. They've already murdered two of them, so it isn't I who am in trouble. It's your husband and the government he represents."

"Twenty-four soldiers who violated my country's borders to conduct an illegal raid and murder several people."

"Terrorists."

"Like you, in my home with a pistol pointed at me," Ayesha said, a little color coming to her cheeks. "Why are you here?"

"To find out the truth," Pete shot back. "To stop the murders."

"You've told me that you and Mr. McGarvey already know the truth. Go home before it is too late."

"It's already too late," Pete said. She stepped forward and jammed the muzzle of the silencer into Ayesha's forehead, just as her phone rang and someone came down the corridor.

FORTY-ONE

McGarvey ordered a car with a GPS from the concierge, who apologized, saying that it would take thirty minutes to arrive. Naisir had obviously flashed his ISI credentials to the manager, so the entire staff was on edge, though if he'd said anything negative about the two Americans, it wasn't apparent in their attitude except that everyone was ultracareful.

He went back to their suite, where he tried to call Pete, but the phone switched to a recording that his call was being forwarded to an automatic voice message system.

Otto called at that moment. "Pete's in trouble."

"I just tried to call her. But her phone switched to voice mail."

"An old Lexus showed up down the street from the safe house, and in the next pass it was in the compound and four guys were getting out."

"Goddammit," McGarvey said. He was afraid of something like this. "Was Naisir with them?"

"I don't think so. These guys were a lot larger than him. But I got the car's tag. I'm running the registration now."

Switching the phone to speaker, he laid it on the bed and got his pistol, the silencer, the spare magazines, and the small bricks of Semtex and fuses. "I want to know when Naisir arrives."

"The Lexus is registered to Zeeshan Manzoor Sial Import/Exports. Hang on."

Mac holstered the pistol, put on his lightweight black blazer, and pocketed everything else. All that was left in the suite was their overnight bags, a few bits of spare clothing, and their toiletries kits. He didn't think they'd be back for any of it.

"I'm not coming up with any actual import or export license applications, but they maintain an account under that name at the Habib Bank AG Zurich in Rawalpindi. I've not cracked it yet, but their business credit cards are platinum. I think I'll go to Zurich and see if it'll be easier to get in."

"Any connection with the ISI?"

"None that I've found so far. My gut feeling is these guys are the city version of the dacoits—bandits, enforcers, tough guys who originally started out in India and Myanmar. They'll work for anyone with money—and they'll do anything from robbing trains, to raping your neighbor's daughter if you get into a feud."

"Kidnapping and murder?"

"Yeah. And they have a reputation of being good at what they do."

"What's your confidence level?"

"That they're dacoits? Ninety percent. I'll have it nailed in a couple of minutes. But listen, Mac, if you go barging in there right now with the four of them on site, plus Naisir's wife, and very likely Naisir himself within the next twenty minutes or so, there'll be a bloodbath, and there's no guarantee you or Pete will come out of it in one piece."

"You're right, but I am going to take a quick pass."

"And then what?"

"I'm going to do exactly what they're expecting me to do. Wait until the middle of the night and then hit them."

The line was silent for a longish moment or two. "By then Schlueter will most likely be there. Seven-to-one odds."

"Actually seven-to-two with Pete. And they'll be overconfident."

"Shit," Otto said. "One of these days you're going to make a mistake."

"Not today," McGarvey said. "Soon as Naisir shows up let me know."

Again Otto was silent for a second or two. "No way I can talk you out of this?"

"I'm not leaving Pete there."

"They won't do anything to her; it's you they want."

"That's right. And I'm not going to disappoint them."

"Shit."

.   .   .

The car turned out to be a chocolate-brown Mini Cooper, with the bigger engine and twin pipes, plus a portable GPS unit suction-cupped to the windshield. McGarvey plugged the address of Naisir's house in the city into the unit. When he arrived, he parked across the street.

Traffic was thick downtown, but orderly, and the impression that he got was of a carefully managed, almost squeaky-clean city, reminiscent in some ways of a Swiss town but with an Islamic flair.

He walked across the street and rang the bell at the front gate. An older man in jeans and a white shirt buttoned at the collar answered the door.

"I'd like to speak to Major Naisir," McGarvey said in English.

"May I ask who is calling?"

"Mr. McGarvey."

"Yes, sir. I will tell the major that you called. Most unfortunately he is not presently at home."

"When do you expect him or Mrs. Naisir?"

"I couldn't say."

He drove over to the government section, where he slowly passed the Pakistan Secretariat buildings on Constitution Avenue. Then he turned around at the bus station and passed the parliament building, the National Library, the Supreme Court, turning on Bank Road. He followed it into the diplomatic section, where he parked in front of the German embassy.

If he had picked up a tail he hadn't spotted it, but he was pretty sure that Naisir had instructed the hotel staff to keep an eye on his activities. They would have reported the car to whatever number they had been given. In addition he'd spotted surveillance cameras on the roofs of all the government buildings, including the German embassy's. If they were watching, they knew where he was. It was even likely that the delay in delivering the car had given the ISI time to plant a GPS tracker. Which was exactly what he wanted.

He got out of the car and sat down at a bench twenty yards away, well out of the range of any listening device that also may have been planted. He telephoned the U.S. embassy and was immediately connected with Don Simmons, the CIA's chief of station.

"Mr. Director, I was hoping that you wouldn't be calling me, but I'm not surprised that you have."

When McGarvey had briefly served as the DCI, Simmons had worked as assistant COS in Cairo. They had met once at headquarters, and again in London at a joint intelligence services conference, where the topic of discussion was the Middle East, which everyone had agreed even then was on the verge of a meltdown. He'd seemed to be a no-nonsense career officer with a limited sense of humor. The work of the CIA was serious business.

"I need to get in touch with Milt Thomas."

"I'll not involve my staff in any clandestine operation you've come here for."

"Nor am I asking for it. I'd simply like him to watch for someone coming in on an Air Berlin flight this afternoon. Routine. As far as I'm concerned he can even report it to his police contact."

"And then what?"

"Give me a call and let me know."

"And then what?"

"Nothing."

Simmons hesitated, but then gave McGarvey a phone number. "If you get yourself into any trouble with the police or the ISI, you're on your own."

McGarvey broke the connection and phoned Thomas, who answered immediately in Punjabi.

"I need a favor," McGarvey said.

"You'll have to clear it with Don," Thomas said in English.

"Already have. I want you to meet an Air Berlin flight this afternoon. See if a woman gets off, and see what she's carrying and who, if anyone, meets her."

"How will I know who she is?"

"I'll send you a couple of photos from my cell phone."

"Do I need to tail her?"

"Depends on who she meets or doesn't meet. But listen up: be careful. This woman is very good, and if Major Naisir is the one to meet her, back off immediately."

"I hear you," Thomas said. "Give me the details."

FORTY-TWO

The neighborhood around the safe house was quiet. It normally was at this hour on a weekday because there were no food or craft stalls here, no restaurants or coffee shops. Nevertheless, Naisir approached with a great deal of caution. His technical department had called with the information from the hotel about the Mini Cooper, and already the calls were filtering in from surveillance cameras in the political section of the city about the American's presence.

"He just finished speaking with someone on his cell phone," Sergeant Salarzai reported. He worked in Naisir's section, and in the few months he'd been at that position he had proved to be a very capable aide. He was one of the few men in the directorate whom Naisir trusted.

"Who did he phone?"

"We don't know. He parked in front of the German embassy and sat on a bench. It's all we have, except that he made two calls, both of them brief."

"Where is he now?"

"Sitting in his car in Jinnah Park not far from your house. He entered a specific address in his GPS, in Rawalpindi, but he drove to the park instead."

Naisir had parked down the block from the safe house, and he instinctively looked in the rearview mirror. "Let me know when he moves."

"Yes, sir. Can you tell me the operational code so that I can log my activities?"

"Later," Naisir said. "Just keep me informed." He phoned Ayesha.

"We have company," she told him.

"The woman?"

"Yes. She had a gun pointed at me, but your four contractors arrived just in time. Everything here is under control. Where are you?"

"Just outside. But McGarvey will show up just as I thought he would."

"Early?"

"I don't think he'll try anything until tonight."

"I'll open the gate for you," Ayesha said.

By the time he got to the end of the block the gate had swung open; he drove inside and parked next to his wife's Fiat and the Lexus. There wasn't a third car, which meant the woman who'd traveled with McGarvey had come in on foot. He'd passed an Aveo parked around the corner—or at least what was left of the American compact car—it had been stripped of its wheels and just about everything else easily removable. Pakistanis were an enterprising people.

Ayesha met him at the door and they embraced. "I think the woman would have shot me," she said.

A chill hand gripped his heart, thinking about what might have happened. "You should not have come here."

"Nonsense. A wife's place is in support of her husband." She came outside and closed the door, out of earshot of the others in the house. "Whatever you think of women in general, do not underestimate the one who came with McGarvey. Even the four dacoits you hired have been unable to intimidate her, and they are very hard men."

"What has happened?"

"She had a cell phone, so obviously she and McGarvey have talked. He knows that she's here."

"That's the whole point," Naisir said. "I want to use her as a bargaining chip; she's of no other use to me."

"And she knows it. She refuses to call McGarvey."

"There are methods."

Ayesha shook her head. "If you mean torture, I don't think they'll work."

"Anyone can be made to talk."

"Not this one, Ali."

"What makes her so special?"

"I'd bet anything that she is in love with McGarvey. And a woman in love will endure anything for her man."

"Including dying?"

"Yes, including dying."

"We'll see," Naisir. "Where is she?"

"Upstairs in the inside bedroom."

One of the dacoits was leaning against the wall at the foot of the stairs. He was very large for a Pakistani, towering six inches above Naisir and easily weighing two hundred pounds. His face was broad, his eyes very dark, with five days' growth of whiskers on his face. He wore jeans and a faded dungaree shirt, a scarf around his neck, very Western. And he looked angry.

"What do I call you?" Naisir asked.

"Sipra will do."

"Where are the others?"

"Jat and Mashud Khel are upstairs watching the front and rear approaches, and Swati is in the living room waiting to begin."

"Probably nothing will happen until sometime tonight. In the meantime I may have another job of work for you. Something perhaps a bit more pleasant."

The dacoit shrugged indifferently.

"Give me just a minute with her, then bring up her cell phone and two glasses of brandy," Naisir told his wife.

"Don't forget what I told you."

"Not to worry. We're just going to have a nice chat," Naisir said, and he went upstairs to the bedroom whose door was closed. It was the one room on the second floor without a window, used occasionally for interrogations. Knocking once, he went in.

Pete was sitting on the floor, her back propped against a wall. She looked up but said nothing.

"The bed would be more comfortable," Naisir told her.

"I hate bedbugs. Filthy creatures. Just like this shit hole of a country."

Naisir didn't bother reacting. "What do I call you?"

"Doris Sampson; it's the name on my passport. Or ma'am."

"You came in with Kirk McGarvey, both of you under false passports. For that you could be arrested and put on trial."

"Please do."

"First I would like you to phone Mr. McGarvey and tell him your situation. I'd like to sit down and have a serious conversation with him."

"No."

"Just one brief phone call."

"No."

Ayesha came in with the phone and two snifters of brandy.

Naisir held out the phone to Pete, but she refused to take it. He handed her a brandy, which she took. She then poured it on the floor and handed the glass back.

"Have Sipra come up here," he told his wife.

She went out in the corridor and called for the dacoit to come upstairs.

"A simple telephone call, and we will leave you alone. You have my word."

Pete looked up at him, a small smile on her lips.

Sipra showed up, very large in the doorway. Naisir handed him the cell phone. "I want her to call Mr. McGarvey. If she refuses, rape her. Maybe she'll change her mind after all."

Pete jumped up. "Wait," she said.

Naisir looked at her indifferently. "No," he said, and he walked out.

FORTY-THREE

☐

McGarvey parked at the bus station a couple of blocks from Naisir's safe house. He picked up the portable GPS unit and tossed it in the back of a pickup truck as it passed by, then went over to the taxi queue and climbed in the backseat of a cab.

"Where may I take you, sir," the driver asked politely in English.

"I'm not sure of the address but I think it's close," McGarvey said, and he gave him the directions he'd taken from the GPS.

It was after lunch already, and although McGarvey hadn't eaten since last night, he wasn't hungry, thinking about Pete. She was a well-trained capable officer, but her specialty was interrogation, not field work. He found that he was beginning to admire her, even though he was worried about her safety.

Just as they passed the safe house the gate opened. A Mercedes shot out of the compound and drove off in the opposite direction, Naisir at the wheel.

Around the corner, they came to a narrow garbage-strewn alley that snaked its way between a dozen buildings to the rear of the safe house. The lane was far too narrow for the cab, and they passed it.

"I think I got the wrong directions. Take me back to the bus station, please," McGarvey said.

"Can you say the house number?" the driver asked.

"No. I was just given directions."

Back at the bus station, McGarvey paid the driver and walked around the corner to a bustling tea shop, where he got a table on the sidewalk and ordered sweet tea. Ten minutes later his phone vibrated. It was Milt Thomas.

"The woman came in early," he said. "I was waiting to pick up another fare when I spotted her coming out of the terminal. For just a second I thought that I might be able to pick her up, but she just got into a Mercedes that was waiting for her."

"Did you recognize the driver?"

"Major Naisir," Thomas said. "But he didn't seem happy to see her. If you want me to follow them I might be able to catch up."

"No, but I might have another problem this evening that I'll need help with. It's something I want to keep local."

"Outside of Langley's purview?"

"Especially Langley's, and Don's."

"I'm all ears."

"Naisir's got a safe house here, just around the corner from the bus station. His wife and four men we think are dacoits are already there. It's where Naisir is bringing the woman he met at the airport."

"They're expecting a war."

"Which I'm going to give them," McGarvey said. "But I'm facing two problems. The first is that Pete is already there and I haven't heard from her since this morning."

"They know that you're coming and she's the bait. I don't know if I can round up some muscle in time, or quietly, but I can come down there and help out."

"We have to keep the CIA out of it, at least officially. But that's going to be my second problem. Once I'm done Pete and I will need to get out of the country in a big hurry, and the airport won't be an option, unless you can arrange a private charter for us."

"There are six contractors working for Executive Solutions scheduled to fly out at midnight. I think I can hold the plane if you're later than that, and there won't be any questions. These guys have been kicked out of the country. Nobody wants them here, not us or the Pakis. So no one will be around to check papers, especially with a couple of extra people."

"That'll work."

"I'll pick you up, but I'll need to know where."

"At the safe house or very nearby." He gave the GPS directions.

"Will there be any cops or ISI muscle?"

"He's using dacoits, so I don't think he wants to involve anyone official. He's on his own here, just like Pete and I are. And I'm count-ing on his being overconfident in numbers."

"One thing, Mr. Director, you're not bulletproof."

"Never have been," McGarvey said.

"How will I know when to come in?"

"I'll let you know, or Otto will. He has a sky bird watching the place, and he'll know when something goes down. But stay loose and no more than five minutes out."

"There's a tea shop just around the corner from the bus station."

"I'm there now."

"Last question, then. How are you planning on getting inside?"

"I'm going to ring the doorbell."

"Are you sure that you don't want some extra muscle?."

"Other than a ride out to the airport, I want you to stay out of this. If you get involved, the CIA is involved, and the White House would come down on the entire Islamabad station like a ton of horseshit. We don't need that right now."

"I hear you," Thomas said.

Mac called Otto and brought him up to speed. "Schlueter's plane got in early and Naisir went to pick her up."

"I wondered where he got himself to in such a hurry. Were you in the cab when he came out?"

"That was me. Anything going on at the house?"

"Everything's quiet. Too quiet. I tried to turn on Pete's phone to listen in, but they took the battery out of it. If you could get Don Sim-mons to send a technical team down I could have them set up some surveillance equipment in the house next door—it's empty."

That was going to be Mac's next question, but he hadn't hoped for that kind of luck. "Which house? Which side?"

"The east side. The one with a common wall. You could get in from the roof. There's only a low barrier separating the two."

McGarvey had spotted the house, but he'd had no way of knowing whether anyone was living there. "They'll be expecting something like that. But I'll use it as a backup route on the way out."

"Okay, Mac, exactly how are you planning on getting in?" Otto asked.

"As soon as Naisir shows up with Schlueter, I'm going to walk over and ring the doorbell."

"They'll kill you on sight."

"They want to know what I know. It's why Schlueter showed up. They want me there, but they want to talk to me first."

"Shit," Otto said.

"If you see something going down and I haven't called, send Milt Thomas in. He's standing by to pick us up and take us out to the airport. But only if there are no cops or anyone else nosing around."

"Shit."

"You already said that."

☐

FORTY-FOUR

Naisir's wife had sent the big man away and then had left herself. That was fifteen minutes ago, and Pete had explored the small room, especially the ceiling tiles, looking for a way out. But the place was tight. And probably soundproof if Naisir used it for extrajudicial interrogations.

Someone came to the door and Pete sat down on the floor in the same spot as before, in time for Ayesha to come in.

"Last chance," Naisir's wife said.

"Why did you stop him from raping me?"

"I thought that I would give you a little time to think about your situation, and then we could talk together, simply as two women."

"Kirk knows that I'm here and he understands the situation."

"You trust him," Ayesha said it as a statement, not a question.

"Yes. And just so you know, he has never once in his career failed at anything."

Ayesha smiled faintly. "Except at his marriage."

Pete resisted the urge to get up and take the woman apart. "Someone killed his family. All of them. He'll do the same here."

"Be that as it may," Ayesha said. "I put the battery back in your cell phone." She tossed it across. "Call him. Tell him that all we want to do is talk."

"Which is why you hired at least the one dacoit."

Ayesha shrugged. "If you know about them, then you understand the seriousness with which my husband takes the mess you created."

"Of your husband's doing. He's paymaster for an operation to kill some of our military personnel."

"Who violated our national borders and murdered innocent civilians."

"Terrorists who ordered the violation of our borders and killed almost three thousand civilians—some of them Muslims," Pete shot back. "We won't forget."

"Neither will we."

Pete switched the phone on but then set in on the floor. Unless the room was shielded from electronic eavesdropping, it was possible that Otto would pick up the signal.

"You will not telephone Mr. McGarvey?"

"No."

Ayesha stared at her for a long time before she turned and left. But she did not close the door.

A moment later Sipra came in and stood watching her, a smile on his thick lips.

Pete got to her feet and circled around to the right, away from the narrow cot, toward the wooden table with two chairs.

"You had your chance," Sipra said in heavily accented English.

"So do you. Just turn around and walk away."

The big man laughed, the sound rumbling deep inside his chest.

She figured that she had one chance, and it was a long shot considering the difference in their sizes. She stopped and spread her hands. "Let's get it over with, pig. That is, if you think you're man enough. But then you've been kissing so much ass all your life to make a few rupees by beating up people that no woman would look twice at you."

His complexion deepened, and he started toward her. He was surprisingly light on his feet, which was worrisome.

Pete feinted left, then right again on the balls of her feet, gliding like a boxer in a ring.

He didn't try to cut her off, instead he stopped in the middle of the room so that whichever way she moved he would only have to step forward to reduce her radius of free space.

She suddenly leaped directly at him, ducking to the left just inside his reach. Her intention was to get on his right side, beneath his hands, and slam a fist into his kidney, maybe slow him down until the opportunity to do what she wanted opened up.

It was like hitting a concrete block, and she saw his left hook coming overhand at the side of her face at the last moment. She could only rear back, throwing her head to the side as his fist landed just above her temple.

She was thrown to the floor, dazed, her stomach roiling, on the verge of vomiting, her head spinning, flashes of light in her eyes.

He ripped the waistband of her jeans open, and, grabbing her legs, he flipped her over on her stomach and pulled her pants and panties down around her ankles.

This wasn't happening! She felt completely helpless, a roaring sound filling her ears.

She looked over her shoulder, as he pulled one leg of her jeans off her ankle, and pulled his trousers down around his knees.

"No," she cried.

As he fumbled with his underwear, she managed to scoot away from him. He grabbed for her, but she heaved herself up on his broad back, grabbed the scarf tied around his neck with both hands, and with her knees in the small of his back pulled with all of her might, twisting her right hand over her left.

He bucked, trying to dislodge her, but her fingers were locked into the scarf, like the reins of a bronco.

He tried to reach up behind his back to grab her and pull her away, but each time she managed to get out of his reach, while still holding tight to the scarf, restricting his carotid artery, stopping the blood flow to his brain.

It seemed like forever before his movements became less violent. Finally he slumped forward on his purple face.

She kept the pressure on with every ounce of her strength until he gave a last shudder. She released her grip, her fingers cramped, every muscle in her body screaming for relief.

Slowly she climbed off him, got to her feet, and pulled up her panties and jeans.

After what seemed like another eternity, her senses came back into focus like a great whooshing coming down around her head.

She checked the corridor, but no one was coming. She went back to the body and searched it, but out of some sense of caution he wasn't carrying a weapon.

Picking up her phone she called Otto, who answered even before she entered the last number.

"Are you okay?" he demanded. He sounded breathless.

"Did you hear it?"

"Yes. What happened?"

"The son of a bitch tried to rape me, so I killed him."

"Mac's on his way. Can you get somewhere safe?"

Pete looked up as one of the other dacoits appeared in the doorway.

FORTY-FIVE

In his Mercedes leaving the airport Naisir was angry with Schlueter for coming back to Pakistan like this, and even more angry with himself for allowing the situation to get so out of hand.

"Why the hell did you come here?" he demanded. He glanced in the rearview mirror to make sure they hadn't picked up a tail.

"To deal with McGarvey," Pam said. "He's still here, isn't he, or have you already taken care of the problem?"

"I met with him this morning at the hotel. He knows about my safe house, and I'm sure that he'll show up sometime tonight or early in the morning."

"The bastard screwed up everything in Norfolk," Pam said. She was angry too. But all of a sudden she looked at him. "How can you be so sure?"

"He brought a woman with him, and we have her now."

"She's a CIA officer. He might cut her loose."

"They came in as husband and wife, and my wife is sure that she's in love with him."

Pam shook her head. "You involved your wife? What the hell were you thinking, Major? Don't you have any conception how dangerous this guy is? If and when he shows up he means to kill you. And if your wife gets in his way he'll kill her too."

Naisir glanced in his rearview mirror again.

"Damn, you're expecting him to come up on your six. You better hope he doesn't, because I can tell you something else. He'll not only come after you; he's already put a plan in place to get out of the country afterward."

"He won't live that long. I can guarantee that. I've hired four guys who know what they're doing."

"Dacoits," Pam said disparagingly. "Shopkeepers."

"These ones are special. There's no way he's going to get around them."

"Unless he gets to us before we reach your safe house," Pam said. "Are you armed?"

"Of course."

"Did you bring something for me?"

"In the glove box."

She took out a bulky Austrian-made 9mm Steyr GB, checked that there was a round in the chamber, and checked the eighteen-round magazine to make sure it was fully loaded. The gun had been de-cocked so it was in its safe mode. "It'd be poetic justice to kill the bastard with this," she said. "The American Army Special Forces used to carry it."

"You're not going to kill him, and neither am I. We'll leave that to the dacoits, who'll also dispose of his body up north."

"Unnecessary."

"He was the director of the CIA, for the sake of Allah. The government of Pakistan does not kill such men. The ISI simply cannot do it, which is why I hired the dacoits. They're outlaws who don't care about the law—religious or secular."

"You hired me to do a job because I'm not a Pakistani. Let me do this now so I can get on with the mission."

Naisir maneuvered through traffic, his thoughts spinning in a dozen different directions, among them his future with the ISI; he'd once entertained the notion that someday he would rise far enough in rank that, along with his wife's connections, he would become the head of the agency. It was still possible, especially if such a spectacular mission as eliminating the SEAL Team Six operators who'd taken out bin Laden were to come to complete fruition. Yet that operation, if it went wrong, could doom him and Ayesha to a prison somewhere, or even an assassin's bullet, despite her family.

"You should not have come," he said at length. "I have the situation under complete control."

"I'm here, and I want to meet him."

"As you wish."

One block out Naisir called his wife to let her know he was close, but she didn't answer until the third ring, and his gorge rose.

"We've had some trouble," she said, and she sounded out of breath.

"Is it McGarvey? I'm just around the corner."

"No. It's the woman. She murdered Sipra. The others want to take her apart, but I convinced them to wait until you arrived. But the situation won't remain stable for much longer."

"Open the gate."

The gate opened as Naisir came down the street, and he drove into the courtyard, the gate immediately closing behind him. Ayesha met him at the door.

"It was your foolish order to have her raped," she said. She was agitated. And she eyed Pam. "What are you doing here? We don't need you."

"I think you do."

Jat, the smallest of the four dacoits was waiting in the hall. The look on his face was neutral.

"Where is the woman?" Naisir demanded.

"This is not what we contracted for."

"Where is she?"

"Upstairs. Swati is guarding her. We demand that she be eliminated immediately."

"You demand nothing," Naisir said.

The dacoit looked at Pam and Ayesha, and his expression darkened. "This is not right."

Naisir turned to start up the stairs, but his wife put a hand on his arm. "There is a further complication," she said. "I put the battery back in her phone and gave it to her. I wanted to try one last time to make her see reason and call off McGarvey."

Naisir held his temper in check. He and Ayesha had had their differences, but he could not honestly remember the last time they'd argued or been cross with each other. She'd grown up with five older brothers, and that pressure, added to her privileged upbringing, had made her a fighter. She was an intelligent, tough, opinionated woman—not without loving kindness and gentleness—but a backbone of pure steel when the need arose.

"She is a trained CIA agent. You should not have done that."

"Nor should you have ordered her rape."

"Stay here," he told his wife. "And you too," he told Pam.

Upstairs Swati was standing in the open doorway to the front bedroom.

Naisir dismissed him, but it took the man forever to finally turn around and leave, an expression of insolence and even hate on his face. He and the others wanted blood.

Pete was seated on the floor, talking to someone on the phone.

Naisir pulled out his pistol as he strode across the room to her and placed the muzzle against her forehead. "Give me the telephone."

Sipra's body had been removed, but the table and one of the chairs were overturned, and there was a light brown stain on the wood floor.

"Got to go," Pete said. She ended the call and handed up the phone. "The last guy who tried to kill me didn't end up so good."

"Who were you talking to?"

"You wouldn't know him."

"McGarvey?"

"Actually, no. So how about either pulling the trigger or taking the fucking pistol out of my face?"

☐

FORTY-SIX

Milt Thomas parked his taxi across the street from the tea shop and walked over to where McGarvey was seated. Just at that moment, Otto phoned.

"I just finished talking to Pete," Otto said. "The body of the dacoit she killed was removed, and a second one was guarding her when Naisir showed up."

"Exactly where is she?"

"I got a good fix before Naisir took the phone and yanked the battery. She's in an upstairs room in the middle of the building, with no outside wall. But before she disconnected she told me that she was sure she heard at least two other voices downstairs, which confirms what we already knew. In addition to Naisir and his wife, there were four dacoits—three of them now—plus the Schlueter woman. All of them are most likely armed, but they're going to want to know what we know before they do anything."

"If they get the chance," McGarvey said. "Milt's here with his cab. Soon as I get Pete out, we'll make our way back here and then out to the airport."

"You're not going to wait until tonight?"

"They'll be expecting me to wait until then. I'm going now. Call if you see trouble coming our way."

"If he was going to call the cops or some of his own people he wouldn't have hired the dacoits, nor would Schlueter have shown up. They want you and Pete dead, after which they'll get rid of your bodies somewhere up in the mountains. It'd be hard to convince anyone that you hadn't just vanished into thin air. Maybe a kidnapping by rebels that went bad,"

A waiter came and Thomas ordered a sweet tea.

McGarvey got to his feet. "Unless something goes wrong, Pete and I should be back here before you finish your tea."

"What if something does go wrong?"

"Walk away from it. Otto will know what to do."

Thomas nodded. "Good luck, Mr. Director."

It took about six minutes for Mac to make it around the corner and to the end of the short block halfway down which was Naisir's safe house. A small pickup truck trundled by, but the neighborhood remained deserted, even though he got the distinct feeling that someone was watching him.

Crossing the street, he took one of the bricks of Semtex out of his pocket, and when he reached the safe house he used the adhesive strip to attach it to the gate just below the top hinge. He inserted an electric fuse into the explosive, setting the timer for ten minutes, then rang the doorbell.

FORTY-SEVEN

A large black bird flew overhead at the same time the sun was covered by a small cloud, and the gate swung open with a slight squeal of metal on metal. For just an instant McGarvey was half-convinced the three things were a sort of omen. Pakistan was an evil place.

But he didn't believe in such things. He had come here initially to kill Naisir or at the very least talk him into pulling the financing from Schlueter. But now he was here simply to rescue Pete. Nothing else was on his immediate agenda. Everything else—stopping the attacks against SEAL Team Six and exacting revenge for the two and their families who had already been murdered—would have to come later.

He'd had nightmares about these kinds of scenarios for most of his adult life. Every woman he'd come to care for, including his wife and daughter, had been killed because of him. Because of what he did. Because of who he was. Who he worked for. The operations he'd carried out.

He started across the courtyard where the BMW, the Fiat, and the Lexus were parked in a row and thought about the people inside: what they wanted, and what they were willing to do to get it. That and their arrogance would be their downfall.

The battered metal front door, its paint chipped, swung inward and Naisir was there, an Italian-made 12-bore Franchi SPAS 12 anti-riot shotgun in his right hand, the muzzle pointed at McGarvey.

"You're sooner than we expected."

"Ordering one of the dacoits you hired to rape the woman I came with changed everything, Major. Hand her over to me and we'll walk away."

"This morning you told me that you wanted to have a talk with Ms. Schlueter."

"That'll have to wait. All I want now is an exchange."

Naisir smiled faintly. "Exchange for what? I have both of the women here."

"Exchange for your life."

"You arrogant bastard," Naisir said, and he racked a round in the short-stock shotgun and pointed it at McGarvey's chest. "I'll shoot you where you stand."

"Do it and you'll end up in front of a firing squad or at the end of a rope, and you know it. Your government would have no trouble sacrificing one of its low-ranking officers to make sure its relations with Washington were not damaged."

"Your bodies will end up at the bottom of some mountain gorge up north."

"You might want to ask yourself what I was doing cruising around the Secretariat and parliament buildings. And why I parked in front of the German embassy, where I sat on a bench and made a couple of calls."

"Doesn't make any difference."

"There are security cameras all over the place up there, so a lot of people know that the former director of the CIA was nosing around. And right about now, they're asking themselves why."

"There is no connection to me."

"I also stopped by your house and left a message that I wanted to speak to you. And the people at the hotel would certainly not hide the fact that you and I met. The real fact of the matter is, the only reason you've made it this far in the ISI is because of your wife's family. Their patronage connections have pulled you along, and the sad part is that you probably are too dumb to understand it."

"For god's sake, if the man wants to talk to me let him in," Schlueter said from inside the front hall.

"Are you armed?" Naisir asked McGarvey.

"Of course I am."

"Give it to me."

"I'll tell you what. My pistol is in a holster under my jacket at the small of my back. If I try to reach for it you can go ahead and shoot me. You can always claim that it was self-defense."

"Kill him now," another woman said. It was Naisir's wife.

"No," Schlueter said sharply. "First we need to know what proof he has. If he wants to trade, it'll be his woman for information."

Naisir came out of the house and stepped aside, the shotgun steady in his hands.

McGarvey moved up to the open door and hesitated just a moment at the threshold. The Schlueter woman, halfway down the short corridor that led to the rest of the house, was flanked by two large men, all of them holding pistols. A third man stood partway up the stairs, a pistol in one hand, while he held tightly to Pete's arm with his other. Ayesha was halfway up the stairs, the only one not armed.

Bringing Pete out of the room where she had been kept was a mistake.

"You okay?" he asked her.

"Just dandy. Did you bring the cavalry?"

"No. But they know where we are."

"You shouldn't have come."

McGarvey stepped inside. "I wanted to talk to Frau Schlueter. Her husband said to say hello."

"Well, here we are," Pam said. "And unless you've brought some proof that I'm in any way involved with the two unfortunate incidents in the States, I'll kill you and the woman."

"Major Naisir and I bumped into each other in Berlin, and after we waterboarded Steffen Engel he mentioned Major Naisir's name. And here you are, the two of you, waiting for me. I wonder why that is?"

"You're a loose cannon, Mr. Director," Schlueter said. "You have nothing; otherwise you would have brought the cavalry. Kill him."

McGarvey reached back with his right hand, grabbed the barrel of the shotgun, and swiveled left out of the doorway. The shotgun went off, spraying the side of the house.

Schlueter or one or more of the dacoits opened fire, at least three rounds striking Naisir in the side of his torso and one in his head just above his cheekbone.

Grabbing the shotgun McGarvey poked it around the corner and fired two quick blasts down the hallway, keeping his aim low and to the left, well away from the stairway.

The returning fire was intense, chips from the concrete block walls flying everywhere, one of them taking a nick out of the side of McGarvey's neck.

The shotgun wasn't silenced, nor were the weapons the dacoits were using; someone in the neighborhood or in a passing car or truck was bound to sit up and take notice and call the police.

"Mac, one out the back door," Pete shouted.

McGarvey stepped back a pace and turned his head to the side. "On my way," he said. He laid the shotgun down and pulled out his pistol, the silencer already attached.

One of the dacoits poked his head out of the door, and McGarvey shot him. The man fell forward on his face, his body twitching.

"Mac—" Pete screamed, but she was cut off.

He rolled around the corner into the house in time to see Pam Schlueter and Naisir's wife turn the corner at the head of the stairs, the one dacoit, his big paw around Pete's head, over her mouth and nose, right behind them.

"Down," McGarvey shouted.

Pete pulled back, her feet over the next step back. The dacoit turned, off balance because of her sudden move, and fired one shot that went wild.

McGarvey fired three rounds, at least two of which hit the Pakistani in the side of the head, driving him further off balance, his knees buckling.

Pete pulled out of his grip and shoved him away, sending his body tumbling down the stairs with a terrific racket.

Turning on his heel Mac went to the door, the last dacoit suddenly there, and they nearly collided. Before the other man could disentangle himself, Mac had the gun out of his hand and pushed him back.

"Leave now and you'll live," McGarvey said.

But the bigger man danced to the left as he charged forward and batted Mac's gun away, sending it skidding across the courtyard. He grabbed Mac in a bear hug, his arms locked as he squeezed.

Mac head-butted him, and the dacoit staggered back, losing his grip. Mac was on him in an instant, driving the knuckles of his closed fist into the man's Adam's apple, crushing it, and blocking air to the lungs.

Still the dacoit tried to reach for Mac, who stepped into him and drove his fist into the man's nose, then the side of his face just below his left eye, and then once, twice, into his chest just over his heart.

But the bastard refused to go down.

The Semtex charge on the gate went off with an impressive bang, and just for an instant the dacoit turned toward it.

Mac hooked a foot around the man's left ankle and pulled his leg out from under him.

The dacoit went down hard, and again Mac was on him with a rage he'd not felt in a very long time, slamming his fist into the bastard's face, which was starting to turn purple, and then his chest again, and a second and third time, putting every ounce of his strength in his blows. Wanting to destroy him, for all the crap that he and the sons of bitches like him were doing. Killing soldiers was one thing, but harming innocent women, and in the case of the SEAL families, even children—that was another thing entirely.

Then Pete was behind him. "Stand down, Mac," she shouted. "He's finished."

In the distance McGarvey was suddenly aware of the sounds of sirens. Lots of them. He looked up.

"Are you okay?" he asked.

She stood swaying, hipshot, favoring her left side. "I think I dislocated my right knee. But we have to get out of here right now."

"What about Naisir's wife and Schlueter?"

"Gone," Pete said. "Over the roof, probably."

McGarvey got to his feet, picked her up, and started for the blown-out gate. "My car is just down the street."

The sirens were much closer now, and as he carried her out of the compound he was in time to see a crowd of at least three or four dozen men and women, some of them carrying clubs, coming at them from the direction his car was parked.

FORTY-EIGHT

Pam Schlueter and Ayesha watched the street from the roof of the house next door, as McGarvey and the woman he'd come to Pakistan with emerged from the gate and pulled up short when they spotted the crowd.

"That'll solve at least one problem for us," Ayesha said bitterly. Her heart pounded painfully in her thin chest. It was too early for her to feel grief about her husband's death at the hands of the American. That would come, but first she needed revenge.

Crouched just below the parapet of the roof she could feel the heat and raw vibrations coming from the German assassin her husband had hired several months ago. Pam kept clutching and unclutching the pistol in her hand.

"We can do nothing for the moment," Ayesha said, putting a hand on the much larger woman's arm.

Pam turned to her, a vibrant hate screwing up the features of her face. "It has ended here. I didn't want that."

"Maybe not."

"You don't understand. I needed to know what the Americans know. I need to know if they have any proof of the payments your husband has made. It would link me to the ISI."

"It's obvious they already have the link, or at least suspect it enough for McGarvey and his woman to come here, to challenge my husband. To kill him."

"Don't be foolish. It was one of your husband's dacoits who fired the shots."

"Had he not come here the dacoits would not have been necessary! The shots would not have been fired!"

McGarvey, the woman in his arms, backing away from the advancing crowd, made a very romantic picture in Ayesha's mind, even though her husband was dead. But Pam was right, of course. Ali had been a fool in so many ways. And he had badly mishandled the entire situation. Especially the operation in the States against the SEALs. Unbusinessmanlike.

"Be that as it may," Pam said. "As soon as it calms down I'm returning to Germany."

"I thought that you wanted retribution?" Ayesha asked, even though she didn't fully understand why yet.

"Your husband is dead; the money will stop."

"*Die Vergeltung*, isn't that what you called it? Payback for the aggression against my country? We would get our revenge, and you would get your payment for services rendered?"

"The money has stopped, you fucking idiot."

"It has not, unless you want to turn away from continuing."

"The ISI will not get itself involved now that your husband is dead, and apparently the Americans know who the paymaster is."

"Was."

Pam, still watching the unfolding situation on the street, started to say something but then looked up, her eyes narrowing suspiciously. "Was?"

"You have a new paymaster."

"I've already told you that the ISI will no longer let itself be involved."

"I'll pay," Ayesha said. "That is, if you still want your retribution. Because I certainly do."

Pam was interested. "It'll take a great deal of money. Perhaps as much as several million."

"Euros or dollars?" Ayesha asked, though it really didn't matter. She had access to as much as she needed. Her father, especially, would understand, as would her brothers. This now was a family affair.

"I'll need a down payment of five hundred thousand euros. Immediately."

"You'll have it within twenty-four hours."

"I'll give you the banking numbers."

"I already have them," Ayesha said. She looked again at McGarvey and the woman. "Before you proceed, your first job will be to kill Mr. McGarvey if he manages to escape today. But not on Pakistani soil."

"He won't get out of this," Pam replied.

"Don't be so sure."

FORTY-NINE

The first of the police were just around the corner when Milt Thomas's cab parted the crowd less than ten feet from where McGarvey stood his ground, still holding Pete in his arms. As soon as the cab was clear Milt started throwing out ten-rupee notes, which immediately distracted the mob long enough for him to draw up and reach back and pop open the rear door.

McGarvey shoved Pete inside first, and as he climbed in, Milt accelerating away, he caught a glimpse of the Schlueter woman and Naisir's wife coming out of the house next door and merging with the mob.

"Otto called, said you guys were in trouble."

"Is that the cops or the ISI behind us?" McGarvey asked.

"The cops," Milt said. "Someone reported an explosion and gunfire and they came running. If you still have your pistol, and especially the Semtex and fuses, toss them out the window as soon as we're clear. For some reason security at the airport has been tightened up in the past hour or so. They're checking everyone's papers real close."

"My things are back at the safe house," Pete said.

"Doesn't matter, I brought both of you new passports, under the names Tom and Maureen Chesson." He handed back an envelope. "We figured that you might be on the run getting out, your old legends burned."

The passports were diplomatic, like the ones they had come in under. To McGarvey's eye they looked perfect, neither his nor Pete's photos exactly matching what they looked like now, which was often a dead giveaway for forgeries. The only problem would come if they were searched. None of their others papers—driving licenses, credit cards, bank cards—matched.

Three blocks away Thomas turned down a narrow street that was bordered on the left by a refuse-littered field. Mac tossed out the Semtex, the pencil fuses, and the two extra magazines of ammunition.

"What about your gun?"

"Back at the safe house."

"Doesn't matter, no serial number, unless they match your DNA with whatever they might come up with from the handle. But I don't think the cops are going to be that sophisticated or quick. And the ISI is going to want to sweep everything under the rug."

"Major Naisir is dead," McGarvey said.

Thomas looked at him in the rearview mirror. "That might become an issue, but not right now. It's going to take them time to straighten out the mess, especially if the ham-handed cops go inside and look around. They'll screw up everything."

"But it's over now, isn't it, Mac?" Pete asked.

"I don't think so. Schlueter managed to get out. I saw her with the major's wife back there in the crowd."

"Will the ISI still be interested in funding her?"

"No, but it's possible she'll find another source."

"The major's wife's family is rich," Thomas said. "And with her husband dead she has the motivation."

"Milt's right," Pete said. "From what little I saw at the safe house she rules the roost. If she's got money, she'll step up to the plate."

Milt looked at them in the rearview mirror. "You're her first target," he said to McGarvey.

"I hope so, because if we get out of here, she'll be mine."

"Ours," Pete corrected.

"You have blood on your neck," Milt told McGarvey. "You'd better clean it off before we get to the airport."

The new airport, called Benazir Bhutto International, the same as the old one, had just opened a year ago, and security at the easiest of times was tight, especially for departing passengers.

This afternoon the lines for cars, taxis, and buses at the passenger dropoff points were not terribly heavy, but there were a lot of police and airport security personnel everywhere. Milt headed across to the separate cargo airlines terminal, where only three trucks were in the queue.

"Let me do the talking," he said.

"Do you have a gun?" McGarvey asked.

"No, and the cab is clean."

"How about your papers?"

"I'm a Pakistani-born American, who came home because he couldn't stand the way of the infidel. It's why I help the local cops whenever I can."

A lot of CIA spies fit the same, unglamorous mold. They were foreign-born American immigrants who were fluent in their native language and who were recruited to return to their homes to spy: China, Russia, Iran, Venezuela, even North Korea, which was the most dangerous assignment of them all because the leadership was so incredibly paranoid and the people brainwashed.

When it was their turn at the security checkpoint, they all handed their papers to an armed guard, while another with a long-handled mirror checked the undercarriage of the cab, and a third with a bomb-sniffing dog checked the trunk.

"What is your business here?" the guard with their papers demanded in Punjabi first and then English.

"I am taking my passengers to the TCS Courier hanger. They are leaving on the London-Heathrow flight."

"They're too late. That plane is leaving sooner than scheduled. Any minute now."

"It's being held for them," Thomas said.

"It's not possible," the guard said. "Anyway you're just a simple taxi driver. What would you know of these things?"

"I'm sorry. I only do as I am instructed."

The guard returned McGarvey's and Pete's passports. "You will have to arrange for another flight," he said.

McGarvey put a hundred-dollar bill in his passport and held it out the window for the guard, who was closely examining Thomas's papers, including a national identity card and his taxi license.

"Perhaps you would care to examine my passport again," McGarvey said.

The guard opened it, looked up at McGarvey and Pete, pocketed the money, and handed the passport back.

"I'll hold your papers," he told Thomas. "Take your passengers to the terminal, and when you return I will have a number of questions for you."

"As you wish," Thomas said.

The TCS Boeing 737 configured as a cargo aircraft was waiting on the tarmac, its engines already spooling. Stairs to the open hatch just aft of the cockpit were in place, a ground crew waiting to remove them.

Thomas pulled up next to the ground crew's pickup truck. "Good luck to both of you," he said.

"What was all that at the checkpoint?" Pete asked.

"Happens from time to time. No big deal."

"If you're connected with what happened at the safe house, you could be in trouble," she persisted. "Mac, tell him."

"If I don't go back, they'll never let this plane get out of Pakistan's airspace. Now get the hell out of here and let me do my job."

"Good luck," McGarvey said, and they shook hands.

"Piece of cake."

McGarvey had to help Pete up the stairs and inside, where they took the last two seats. The others were occupied by a half-dozen contractors, one of them a medic who even before they had taken off put Pete's knee to rights by popping the kneecap back in place.

"That helps," she said gratefully.

"What happened?" he asked. He was a man in his late thirties or early forties, mild-mannered with a southern accent.

"Trust me, you don't want to know," she said.

McGarvey phoned Otto, who answered on the first ring. He'd been standing by for the call. "We're on the way out."

"How'd it go?"

"Could have been better. But Milt might be in some sort of trouble."

"The embassy is working on it. They're getting him out of Islamabad tonight. We're just waiting till your flight clears Pakistani airspace. A company plane will be standing by for you at Heathrow."

"I'll tell you all about it once we're over the Atlantic."

"But it's not over?"

"I don't think so," McGarvey said.

Germany

Pam Schlueter got back to Berlin a day and a half later, bone-tired and a little bit discouraged because of her abject failure in Pakistan and the death of her paymaster. She didn't think for one minute that Ayesha Naisir would ever make good on her promise to pick up the tab for the rest of the project. And all that was left in her mind was her own revenge, first against McGarvey and second against her ex-husband—a job of work she should have accomplished long ago.

It was early evening under a cloudless sky when she emerged from the Air Berlin arrivals gate at Tegel Airport, and went through customs carrying only her passport and a single carry-on bag containing a couple of items of clothing, all of which she had purchased in Islamabad.

She had half-expected to be questioned by the airport immigration people, but she was passed through without comment. Outside, she held back for a few moments to watch the area around the taxi stand, again expecting to spot a cop or BND officer waiting for her. Those guys almost always stood out.

But again no one had come for her. It was as if Rawalpindi never happened; not the kidnapping of a CIA officer and not the shootout with the former DCI. It was surreal, and all the way to her apartment in the city she had a hard time controlling her jitters.

She had the cabbie pull up a block away. After he was gone she walked the rest of the way, passing her building and suddenly turning around at the end of the block to see if she was being followed. But no one was there, and no car or truck out of the ordinary. Only normal traffic for this time of the night, mostly Turks, Greeks, and a few Muslims, mostly from Africa.

She took the stairs to the third floor and listened with her ear to the door for several long beats, but all was quiet, except for some sort of wailing music from the apartment below, sounded Oriental to her, and voices from the apartment just above hers.

The entire building smelled of leaking sewer pipes, boiled lentils and chickpeas, and the ever-present garlic. The irony of it all for her was that she was a millionaire now. Even if she cut and ran, dropping everything, she could retire comfortably somewhere, and if she lived carefully the money she'd already accumulated would last a lifetime.

But she couldn't. What was coming next would be her retribution.

Inside her tiny one-room apartment, she tossed her bag on the narrow bed, turned on the small table lamp, and found her loaded Glock 26 pistol and silencer in the small *Schrank* that held her few clothes. For the first time since leaving Pakistan she felt reasonably safe. If someone came here wanting to arrest her, they would pay dearly with their lives.

She took off her light khaki jacket and hung it up at the same moment someone tapped lightly on her door.

Pistol in hand she stood to one side. "Yes?" she said.

"It's me," a woman responded.

For just an instant Pam wasn't sure whether her hearing was playing tricks on her. She knew the voice. Holding the pistol out of sight behind her back, she opened the door.

Gloria, her U.S. contact, stood there, an awkward smile on her plain oval face. The woman was shorter than Pam, and a little on the dumpy side, but like the only other time they'd met, she seemed happy and relieved all at once.

"I found out about the trouble in Paki land, but then nothing else," the woman gushed. "Christ, I didn't know if you were dead or what. I had to come personally and wait for you."

Pam stepped aside to let the woman in. "It wasn't necessary for you to come all this way. To take the risk."

"No risk, believe me," Gloria said. Her voice was nasal and a little high-pitched, and her eyes darted all over the place as if she was afraid that something was going to jump out of the shadows and bite her. "You can't image how much we depend on you."

Pam laid her pistol on the small table, and then took Gloria's coat and large shoulder bag and set them aside.

The woman's eyes were round, looking at the pistol. "Were you expecting more trouble?"

"Trouble, yes. But not you. What the hell are you doing here?"

"I had to make sure that you weren't dead."

"You've already said that."

"The others suggested that I come. My sources. But they don't know the reality. To them it's just a game we play."

Pam had suspected from the start that Gloria had her sources. In her position it had always been impossible for her to know everything she knew without help. But she'd always thought that "the others" were just friends, acquaintances, someone in Gloria's social network, even though she'd known intellectually that such a simple explanation wasn't likely. But "sources" implied a network with structure. And yet she was here, and she was suggesting that the others—almost certainly bored housewives of important government officials—were in it as a game. To them it wasn't real.

"The others?"

"They're all over Washington, inside the Pentagon, you wouldn't believe." Gloria stopped. "I can't give you their names. You have to understand."

"I do," Pam said. "You, I understand; we have a bond. But what about your friends in high places?"

Gloria shook her head. "Just next to men in high places."

"All women?"

Gloria nodded.

"Battered women?"

Again Gloria nodded, a real sadness coming into her eyes. "And jilted women, and trivialized women, and ignored women. And after I tell them about you, how you're fighting back, they don't have one bit of trouble helping with little bits of information now and then. They figure—just like I do—that if you can make it on your own, so could they."

Pam had understood Gloria almost from the beginning when they had accidentally met in Washington. But she'd never been able to figure out how the woman got her information, some of it startlingly secret, until now. And she understood the risk involved, the least of which would be prison.

She reached out and Gloria came into her arms; They held each other close for a long time.

"It's all right," Pam said softly. She brushed a kiss on Gloria's cheek. "It'll be okay now, I promise."

Gloria looked up. She was crying.

Pam kissed her on the lips, and Gloria responded, shuddering and passionately kissing back.

They undressed each other and went to bed, where they made love very slowly but with a huge, pumped-up passion that seemed as if it had been building forever. At one point Gloria cried out, but softly, all the way from the back of her throat.

When they were done, Pam covered them up and they held each other closely, finally going to sleep, both of them exhausted.

Sometime just after three in the morning, Pam woke up, her heart pounding. She disentangled herself from Gloria and got out of bed. At the window she looked down at the street, which was completely devoid of traffic at this hour. No suspicious cars or vans were parked half up on the sidewalks. No one was lurking in the shadows as far as she could tell.

After a while she got a bottle of schnapps and a small glass from the cupboard, and then powered up her laptop. While it was booting up she poured a drink, tossed it back, and poured another.

She checked her in-box but there were no messages from any of her operators; they were laying low for the time being. Next she checked the half-dozen banks she maintained as close as Luxembourg and as far as the Cayman Islands. When she came to her account with Haddad Commercial Bank Offshore on Jersey in the Channel Islands, she sat back. Five hundred thousand euros had been deposited last night, shortly after she had left Pakistan.

She stared at the screen for a very long time. Then she shut off the machine, finished her second glass of schnapps and went back to bed. In the morning she would tell Gloria exactly what she needed.

PART
THREE

The Next Five Days

FIFTY

□

Otto had arranged for one of the CIA's Gulfstream VIP jets to pick them up at Heathrow and take them across the Atlantic. They landed at Joint Base Andrews in the middle of the night and taxied over to the navy hangar the company used.

Marty Bambridge was leaning against a big Cadillac Escalade, a scowl on his face. Two men in dark Windbreakers stood nearby, and two others were waiting at a second Cadillac.

"Looks like we have a welcome home committee," Pete said from her window seat. "And Marty doesn't look happy."

"Has he ever been?" McGarvey asked. He'd figured the sort of reception they'd get, especially if Bhutani, the ISI's director general, complained to Page. But the DCI's private phone line was one area where Otto never hacked. It was a point of honor.

"We may have had some certifiable idiots on the seventh floor, but they were patriots doing the best they knew how," he'd explained once.

They thanked the pilot and crew, who had treated them to a late breakfast last night then left them alone so that they could get some rest.

McGarvey went down the stairs first. Pete, whose knee still bothered her, hobbled after him. She'd refused his arm.

"I won't give the bastard the satisfaction," she'd said.

Marty came over to them. "I'm not going to start anything with you two this morning, except to tell you that you're staying on campus in one of the safe houses. You'll be debriefed after breakfast, after which it will be decided what the hell to do with you."

"By you?" Pete asked.

"That will be way above my pay grade, but the White House has been made aware of your little escapade, and no one over there or on the seventh floor is particularly pleased."

"Has the media gotten hold of it yet?" McGarvey asked. In this case he couldn't blame the deputy director of operations for being angry. The man was caught between a rock and a hard place.

"Thank God, no. But no one expects that to last much longer."

"No one's linked the two dead SEALs with the bin Laden operation?"

"The navy has, of course, but apparently there are some other complications."

"I expect there have been," McGarvey said. Captain Cole was one of them, and the SEAL Team Six guys were the other. They were cutting off their noses to spite their faces. It was crazy, and yet Mac could see it from their perspective. They were proud, they were tough, they were DEVGRU operators, the meanest sons of bitches on the planet.

"I hope you're not going to be difficult tonight. It's too late and I'm too tired to put up with your shit."

"We'll go along for now," McGarvey said.

"Good," Bambridge said. "You'll ride with me. Ms. Boylan will ride in the second car."

"No. And we won't be separated at the safe house."

Bambridge's anger immediately deepened. "I don't want to force the issue, goddamnit."

"No, you don't, Marty. And neither do we. We'll sit still for the debriefing, and then we'll get out of the company's way. But you have to know that the problem hasn't gone away, even though I was personally responsible for the deaths of an ISI officer and three of the four dacoits he'd hired to kill Pete and me. That was after they'd kidnapped her and tried to rape her."

"I killed the bastard," Pete said.

Bambridge shook his head. "God save us all," he said. "Backseat in my car for the both of you."

One of the security officers opened the door for them. "Welcome back, Mr. Director. Rough op?"

"It had its moments. Davis?"

"Yes, sir."

"How are your wife and son?"

"Just fine, sir. Thanks for asking. But we've added a girl."

"Congratulations."

"Jesus," Bambridge muttered.

The safe house, one of several on campus, had once been someone's home out in the Virginia woods just up the hill from the Potomac. Three bedrooms upstairs under low-hanging eaves, and downstairs a kitchen, living room, and the dining room, which had been converted into a soft interrogation or debriefing conference space, with a table for six. A flip of the light switch turned on an electronic suite of equipment: everything said or done in the room was recorded by six cameras and several sensitive microphones mounted in full view on the walls and ceiling. In addition, body temperatures of everyone in the room were continuously monitored, as were facial expressions, which were measured against a series of parameters that Otto had designed to detect stress. The equipment was more reliable than a lie detector apparatus.

The entire house was in a Faraday cage—wire mesh inside the walls and ceiling that made cell phones or any sort of Wi-Fi equipment useless.

They had been left alone, on their word that they wouldn't run off. Shortly after dawn a company chef came over and fixed them coffee and a full breakfast of eggs Benedict, hash browns, and orange juice.

Toiletries and fresh clothes in their sizes had been brought over—jeans, polo shirts, and underwear.

At eight sharp, Bambridge, along with Pete's former partner, Dan Green, showed up. As a team they had been the CIA's most effective interrogators, until she had been bounced over to the National Clandestine Service. She hadn't been given a field assignment after she had joined forces with McGarvey a couple of years ago on an operation here in the Washington area. For that reason, among others, she'd been out of favor with the DDO.

Green who was a short little man, under five feet, with a head too large for his slight body, and wide, soft brown eyes that seemed to understand and completely sympathize with everyone, came into the front hall with a big smile. He and Pete embraced.

"I heard that you and Mr. McGarvey were back in town and I had to come over to at least say hi," he said.

"I'm glad it's you," Pete said. "We can get this over with in an hour."

"Don't be so sure," Bambridge said.

"Ms. Boylan doesn't know how to lie, sir," Green said.

The four of them went into the dining room, and Bambridge made a show of flipping the switch. When they were settled around the table, Green began.

"Mr. McGarvey, let's start, shall we, with a simple narrative outline of the facts, the times and places, the casualties, the circumstances. The to-and-fro details. We'll fill in the blanks later, if you don't mind."

"It didn't turn out the way we wanted it to," McGarvey said.

"These sorts of things never do, do they?"

McGarvey ran through everything, including the business in Norfolk and the interrogation of Steffen Engel, which led them to Pakistan and the business at Naisir's safe house. It took less than ten minutes.

Bambridge was obviously uncomfortable, but he kept his agitation to himself and said nothing.

"Anything to add or subtract?" Green asked Pete.

"Only that the bastard major ordered one of his goons to rape me. But I killed him instead." She looked pointedly at Bambridge. "I'm pretty sure that wasn't in the ISI's playbook."

"And the major's wife and the German terrorist, Pamela Schlueter?"

"They're at large," McGarvey said.

Green turned to Bambridge. "I'm finished, sir."

"I have a few more questions," the DDO said.

"They are telling the truth."

"You can't be sure."

"Yes, sir, I can," Green said. They all got up and Green and Pete embraced again. "You were limping. Are you okay?"

"I banged up my knee a little, nothing serious," Pete said. "May and the kids are fine?"

Green smiled. "Do you have any idea what an orthodontist charges for braces?"

"Not a clue."

"Don't ask," Green said. He shook hands with McGarvey. "Good to see you again, sir. And good hunting."

FIFTY-ONE

☐

Bambridge drove McGarvey and Pete over to the Old Headquarters Building, busy with the morning shift arriving, and upstairs they went to the director's seventh-floor office. Walt Page and Carleton Patterson were waiting for them and Otto breezed in a moment later.

"Am I late?" he asked.

"No," Page said and he directed them to have a seat. His expression was even sterner this morning than normal. His was a banker's face in the middle of a financial meltdown.

McGarvey and Otto had talked at length over the Atlantic last night about the situation here, the only puzzle being the assassination of Wolf at the hands of some unknown gunman. The biggest question of all was the BND's reluctance to find out why he'd been killed. Apparently he was at the wrong place at the wrong time, and he was robbed and his car stolen. The stripped VW Jetta was found the same day in an industrial section of Berlin. Case closed.

It was their relationship with Pakistan—similar to that of Washington's. The ongoing fight against the Taliban was primary: all other considerations were off the table.

"We're in a difficult situation, for which I'm expected to give some advice to the president as quickly as possible," Page said. "The fact of the matter is I have nothing of value to tell him."

"The situation with the attacks on SEAL Team Six team is not over," McGarvey said, but Page raised a hand.

"If you're right about that, which you very well may be, it's not the situation I'm talking about. Pakistan and India have been rattling sabers over the past twenty-four hours. As of early this morning our surveillance satellites detected the activation of missile installations along the border with Kashmir. Pakistan's Ra'ad ALCMs and India's new Nirbhays, both of which are nuclear-tipped, are at the ready or will be very soon."

"It's happened before," McGarvey said. "And you can't tell me that we had anything to do with the escalation."

"It can't have helped," Bambridge told Page. "I assume that you've had the time to read the transcript of their debriefing this morning."

"Yes," Page said.

"And so have I," Patterson said. "Nothing in it would indicate some flash point being crossed, though their actions at this time, as Marty suggested, could not have helped. A gun battle between an ISI major and his wife, plus another woman, and the former director of this agency and one of our current employees was a political slap against President Mamnoon Hussain. The fact that you entered Pakistan under false passports—diplomatic passports—was another serious slap against this agency and the White House."

"The president's national security adviser knew the score," McGarvey said, though he didn't know why he was defending himself.

"Yes, and he told you that you would be on your own," Page said. He was angry. "But not that you would drag along Ms. Boylan, not that you would use our assets on the ground, or borrow one of our Gulfstreams and crew to pick you up in London."

"That was my doing, Mr. Director," Otto said.

"That's beside the point. Our Islamabad station is in shambles and Don Simmons has threatened to resign just when we need him the most."

"Did Milt Thomas get out?"

Page was vexed. "Yes. He managed to make it overland just outside Peshawar, where an army helicopter picked him up and flew him across the border to Jalalabad. Also a consequence of the mess you created. As it was they made it across the border minutes before a pair of Pakistani fighter jets showed up."

"He's a good man. None of it was his fault."

"No," Page said sharply. "Yours."

"Yes," McGarvey said, suddenly sick to death with all the bullshit. Page was a good man, but he was too caught up in the political consequences of dealing with a crisis—not of his making, or of anyone else's in his office—that he had lost sight of the reality of the situation.

"That's a refreshing change," Bambridge said.

"The saber rattling between Pakistan and India is just that. Showmanship for their electorates. Pakistan's president is under a lot of pressure because the country is falling apart. Their financial structure is crumbling, electricity is a major problem even in the bigger cities—Islamabad included—and although we're winning the war against the Taliban, a sufficient percentage of his electorate support the terrorists to the extent that they resent our drone strikes. So what's a beleaguered head of state supposed to do? Fix the problems? Impossible in the short run. So he does the next best—shift the focus elsewhere."

No one said anything.

"I sat in your chair, Walt, and I didn't much like it," McGarvey continued. "Tell the president what you know and leave the speculation to someone else. This is the Central Intelligence Agency—not the Central Second-Guessing Agency. Leave that to the national intelligence director; she seems to be good at it."

"So where does that leave you at this point?" Page asked.

"Has there been any direct response from anyone in Pakistan about what went down?"

"None. Pat Garrick assured me that there've been no phone calls or e-mails in the past thirty-six hours concerning the—incident." Air Force Lieutenant General Patrick Garrick was director of the National Security Agency, which monitored just about everything electronic just about everywhere.

"About what I expected."

"John wants to have a chat with you." John Fay was the president's national security adviser.

"I'm not going to have the time," McGarvey said, and he got to his feet. "If there's nothing else, Mr. Director?"

Bambridge was pissed off, but Page held him off. "Tell me that you're not going back to Pakistan."

"I'm staying here. They're coming to me."

"You're convinced that the attacks against the SEAL Team Six will continue?" Patterson said. "Even though they know that you have become personally involved?"

"I think so. Partly because they believe that neither the CIA, the FBI, nor the ONI are willing to get involved."

"Could be the two murders are isolated incidents?"

"No," McGarvey said. "I'm going to need Ms. Boylan and Otto."

"Not a chance in hell," Bambridge said.

"Try to stop me, sir, and I'll resign," Pete said, getting up.

Otto was grinning ear to ear as he got to his feet. "You wouldn't want me to resign. Be your worst nightmare."

"You're convinced the threat is real?" Page asked.

"Yes, I am."

"What next, then?" Patterson asked.

"We're going to try to save these guys from themselves."

FIFTY-TWO

Page's advice to Bambridge was to stay out of McGarvey's way. And after his DDO was gone, he asked Patterson to remain. "I'd like an extra set of ears."

"Do you think he'll take your call?"

"Won't hurt to try," Page said, not at all surprised that the company's general counsel had suspected what was coming next. "We've talked before. Unofficially."

Patterson nodded.

Page phoned the ISI's director general on an unofficial private line. It was a little past four in the afternoon in Islamabad, and the call was answered on the second ring.

"Good afternoon, Tariq. I hope that your day was not as difficult as mine has started out to be."

"Good morning, Walter. My day has been interesting, but then it is an expected part of positions men like us manage to get ourselves into."

"How are Maryam, and your children and grandchildren? In good health, I hope?"

"Yes, of course, thank you for asking. But I don't spend as much time with my wife these days as I would like; she is almost always with our daughter and the two babies."

"She must be in her glory."

"And Betty is well?"

"Yes, I'll send her your regards."

"Please do," Bhutani said. "What is on your mind, my friend?"

"The developing situation in Kashmir. It has us concerned."

"It has been a running debate for some years now; you know this as well as anyone. But I can assure you that there will not be a war any time soon."

"I thought not."

The line was silent for several beats, until Bhutani came back. "Kashmir is not the reason you telephoned. What is on your mind, Walter?"

"The recent trouble in Rawalpindi. I've been told that one of your officers had been shot to death in some altercation."

Bhutani chuckled. "I must congratulate your Mr. Simmons and his agents for their fast work. Our Federal Investigation Agency is conducting an independent inquiry. The first reports I've seen indicate that Major Naisir was gunned down by bandits. We call them dacoits. Very probably hired by enemies of the major's wife. Her family is wealthy, and wealth always attracts its adversaries. I'm told that there have been incidents of the same nature in the past, and unfortunately there may be others in the future."

"It is unfortunate," Page said.

"What concern is the death of one of my junior officers to the CIA?"

"We were trying to track the whereabouts of one of our citizens—Indian-born—who we think might be dealing in arms smuggling to the Taliban fighters on the border. We traced him as far as a hotel there in Islamabad, and perhaps he was in Rawalpindi on the day of the shooting. I was hoping that if he was involved, you would let us know."

"Yes, we too are investigating this man. Poorvaj Chopra. He has disappeared, and it may be possible that he was involved, but there have been no witnesses."

"If an American citizen was involved, then you have my apologies, and a promise that I'll do everything within my power to see that it does not happen again."

"But then it is an internal problem, one that we will handle. Once he is arrested, he will be placed under the jurisdiction of our legal system."

"If he were to reach our embassy, however, he would be placed under arrest, and I would hope that he could be brought back to the United States to stand trial."

"That would be a matter for our governments to decide," Bhutani said.

"Of course."

"Is there anything else that we need to discuss?"

"No, but thank you for your assurance on the situation in Kashmir. May I pass it along to the White House?"

Bhutani hesitated for just a beat. "Merely as my opinion, Walter. My job, like yours, is merely to gather information and offer advice. Whether our governments actually take such advice is another matter."

"I understand, Tariq. A pleasure talking with you."

"Likewise," Bhutani said, and he rang off.

"He knows that Chopra does not exist," Patterson said. "I could hear it in his voice. It's very difficult to lie in a language other than your own."

"But he didn't name McGarvey."

"It would not have accomplished a thing, except to admit that there might be something to the story that Pakistan is financing an operation against SEAL Team Six."

"Even the White House and the navy can't accept it, because of Pakistan's tacit acceptance of our drone strikes, and now because of Kashmir. The situation is too incredibly delicate."

"I agree. So what do we do?"

"Just like I told Marty, stay out of McGarvey's way."

"We can't support him."

"No," Page said. "But Otto will and so will Ms. Boylan, and I'm sure that Otto's wife still has her connections. The real problem is the same as it has always been. There's not much that we can do for him."

"One of these days he'll find himself outgunned," Patterson said gloomily. He got to his feet. "I'm getting too old for this."

"So am I," Page said. "Let's hope Mac isn't."

FIFTY-THREE

☐

Ayesha walked up the gentle slope in the Islamabad Graveyard, past row after row of stones and tablets back to where her husband had been buried the morning after his death, as was Islamic custom. It was early evening. The lights of the city were behind her; only the lights of the PAEC General Hospital were visible up the hill from her.

She'd parked her car at the side of the Faqir Aipee Road, just off the Kashmir Highway and had gone the rest of the way on foot. She was leaving for Germany later this evening, her packed bags in the car. It was possible that she would never be able to come home, and she wanted to say good-bye one last time to her husband.

He had been a good man to her, never resenting her family's fortune or her advice. In fact she believed that over the past several years, since the incident with President Musharraf, he had actually depended on her. And for that she felt the loss all the more keenly.

But she did not cry. She'd been the only girl in the family, and she'd grown up tough, entirely capable of holding her own among men. Her father and uncles and brothers never cried, nor did she.

She got to his grave site and stepped to one side of the simple headstone. He could have been buried in the military cemetery, but he'd once told her that he belonged here with the common people. He was no hero, nor would he ever be, so he felt it wasn't right that he should be buried with soldiers who'd died on the battlefield. Nor did he want to be buried in the private cemetery where Ayesha's people were laid to rest.

So here he was. A common man: in fact one of the last to be buried in a cemetery hardly a half century old and already full.

"He should not be here," General Bhutani said behind her.

She turned. "You startled me, General." Two bodyguards stood a few meters away.

"It wasn't my intention, Ayesha. But he deserved a soldier's burial."

"He wanted it this way, but not so soon."

"I agree. Too soon. And for the wrong reasons—still another affront to our dignity."

She looked again at her husband's gravestone. "Why did you come here, at this particular time? Certainly not to visit the grave of a simple major?"

If Bhutani took any offense at her tone, he did not show it. "I was told that you were leaving for the airport, and I wanted to talk to you in person—not on the telephone—before you left."

"You followed me?"

"Yes. And I wasn't surprised when you stopped here."

Bhutani and his family were crude, in Ayesha's father's opinion. Only a generation or two from simple mountain tribespeople. Lacking in manners and modern sensibilities. Perfect for the role of ISI director. And in many ways, in her estimation, exactly the same as McGarvey, the former director of the CIA. Violent men, devious, skulking around, peering into other people's lives for some prurient interests in the name of national security. And she was sure that her expression showed her contempt, because his face darkened.

"Why are you going to Germany? What's there for you so soon after your husband's death? The rug business?"

"A vacation before we and India destroy each other over petty religion. I have a plane to catch. I don't want to be late."

"It will be held if you are not on time," Bhutani said, his tone harsh now. "Or not, if I have you taken in for interrogation."

"I don't think you would want to do that, General Bhutani. The consequences might not be to your superiors' liking."

"A risk I am willing to take in order to convince you that I am on your side. I know about Ms. Schlueter and the operation your husband hired her to run, just as I know about her part in the incident in Rawalpindi. She is back in Germany now, and I believe that you are joining her there, perhaps to avenge your husband's death by continuing the mission."

"And which mission is that?" Ayesha demanded. Her heart pounded. Buffoon or not, Bhutani was powerful.

"Retribution for the American raid at Abbottabad. Two have been eliminated; twenty-two remain."

"I would think that you would have your hands full spying on India to bother with something so insignificant."

"Not insignificant to some in our government who want to see such a thing happen. Of course your husband understood the delicate balance we have to maintain between ourselves and Washington and between us and our population."

"You didn't support him."

"But we did, to the extent that was politically possible."

"He's dead!"

"He was a soldier; he understood the risks."

"Now you want me to take up the battle."

Bhutani smiled wryly. "Isn't that why you're flying to Germany tonight?" he said. "We can support you financially, and with intelligence information, but the actual operation will have to be carried out by whoever Ms. Schuelter hires. They're expendable."

"As am I?"

"Yes," Bhutani said.

Ayesha held her silence for a moment. She hadn't expected the ISI director to be here, though what he was telling her *was* expected. But now that it was in her face, to some extent even more than the fact of her husband's death, when she was on the verge of flying to Berlin, it was superreal for the first time. People were going die—possibly she herself.

She glanced again at her husband's grave. "What are my chances?"

"I don't know, but I expect they will be near zero for the entire mission unless you convince Ms. Schlueter to first take care of one thing."

"Mr. McGarvey."

"Yes. You must do everything within your power to eliminate the man, and my agency will supply you with money."

Ayesha looked at him. She was a businesswoman. "How much money?"

"Unlimited," Bhutani said. "Kill McGarvey."

FIFTY-FOUR

Ayesha phoned Pam from the airport to tell her she was in Germany. It was midnight local time, and she asked for directions or for someone to pick her up.

"What the hell are you doing here?"

"Protecting my investment. Did you receive the money?"

"Yes, and we're making plans at this moment. Go home, Mrs. Naisir. Grieve for your husband. Help your family with their rug business and leave this sort of thing to me."

"You didn't do so good in Rawalpindi."

"Because of the setup, which was your husband's fault. I'm sorry, but you and I were lucky to get out of there alive, and I think you understand that. Go home."

"If you force the issue, I'll send no more money. You'll be on your own. In any event I have some other news for you, and a direct request from someone very important, but we have to discuss it in private."

"You have no idea how difficult you're making the situation by coming here," Pam said.

"It's your call," Ayesha countered. "I can get a hotel room for the night and fly home first thing in the morning, in which case you're going to gain some powerful enemies. Either that or you can come pick me up."

"What airline?"

"Air Berlin."

"Fifteen minutes," Pam said, and hung up.

Ayesha finished her tea. Then she shouldered her carry-on bag and went down to the baggage claim area to wait at the doors, not at all sure exactly why she had come to Berlin, except that she wasn't used to giving away her money without maintaining some control.

Pam arrived in a beat-up red Mercedes that had to be at least twenty years old. Ayesha got in. "We have a lot to talk about," she said.

"We certainly do," Pam said. "We're meeting with my operators tonight, and they're going to have some pretty tough questions about why you're sticking your nose into this business. And they have the right to some straight answers because their lives are on the line."

"The situation in Pakistan right now is very tense."

"Your government can't seriously be thinking about going to war over a worthless piece of real estate."

"Probably not, but our relations with the United States have weakened."

Pam glanced at her. "Who knows you're here?"

"General Bhutani."

"The director of the ISI?"

"Yes, and he's agreed that the service will pick up the cost of the operation. He made an offer of unlimited funding, but with one condition."

"Which is?"

"That we kill McGarvey before finishing with the SEALs."

The abandoned warehouse in Spandau, Berlin's industrial sector, had once housed the manufacture and storage of high-voltage transformers and heavy-duty electrical switches dating back to before World War II. For a time, after the wall had come down and the two Germanys had reunited, the sprawling and partially damaged facility had been used to temporarily billet and process the hundreds of thousands of internal refugees fleeing the former east zone.

It had been closed down five years ago, and now only some Turkish, Polish, and Romanian squatters came and went. It was scheduled to be demolished sometime in the coming months. In the meantime the police never bothered with the place.

Pam drove in through an open service door and parked at the foot

of some stairs that led to what had been a foreman's office overlook-
ing the work floor.

Two men armed with 9mm Uzi submachine guns waited just
inside the door. Two others were spread out against the back wall of
the room beyond three metal desks, a couple of file cabinets, and a
large drafting table. Many of the ceiling tiles were down, and the
floor was littered with debris and animal droppings. Only the background glow from the city penetrated the windows, many of which
were broken.

Pam explained that Ayesha had come not only with additional
money but with instructions, which the four men didn't want to
hear. But they lowered their weapons.

Felix Volker, one of the two at the door, looked Ayesha up and
down. "Money's good, but I'll be fucked if I'll take orders from some
raghead broad."

"Then leave now while you still can, Herr Volker," Ayesha shot
back.

"Son of a bitch, how do you know my name?" Volker demanded.
He looked at Pam. "Is it you with the big mouth?"

"No."

The general had given Ayesha a dossier on the men Pam Schlueter
probably had working for her. He had gotten it from Ayesha's husband, who had gotten it from Pam herself. "Herr Bruns," Ayesha said
to the other man just inside the doorway. "Herr Woedding, Herr
Heiser."

"So you know our names, so what?" Woedding said. He was toy-
ing with the safety catch on his weapon, a wildness in his eyes, as if
he were about to crack up.

"The intelligence service of my country is pretty good. They've
agreed to help with the first part of the mission, after which you
would be on your own, except for the funding."

"Apparently it didn't do your husband or the street muscle he
hired any good. It got them killed."

"One man."

"Yes, Kirk McGarvey, the former director of the CIA, and once
upon a time a pretty good shooter in his own right."

"He killed my husband, and we want him dead. Job one."

Woedding looked at the others. "Maybe we'll kill McGarvey, as you wish, then take our money and run."

"We'd find you."

Woedding shrugged. "We're pretty good."

"We have no gripe with the SEAL Team Six guys," Heiser said. "They were just soldiers like us."

Nothing like you, Ayesha wanted to say, but didn't. "With McGarvey out of the way, I can't see you turning down the money."

"You weren't specific," Pam said. "How much money?"

"Name your price, Frau Schlueter. We'll double it."

FIFTY-FIVE

☐

Walter Page's limousine was admitted through the White House West Gate a few minutes past six in the afternoon. He was met at the portico by John Raleigh, an aide to John Fay.

"Good afternoon, sir. They're waiting for you in the Situation Room."

Fay had called him at two requesting the meeting. He'd only said it had to do with the Kashmir situation but wouldn't elaborate. Page had spent most of the afternoon in the Watch down the hall from his office where five analysts dealt with a constant stream of information coming from U.S. satellite assets and other intelligence resources from around the world.

All he'd learned was that India and Pakistan continued to mobilize their forces along the border, but to this point there'd been no accidents, no exchange of artillery fire, as had been common for several years.

The only disquieting facts were that both sides had a significant portion of their missiles fueled and made ready, and that a small contingent of Chinese military advisers had arrived in Islamabad early this morning.

Raleigh left him at the open door to the Situation Room in the West Wing. The mood among the people around the long table was subdued. The president had not yet arrived, but his chief of staff was already seated, as were a stern-faced Fay, the secretary of state, the director of the National Security Agency, the director of National Intelligence, the chairman of the Joint Chiefs, the secretaries of Defense, Treasury, Interior, Homeland Security, the ambassador to the

UN, and the attorney general. The thirteen, plus Page, constituted the majority of the Security Council.

Most of the others looked up and nodded when he came in and took his seat.

Madeline Bible, the director of National Intelligence, was seated next to him. She leaned over. "What's this about the Chinese in Islamabad?"

"I just got it myself, and our confidence is not all that high. I was going to ask what you'd heard and what your sources were."

The president came in and everyone rose. He swept to his chair and motioned them down. "Thank you for coming on such short notice. As you all know, the situation in Kashmir between Pakistan and India has ratcheted up overnight. I'm told that a shooting war has become a real possibility."

"I'm afraid that's the conclusion my people have come to," Bible said. "I've prepared a brief summary, which outlines the intelligence data we've collected over the past several months." She passed copies of the thick spiral-bound report to the president and the others.

"Give me the highlights," Langdon said.

"Until this morning I would have advised that the chances of an all-out conflict were less than twenty percent. Something under the normal level over the past several years. But we learned that a delegation of high-ranking Chinese military officers arrived in Islamabad this morning and met with President Mamnoon Hussain and his cabinet, including his military advisers. Though the exact content of that meeting is unknown, we must presume that the Chinese have offered their help in the form of advice, possibly of a strategic nature."

"No," Page said out loud. "I'm sorry, Madeline, but that's reckless."

She started to object, but the president held her off.

"Walt?"

"My people tell me that the Chinese may have sent a peace delegation. Zhang Wei and Xiang Pandi are with the group."

"I'm not sure I know the names."

"Intellectuals," Dr. John Boettner, the secretary of state, said. "Doves. Peace advocates. They've argued in some of the journals that a nuclear war between Pakistan and India over Kashmir could easily spread east over the Himalayas into China."

"Words are cheaper than bombs," Bible said.

"It would be in their best interest to prevent a nuclear exchange," Page said. "In addition I spoke with General Bhutani yesterday afternoon, and he assured me that there would be no war."

"That was an unauthorized contact, Walt," Fay said.

"My call was unofficial and was about another completely separate matter."

"Yes?" Fay prompted when Page didn't continue.

The president interrupted. "You have something of a personal relationship with the general, isn't that right?"

"Yes, sir. I've been to Islamabad twice to see him, and we met again in New York at last year's Global Conference on Intelligence Issues. When I spoke to him yesterday I couldn't detect any stress in his voice."

"Were there translators?" Bible asked.

"No, his English is adequate. But my people tell me that it's difficult at best to lie in a language foreign to your own."

"I know some pretty good liars," Bible said.

I'll bet you do, Page wanted to say, but he held his tongue. He didn't like the woman, and it had nothing to do with her gender. She was a politician first, an intelligence director second.

The president turned to the chairman of the Joint Chiefs, General Bruce Ringers, who'd held just about every important post in the military since his graduation from West Point thirty-five years ago, including combat roles in Kosovo, the first and second Iraq wars, and briefly at the beginning of the conflict in Afghanistan. He and Secretary of Defense Matthew Koratich were close personal friends, and the secretary-chairman working relationship was better than any in history. Under the two men things were getting done—including the top-down reorganization of the entire military-industrial juggernaut.

"What's your assessment, Bruce?"

"They've been there before, and each time they've backed off before things could go too far."

"I hear a but in there."

"Yes, sir. Having that much military hardware in such close prox-imity is inherently dangerous. Sooner or later someone will make a mistake, which could touch off a conflict. In this case an exchange of nuclear weapons, even if only theater size, could touch off a much larger regional war. The casualties would be massive."

"Surely that's not their intent?" the president asked.

"No, sir," Koratich said. "But as Bruce said, mistakes will happen sooner or later."

"The Chinese have sent a delegation to Islamabad. Maybe we should send someone to New Delhi. Or if the situation is already dangerously close to the brink, you might want to telephone Prime Minister Narendra Modi."

"I'll do both," Langdon said. He turned again to Ringers. "What's our military response?"

"If you mean go to a DEFCON 4, I'd advise against it. Not unless you would want a measured response if hostilities actually start."

"Christ, no," the president said. After a beat he got to his feet. "Keep me advised," he said, and he left the room.

Page was the last to head down the corridor when Fay pulled him aside. "The president would like to have a brief word. We'll meet him in the Oval Office."

"I've had no update on McGarvey," Langdon said. "I assume he went to Pakistan. Is he back safely?"

"Yes, sir," Page said. He went through everything that had hap-pened in Islamabad and at the safe house in Rawalpindi, including McGarvey's opinion as a former DCI that the current issue over Kashmir was merely saber rattling by President Mamnoon Hussain to appease a population sick of power outages and an economy that was in meltdown.

"Nothing was settled by his going to Pakistan?" the president asked.

"No, sir, except that an ISI major who apparently was the paymas-ter for the group that has already killed two of the SEAL Team Six operators and their families was himself killed in a shootout."

"Then it's over?"

"McGarvey doesn't think so."

"What's next?"

I think he's going to offer himself up as a lightning rod."

FIFTY-SIX

□

KLM Flight 1824 from Berlin landed at Montreal's Trudeau International Airport a few minutes before five in the afternoon after a ten-and-a-half-hour flight. All but the first class passengers looked shell-shocked.

Ayesha was traveling under a very good British passport that identified her as Suzanne Reynolds from London. She went through customs and immigration with no trouble and headed down to the rental car counters as planned.

Pam was four passengers behind her, traveling under a U.S. passport identifying her as Janice Whittaker from Milwaukee.

"Do you have anything to declare?" the agent asked her, looking at her customs form.

"No," Pam said, keeping her face straight. It was possible McGarvey had come up with a photo of her, but it wasn't likely that it would have been distributed to airports here in Canada. Before they had left Berlin she had dyed her hair dark brown and had her passport photo taken wearing glasses.

The immigration officer stared her for several long beats, but then handed back her passport. "Welcome to Canada, ma'am."

Downstairs Ayesha was waiting near the Hertz counter on the ground floor of the parking garage. She looked nervous. "Was there a problem?"

"No."

"You were delayed."

"You should have stayed in Islamabad, if you're going to act that way. This is the easy part."

"I'm sticking with my investment. I won't get in the way."

"You're already in the way," Pam said, and she got in line for a car.

Ayesha's husband had been made of the same stuff as his wife. He had been the paymaster and he had stuck his nose where it hadn't belonged because he wanted to be the one in charge. He had made a mistake by coming face-to-face with McGarvey, and it had ended with his death. It had been so stupid. But without his connection to the money there would not have been an operation, a fact he had pointed out to her from the beginning. Now she was stuck with the woman.

Pam looked back at her and smiled. Perhaps the woman would be shot to death in the end after she had made the final payment. Like husband, like wife.

The car was a Ford Fusion with a full tank of gas. Forty-five minutes after they'd touched down, they were merging with heavy work traffic on Highway 20, heading north toward the Highway 10 Pont Champlain Bridge across the St. Lawrence River that would lead to Highway 15 south, and shortly thereafter the U.S. border and Interstate 87.

"We need to get something perfectly clear before we hit the border," Pam said. She'd been checking her rearview mirror since they'd left the airport. So far as she could tell they were clean.

"Don't lecture me," Ayesha shot back.

"I will and you'll listen, because our lives depend on it. The guys you met in Berlin are professionals. All of them ex-special forces with the German army. Some of the best badasses in the world, and they won't stand for any of your rich-girl shit."

"But I'm the one with the money."

"Money is important, but they value their lives more. If for one instant they think that you're leading us down a back alley with no way out, they'll kill both of us with no compunction and run."

"I said that I'd stay out of the way."

"More than that, keep your mouth shut."

Ayesha turned away for a moment. "Why are you constantly looking in the rearview mirror?"

"Because McGarvey is a sharp bastard, and by now he's probably guessed that I'm coming after him. In fact he may be counting on it. And I wouldn't put it past him to have someone looking for me."

"For us," Ayesha said quietly. "I'm doing it for my husband; you're doing it for money."

"For more than that. Much more."

Traffic had thinned out just before the border, which was about fifty-five miles south of Montreal, but then bunched up at the checkpoint. On the Canadian side they had to show their driving licenses and the car rental contract when it was their turn. They were ten cars back.

"Busy today," Pam said, handing their papers out the window.

"They're looking for someone," the border patrol agent said.

"Anyone specific?" Pam asked, hoping that Ayesha wouldn't panic.

"They've been paranoid since 9/11."

"Can't blame us."

The agent looked up and smiled. "I guess not," he said. He looked at Ayesha. "You okay, ma'am? You look a little green."

Pam didn't have a pistol, and they were pretty well stuck here, with no way back and no way forward.

Ayesha smiled weakly. "We just came crossed the Atlantic. Calm flight. But I get airsick no matter what."

The officer nodded. "My wife's the same way, and nothing helps." He handed back their papers, stepped aside, and waved the next car forward.

Pam drove the several yards to the line on the American side. "You did good," she said. "But you don't have much to worry about. If they catch you they'll merely send you back to Pakistan. I'm a different story."

The wait was nearly a half hour, and the line behind them was long enough that cars were backed up on the Canadian side. When it was their turn at one of the lanes Pam handed their papers out the window to the border agent, while another used a mirror on a long handle to check the undercarriage.

"Open the trunk, please," the officer said as he looked over their passports and the car rental contract.

Pam opened the trunk and a third officer went around to the back.

"Where were you born?" the officer asked Pam.

"Milwaukee."

"Still have relatives there?"

"My mom and dad are dead, and I have no brothers or sisters. Friends."

"Where do you work?"

"In the bottling plant at Schafer's Brewery. It's on Wisconsin Avenue."

"What was the purpose of your visit to Canada?"

"Honeymoon. We got married last week."

The customs officer looked at her, and then at Ayesha, who was embarrassed. After a beat, he handed back their papers. The officer at the rear closed the trunk lid and the one with the mirror stepped aside.

"If your partner is going to live here, she'll need a green card."

"Yes, sir," Pam said and the officer waved them on.

Ayesha started to say something, but Pam held her off until they were well out of sight of the border crossing and on the open interstate.

"We're partners, so don't forget it."

"But why? It's disgusting, and illegal."

"Not here, but I wanted to give the asshole something to focus on other than our papers. And it worked."

FIFTY-SEVEN

They were temporarily bunking at the Renckes' off-the-grid house on a pleasant street in McClean across the river from Falls Church. The company knew that Otto had his bunker, but no one on campus thought it was such a good idea to go looking for it.

McGarvey had taken Pete over to All Saints Hospital in George-town to get her knee looked at. The small facility tucked away on a side street was used to treat wounded intelligence service officers—mostly from the CIA—in secret. Luckily, it was nothing more than a dislocated kneecap that would heal itself in time.

They stopped afterward at their apartments and got fresh clothes, and in McGarvey's case, his go-to-hell kit of spare Walther and magazines, several sets of IDs, and cash—in case he needed to get out of the country in a hurry.

"You think it could come to that?" Pete had asked.

"If we miss Schlueter I might have to follow her. And there might not be enough time to get my things."

It was early evening by the time they got back. Louise was doing steaks on the grill in the backyard.

"She does the cooking. I open the beer and wine," Otto said, grinning.

The weather was pleasant and they sat at a picnic table out on the patio. Otto had taken to smoking cigarettes—three each day—but although Louise was on his case she really didn't push it. Smoking was bad, but it had replaced his old habits of drinking heavy cream by the quart and eating Twinkies by the dozen. He'd actually slimmed down and looked pretty good.

Mac and Pete slept in separate rooms, Louise's doing, and no one mentioned anything about it, though everyone, including Mac, felt the tension and the way Pete looked at him.

"There's been nothing from the Pakistanis about the incident, which isn't all that surprising considering what they're facing right now," Otto said. "So what's next?"

"The White House and the company are staying out of our way for the moment, and the navy is ignoring the whole problem," McGarvey said. "All but three of the guys are out of the service, none of them retired, and so far none of them has asked for help."

"Proud," Louise said.

"Yeah."

"Remind you of anyone we know?"

McGarvey was at a loss.

"She means you, Kirk," Pete said.

He guessed that they were right, but it was neither here nor there. "Schlueter and her team are coming back to finish the job, and I think that the ISI will continue to finance them. And the timing is probably good considering the fact that our focus is on the situation between them and India, especially now with the Chinese involved."

"Their first target has to be you," Otto said. "You stopped them once in Norfolk, and you threw a monkey wrench in the works in Islamabad."

"Right. And I'm going to make it easy for them. I'm going to be right out in the open, so as far as they're concerned they'll be getting two for one."

"We're going to make it easy for them," Pete said.

"No."

"Have Marty fire me and I'll tag along as a civilian."

McGarvey started to press his protest, but Louise interrupted.

"What do you have in mind?" she asked. "Something here in Washington where we can control the situation?"

"Norfolk. Greg Rautanen—the Ratman—one of the SEAL Team Six guys. He's married but they don't have any children, and right now his wife is living with her sister in Seattle. He's screwed up, and maybe an alcoholic, and probably on the verge of having his house foreclosed."

No one had to ask how he'd come by the information, because it was obviously Otto's doing.

"Why him?" Louise asked, not liking what she was hearing.

"No family close at hand, no friends, no social or neighborhood ties. He's a lone wolf. If it's just the two of us, the collateral damage will be minimal—zero if I can help it. And the guy was a SEAL Team Six operator."

"Okay, so you want them to come after you," Louise said. "I see that. But first you'd have to advertise where you are. How?"

"Dick Cole."

"DEVGRU's chief of staff?" Pete asked.

"Acting chief of staff," Otto clarified. "There're some unspecified issues in his file, which means it's just a temporary assignment until he screws up again, at which time he'll be dumped. He's already been passed over twice for his first star, and the third time is the deal breaker."

Louise was shaking her head. "What good will it do telling him what you're up to?" she said. But then she suddenly got it. "You think he's a leak?"

"Schlueter knew too much about my movements," McGarvey said. "Cole did a stint in the Pentagon, and I'm betting that he still has some contacts over there willing to do him a favor from time to time."

"Only the CIA knew what was going on. He'd have to have a friend in Operations."

"Which he doesn't, as far as I can determine," Otto said. "I've doubled-checked everyone on Marty's staff who could have had access to that kind of stuff."

"Another Snowden—maybe a contractor?" Pete asked.

"I don't know," McGarvey admitted. "But my first impression in his office was that the guy had some agenda of his own, and he was seriously pissed off at me for coming to him with questions about his ex-wife."

"I'm sorry, but if that's a hunch, it's one of your worst," Louise said.

"I'll find out when I talk to him again and tell him what I'm going to do, and why."

"Which is?" Otto asked.

McGarvey hadn't told anyone what his plan was, though he sus-pected that Otto had probably figured it out when he'd been asked to find one of the SEAL Team Six guys who was alone for the moment. And maybe someone who was screwed up and had been written off because of it. None of the guys were homeless yet, but Rautanen was close to becoming so—one of the 25 percent of homeless men who were combat veterans. No one gave a damn about them, not the military in which they had served or a nation for which they had laid their lives on the line.

"I'm going to tell Cole that Schlueter is coming after me, as well as the SEAL Team Six operators, and I'm going to use him as bait."

Louise took a deep draft of her beer. "Now, why didn't I think of that," she said.

Pete was nodding. "I'll cover your back."

FIFTY-EIGHT

Coming through customs at Mexico City's Benito Juárez International Airport Felix Volker was in a rare good mood. Today was his thirty-ninth birthday. He was fit, he was going into an op that wasn't going to be easy—therefore it would be satisfying—and when it was done, he would be a rich man, relatively speaking.

He'd been born to a factory worker father outside of Leipzig in what had been the war-shattered east zone, and a mother who spent her days reading smuggled American movie magazines rather than cook or clean. His two older sisters—dead now for all he cared—had taken after their mother and were nasty-tongued slobs who had taught him all about sex, starting when he was about five.

Felix had made his way across the border into the west in the woods south of Lubeck with his uncle Bruno a year before the fall of the wall when he was thirteen. For the next four years he bounced between construction jobs and some state-sponsored welfare programs until he was eighteen and could join the Bundeswehr, where he had been taught to kill with a variety of weapons, including his bare hands, and where he had learned to love the smell of blood and the other bodily fluids that leaked out of a man at the time of his death.

At times, waking in the middle of the night with an erection, he remembered his dreams; they were never about sex, but always about killing. And when he was in the middle of the act of assassination, he always became sexually aroused. Fucking Pam at her tiny apartment had meant nothing more to him than a stylized act of murder.

At the time of his other-than-honorable discharge from the KSK the shrink had recommended that he seek psychiatric help. "You end up killing your family—your father and mother and especially your sisters—over and over again, with nothing to show for it. In the end you will certainly destroy yourself."

In the end Volker had waited until the army psychiatrist had gone on a skiing holiday with his mistress outside of Munich and had killed them both in their chalet bed in the middle of the night.

The military investigators had questioned him, but in the end they left him alone, figuring that the doctor had probably been murdered by the husband of his mistress, himself a psychiatrist. Nothing ever came of it.

He took a cab to the Royal Hotel in the Zona Rosa, where he had a quick lunch, and then took a cab back out to the airport, where he was dropped off at the Air Canada entrance. When the cab was gone he walked down to the American Airlines counter, where he checked in electronically.

Fifteen minutes later he showed his boarding pass and passport to the security agent and was passed through the electronic scanning devices back into the international terminal.

Walking down to his gate for the flight to Atlanta, his heart rate never rose above fifty—about the same as when he killed someone. It was another aspect of his physiology that had baffled the KSK shrink. Whenever he was in a high-stress situation—on the battlefield or in bed having sex—it was always the same. His heart never worked hard. It was as if he didn't care. Which he didn't.

The flight to Atlanta was uneventful, and once he was through customs with just his one carry-on bag he took the shuttle over to the Hilton, where he checked in under his work name, Tomas Spangler, a Swiss citizen from Bern, paying for it with an American Express gold card.

The room was nice. Upstairs he ordered a roast beef sandwich and a couple of beers from room service, and while he waited he stared indifferently out the window toward downtown several miles away.

While on an op he'd lived for short periods in luxury hotels as well as shit holes. He'd never cared which. He'd also slept in bombed-out buildings, under a tarp in a construction zone, behind a pile of rocks in a battle zone in Afghanistan, and aboard a stinking freighter. That he was in the United States didn't matter either. The location, that is. He was here to do a job, after which, depending how big his payday was, he would take a couple of years off, though he had no earthly idea where he might hole up or exactly what he might do—nothing except killing interested him much.

When the sandwich and beers came he gave the man a nice tip and went back to the window to stare at essentially nothing, while he mechanically ate his meal and drank the beers.

Afterward he used his encrypted cell phone to call Pam. "I'm here."

"When will you be in place?"

"Tomorrow. What about the others?"

Pam didn't answer; she was gone.

First thing in the morning Volker checked out and took the shuttle back to the airport. He rented a Ford Taurus at the Avis counter, using the Spangler credit card, ID, and international driving license. By eight thirty he was on I-85 heading northeast toward Norfolk.

He tuned to a country-and-western station and matched his speed with most of the other traffic. The morning was bright and sunny, and for the first time since he could remember, he was actually horny. And he smiled.

FIFTY-NINE

Driving through the night, stopping only at rest areas and gas stations, where they refueled the car and got sandwiches and drinks, Pam pulled into the parking lot of an IHOP just off I-66 in Arlington at nine in the morning. The parking lot was nearly full.

Pam was hopped up on adrenaline, and even if they had stopped somewhere for the night she knew that she would never be able to get to sleep. Not now that they were getting so close. And especially because she was going to come face-to-face with Gloria again.

Ayesha, who'd slept most of the way, except when they passed well to the west of New York City before connecting with I-95 south, woke up when they stopped. "Where are we?"

"Outside of Washington."

"But what is this place?"

"We're meeting someone here for breakfast," Pam said.

"Who?"

"A friend."

Gloria sat in a booth near the back. She was a mousy-looking woman, somewhat dumpy, with short, light brown hair, thin lips, and close-set eyes. She was dressed in jeans and a light top. When she saw them her eyes widened like a deer caught in headlights.

"Hello," Pam said.

Gloria took a moment to speak. "You didn't say you were bringing someone."

They sat down. "Ayesha Naisir."

"The major's wife. Jesus Christ, how could you bring her here? Considering the situation."

"She's providing the operational funds now. It was she who put money into your account."

"I thought it was you," Gloria said. Her voice was reed-thin and high, almost like the upper-register notes in a clarinet, but soft. She leaned forward. "This is not good."

"I'm sorry, who exactly are you?" Ayesha asked.

"You have my bank numbers, that's enough."

"It was a blind account. No name."

"Yes," Gloria said sharply. "And it will remain that way even after your silly countrymen blow themselves and India off the map. Have you any comprehension what's about to happen, unless the Chinese manage to convince President Mamnoon Hussain to stand down?"

"There'll be no war."

"I wish my government were as sure as you are, Mrs. Naisir. But here you are, a long way from home, about to finance the mass murder of some American heroes."

"You're an American, helping with the murders," Ayesha shot back. "Where is a logic that Allah would understand?"

"Fuck you and your prophet and all your people."

Ayesha started to rise, but Pam held her back. "We don't need this," she said. "We have a job to do." She looked pointedly at Gloria. "Including what I promised you."

"I won't wait much longer."

"You won't have to."

Gloria hesitated, but then she lowered her eyes. "The money's under the table in an attaché case. One hundred thousand. I've written down the address of a gun shop in Richmond whose owner will cooperate. She'll supply you with whatever you want, no paperwork. But the price will have to be right."

Pam reached down and found the handle. "What about Norfolk?"

"A couple of detectives are investigating the murder of the one guy and his family. ONI is on it too, but they're not making much progress. They're thinking a home invasion gone bad. Because that's probably what they've been told to think."

"By whom?"

"I don't know," Gloria said. She was bitter all of a sudden. "It wasn't those boys' fault. They were just following orders. God, duty, honor, country. Hoo-rah."

"What about McGarvey?"

"He's back here. A CIA jet picked him and the woman up in London and brought them to Andrews, where they were met by someone from the CIA. Probably the DDO and a couple of his goons."

"I met the woman," Pam said. "Any idea who she is?"

"Pete Boylan. She worked as an interrogator until she was transferred to the Clandestine Service. But I haven't been able to find out much more than that about her."

"Are she and McGarvey lovers?"

"There's speculation."

Pam was sure of it, because of McGarvey's zeal storming the Rawalpindi safe house to rescue her. All very romantic. "Where'd he go after Andrews?"

"To Langley overnight, but then he disappeared."

"Where?"

"Unknown, but almost certainly he's with his friend Otto Rencke, who's the reigning computer geek at the company. You might want to take care with McGarvey's violence, but you'd better take special care with Mr. Rencke's computer expertise. The man is a black-magic witch."

"If he moves I want to hear about it immediately."

"There's something else," Gloria said. "But we're not sure what it means."

"Yes?"

"Petty Officer Greg Rautanen, he's one of the SEAL Team Six guys. Lives alone, a drunk, screwed up. Anyway, the ONI opened a new file on him. Some inquiries we apparently made, and it put up a red flag. Whoever hacked his file didn't do a good enough job of it to hide their tracks."

"Doesn't sound like this Rencke character."

"That's just it; my sources said it looked as if the hacker came in with a sledgehammer on purpose. He wanted to be burned. Maybe he wanted to let someone know that Rautanen had been singled out for some reason. It maybe was a message."

Pam saw it. "The son of a bitch," she said softly.

"What?" Ayesha asked.

"He knows I'm coming," Pam said. "He doesn't know when or exactly where, except that it'll be in Norfolk. So he opened the door for me with this Rautanen guy. 'Here I'll be,' he's told me. 'Come get me.'"

"If he's expecting us, we need to come up with another plan," Ayesha said.

"On the contrary. We're going to do exactly what he wants us to do," Pam said. "What he thinks we were going to do all along."

SIXTY

□

Greg Rautanen's tiny bungalow was across Lake Edwards from where Steffen Engel had been taken down, and just down the block from a large apartment complex. The entire neighborhood was run-down, trash everywhere, most of the buildings in disrepair. And despite the fact it was just ten in the morning, knots of desperate-looking black kids, most of them in their teens, were hanging out on just about every corner.

McGarvey and Pete had flown down to Landmark Aviation at the Norfolk Airport where Otto had a new rental Hummer waiting for them. "Tough neighborhood," he'd told them. "The car might impress the kids, but I don't know how Rautanen will react, seeing the same kind of vehicle he used in the service."

"He might freak out?" Pete asked.

"The guy's screwed up, but there's no knowing how bad he is. A lot of them come out so hyperaware that a car turning the corner down the block could trigger the memory of someone coming at them in a car loaded with explosives. He could react pretty violently to defend himself. A lot of them come out of the service as gun nuts, but some don't want anything to do with any kind of weapon. They even barricade themselves inside their houses on the Fourth of July. Most of them have nightmares—even waking nightmares. Somebody happens to walk in on them during an episode like that and it could get hairy. Chronic detachment, lack of sleep, depression, of course, fear of any kind of a crowd, like in a mall or a movie theater. It's why a lot of them end up getting divorces or going on the streets and living alone under a bridge or in the woods in a cardboard box."

"And this Rautanen is like that?" Pete had asked.

"Probably," Otto said.

"We're going to use this poor guy?" Pete asked. "Put him on the firing line as bait?"

"He's already on the firing line," McGarvey told them. "Schlueter and whoever she's hired are coming after me, but they also mean to kill as many of the twenty-two SEALs who are left—and that includes Greg Rautanen."

They passed Rautanen's house and at the end of the block turned around and came back. The lawn had not been tended in a very long time. An old kitchen range was lying on its side next to the short dirt driveway. A ratty old pickup truck with plates that were two years out of date was parked in the carport. The yard was filled with full trash bags.

McGarvey drove up and parked in the street, but left the engine running.

"We can't use this guy, Mac," Pete said. "It isn't right."

"I don't know how long this is going to take, but if something starts to go down, beep the horn."

They were a block away from the apartment buildings where a half-dozen kids were watching them.

"Don't use your weapon unless there's no other choice," McGarvey said. "I don't want to get into a shootout with a bunch of kids. End up as a race riot."

Pete was looking at them. "This could go south in a New York minute," she said.

"In more than one way," Mac agreed.

He got out of the Hummer and went up to the house. The front door was slightly ajar. The curtains were drawn and no lights were on inside. The place smelled of rotting garbage, and maybe pot.

McGarvey eased the door a little farther with the toe of his shoe. "Greg," he called softly.

No one answered.

"My name's Kirk McGarvey. I used to work for the CIA, and right now I'm here to help you."

"Get the fuck out of here."

"Two of the operators on Neptune Spear have already been taken down. The bad guys want the rest of them. Makes you a target."

Mac heard the distinctive sound of a shotgun being racked. It was an attention getter, and Mac's gut tightened. No telling how far over the edge the guy was.

"You have exactly two mikes to make a one-eighty," Rautanen said.

"I'll wait in the truck with my friend if you want to call someone and verify who I am. You might want to try Captain Cole."

"He's a prick."

"You've got no argument from me. But I shit you not, Ratman, your ass is seriously on the line here. There's a world of hurt coming this way, and I'm here to watch your back."

Rautanen was silent for a long time.

"Ratman?"

"Shut the fuck up, only my friends have the right to call me that. Who's the broad?"

"She's a CIA Clandestine Service officer who's going to watch both of our backs."

"I don't need you."

"Like Pete Barnes and Brian Ridder and their familes?"

"It's just me," Rautanen said, and McGarvey could hear the desperation in the man's voice. "And no one gives a shit, because I can take care of myself."

"If they can find you here, which they will, they'll find your wife in Seattle."

Rautanen didn't reply.

"Hiding won't help. It's why I'm here. I want to use you as bait."

The house was silent.

McGarvey pushed the door all the way open, at the same time Pete hit the horn. He turned around, the barrel of the 12-bore Ithaca Stakeout shotgun inches from his face.

"She opens fire it'd be a reflex reaction—my finger on the trigger," Rautanen said, a crazy look in his eyes. "You'd be one dead motherfucker."

"We'd both be dead, and your problem would be solved," McGarvey said. "Your problem. It'd still leave the other guys."

Pete had gotten out of the Hummer, her .45-caliber Wilson conceal-and-carry pistol in a two-handed grip.

"Your Ithaca is starting to attract some attention," McGarvey said.

Pete started to come forward, but McGarvey waved her off. "So either shoot me or let's get inside and I'll tell you what I have in mind."

Rautanen glanced at the kids down the block. "They won't come anywhere near my place. They think I'm crazy. And you know what, McGarvey, I am outta my fucking skull."

"My friends call me Mac. Lower your weapon and we can talk. But we need to get some shit straight ASAP, because I think whatever is coming your way will probably happen tonight."

Rautanen's hand steadied and he moved close enough so that the muzzle of the shotgun touched the bridge of McGarvey's nose.

"Mac?" Pete said urgently. She moved forward so that she was only a couple of feet away, her pistol aimed at the side of Rautanen's head.

"It's Greg's call," McGarvey told her. He shrugged. "So shit or get off the pot, Mr. Rautanen."

After a moment, Rautanen grinned and lowered the shotgun. "Friends call me Ratman," he said. "You want a beer?"

SIXTY-ONE

□

Felix Volker got off I-95 at Kenly, North Carolina, a town of around one thousand people a few miles southeast of Raleigh. He turned off not so much that he was hungry, although it was just before noon, but because he was tired of driving and he wanted a drink. Tonight, when he got to Norfolk and hooked up with Schlueter and the others, there'd be no alcohol. He was too thirsty and too keyed up to wait until after the op.

He took the narrow county road under the interstate northwest and followed his nose to a small redneck country bar. A few pickups were parked in front—gun racks in the rear windows, a hunting dog in one chained to a ring. The dog put up a baying when he pulled up and got out of his rental car.

Tobacco and corn fields stretched out in either direction across the relatively flat coastal plain that ran one hundred miles all the way down to Pamlico Sound and the Atlantic Ocean where the tourists went.

The day was already beginning to heat up, and by this afternoon he figured the lowlands would be unbearably humid. It was something he didn't like. Germany's climate was mild, especially south around Munich, and even farther north in Franconia around Nürnberg where he'd lived for a couple of short stretches. Snow in the winter, but nothing extreme. Warm in the summer, but not hot. *Schon.*

He was dressed this morning in dark jeans, a dark polo shirt, and thick-soled walking sandals. He left his black jacket in the car and headed toward the front door, when a couple of thickly built young men—maybe in their early twenties and farmers by the look of them—came out.

"Well, son of a bitch," one of the kids said as Volker passed them and went inside.

The bar ran across one-third of the room. To the right there was a pool table, a dartboard against the rear wall, and an old-fashioned jukebox in the corner. The men's room was to the right, the women's to the left. Two older men in bib overalls were seated at the bar, behind which was an older woman with long gray hair.

Volker took a stool away from the two men, who turned and looked at him as if he were someone from a different planet.

"What'll it be?" the bartender asked. Her accent was very southern, difficult for Volker to understand.

"A beer, please. Dark, not so cold."

"Sam Adams," the woman said. She poured it from a tap and set it down. "Two dollars."

Volker paid her, and took a deep drink. It was too cold and weak, almost like water to him, but it was okay. "*Danke*," he said.

"You're German," she said.

He nodded. "Just passing through. I was thirsty."

"Are you hungry? We have burgers and pizza. Frozen, but not so bad."

"No. Just time for one beer and then I have to be on the highway to Atlanta."

The two farm boys came in, big grins on their faces, and came to the bar. "Better give us a beer, Maudie," the taller, stockier one said. His massive head sat on a thick neck and broad shoulders.

"Thought you boys had to get back to work," the bartender said, but she poured them a couple of beers.

"Wanted to say hi to the gentleman with the girly footwear," the other one said. His face was round and filled with freckles. "Hadn't seen him around here before."

"I don't want any trouble in here, like Friday."

Volker sipped his beer but didn't look at them. They wanted trouble, of course, and he was of a mind to give it to them. But it would be foolish on his part, as well as theirs.

"Not very polite, you son of a bitch," the big one said. "Didn't your mama teach you nothing?" He grabbed Volker by the arm and tried to pull him around.

Volker put his beer down, turned, and smashed a tremendous right fist into the kid's face, just above the bridge of his nose, driving him backward on his butt, blood gushing down his chin.

"Jesus," the bartender said. She took a cell phone out of her pocket, but Volker reached across the bar and took it from her.

The second kid hit Volker in the side of the neck.

This is not why he had come to America, to have a duel with a couple of country boys. It would have been much easier if he had been allowed to have his one beer and drive away. But it was too late for that now.

He broke the bartender's cell phone on the kid's forehead, then slammed the doubled-over knuckles of his left hand into the boy's Adam's apple, crushing his windpipe.

The two old men sat where they were, slight smiles on their weathered faces.

The kid staggered backward, clawing at his throat, trying desperately to breathe. His face was turning beet red, and Volker figured he'd be on the floor unconscious in about ten seconds and dead within a minute or two.

The bigger farm boy got to his feet and charged, but Volker turned and stepped into him, shoving him up against the bar. Reflexively, after hundreds of hours of hand-to-hand combat drills, Volker used his bulk to get the kid turned completely around, grabbed his head, and twisted sharply, the spinal column where it attached to the base of the skull breaking with an audible pop. The boy dropped to the floor like a stone.

Volker looked up as the woman disappeared out the back door. He finished his beer. Then he went over to the old men who had not moved and broke both of their necks, letting their bodies crumple to the floor.

He looked out the front door to make sure that no one else had driven up. Then he crossed the barroom and went out the back door in time to see the woman come out of a small house fifteen meters across a backyard, her purse in one hand and a baseball bat in the other.

She spotted him and fumbled in her bag as she sprinted to a dusty Saturn SUV, its blue paint badly faded in the southern sun.

Volker reached her just as she got to the driver's door.

She dropped her purse and swung the bat, just missing the side of Volker's head. She was frightened but determined. Volker figured she had to be at least in her late fifties or early sixties and had more spunk than the two farm boys put together. It was a shame.

He snatched the bat from her hands, and as she spun around trying to get away he swung it one-handed into the side of her head, cracking her skull, driving her against the side of the car.

She raised a hand to ward off the next blow, the bat breaking her arm, and her legs started to go out from under her.

Methodically, with not much feeling, Volker hit her in the head again, knocking her to her knees.

Barely conscious, she could only whimper, no fight left in her.

Volker swung the bat, hitting her in the temple. Her head bounced against the car door, leaving a long bloody streak as she fell face-first into the dirt.

For a long time Volker looked at her. He couldn't tell if she was still breathing, but it was of no matter. She was dead, or as good as dead.

He glanced at the back of the tavern. Too easy, he thought, dropping the bat. Norfolk would be more interesting.

SIXTY-TWO

This time around Dick Cole met McGarvey in front of admin. It was noon, and McGarvey half-expected the captain to take him to lunch at the O Club so they would be on neutral ground, with witnesses in case something went wrong. Instead Cole walked around to the east side of the building and headed in slow trot down a dirt path toward some woods a hundred yards away.

No one was in sight, but in the distance—in the direction they were headed—the sounds of automatic weapons fire and the occasional sharp crack of a small breaching explosion drifted up to them.

Cole, dressed in Cryes and bloused boots, ran with an easy gait. McGarvey wore jeans, a light-colored polo shirt, and Topsiders. He'd been required to leave his pistol in his car outside the front gate. The day was warm and the path downhill was easy.

They ran in silence for a few minutes until they reached the woods, where the path split off in two directions. Cole took the route up a fairly steep hill.

"If you need to pull over let me know," Cole said.

Rautanen was right—the guy was a prick. There were lots of his type in the military and as civilians in government; this didn't make them bad, just self-important assholes.

McGarvey picked up the pace. "No, thanks," he said.

If Cole was irritated he didn't show it; he just matched the pace. "I was a little surprised to get your call. What can I do for you this time?"

"I came down to let you know what I'm going to do. See if you wanted to coordinate efforts. They were your guys, after all."

"I understand what you're saying, but there's no way in hell any military organization on this planet, now or ever in history, could hope to keep track of all of its discharged—retired or otherwise—personnel. Logistically it's impossible. Surely you can understand."

"These guys were special, captain."

"Nothing I can do."

"They did a tough job for us, and now we're just tossing them aside."

"I'm following orders," Cole shot back.

McGarvey had heard the same excuse before. Lots of times. "I figured you'd say something like that."

Cole pulled up short and glared at him. "What the hell do you want me to do? Why the fuck did you come back here?"

"Just to let you know what's in the works."

"If it's about my ex-wife, forget it. I told you before, she's not involved. It's not like her. She's a bitcher, not a doer."

"I hear you," McGarvey said. "Do you want to know what I'm planning?"

"Frankly, no," Cole said, and he took off up the hill.

McGarvey kept the pace. "His name is Greg Rautanen. A chief petty officer, out of SEAL Team Six for about three years now."

"Never heard of him."

"He was one of the operators on Neptune Spear. Bit of a basket case now. Wife left him, so he's all alone."

"A lot of operators come through here."

"He's agreed to work with me."

"Doing what?"

"The same people who took out Barnes and Ridder and their families are coming back to finish the job. Only this time it's me they want. And I'm going to make it easy for them. Rautanen and I are going to hide in plain sight."

"Here in Norfolk?"

"That's right. Possibly tonight."

Cole stopped at the crest of the hill. Below them was an urban battle setting of a dozen concrete-block buildings Six operators appeared around the corner of one of the buildings. One of them did something to a door, then swung wide away from it. Three seconds later the breaching charge blew the door inward, and the six operators charged inside.

"You're planning on instigating a firefight in some neighborhood, maybe get some innocent people killed?"

"Some innocent people have already been killed."

"I suppose I could call the ONI, but I'd be wasting my time. The local cops might be interested. But maybe I should just keep my mouth shut and let it play out like you think it will. Get yourself and Ratman killed. For what?"

Bingo, McGarvey said to himself. "Because someone cares."

Cole bridled. "Listen, you son of a bitch."

"I'll find my way back," McGarvey said.

He turned on his heel and jogged back down the hill and up the other side to the admin building where Ensign Mader, who had picked him up at the front gate, was waiting beside his Hummer.

"Where's Captain Cole?"

"He wanted to watch the end of a training evolution on the other side of the hill."

The ensign, who'd been smoking, field-stripped his cigarette, placing the filter in his pocket, and drove McGarvey back to the main gate.

"The captain was seriously pissed off the last time you came down here. Took it out on us."

"That's your problem."

"What the hell are you doing here, sir?"

"Ask the captain."

"I'm asking you, sir."

"Stay out of it, Ensign," McGarvey said harshly. "There's some serious stuff coming down that's way above your pay grade. And when the shit hits the fan, which it will, anyone nearby is going to get dirty."

But Mader was young and gung ho. "These are my people," he shot back angrily. "I'm not just some fucking drill instructor. I go out on deployments. I've been plenty dirty before. And I expect I will be again."

"We all will," McGarvey said. But there was no way in hell he was going to tell the kid that he suspected Cole was selling them out. He just couldn't think of a reason for it.

SIXTY-THREE

Shockoe Slip was a section along the James River not far from downtown Richmond where tobacco warehouses used to do a bustling business. The once-seedy district had been turned into a fairly prosperous area of restaurants, shops, and apartments. Most of the warehouses still existed, though they no longer contained tobacco.

It was three when Pam happened to look across the street from the sidewalk café where she and Ayesha had been sitting nursing sweet ice teas for nearly two hours in time to see three Hispanic-looking kids in their very early teens beating up on a black kid who was maybe eight or nine years old.

"That never happens in Islamabad," Ayesha said. "The tension between black and white has to be an embarrassment to Washington."

Pam had listened to her crap the entire way from Montreal. "The Sunnis don't kick the shit out of the Shi'ites? Give me a break."

"That's different," Ayesha flared.

The young black kid got out from under his tormentors and disappeared around the corner, but no one on the street, in passing cars, or in the restaurants seemed to notice or care.

"I don't like this place," Ayesha said. "May we leave?"

"Not yet," Pam said. The three Hispanic kids had walked away as soon as the black kid had disappeared. It had been too easy, she thought. Too staged. They hadn't followed him.

A police car cruised past, and as it rounded the corner where the kids had gone, its lights came on and its siren whooped twice.

Thirty seconds later the black kid walked past. "Yo, ladies, Ludlow is waiting," he said without slowing down or looking at them.

Pam laid down a twenty-dollar bill, and she and Ayesha got up and headed after the kid, keeping back a little, until he went down one of the narrow alleys that ran along the riverside. And then they caught up.

"Friends of yours across the street?" Pam asked.

Close up the kid was small, but he had the facial expressions and features of a teenager who'd spent a long time on the street.

"They're ragheads, but they're okay," he said. He looked pointedly at Ayesha. "Wanna fuck when we're done with business?"

"No, she doesn't, you little bastard," Pam said.

The kid laughed. "You can call me Fredrick, but it's true I never did know my ol' man."

They came to one of the old tobacco warehouses, in a neighborhood of similar three-story buildings that had been converted to apartments or condos. Fredrick punched a code into a door reader. Inside they walked to the rear of the building and took an old freight elevator down to the level of the river's loading docks.

On the ground floor the lobby had been tastefully painted in soft tans and greens, carpeting, even a small, modern chandelier hanging from the high ceiling. But down here the stone walls were dank and dirty, the floor covered in old uneven planks that were worn down in a path.

At the end of the corridor the kid opened a thick steel door that moved aside on rollers. "Ludlow's waiting inside for you," he said. He gave Ayesha another smile. "You change your mind, let me know, I'll be around."

The warehouse room was large, with steel shutters over the windows and loading doors facing the river. A dozen safes were arranged along two walls, while a long table covered with a green felt cloth dominated the center. There were no chairs or filing cabinets—nothing else, except lights dangling from the ceiling.

Ludlow, the only name Gloria had given them, came toward them out of the darkness in a corner. He was possibly the tallest, thinnest man Pam had ever met. At nearly seven feet, and perhaps one hundred fifty pounds or so, she thought he might have been a performer in a circus or carnival somewhere—a moko jumbie who didn't need stilts. But he was old, somewhat hunchbacked, and his crinkly gray hair, narrow black face, and sunken cheeks and jowls made him look like a clown who made you want to cry.

He stopped within arm's length and offered them a thin smile.

"Ms. Pamela, Mrs. Ayesha, a certain party informed me that you might wish to do some business today," he said. "You will be engaging in an operation in the open, or will stealth be important?"

"Stealth," Pam said. Gloria had promised that this guy was one of the best in the business.

"And how many persons will need to be armed?"

"Five, including me."

"And what of Mrs. Ayesha, perhaps a small defensive weapon?"

"Yes," Ayesha said.

"No," Pam said. "The lady is to be a distant observer."

They had talked about it on the way down from Washington. Ayesha's argument was that she was paying for the op and she wanted to be a part of it. She wanted to kill the bastard who'd caused her husband's death. Pam's argument was that she had no idea of the level of firearms training Ayesha had received, and she didn't want an amateur in her group with a deadly weapon in hand.

Ludlow waited politely for Ayesha to object. When she didn't, he nodded.

"May I be told the nature of your operation?" he asked Pam.

"Assassinations, most likely at close range and most likely in quiet neighborhood settings."

"I see. And may I know if you would like suggestions, or have you already determined your equipment needs."

"Glock 26 pistols, nine-by-nineteen. Five of them, along with suppressors, and four magazines of ammunition each."

Ludlow neither approved nor disapproved; he merely nodded knowingly. "You have a choice of magazine capacity—ten rounds, twelve, fifteen, seventeen, nineteen, or thirty-three. Although I must advise that because of the compact nature of the really very excellent little weapon, magazine capacities of above fifteen rounds defeat the general purpose of conceal-and-carry."

"Fifteen-round magazines will be sufficient."

"Now then, we come to the matter of holsters."

"Simple thumb-break paddle holsters will do. Four right-handed and one lefty." Hesier was left-handed.

"Knives, garrotes, or other specialized equipment?" Ludlow asked. "I can't imagine that you will be needing flash-bang grenades or any other noisemakers in the setting you describe."

"No," Pam said. "But I will need five Ingram MAC 10s, with suppressors, and four 30-round magazines of the .45 ACP rounds. Shoulder stocks will not be necessary, though leather slings to carry the weapons beneath coats or jackets could come in handy."

"A fine submachine gun, though not particularly accurate beyond ten feet, especially with the suppressor."

"Accuracy beyond that distance will not be an issue."

"Anything else?"

"How soon can you have the equipment here?"

"Oh, everything you require is already here," Ludlow said. "How soon can you have the cash?"

"How much?"

"Fifty thousand dollars."

Ayesha started to object, but Pam held her off.

"Do you have a secure Internet connection?"

"Yes."

"I'll bring the car around, and Ayesha will take care of the payment. But the transfer will not go through until I have personally inspected everything."

"Nor will I release the equipment until I have confirmation of the transfer."

"Then we have an agreement," Pam said.

"Of course."

SIXTY-FOUR

□

McGarvey and Pete had checked into a Marriott Courtyard near Cape Henry, the section of the coast where the settlers on their way to Jamestown first landed on the mainland. Pete had agreed to wait until he came back from meeting Cole. She was in the lobby having a cup of coffee when he showed up.

"How'd it go?" she asked. She was excited but trying not to show it.

"About how I expected it to go," McGarvey said. "Did you get any lunch?"

"No."

They went out to the Hummer, which McGarvey had parked under the overhang. He drove over to a 7-Eleven, where he bought a six-pack of Bud, and then to a McDonald's, where they got burgers and fries, and he drove to the park. They had to pay for a sticker to get in.

The day was bright. They sat at a picnic table eating lunch. The ocean a deep blue and unusually calm. Not far away a cross commemorated the site marking the spot where British North America, and eventually the United States, had begun.

"I'm sitting here twiddling my thumbs. What'd he say?" Pete demanded.

"His hands are officially tied. 'We can't keep track of every GI who ever served.' Said he didn't know Rautanen, but he let it slip he knew the guy's handle."

"What's next? This isn't going to happen unless he's the leak, which I find hard to believe. He may be an asshole, from what you said and from what Rautanen told you, but that doesn't mean he's selling his guys out." Pete looked away. "This just doesn't make any sense, Mac. I talked to Otto about it while you were gone. He said Cole doesn't appear to have any financial problems. No mistress. He's married, apparently happily, at least his wife hasn't filed a restraining order against him or anything like that. He's been passed over for his star, but his last two psych evals don't show anything except a mild resentment and frustration that he hasn't been promoted. He knows that the third time's a charm, but he's not going nuts over it."

"Agreed," McGarvey said. Driving away he'd come to the same conclusion. But he was missing something. He could feel it.

Pete looked out at the ocean. "Nice day, pretty view, but what the hell are we doing sitting around?"

"Waiting for someone to make their first move."

"As in going after Rautanen?"

"That, or something else."

"You're not making any sense, Kirk. What, 'or something else'? You told Cole that you were here to provoke an attack against Rautanen. What do you think he'll do about it?"

"I hope he sends someone to take Rautanen into protective custody, which would prove me wrong about him."

"Then what?"

McGarvey followed her gaze out to the southeast, where a very large ship heading north was low on the horizon. It was too far to make out any details, but he thought it was either a container ship bound for New York or a naval vessel on its way here. Or neither. Or both.

His cell phone vibrated. It was Rautanen.

"You nearby?" the ex-SEAL asked. He sounded stressed.

"Fifteen, maybe twenty minutes. What's going on?"

"A car has made two passes. Government plates. Two people inside."

"Are they in sight now?" McGarvey asked. He got up and motioned for Pete that they were leaving.

"Could the people coming after me fit that profile?"

"Possible, but I think it could be SPs coming to take you into protective custody."

"Your call," Rautanen said.

"If they come back, don't let them in until I get there," McGarvey said. "But for Christ's sake don't open fire unless they shoot first."

"Best you boogey—they just pulled into my driveway."

"On my way," McGarvey said. "I'll call you right back."

"Is Rautanen in trouble?" Pete asked

"Probably not, but I want to make sure. Drive."

As Pete headed out of the park toward I-64, McGarvey got on the phone to Otto and explained the situation.

"Did you get a number on the plates?"

"Stand by." Mac put Otto on hold and redialed Rautanen. "I need the number on the car's tag."

Rautanen gave it to him. "They're just sitting in their car. Looks as if one of them is talking on a cell phone."

"You don't want to shoot these guys."

"Incoming rounds have the right of way."

McGarvey got back to Otto and gave him the tag number. "One of them is apparently on a cell phone."

"ONI," Otto came back moments later. "Lieutenant Kevin Hardesty and Chief Petty Officer Caroline Cyr."

"Can you hack into their phone call?"

"Just a mo," Otto said. He was back. "They just hung up, but they were talking to someone in Cole's office."

"Cole himself?"

"Unknown," Otto said. "But the two in the car are not your bad guys, so there better not be any shootout."

"We're on the way over there right now," McGarvey said. "Anything new on Schlueter or anyone else associated with her?"

"No. But if she and the guys she hired are as good as you say they are, they could have gotten across our border without raising any flags. I have to assume they're carrying first-class papers."

"The problem will be weapons. They'll have to come up with the hardware somewhere. And if it were up to me, I'd wait until I was close. Reduce the chance of some cop stopping me for speeding and decide to look in the trunk."

"I'll get back to you," Otto said, and he hung up.

They reached the busy interstate and Pete kept up with the fastest cars, about ten miles over the speed limit.

"Looks like they're ONI," McGarvey told her.

"Cole's off the hook."

"I don't know," McGarvey said.

"What are you thinking, Kirk? Is he playing with you?"

"Anything's possible. He knows I've been in contact with Rautanen, and he has to figure that I would expect him to send someone over to pick the guy up, just in case I was right."

"Which he's done."

McGarvey nodded. But nothing was adding up for him. Something was missing. Something just beyond his ken. It was just a hunch, but he'd learned a long time ago to listen to his instincts.

He phoned Rautanen again, but this time no one picked up.

SIXTY-FIVE

□

Fredrick slid into view out of a door adjacent to Ludlow's warehouse when Pam pulled up with the car and got out. A trolleybus half filled with tourists rattled by and chugged up a short hill at the end of the block.

"You ladies made a deal; that's a good thing," the kid said.

"What's it to you?" Pam demanded. She didn't give a damn about the money that wasn't hers in the first place, but she hadn't heard from Gloria, and this close to Norfolk she didn't want to walk into an unknown situation.

"Ludlow says come help the ladies load the goods. Tonight we celebrate."

Ludlow had unloaded all the weapons from the safes and had laid them out on the felt-topped table, along with three padded ripstop nylon bags with shoulder straps and locks on the heavy-duty zippers

Ayesha stood at the other end of the table, a laptop in front of her. "Do I transfer the funds now?" she asked.

"Not yet," Pam said. She picked up one of the Glock 26s, ejected the magazine, and ejected the round in the chamber. Holding the slide with her right hand, she pushed the release button just forward of the trigger guard; the slide came backward and up, off the pistol's frame. She took out the spring and then the barrel and closely inspected each part.

"Are you satisfied?" Ludlow asked.

Fredrick had closed and relocked the service door and stood to one side.

"With this weapon, yes," Pam said. "May I trust you that the rest of the equipment is in order?"

"Of course. It would be bad for my business otherwise."

"Bad for your life if you were lying."

Pam ejected the rounds from the magazine, counting out the full fifteen. The spring seemed tight. No dust or old gun oil clogged the mechanisms. The weapon was new or nearly new and had been expertly cared for.

Pam reloaded the magazine and reassembled the pistol. "Pay him."

Ayesha and Ludlow hunched over the laptop as Pam inserted the magazine into the handle and jacked a round into the firing chamber.

"Ludlow," Fredrick cried.

Pam turned as the boy pulled a SIG Sauer from beneath his jacket. She shot him once, hitting him in the middle of the forehead. He went back hard against the door and fell to the wood planks.

Ayesha shouted something.

Ludlow, his arm around her chest, using her as a shield, a SIG's muzzle pressed against her temple, seem unfazed. "He was a good boy," he said. "No need for him to die."

"I didn't trust him."

"How shall I explain this to Gloria?"

"Tell her the truth."

"And what now?"

Pam lowered the pistol, so that the barrel was pointed toward the floor away from her. "You have your money, and as soon as we load the weapons into our car we will leave. If there is to be a second time, do not send an assistant. I deal only with the principals."

"But then I could shoot you, and this woman. In the end I would have the money and the merchandise."

"How would you explain it to Gloria?"

"I would tell her the truth," Ludlow said.

Pam nodded. "It's not necessary, Herr Ludlow," she said. She transferred the pistol to her left hand, and holding out her right she stepped closer. "Let's shake hands on the deal, and the woman and I will be on our way."

Ludlow's eyes were narrow, but he started to lower his pistol, when Pam fired one shot catching him in his left eye. His pistol went off, the shot ricocheting off the front of a safe, and he fell back, dragging Ayesha to the floor with him.

Ayesha struggled desperately to disentangle herself from the man's body. Pam kicked the pistol away, sending it skittering across the floor.

Ayesha got to her feet, deeply frightened and boiling mad. "These people were helping us," she screeched. "We made a deal in good faith."

"This isn't the rug business," Pam said. "I wanted no witnesses."

"What about me?"

"You're my paymaster. I want this operation to be completed and for you to go back to Pakistan and report to the ISI that the contract is finished. I don't want to look over my shoulder for the rest of my life expecting one of them to come gunning for me."

"Fine," Ayesha said. "You can load the weapons in the car while I get my money back."

Thirty minutes later they had connected with I-64 east of downtown, and Ayesha sitting low in the passenger side, stared at the traffic, the buildings, and the power lines, her shoulders slumped, her head down.

"Are you okay?" Pam asked.

"I've been to Moscow and Beijing and London and Paris, but this is different."

"It is different."

Ayesha turned to her. "No, I mean *different*. Moscow is fast, Beijing is frantic, and London and Paris are European. But this place is angry, indifferent. No one cares."

Pam was anxious, not hearing from Gloria yet, but her mood softened a little. "It just looks that way to an outsider."

"You're a German—an outsider."

"I was married to an American naval officer. I lived in Washington."

"But you didn't love him. You got a divorce."

"He was a pig, I agree, but some of the others were kind to me. They understood."

"Other women?" Ayesha asked. "We understand what it's like to be alone in a crowded room."

"Men too. Grocery clerks, a kid at the Wendy's, the guy and his wife who delivered our newspapers, the guy who came to fix our air conditioner, even a cop who stopped me once for speeding on the Beltway."

"Sounds like you were brainwashed. Why did you leave?"

It was easier to remember the bad parts, the things that had nurtured and fed her hate. But sometimes she remembered some of the good stuff. Little League baseball had almost made her want to have a child of her own. The mother and daughter selling Girl Scout cookies almost made her want to climb out of her shell and volunteer—Dick had told her once that America was the land of volunteers. It was a concept that most Europeans didn't get.

But the television was bad, especially the sports matches—baseball and football, which really wasn't football at all—that Dick had loved beyond everything but porn.

The food was mostly bland.

The beer was like ice water.

Even the German country bread from the deli was little more than ground-up cardboard. The cheese bland, the butter pale and tasteless. And everything was laced with tons of salt and even more sugar.

And every once in a while, Pam wanted to say: So what? Who gave a damn? Friends told her that if she wanted authentic German food she could order it online, she could watch movies or television programs on her laptop, and she could get *Stern* magazine and the *Berliner Zeitung* newspaper delivered to her door, so quit griping.

But she'd never been able to get over her hate.

Her encrypted cell phone chirped. It was Gloria.

"His name is Greg Rautanen. McGarvey and the woman operative he's with are making their stand there"

"What about the navy?" Pam asked. She was having a hard time concentrating on her driving. They were so damned close.

"The ONI is making a move to take him in for protective custody."

Something gripped Pam's chest. "They know it's me coming?"

"They've known it all along," Gloria said. "Or at least some of them have. They want you to fail, but they're willing to let you go at it in order to make a point in Washington."

"Which is?"

"Doesn't matter. What does matter are your plans. Did you make the merchandise connection in Richmond?"

"Yes. I need the details on Rautanen's location and his background."

"I'm sending it to your cell phone. But take care with McGarvey. He may be a has-been, but he's still very dangerous."

"I mean to kill him."

"Good," Gloria said. "Tell me, how did Ludlow look to you?"

"When I left him?"

"Yes."

"Dead."

SIXTY-SIX

At Rautanen's place a government-issue gray Ford Taurus was parked in the driveway. Pete pulled up and parked on the street. The crowd of blacks at the corner by the apartments had grown, but it didn't look as if they were getting set to make a move.

"Stay here," McGarvey said.

He jumped out of the Hummer and pulled his pistol as he hurried up the driveway and looked inside the ONI car. There were no signs of violence in the car or on the gravel driveway leading from it up to the house.

Pete came up behind him. "Last time I stayed back it nearly didn't work out in your favor," she said. She'd drawn her weapon.

"Greg knows we're coming, and I don't think he'd get into a shoot-out with a couple of ONI guys trying to bring him in."

"Depends on how screwed up he is."

Mac went up to the front door and knocked with the butt of his pistol. "It's me," he said.

"Door's unlocked," Rautanen said from inside.

"Everything okay?"

"Five-by-five."

"We're coming in," McGarvey said. He holstered his pistol and motioned for Pete to do the same.

The two ONI officers, in civilian clothes, were seated next to each other on the dilapidated old couch. Rautanen was perched on the arm of a matching easy chair, the Ithaca cradled loosely in the crook of his right arm. He was dressed this time in his desert-tan battle uniform, a navy-issue SIG Sauer P226 holstered on his chest.

"About time you guys showed up," he said. "I was thinking about shooting these two for the hell of it. Not really sure exactly who they are."

"Lieutenant Kevin Hardesty and Chief Petty Officer Caroline Cyr," McGarvey said. "ONI, here to take you into protective custody on Captain Cole's orders."

"You have to be Mr. McGarvey," Hardesty said. He was lean, built like a soccer player, with seriously dark eyes and a demeanor to match.

"Yes, and this is my partner, Pete Boylan."

"First of all, we don't like people pointing guns at us," Hardesty said. "Especially when we're here to help."

"I don't like people barging in on me, unless you think I'm breaking some navy reg," Rautanen shot back. His temper was flaring. "Anyway I'm no longer in the navy."

"We're here trying to do you a favor. Captain Cole suggested—not ordered—that we come out to talk to you about a situation that Mr. McGarvey thinks might be coming your way."

"There's no proof yet," Caroline Cyr said.

"Don't be stupid," McGarvey shot back. "Barnes and Ridder and their families were shot to death. How many more bodies do you guys want to see piled up until your bosses decide to stop covering their bureaucratic asses?"

Hardesty started to say something, but Caroline held him off. "We're not the bad guys, Mr. Director. And, yes, we were briefed on you and what you think has been going on. And we were sent here to try to defuse the situation by taking Chief Rautanen into protective custody until the situation stabilizes."

"The situation won't stabilize. If they miss Ratman tonight, they'll go after the other guys."

"What other guys?" Hardesty said.

"If you don't know that, asshole, what the hell are you doing here?" Pete asked.

"Following orders."

"We're not. In fact tonight some people are going to die here, and we're going to kill them. Maybe you oughta call for reinforcements, or maybe call the cops on us, because it's not going to be pretty."

Hardesty tried to say something, but Pete cut him off.

"Maybe if you guys had been on the ball the other two guys and their families wouldn't be dead now." She was on a roll, her eyes flashing. "This isn't how we're supposed to treat the folks who go out there and put their lives on the line for the rest of us. Why don't you pick up a rifle and hump your ass off to the Anwar Province or someplace tropical like that."

"Did you take their guns?" McGarvey asked.

"No, sir," Rautanen said, grinning.

"Get out of here," McGarvey told the two ONI officers. "We appreciate what you're trying to do, but more's needed. The attack on our guys stops tonight."

The ONI agents got up, and at the door Caroline turned back. "You think that something's going down tonight?" she asked.

"It's possible," McGarvey said.

"Is there anything we can do for you, short of sending reinforcements."

"Tell me what your specific orders are, and who gave them to you."

Caroline smiled and shrugged. "Ah, well, good luck, you guys. I wish there was something we could do, I really do."

After they walked out Rautanen went to the window and parted the curtain. "I don't think the LT is real happy with his chief," he said. He turned back. "They were here for show, no way in hell they wanted to take me in. Weren't even surprised when I jumped them out front. Didn't try to talk me out of anything."

"I'm not surprised either," McGarvey said.

Rautanen laid the shotgun on the coffee table and perched again on the arm of the easy chair. "So what's the op tonight? Who's coming after me, and why?"

"A group of German contractors hired by the Pakistani ISI, which wants payback for Neptune Spear."

Rautanen broke out in a big grin. "No shit," he said. "Are they after all of us?"

"With you it'd be three down, twenty-one to go."

"Plus one."

McGarvey shook his head. "Who?"

"The dog. Don't forget the dog. He was right there with us, man."

McGarvey let it ride for a beat. "These guys are good. German KSK. They don't have a hard-on for you guys, but by the same token they don't give a shit. It's just another day at the office."

"Good. Makes it professional. Nice and clean, nothing ambiguous. No second thoughts, no touchy-feelies, no hesitations. You see the shot, you take the shot."

"Could get hairy," Pete said, trying to bring him down just a little.

But Rautanen's grin broadened. "Good. So what's the op plan?"

"Tell me what you know about the apartments up the street. The layout, the people," McGarvey said.

"No place you want to be," Rautanen said. "Good people, most of them, but the kids are seriously pissed off, and I don't blame them. It's why I act crazy all the time, keep this place looking like a shit hole, so they'll stay away."

"Has it worked?" Pete asked.

Rautanen grinned. "Here I am."

SIXTY-SEVEN

☐

When they checked in at what had been a Motel 6 on North Military Highway in Virginia Beach, the old guy who was the desk clerk gave Pam and Ayesha a knowing smirk. The place was run-down, in a seedy neighborhood, and attracted all kinds of clientele.

They drove back and parked in front of the end room. Ayesha held her silence until they got out of the car.

"What kind of horrible place is this? We could be in Rawalpindi."

"We just were, remember?" Pam said. She had no sympathy for the woman, none whatsoever, but she had been telling the truth when she promised to make sure Ayesha got back to Pakistan in one piece. It was for self-defense if nothing else.

They carried the heavy bags inside and flopped them down on the twin beds. The room was reasonably clean, though the sink ran slow when Ayesha splashed some water on her face. The mirror was cracked and one of the fluorescent tubes was burned out.

"My four operators are in the next two rooms," Pam said. "I'm going to get them together for their briefing. I suggest that you remain here until I come back for the equipment."

"I'm not staying here alone."

"Listen to me, bitch. I'm trying to carry out this op while at the same time keep you alive. These guys won't want to deal with you. For all they know you're a spy for the ISI who'll turn them in when this is all over. It'd be easier for them to kill you now so that they won't have to look over their shoulders for the rest of their lives."

"Like you."

"That's right. The ISI knows who I am, which is why I want to make sure that you get home safely."

"Interesting," Ayesha said. "They'll want me dead to save their own necks, and you want me alive for the same reason."

"So stay here."

"No," Ayesha said. She hefted one of the bags. "Let's see how my money is being spent."

Pam considered the woman for a long beat. Without her cooperation the money would dry up. Reestablishing a tie with the ISI would take time, even if it could be done now, considering the tense situation with India. And working with the devil you knew was almost always better than working with one you didn't.

"Put the bag back on the bed and stay here, I'll be right back."

"I said I won't be left out of this."

"I'll bring my people here. They'll have to find out about you sooner or later—might as well get it done now."

"Don't ignore me. I have just as much reason for retribution as you do. Maybe more."

Pam went to the next room and knocked discreetly on the door. "It's me," she said.

The door opened on its safety chain. Volker was there with a shotgun. "Who is the woman you brought here?" he demanded.

They had maintained a lookout. It was something she hadn't thought about. To this point no one but she and the four operators—Volker and Bruns in this room and Woedding and Heiser across the hall—knew about this place. "Our paymaster from the ISI."

"Get rid of her and then we'll talk."

"Where'd you get the shotgun?"

"A little bar in North Carolina. No witnesses."

"The gun will be reported stolen."

"No," Volker said. "Get rid of the broad."

"If you want in on this op, it's on for tonight," Pam said. "I'll see your ass next door in five."

She went across the narrow corridor and knocked on 122. "It's me."

Heiser opened the door a crack. "Is it time?"

"I'm in one-twenty-five. Briefing in five minutes."

Heiser closed the door.

.   .   .

Volker left his shotgun behind, but he and the other three men kept on their feet, their body language tense. Fight or flight, they left their options open.

"The woman's name is of no importance; she is our paymaster and nothing more," Pam said. She too was on her feet. The weapons were laid out on the bed between them.

Ayesha stood at the open bathroom door. She had the good sense to say nothing.

"She will not be on either assault team tonight, and before first light all of us will be long gone from here, in our separate directions, considerably richer than we are at this moment."

"What guarantee do we have that when this is over she won't out us?"

"None, other than your own tradecraft and the money, which will allow you to go deep."

"And if we don't wish to stay 'deep', as you put it, forever?" Heiser asked.

At twenty-four he was just getting started. The thought of such an early retirement didn't sit well with him, hadn't from the beginning. It was something Pam had understood the first time she met him.

"That would be entirely up to you," she said. "But once the dust settles, which it surely will—even 9/11 has faded in the minds of most Americans and Neptune Spear will fade in the minds of the Pakistani government—there will be other operations."

"With you?"

"We'll see," Pam said.

After tonight she would be faced with one last operation—hers personally, with Gloria's help—and she would go permanently to ground somewhere. Possibly in Germany, after some plastic surgery and some bulletproof identity documents, which a lot of money could buy. She would go back to being a small-town girl. Maybe buy a *Gasthaus* somewhere outside of Munich.

Or maybe she would set up in Frankfurt or Luxembourg or even Zurich as an investment counselor for a specialized clientele. A money laundress and financial expediter for guys like Heiser. It would be the dolce vita: nice clothes, nice cars, nice apartments, fine restaurants, vacations to the Caribbean or South Seas. A boy toy who wouldn't beat on her.

Anything was possible with money and retribution under her belt.

Volker looked at Ayesha. "If this goes bad and the ISI goons start coming for me, I'll get past them, and you will be my first kill."

Ayesha shrugged. "Do you want the money or not?"

Volker nodded at length.

"Then do as you're told and keep your fucking mouth shut."

The tension level in the small room rose palpably.

"Kirk McGarvey will be our primary target for tonight. The ST Six operators will be secondary."

"He's here?" Bruns asked.

"Yes. At the home of one of the Neptune Spear operators, just a few miles from here. He knows we're coming, and he's offered the operator as bait."

"Shouldn't be too tough for the four of us to take them down," Bruns said.

"Tell that to Dieter and Steffen," Pam said. "But they went in blind, something we won't do."

"We're listening," Volker said.

SIXTY-EIGHT

Sitting at the kitchen table in Rautanen's house, McGarvey methodically cleaned and oiled his Walther PPK. He unloaded and reloaded all three six-shot magazines of 9x18mm shells, making sure that the spring in each was not jammed. Finally he reloaded the pistol, jacking a round into the firing chamber, then removed the magazine to load another round, making his pistol a six-plus-one shot.

Pete sitting across from him watched in silence as he pocketed two of the magazines, holstered the pistol at the small of his back, and set the silencer tube aside.

"What can I say to talk you out of this," she asked at length.

"We've come this far, and I sure as hell won't turn around and walk away."

"I understand, and I'm not going anywhere. I'm just saying that we should call for backup."

"They'd spot it and sit on their heels. Time's on their side."

Rautanen had been watching the street from the living room window. It was finally dark. He came back to the kitchen and opened a Coke. "Nothing yet."

"You up for this?" McGarvey asked.

Rautanen laughed but nodded. "You bet your ass, but I think that you're crazier than I am."

"Tell him," Pete said.

"Do you have anything other than the Ithaca and the SIG?" McGarvey asked.

"A KA-BAR, if it comes to that."

"How many rounds for the guns?"

"Two boxes of double-ought shot, two of slugs for the Franchi, and a couple of boxes of hollow points for the pistol."

Schlueter would be sending at least three or four shooters tonight, and after what had gone down in Rawalpindi he was sure that her primary target had changed from the ST Six guys to him. Once he had been eliminated they would go on with the op.

"How about you?" he asked Pete.

She nodded. "In for a penny, in for a pound, my dad always used to say."

"No silencers," McGarvey said. "I want this noisy."

"But we don't know when," Rautanen said. "Could be an all-nighter, and maybe not go down until tomorrow night or the next."

"Unless we set the time," McGarvey said. He phoned Otto, and put it on speaker.

"Is it a go for tonight?" Otto asked.

"I want you to start calling all the Neptune Spear guys right now, even the ones on active duty if you can get through to them."

"I can," Otto said.

"Tell them that we think that one of them will come under attack sometime tonight, so sit tight and keep a sharp watch."

"What do I tell them about you and Pete?"

"The truth. We think that Ratman could be the primary target and we're setting a trap. But make them understand that Schlueter's KSK operators might try to draw me out by attacking one of the others. They want to get me into the open and take me down."

"All you have is a pistol," Otto said. It was clear he didn't like the idea.

"Do it."

"You'll be outnumbered, even with Pete and Rautanen."

"Do it," McGarvey said, and he rang off.

"That didn't sound encouraging," Pete said.

McGarvey called Cole's home phone. A woman answered after three rings, and he asked to speak to the captain. "May I say who is calling?"

"Kirk McGarvey."

"Yes, just a moment."

McGarvey got the oddest sensation in just those few words: the woman not only knew who he was but had been expecting his call. Which was nonsense.

Cole was on the line almost immediately. "Who the fuck do you think you are calling me here?"

"I'm at Ratman's house. I think someone will try to take him down tonight and I'm going to stop it."

Cole hesitated for several beats. "If you really thought something like that was going to happen, you'd have the bureau surrounding the place. The state, county, and local cops would be in on it. SWAT teams. The whole nine yards."

"The navy officially doesn't believe the story, so what makes you think the bureau or anyone else would?"

"I passed it along to the ONI."

"Yeah, I met them."

"You didn't let them take Rautanen where he'd be safe. So what do you want from me?"

"To let you know what's about to happen."

"You're just as bad as Rautanen. It's a wonder the both of you aren't out on the streets."

"Most of those guys are there because in the end it's a lot easier dealing with the aftermath of three hundred plus days out of every year on deployment. Blown-out knees, bad hips, ankles shot, shoulders beat up, not to mention their mental state," McGarvey said bitterly. He hung up before Cole could respond.

"I told you he was a by-the-book prick," Rautanen said.

"Do you and any of the other guys ever get together for a beer or something?" McGarvey asked.

"I've never gotten around to it. And I doubt if most of the others do. Doesn't seem to be any point. By the time the guys get around to quitting, their wives have about had their fill. They pretty much keep them on a short leash." He shrugged. "Or bug out."

"No contact with any of them? Not even the occasional phone call?"

Rautanen was about to say no, but he changed his mind. "Tony Tabeek. He and I used to hang around. He called last year after I became a bachelor and asked how I was holding up. I thought it was nice of him."

"Is he here in town?"

"Over in Virginia Beach."

"Call him," McGarvey said. "Tell him you got a call from a guy named Otto who warned you that the rest of the Neptune Spear crew might come under attack sometime tonight. You just wanted to give him the heads-up. Do you think he'll listen?"

"We were on Chalk One together. He'll listen."

Pete handed him Mac's cell phone. "They won't be able to trace your call."

"I want him to use his home phone."

Rautanen grinned. "They've got my phone bugged?"

"I'm counting on it," McGarvey said. "But wait ten minutes until we're sure that Otto has had a chance to get to him."

"Anything else?"

"Tell him that I'm setting a trap."

Rautanen hesitated a beat. "Do you think they'll buy it?"

"They will when you tell Tabeek where I'll be waiting."

"Standby one," Rautanen said. He got up and left the kitchen.

"I'm frightened," Pete said, her voice low.

"You'll be okay here. It's me they want."

"Not for me. I'm afraid for you."

McGarvey reached over and touched her cheek, and she flinched. "We're going to finish it tonight. No more looking over our shoulders to see who's coming up behind us. No more worrying about these guys."

Rautanen came back and laid a pair of black night-fighting camos and a black watch cap on the table. "You'll need these."

SIXTY-NINE

☐

Pam and Ayesha had dinner at a KFC a few blocks from the motel, while Volker and the others spread out to two different places to get something to eat. They were all dressed in ordinary street clothes—jeans and pullovers or baggy shirts.

Their weapons were still back at the motel where they would meet at nine sharp for their final orders. They wanted to minimize the time on the streets when they were armed in case of a routine traffic stop.

The cell phone in Pam's hip holster buzzed. It was the special program in which the contact information on the remaining twenty-two Neptune Spear SEALs was stored. Every call to their numbers showed up on her phone. Earlier she had intercepted the phone calls from Otto Rencke. This time the call to Tony Tabeek came from Rautanen's house phone.

"Yo, Tank, this is the Ratman."

"You got the same call from the CIA?"

"Yeah. Why I called. We're going to try to head off the shit over at my place. Bait and switch."

"I'm listening."

"You know the apartments up the block from here?"

"Yeah?"

"Got a guy named McGarvey, ex-CIA. He figures that I'm number one on their hit list. He's going to set up at the apartments, and when they come in he'll be at their six."

"If that complex is what I think it is, your guy's got balls." Tabeek said.

"It is and he does," Rautanen said.

"What do you want from me?"

"Nada. Just giving you the heads-up, because he thinks you might be next after me."

"What about the captain?"

"Cole? He's a pussy. We're on our own, man. Keep a sharp eye."

"You too," Tabeek said.

Pam hung up.

Ayesha was staring at her. "What is it?"

"Tonight's operation just got easier," Pam said.

She speed-dialed the other four, Volker first.

"Problems?" he asked.

"Just the opposite. Get back to base. We're a go."

She gave the same message to the others, and she and Ayesha got in the Fusion and headed back to the motel. It was a weeknight, but traffic was still heavy. The bars and other dives that always surround a military base like a cloud of meteors were already busy with guys who were off duty.

"Tell me what's going on," Ayesha said. She seemed excited, a glow in her eyes.

"McGarvey's made a mistake," Pam said. "He thinks he's set a trap for us, but instead he's the one who's backed into a corner." She explained what she'd overheard and what her plan was.

"Is he that foolish?" Ayesha asked.

"He wouldn't be if he knew that I was monitoring the phone calls to all the ST Six guys."

"He's CIA—he must have a lot of resources at his disposal. Enough to possibly predict that you have the ability to monitor such phone messages. Maybe he's set a trap for you."

"You don't know what you're talking about," Pam said angrily. But something nagged.

"I was married to an intelligence officer who knew all about the CIA, and who liked to tell me about his days. And McGarvey did find us at the Rawalpindi house."

"This time is different."

"How so?" Ayesha asked, her tone insinuating and irritating.

"There will be me and four of my operators."

"We had you, my husband, and four dacoits, plus we had the

woman as a hostage, and we were on familiar ground, and yet McGarvey managed to win the day. What makes you think this evening will be any different?"

"Your husband wasn't a field officer, and the dacoits he hired were amateurs. In the end both you and the woman were liabilities."

Ayesha looked out the window as they pulled in to the motel's parking lot. "Your kind always has excuses."

Pam slammed on the brakes at her parking spot. "I don't need your shit!"

"But you need my money."

"You're staying here until we're back."

"I'm going as an observer."

Pam was on the verge of killing the stupid woman herself and putting the body in a Dumpster somewhere. "What if you get yourself shot by McGarvey or the CIA bitch at Rautanen's, or even one of my guys? How the hell do I explain it to the ISI? We'll need the money to continue with the op after tonight."

"They'll probably be glad to get rid of me," Ayesha said. "Believe me, they're just as interested in finishing this thing as you are."

"I don't have a spare weapon to give you, even if you knew how to use it."

"As it turns out, I'm a fine shot. My husband taught me."

Pam looked at her in the dim light. "There is an American expression that I learned when I lived here. You might take heed. Be careful what you wish for—you just might get it."

Volker and the other three showed up at Pam's room ten minutes later. They were pumped, ready to shoot someone.

"It's a go for tonight as I expected it would be," Pam told them. "But it's likely to be much easier than I first thought it might be. For starters we won't have to split our forces."

Her original plan was to have one of her operators make an attack on one of the SEALs who lived within ten minutes' driving time of Rautanen's house with the idea of luring McGarvey away. Pam and the other three would be standing by, and as soon as he walked out of the house they would nail him.

"What has changed?" Volker asked.

Pam told him about the intercepted phone calls, including the one that Rautanen had made to Tabeek—one of the operators who'd been on Chalk One.

"It could be a setup, if he knows we're monitoring their calls."

"Even if he does, he's going to do exactly what we wanted him to do in the first place. Only he'll believe that we're making an assault on Rautanen's house. He won't expect us to come up on him from all directions, leaving him no way out. The Americans in the first Iraq war talked about shock and awe. Well, we're going to give the bastard a shock-and-awe campaign that he won't walk away from."

"What about the rest of the operation?"

"McGarvey's first, and then we reevaluate the situation in front of us," Pam said. "But if it looks as if it's falling apart, we'll do a one-eighty and get out. You have your escape routes and documents. Drop the weapons in place—they're untraceable—and walk away."

"There is a lot of money you promised us," Heiser said.

"Trust me: once McGarvey has been eliminated the operation will continue. Perhaps not tonight, perhaps not until the dust settles, which it eventually will. But we will finish what we started, one SEAL operator at a time."

"Okay, what's the tactical plan?" Volker asked.

"I'll show you," Pam said and she brought up a map on her smart-phone, shifting the view to the side of the apartment complex facing Rautanen's house. "The lake is north and the SEAL's house is east of the apartments, so we'll come in from the west and split up once we spot him."

"Will he be outside or inside one of the apartments?"

"Unknown," Pam said, and Ayesha interrupted her.

"I'll go in first and do a recon," she said, and the others simply looked at her.

SEVENTY

McGarvey crossed the backyards of the three houses between Rautanen's and the edge of the apartment complex. Two of the small
ranch styles had been foreclosed on and abandoned, but the middle
one was still lived in, though no lights shone from any of the windows this night.

A half-dozen or more black kids had started a small trash fire just
off the street at the front of the parking lot. A boom box sitting on a
dilapidated folding chair was playing some tuneless rap song the
sounds of which echoed off the front of the building.

What little traffic there was at this hour did not linger, even
though it was early—before ten o'clock. The drivers counted themselves lucky if they got through this neighborhood without trouble.

Some old junk cars were parked at the rear of the complex. Two
of them were up on concrete blocks, minus their wheels. Another
was totally trashed; all of its windows broken out and its seats and
dashboard cut apart. One had its trunk lid open.

Some of the windows in the half-dozen three-story buildings
were lit, but most of them were in darkness. Laundry hung from the
railings on several small balconies. Stopping just at the corner of the
first building, McGarvey got the distinct sense that he was being
watched. Yet the entire complex, like the neighborhood, had the air
of abandonment.

From where he stood he had a good sight line of the west side of
Rautanen's house, including the carport and the Hummer. The lights
were out: Pete was watching from a bedroom in the rear, and Rautanen from a living-room window in front.

In the far distance a fire truck siren echoed across the lake, and somewhere he thought he heard a train whistle. Night sounds, lonely. Most good people were at home watching TV or getting ready for bed. The predators were out prowling like wild animals in the dark, looking for prey.

Stepping around the corner, McGarvey walked to the front where the black kids stood around the fire in a small metal barrel. It wasn't cold outside; the fire was merely something to do, a gathering place for them.

The kids turned around, and one of them shut off the music.

"Good evening, gentlemen," McGarvey said. He stopped about ten feet out. "Got a question for you. Fact is, I need your help."

For several long beats the kids—who ranged in age from their midteens to maybe nineteen or twenty—were silent. One of them pulled out a knife and another a pistol, which looked to McGarvey like an old .38 Saturday Night Special.

"We're going to help you into the ground, you dumb sucka," the older one said.

The kid with the pistol took a step forward.

"You know the guy lives in the house at the end of the block?" McGarvey said. "The one you think is nuts? He needs your help."

All of them laughed.

"You've heard of bin Laden," McGarvey said, addressing the older kid. "The guy down the block was on the team that went over to Pakistan to take care of him."

"So?"

"Their government has sent people over to kill him—name's Greg."

"Just get your honky ass out of here before we waste you."

"The people are coming here tonight. If you get in the way they'll kill you. Thing is, I'm pretty sure they know that I came over to set a trap for them, so I'm number one on their hit list. And they're carrying more than a couple of knives and one shit-hole pistol that'll probably blow up soon as the trigger's pulled. It's why I need your help—so that I'll have a chance to stop them from pulling it off."

"What's it to us?" the one kid said. A couple of the others looked over their shoulders down the street.

"Thing is, these people have already killed two of the SEALs who took out bin Laden. That, and they murdered the families. Like I said, I'm here to stop them."

"You a cop?"

"I used to work for the CIA."

The older kid—their spokesman—was impressed. "No shit?"

"No shit," McGarvey said. "So this is what I want you guys to do for me."

The kid with the gun came forward all of a sudden, the pistol pointed straight out.

Before the kid could react McGarvey snatched the pistol out of his hand. The one with the knife started forward, but the older kid put out an arm and stopped him.

"He didn't come here talking all his honky bullshit for nothing," their spokesman said.

"That's what it is, nigger, honky bullshit," the kid who'd had the pistol slammed back.

"Maybe, but this time's different."

McGarvey held out the gun, handle first. "I'd get rid of this before you get hurt."

Slowly the younger kid took the gun. He turned and walked back to the fire, but he didn't put the pistol back in his belt.

The entire city seemed to fall silent, except for the crackling of the small fire, which gave off black smoke and the acrid odor of burning rubber. McGarvey had been in a lot of foreign places in a career of a couple of decades, but here and now it almost seemed as if he were on another planet—yet still in his own country.

"So what do you want?" the older kid asked.

McGarvey told him. None of them were happy.

SEVENTY-ONE

□

Ayesha hid in the shadows twenty feet from where McGarvey stood with the black kids on the corner. She could hear them talking, but she couldn't quite make out the words, except when one of them called the other a nigger. She knew enough, though, to keep out of sight: the tension was palpable. And when McGarvey handed the gun back to the kid, she'd almost turned around and walked away.

The scene was way beyond her understanding. Everything she'd ever read about the situation between blacks and whites in the United States, everything she'd seen on the television and heard on the radio, had led to the belief common in Pakistan and most other places around the world: that America was on the verge of a race riot.

It didn't seem to her to be anything like that. McGarvey was outnumbered, but except for the kid with the gun, nothing had happened. It looked to her like they were having an ordinary conversation.

It came to her all of a sudden that the conversation McGarvey was having with the black kids was anything but ordinary, and again she had the sudden urge to turn around and get out of there.

Her cell phone vibrated in her jeans pocket. She stepped farther back into the shadows next to the apartment building's entrance and answered it. "Yes."

It was Pam and she sounded stressed. "What's the situation?"

"McGarvey's here. I'm about twenty feet away from him and some black kids. I think he's enlisted them."

"Enlisted them? What are you talking about?"

"They're going to help him. Probably act as lookouts. You were right that he'd be here waiting for you, but wrong that if the blacks caught him there would be trouble."

"Where are you exactly?"

"I'm at the front entrance to the building nearest the houses. Rautanen's is four doors away—about fifty meters from here."

Pam had dropped her off about a block away, and she'd made it this far on foot. The other four operators on the team had parked even closer and were standing by to strike, with enough firepower to take out McGarvey and the black kids ten times over.

It was retribution for the strike on bin Laden, the violation of Pakistan's borders, but more than that for Ayesha; this evening it was supposed to be retribution for her husband's death. But now that she was this close she found that her feelings were flat. Retribution would not bring Ali back to her—nothing on this earth would. All that was left was for her to someday join her husband under Allah's pure light in paradise.

Trouble was, she didn't really believe in all that nonsense. If there was a paradise, it was here on earth, among the living.

"Have you been spotted?"

"No."

"How many blacks are with McGarvey?"

"Seven. But most of them are kids."

"Are any of them armed?" Pam demanded.

"McGarvey took a pistol away from one of them, but then he gave it back."

"What?"

"He gave it back to the kid," Ayesha said. "Look, I'm getting out of here."

"Stay there. We're on our way. Just keep your head down."

Ayesha cut the connection.

One of the black kids had grabbed the boom box and headed around the corner with a couple of the others. McGarvey had disappeared around the corner of the building, but the rest of them headed directly toward the front entrance where Ayesha was standing.

She turned and headed as fast as she could run down the length of the building, staying as much as possible in the deeper shadows. Thankfully all the streetlights were out and she nearly made it to the corner, when one of the kids behind her shouted something she couldn't make out.

Ducking around the corner she tripped on some trash and fell on her face, scraping her elbows and smashing her chin into the broken blacktop, blood in her mouth.

She scrambled to her feet and ran headlong to the rear of the building and around the corner, where she pulled up short, gasping for breath. Twenty meters across the rear parking area was another apartment building; there were others to the left. To the right, was a narrow strip of what once might have been grass but was now mostly bare dirt and some weeds and trash. This was where the coordinated attack on Rautanen would take place once Pam's team had taken care of McGarvey.

No direction was safe. She wanted to get out, find a street where she could get a cab back to the motel for her things and then to the airport where she could rent a car and get clear of the city. Anywhere. She had the credit cards, the passport and other documents, and plenty of money to get out of the country. Anywhere. Perhaps back to Canada, or even Mexico, and from there she could make her way home.

"Who the fuck are you?" someone said to her left.

Ayesha turned. A tall black man, young, maybe twenty, with the menacing look of a Taliban fighter, was two feet from her. Her heart stopped and her legs suddenly went so weak she thought she wouldn't be able to keep on her feet for another second.

"McGarvey," was all she managed to say.

□

SEVENTY-TWO

McGarvey had just come around the rear corner of the building when he heard a woman cry his name. The blacks he'd talked with had dispersed—some of them inside the buildings where they would take up positions on the balconies as lookouts, others on the west side of the apartment complex.

The nearest one to him was the kid with the gun, still out front watching to the east, toward Rautanen's house.

Everyone was pretty much within hailing distance to warn him their company had arrived.

He pulled out his pistol. Trailing his left hand against the side of the building he hurried in the direction of the woman's voice. It was dark back here and he was within thirty feet of the east side of the building before he could make out the figure of a slightly built woman, two black kids towering over her, holding her against the wall.

They didn't spot him until he was ten feet away. One of them turned, a machete in his hand. "Who the fuck are you?" the kid demanded. He had a Caribbean accent, maybe Haitian.

"The woman's with me," McGarvey said. He held his pistol more or less out of sight at his right side. "Back away and nothing bad will happen here tonight."

The other kid, whose left hand was on Ayesha's chest, holding her against the wall, raised a knife to her throat. "Motherfucker, I'll slice the bitch."

"I don't think so," McGarvey said, raising his pistol.

The kid with the machete laughed. "So she dies," he said. "In the meantime I'll have half the hood down here covering your honky ass."

"Right now a world of shit is about to rain down on this place. At least four German Special Forces guys armed with automatic weapons are coming this way to kill me, and they won't give a shit who they have to take down to do it."

"Bullshit."

All of a sudden McGarvey recognized the woman. "Didn't expect to see you here," he said. "Though I can guess why you came."

"I came looking for you," she said.

"You found me."

"I told Pam that you were talking with some kids out front. They're less than a block away."

"Voodoo bullshit," the kid with the machete said. He was high on something.

"Why do you suppose she's really here?" McGarvey asked. "Why do you think someone like me is here? To shake up dumb sons of bitches like you and your pal who're only big enough to shove a woman around?"

The kid with the machete suddenly lunged forward, raising the blade as he came.

McGarvey side-stepped him at the last moment. Just as the machete was coming toward his head, he slapped the kid's hand aside and grabbed him under his arm, just above the elbow, and then shoved him against the building.

The kid was like a wild man, bouncing all over the place, kicking, screaming incoherently.

"I'll slice the bitch," the kid holding Ayesha said.

McGarvey brought his gun around and shot the kid with the machete in the left kneecap. He grabbed the blade and twisted away as the kid howled and dropped to the ground, holding his destroyed knee with both hands.

McGarvey tossed the machete away and strode to Ayesha's side, pointing his pistol at the kid's head. "You're dead in three seconds."

The kid froze.

"Three, two, one—"

The kid suddenly released Ayesha and stepped back.

"Drop the knife and help your buddy get the fuck out of here before the shit hits the fan."

The kid did as he was told. Warily eying McGarvey, he hustled to help his friend up, and the two of them limped across the parking lot to one of the buildings in the back.

"Mac," Pete called from behind him

He turned as Pete came around the corner, her pistol drawn. "Otto monitored a call from her cell phone to Pam. They're on their way."

Two of the black kids came around the corner right behind her.

"She's with me," McGarvey told them, and they pulled up.

"They know you're here," Pete said.

"That's what I wanted to happen," McGarvey said. "I want you to take her back to Rautanen's and keep your head down."

Pete suddenly reared back. "Mac," she shouted.

McGarvey turned on his heel in time to see Ayesha just about on top of him, the kid's knife in her right hand, coming in for the kill. He feinted to the left as she lunged.

Pete fired one shot, catching the woman in the chest just below her left breast.

Ayesha's momentum carried her into McGarvey and her legs gave out from under her, the knife slipping from her hands.

He helped her to the ground. Her eyes fluttered and she said something indistinct.

He lowered his head so that his ear was at her mouth. "What is it?"

She said something in Punjabi, her voice barely audible.

"In English," McGarvey said.

"For Ali," she whispered. "It was for my husband. Always for him."

She stopped breathing at the same moment automatic weapons fire, what sounded to McGarvey like a suppressed MAC 10, raked the side of the building inches from where he was down on one knee.

SEVENTY-THREE

□

Pam heard the barely audible gunfire from the east of her position in the middle of the apartment complex. It was either Volker or Woedding. She'd sent the two of them between the buildings in the direction of Rautanen's house, while Bruns and Heiser had split off to the rear of the second row of buildings, hoping to catch McGarvey in a flanking position.

They'd left the cars at the edge of the complex and had come the rest of the way on foot—the four operators forward while she hung back in case McGarvey tried to make an end run.

She'd set up a common number on their encrypted cell phones. She keyed it. "Report," she said softly.

"He's on the east side with the woman," Volker responded. It sounded as if he was running.

"Is he down?"

"Negative, but we hit two of the blacks with him."

"What's your situation?"

"We're across the parking area."

More suppressed gunfire came from that direction, followed immediately by several unsilenced pistol shots.

"He and the broad just went inside the building. We're taking fire."

"Klaus, Friedrich, *kommt!*" Pam called.

"We're twenty-five meters behind the building," Bruns responded. "We'll try to get in from the rear."

"Good. Felix, copy?"

"*Ja.*"

"What about Ayesha?"

"She's down. The woman with McGarvey shot her."

Just as well, Pam thought. She would worry about the money later. "I want this op over with now. McGarvey's making too much noise."

"That's his intention," Volker radioed back.

McGarvey and Pete huddled just inside the doorway of the apartment building across the parking lot from where Ayesha's body and the bodies of the two black kids who had agreed to help out were lying.

Pete was on the phone with Otto. She handed it to McGarvey.

"There's been a fair amount of phone traffic, but they're using a military-grade encryption algorithm, which is going to take my darlings a minute or so to figure out. But I'd guess that they're going to try to flank you. They can't be happy with all the noise you're making."

"Have the cops taken any notice?"

"Not yet. Do you want me to give them the heads-up?"

"No."

"Goddamnit, Mac—"

"If some patrol officer shows up he's going to get himself killed. And by the time a SWAT team is organized this'll be a done deal. One way or the other."

A half-dozen incoming rounds blazed through the open doorway, ricocheting around inside the entry vestibule. McGarvey reached around the corner and emptied his magazine in the general direction of the two shooters.

"Go upstairs and try to find a balcony on the first or second floor, if someone will let you in," he said as he changed out magazines. "If not, cover me from the landing."

"I'm not going to leave you alone."

McGarvey grinned. "You know this isn't going to work for us if you're all the time arguing with me."

"Chauvinist."

"Just keep your ass down. I want to end this crap tonight."

She pecked him on the cheek. "For luck," she said. She hurried past the elevator door, which had an out-of-order sign on it, and bounded up the stairs two at a time.

The cell phone burred. It was Otto again, and he was excited.

"You've got two guys in front of you, and I think two more are coming up on your six."

McGarvey looked over his shoulder at the same time someone out front opened fire, but with what he was sure was a Heckler & Koch 416 with a suppressor, one of the weapons of choice for SEAL team operators.

Rautanen.

Volker took a hit high on his right arm before he knew someone was coming up from the east; he managed to roll left out of the line of fire. Automatic weapons fire from a silenced light submachine gun kicked up dirt and bits of pavement all around him, while at the same time McGarvey or the broad fired a half-dozen pistol shots from just inside the building across the parking lot, two rounds whizzing past his head so close he could feel the shock waves.

"Bastard," Heiser said, crouching beside him. He fired a sustained burst from his MAC 10, walking the rounds out and up, at least three finally catching the ex-SEAL in the leg, lower torso, and upper chest.

Rautanen went down heavily and lay still. It was impossible for Volker to tell from this distance if the guy was dead or not, but he was down, which for the moment was all that mattered.

"You okay?" Heiser asked.

"Nothing serious," Volker said. Awkwardly he keyed his cell phone. *"Klaus, wo ist?"*

"Ready to go in. Give us distracting fire."

"On three," Volker said. "They're going in," he told Heiser. He waited two counts, then got up on a knee and began firing measured bursts at the open doorway. Heiser followed suit.

Pam was on the phone, but he ignored her call—the time for bullshit orders was over.

McGarvey hunched around the corner, his back against the wall, as the incoming rounds bounced all over the place. It was covering fire for whoever was coming down the hallway from the rear door.

A figure loomed large in the darkness and McGarvey emptied his magazine down the narrow corridor. He changed out the magazine, recharged his weapon, and was about to fire, when a round slammed into his side just above his hip. He felt an incredible burst of pain.

Pete suddenly appeared, firing her pistol around the corner from the elevator door. One of the Germans grunted, but kept firing.

McGarvey's phone vibrated again at the same moment the firing from the front of the building intensified a half-dozen times over. There were more than four of them, he thought, his head buzzing.

He emptied his last magazine down the corridor, as Pete changed out her last one.

Someone in dark night-fighter camos appeared in the doorway, an H & K at ready arms. For just an instant he thought it was Rautanen, but he was sure that the SEAL was down.

"Pete, get down," he shouted, at the same time as he threw his pistol at the man's face. As he began to lose consciousness he got the strangest impression that the guy in the doorway was Dick Cole, with two other similarly dressed figures right behind him.

Pete was there over him as he slipped away, his only regret at that moment was the fact that he had only one kidney and he was sure that the round he'd taken was right there. And being on dialysis for the rest of his life was never what he had in mind.

SEVENTY-FOUR

The room was dim. As McGarvey began to wake up he was conscious of a familiar chemical smell. He thought that he might be at All Saints, which was the private hospital in Georgetown that took care of seriously injured intelligence officers.

Somewhere in the distance he heard voices speaking in very low tones. One of them was a woman's voice which he recognized as Otto's wife, Louise. She sounded insistent.

His mouth was gummy and it was hard for him to focus. Everything seemed blurred at first, until gradually he began to make out that he was in bed in a hospital room. The blinds to his left were drawn; even so, he knew it was night.

He tried to turn, but a huge pain slammed his side, and he remembered that he had been shot in the kidney. Two down, zero to go.

A host of other thoughts came tumbling into his head, chief among them Pete. She'd been right there in the middle of it in the apartment building's vestibule when he'd been hit, and he hadn't been able to do a damned thing for her. That hurt even more than his wound.

Dr. Alan Franklin, chief of surgery at All Saints, walked into the room, a smile on his hound dog face. "How're you feeling?" he asked.

"Like someone who's been shot in the side. How's Pete?"

"Ms. Boylan is one tough woman, she's already pushing to get out of bed, and she can't see why she shouldn't be in here with you," Franklin said. He'd worked on McGarvey a couple of times before and he was damned good at what he did. Any hospital in the country would appoint him chief of surgery if he'd only ask. But he was comfortable here. His kind of people, he liked to say. Interesting injuries.

McGarvey was alarmed. He tried to sit up. "Was she hurt?"

"No. And if you don't take it easy you'll end up back in the operating room."

McGarvey lay back, a little woozy. "What happened?"

"A long shot, actually, but you and Ms. Boylan are both O positive and your HL antigen profiles were within the ballpark. She stepped up to the plate for you and I did the operation this afternoon. About nine hours ago."

"What are you talking about?"

"Your remaining kidney was damaged beyond repair, so Ms. Bolan donated one of hers. Saved your life."

"I want to see her."

"In the morning. Right now you need to rest."

"Come on, doc, I just woke up. I have to pee—"

"You're catheterized."

"I'm hungry."

"I'll order up some broth and maybe some Jell-O."

"How about a beer, or better yet a Rémy?"

Franklin laughed, and it was the best sound Mac had heard in a while.

"Broth and Jell-O it is. In the meantime I heard Louise out in the hall, which means Otto's out there too. I want five minutes with them."

"Five is all you'll get. The button on the controller by your hand is a morphine pump. Press it if you need some relief."

Franklin left and before Otto and Louise were allowed in a nurse took Mac's blood pressure and checked his urine output. She gave him a smile. "You'll live."

"Yes, he will," Louise said, breezing in. She gave Mac a peck on the cheek.

"Close the door," McGarvey said.

Otto did. He pulled a beer from his pocket, popped the tab, and handed it to McGarvey, who took a deep drink. It was great.

"What about the Germans?"

"All four of them are dead," Otto said. "Dick Cole came with four ST Six guys and it was over before it started. BND doesn't want the bodies. They suggested we cremate them and dump the ashes. Happened earlier this morning."

"Rautanen?"

"He was wearing his Kevlar. Took a hit in the leg and groin, but he'll survive. He's in the Naval Medical Center at Portsmouth. Says to say hi."

"How about the kids from the complex?"

"Three of them are down—two KIA, the third in critical. Cole had him taken to Portsmouth with Rautanen. Least we could do."

"What about Ayesha Naisir?"

"Her body is on the way to Pakistan as we speak. I think the ISI will stage a robbery attempt or something like that in Rawalpindi. She was shot to death along with her husband."

"The White House?" McGarvey asked.

"The incident never happened," Otto said. "But John Fay sends his regards, said thanks."

"Pam Schlueter?"

"No trace."

"She'll turn up sooner or later," McGarvey said. "But Dick Cole. If he wasn't the leak, who the hell was?"

"We may never know."

The door opened and Pete, came in in a wheelchair, Louise helping her. "I heard that you were awake," she said, coming to McGarvey's side. "We have about five minutes before Franklin or one of his nurses catches us. So how do you feel?"

"Pretty good," McGarvey said. "You?"

"Never better," Pete said. She took the beer from him. "If this is going to work between us, you're going to have to learn how to share."

SEVENTY-FIVE

□

Gloria, her feet propped up on the lower rungs of a stool, sat at her kitchen counter talking to Pam on her cell phone. With Dick upstairs it was too dangerous to use the house phone, but it was a call she couldn't avoid. She was furious.

"Where are you at this moment?" she demanded.

"Athens, but I'm not going to say here."

"I can find out."

"Don't."

"You blew it, and then you didn't finish the most important part of the job. The one I was expecting from you. You need to come back immediately."

"Don't be a fool. They know my name."

"McGarvey is probably dead."

"It doesn't matter," Pam shouted. "It's not only the CIA who knows my name, it's the Pakistanis. Major Naisir got himself killed and so did his wife. Those ISI bastards will at least want their money back."

"Give it to them."

"They won't go away, and money is the only thing that'll keep me alive until the situation stabilizes."

"Then what?" Gloria said. "I need this." She was pleading.

"I won't forget you. I'll be back to finish it."

"When?"

"I don't know," Pam said. "In the meantime I'm getting rid of this phone and all my Internet connections, so you won't be able to reach me. But I'll be there, I promise."

"You can't quit," Gloria said. But Pam had hung up.

Her husband, Dick Cole, came in wearing a bathrobe. "Who can't quit?"

She turned and smiled. "Just a silly girlfriend of mine, who wants to quit her job just when it was getting interesting." More than anything in the world she wanted him dead.

Cole shrugged indifferently. "Do you want to do some porn and fool around? I got a couple of new movies."

"Sure, sweetie," Gloria said, her heart aching. "I'd like nothing better."

EPILOGUE

◻

Island of Serifos
Three months later

McGarvey had been alone again long enough now on his island re-
treat that he no longer saw any value in it. Pete had stayed with him
for the first few weeks, but he'd sent her back to her job at Langley to
keep her ear to the ground.

He ran every day across the rugged hilly terrain, along cliffs that
plunged into the Aegean, up steep stairs that the Greeks and then the
Romans had carved to their temples, and back down to the town,
where he sometimes had lunch and a half bottle of good retsina. He
was up to five miles a day now, and sometimes he swam in the sea
for an hour or so, pushing himself as he always had.

A couple of days each week he hiked up from where he stayed in
the lighthouse that had been converted into a comfortable apartment.
He shot his pistol at small targets, bottles, bits of newspapers or magazines, even a cigarette pack he'd picked up in town. His accuracy
with the Walther became very good up to three hundred inches.

He sat this noon at the tavern by the ferry dock as the boat from
the mainland pulled up and the passengers, mostly tourists at this
time of early fall, disembarked.

Time to go home, the idle thought crossed his mind. Physically he
was back to nearly one hundred percent, and he was beginning to
chafe at the bit sitting around here. And as was often the case with
him, he was beginning to feel that something was coming his way.

Not Pam Schlueter, or the ISI—but something or someone else.
Something just beyond his ken.

Louise said that it was an instinct for survival honed after a lot of years in the field, and Otto agreed. But he thought it more likely that every time he got bored he looked for something to do. Some nut to crack. He'd been doing it for so long, and he'd lost so much, that it was a way of life. His life.

"It's what I am," he'd once told a DDO who'd tried to figure him out.

"An anachronism," the deputy director had called him.

But the man had been gunned down when he'd stupidly stuck his nose in the middle of an operation.

He raised his wine glass, but then stopped. Pete was getting off the ferry, trailed by Marty Bambridge, who looked anxious even from this distance.

They walked across the quay to the line of waiting taxis, but while Marty was negotiating with a cabbie Pete scanned the waterfront cafés, finding McGarvey sitting alone at a sidewalk table.

She smiled and nodded, and then said something to Bambridge, who did a double take before he too spotted McGarvey. They had to wait for a break in traffic before they could cross the street.

"At least we don't have to climb all the way up the godforsaken hill to your lighthouse," Bambridge said by way of greeting.

"Hi, Mac, you okay?" Pete said.

He got up and they embraced. "A little lonely."

"Me too."

They all sat down, and when the waiter came over Pete ordered a retsina while the DDO asked for a Coke.

"We have a developing problem," Bambridge said. "It's why we came over to talk to you."

"I thought that I was persona non grata in Washington," McGarvey said, though he didn't really know why he was being so irascible, except that he was still tired from dealing with the political bullshit. Lead, follow, or get the hell out of the way. But it was never that simple.

"There's a serial killer loose inside the CIA headquarters campus," Pete said. "We need your help."